Betrayed

Farseen Chronicles Book 3

N. R. Tucker

Betrayed

ISBN – 978-0-9906777-5-8

Farseen Map

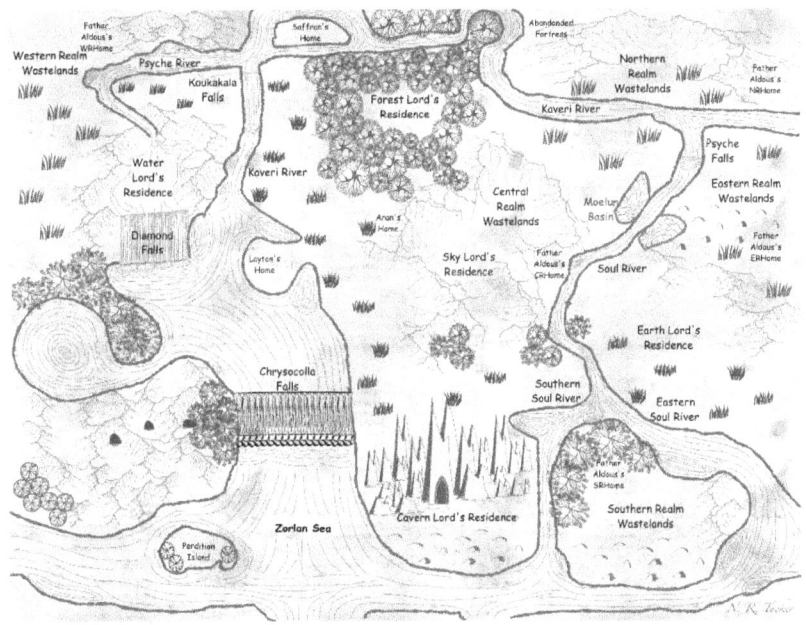

Chapter 1

Siri and Tempe fired in unison, four preternaturals fell to the ground. The darts were loaded with a sleeping potion and the first of thirty-two injections delivering the antidote to the Crystal virus. Reloading her dart guns, Siri cast a sleep spell toward two wizards, who shrugged off the spell and prepped spells of their own.

Focused on the two wizards, Tempe modulated her enchantment, "Slumber." Both wizards fell to the ground, asleep. One even snored. There were still enemy wizards in play. Since her team members had wizard blood, Tempe couldn't drop all wizards in the room. She didn't have enough control over the modulation of her voice to protect her team from the enchantment. Siri acknowledged Tempe's assist with a quick salute, and fired her reloaded dart guns, dropping two infected shifters just after they shifted into their other form.

Tempe dropped her empty dart guns and adopted a fighting stance as a large male fae ran toward her. The fae fought with all the cunning of a brick wall. He jumped and landed on her. She hit the ground with a thud forcing the air out of her lungs. She took a deep breath and coughed as she sucked in dust. Unable to throw the guy she used a tactic that never failed. She grabbed his balls and squeezed hard. As most males would, the fae emitted a high-pitched squeal and rolled off her. Tempe called wind and threw the fae into a wall.

As she stood, Tempe felt a spell roll harmlessly over her spell protected clothes. She looked over in time to see Siri shoot a dart into the witch's neck. The unconscious witch dropped to the ground.

Three shifters shifted and snarled, showing their wolf teeth. Using her rune weapon, Tempe pulled fire and circled the wolves. The large fae regained consciousness, charged Tempe and tackled her, again. They slid across the floor, exchanging unfocused punches that hurt less than the burn of sliding across the floor. It was enough of a distraction to make Tempe lose focus and the fire circle dissipated.

The wolves charged Siri, the closest intruder to them, while her darts dropped two of the three remaining witches. The third she tossed into the wall before using wind to fly over and behind the wolves. Loading her dart guns, again, she landed solidly on the floor, and turned her guns on the wolves. She got two but the third turned and clamped down on her arm.

As the fae and Tempe unfolded from each other, Tempe focused on the wolf, modulated her voice, and enchanted the remaining wolf to sleep. She didn't see the large fae fist that met her jaw in a nice solid blow.

When she opened her eyes, a short woman stood over her, hand extended. Tempe almost waved Brandi's hand away, but another round of dizziness hit, so she grabbed the proffered hand and stood. Looking around, she noticed her sparring partner was down, obviously Brandi's doing. The wolf had a dart in his neck and Brandi had one of Tempe's dart guns in her hand.

Siri finished dressing her wound and proceeded to clean up her blood. Another spell caster could use blood for a vast number of spells.

While Tempe and Siri had taken out the shifters, wizards and witches, Brandi, a shifter, witch, vampire amalgamation, had quickly and efficiently beheaded the vampires in the room.

Tempe said, "We need dart guns to fire more than one dart per load."

"Yep, the High Coven's Weapons Division is working on it," Siri replied.

Tempe grinned and looked for the vampires. True to form when Brandi was around, the vampires were dead and beheaded in a pile in the corner. Brandi always threw the vampires she killed into a pile. Tempe didn't know if it was for aesthetics or to make the clean up easier. Since vampires only turn to dust in the Farseen sun Tempe pulled out her rune weapon, focused, and said "lumifar". There was a high level of satisfaction in watching the vampires turn to ash. Gotta love a spell that cleans up after itself.

The vampire ruling elite provided any vampire caught by the virus with their final death. The task force decided it was a waste of time and energy, not to mention downright dangerous, to keep the vampires undead until their vampire executioner showed up to send them to their eternal death. The high wizard and shifter sovereign informed the vampire protectorate of their decision and he had not objected. In fact, Gwaednerth didn't respond at all.

This nest, in a rundown neighborhood in Chicago, had a mixture of infected fae, shifters, witches, and vampires. It's the first time they've seen vampires mixed in with the rest of the infected, but their intelligence had been right. In the past there were always two nests near

2

each other, one for vampires and one for everyone else. Perhaps the new version of the Crystal virus made vampires more compliant and less likely to feed on their compatriots, or perhaps the virus made the infected taste bad.

A field blood test verified the nest was infected, even though the virus no longer gave the infected the thick black rim around the irises. Physical identification would be harder in the future.

Raven and Ryan had been assigned guard duty outside and helped load the unconscious into the vans. Siri hopped into Ryan's van to drive while Ryan guarded the prisoners. Brandi drove Raven's van of prisoners. Tempe shifted to her falcon and flew recon as they drove to a private landing strip. They flew to the facility where the infected would be kept for the sixteen days required to eliminate the infection from the host. Once they completed the series of antidote injections, they would be given the inoculation and could never be put under the influence of the virus again.

The inoculations were given out as quickly as possible, but it was proving to be hard to locate everyone, especially those in the preternatural community who didn't wish to be found.

*****

Under Citlali and Murdoch's watchful eyes, the plane pulled into the hanger next to the loading dock. They stood on the walkway ready in case there were problems. The facility in northwest North Dakota, near the Canadian border, was surrounded by a whole lot of nothing. The detainment center or rehab facility – title dependent on who was speaking – was manned by a team of wizards, fae and shifters who would guard the prisoners until the drug was out of their systems and protect them in case the Shadowed showed up.

"It's good to see you, old friend," Tempe said to Citlali with a half bow.

"Watch your mouth, shifter. You have at least three thousand years on me," Citlali replied with a smile. The former high wizard had retired a few centuries back when she decided she was getting slow and turned the reigns over to Nova, the current high wizard. Wizards age more slowly than humans but they still age. Slower but still a deadly threat, Citlali offered to run the rehab center with the help of her descendant, Murdoch.

Tempe was half fae, half shifter and for both species aging halts around the age of thirty. Not immortal, either species can be killed, but unless it's a deathblow recovery would eventually happen. She was almost seven thousand years old and would always look thirty.

Siri was a fae/wizard mix, working for the highest bidder as a hit man, but she had standards and was picky about her jobs. Since this drug, and other drugs like it, came into being she had been working full time for the high wizard coven.

"Siri?" Tempe asked as they helped unload the infected. "Have you tested Kacy and Kenley?"

Siri currently lived in Scotland with Tempe's son, Devlin. Devlin's father had wizard blood and Tempe hadn't known. Her other two children, who make up the rest of her fraternal triplets, were also to be tested.

"Yes," Siri smiled serenely as she and Ryan loaded another infected onto a waiting stretcher. Ryan and Raven smiled.

"And?" Tempe asked when she couldn't stand it anymore. They loaded another infected onto a stretcher in the nearly bus sized cart for transportation to the recovery wing.

"And, both show real wizard talent. I suspect their father's father or mother was a strong wizard." Siri stopped and glanced over at Tempe, "You didn't know?"

"I never met them. I know his dad was a shifter but Winford never talked about his parents and they were dead before we met. During the dark ages few talked about having witches or wizards in the family even with other members of the preternatural community," Tempe shrugged.

Tempe waited a few minutes but was finally forced to ask, "Are you going to continue to train Devlin and what about Kacy and Kenley?" she growled. She might as well be talking to the wind.

"Your children will let you know what they decide." Siri walked off to talk to Citlali and left Tempe standing with her mouth hanging open.

"You are too accustomed to everyone answering your questions, mostly before you ask them." Murdoch stated with a grin. Ryan and Raven laughed.

"Yes," Tempe responded curtly and walked off. Over her shoulder she commented, "If my nephew and sister are going to laugh at me they might want to do it where I can't see them. Most people think I have something of a temper."

Ryan attempted to wipe the smile off his face and failed. Raven didn't even bother.

Following Siri, Tempe switched to a new topic. "The three witches chanting together seemed stronger than I thought witches were. Are you sure they aren't wizards?"

Siri stopped walking and looked at the shifter in surprise, "You've never dealt with a coven, have you?"

"Until the freed fae war and the Shadowed entered my life, I rarely dealt with wizards or witches and most were rogues, working alone. I know wizards together are stronger than if they are solo, hence the covens. Is the same true for witches?" Tempe asked.

"Very much so, and the number matters. Three, five, seven or thirteen are the optimum numbers for a joint spell for witches or wizards. And here's another tidbit, a wizard can use a wizard or witch coven numbering thirteen to multiply his or her power significantly, but all participants must willingly offer their power to the wizard," Siri explained.

*****

Once the infected were settled and reports were filed, Siri flew back to Scotland while Raven returned to New York City and her modeling career. Ryan, Brandi and Tempe flew back to the Smoky Mountains.

The trio landed at a private airstrip and piled into Ryan's pickup truck. He got a good deal – according to the guys in Eli's clan – on a Ford Ranger 4-door pickup and was happy as could be. If he had a girlfriend right now she would be jealous... of the truck.

"How's my girl?" Ryan patted the dashboard of his truck.

"Have you named her?" Brandi's expression was more smirk than smile.

"No name could do her justice," Ryan replied seriously as he backed out of the parking space, shifted gears, and headed for home.

Tempe shook her head. She loved driving her sporty BMW convertible, but she has never understood the male love affair with pickup trucks. They're great for hauling, but other than that, she didn't get it.

As they neared Eli's, Brandi motioned toward an intersecting road. "Can you drop me off at Half Acre? We landed later than I expected. I'm scheduled to meet Willow there."

"Sure." He cut down the road and headed for the halfway house the high wizard set up for preternaturals the Shadowed had used as test subjects.

When Ryan and Tempe finally arrived at Vitvarg Farms, Eli's home, they grabbed their stuff and headed for the house. Bryce pulled his SUV in the driveway and parked next to them. Tempe waited for him and though Ryan waved, he walked on into the house.

"How was the trip?" Bryce asked as he grabbed his briefcase and suit jacket. Bryce was the local DA. He dressed for success and looked extremely good doing it. His skin tone and straight black hair confirm his Native American heritage while his blue eyes were a nod to his Irish father. At almost six and a half feet tall he was impressive looking.

"Same as before. We were successful," Tempe responded after a nice long kiss.

Once upstairs in their sound proof room Tempe voiced her concern. "We find a nest of infected individuals, a task force goes in, rounds them up, and then we take them to the rehab facility. I'm beginning to think someone is infecting people just to keep us busy while they work on their master plan."

"Do you have actual proof or just a feeling?" Bryce asked in his best cross-examination voice as he loosened his tie.

"A feeling," she responded as she chewed her lower lip, a bad habit she couldn't seem to shake. "I can't explain it but the wizards should have been able to find the new Shadowed facility, unless the Shadowed moved to the Farseen or they have a cloaking spell the high coven can't breach. The fae have assured us there's no Shadowed facility there but I don't know if they looked everywhere." Tempe whispered, "I think this alliance would work better if the shifters, wizards and fae actually trusted each other."

Bryce pulled her into his arms for a real welcome home kiss before they both sat down at their desks to work. He dove into paperwork for the DA's office. Tempe took care of alpha clan business.

After a good amount of time spent staring at her laptop, trying to see a pattern, Tempe had to admit it didn't make sense. She reviewed the data in various formats. A map marked with locations where the infected were found provided clues but no answers. A spreadsheet of the data, sorted and filtered in many ways, was equally useless. The result was she found no pattern. Tempe was so desperate she tried to determine if the lack of pattern was a pattern. It was with relief she heard the call for dinner.

Chapter 2

After dinner Bryce and Tempe drove to the Harmony Bar. Since it's the local hangout for the preternatural community, Eli had a member of his cyngor there most nights in case the manager, Theo, a shifter from Eli's clan, needed assistance. When Bryce pulled the duty, Tempe normally went with him. They finally found a parking place and walked in, or at least attempted to. The place was packed. They forced their way to the bar and the two seats usually waiting for Eli's rep. It was standing room only.

Adelia and Odelia, twin sisters and wizards, stood watch behind the bar as they served drinks. When they walked up Odelia poured Bryce his favorite beer and then she poured Tempe a glass of wine.

"What's the occasion?" Tempe sipped her wine and turned to face the crowd, leaning on the bar. It was a Wednesday night for pity's sake.

"Some shifters are running the Appalachian Trail, north to south. They're almost done and stopped here to rest for a couple of days. They rented out the place for the evening as a preternatural-only night so there are no humans here."

That explained why there was a bouncer of sorts at the entrance. Bianca was able to identify if someone was normal human or other. She didn't get the full range of powers, but she could identify them as preternatural. She was also gifted with avoidance spells. Tonight, that meant humans suddenly remembered something they had to do or somewhere else they needed to be.

"Are two of them those stunning twins?" Bryce asked.

Tempe looked over and sure enough, a set of twins was sitting at a table and even in a room of preternatural good looks,

7

they stood out. Bryce was right, they were stunning. Both were tall with black hair, brown eyes and exquisitely proportioned bodies.

"Yep," Adelia replied as she poured drinks and handed them off to a waitress. "Kalen asked how to get in touch with you, Tempest."

Bryce looked at her in surprise and she shrugged her shoulders, "I don't know him. It's not like anyone would forget that face."

"Or body," Adelia added wishfully looking at his muscular arms and legs. "Well, he's coming this way. Someone must have told him you arrived."

Sure enough, Kalen and his sister made their way over. When they reached the bar the sister extended her hand, "I'm Kala Porter and this is my brother Kalen. You're Tempest, right?"

"Hello, and yes I am," Tempe replied, shaking the extended hand.

"We wanted to thank you," Kalen smiled.

Interesting. Normally people told Tempe she destroyed their family for some action she took for the sovereign. "What did I do to warrant your thanks?"

"Our cousin, Arleth, was one of the shifters you rescued from those awful wizards."

"Wizards aren't awful!" A big biker guy growled and stood up, flexing his impressive muscles. Others joined him. The bar patrons started sorting themselves into wizards and shifters.

Tempe noticed a couple of witches from the local coven edging toward the door, smart witches. Wizards were significantly more powerful than witches and if the fur flew, a lot of shifters wouldn't bother to distinguish between wizards and witches. A handful of fae also headed out the side door, probably didn't want to get involved in a fight that wouldn't benefit them.

"I didn't say all wizards, just the ones stealing people off the street. Although, it seems wizards should be able to clean up their own mess," Kalen responded indignantly.

The sorting was complete. Tempe noticed with regret there were just as many wizards as shifters. It would be a nice, even bar fight.

Theo, the bar manager, came out from his office while most of his staff assumed what could only be their assigned defensive positions in case there was a fight. Harmony bars only hire members of the preternatural community. Tempe's sister, Bliss, and her husband, Geno, own the international chain. They catered to the preternatural community.

At the entrance to each bar hung a copy of the actual Treaty of Harmony for all to read with a plaque that decrees 'By entering this bar you agree to abide by the Treaty of Harmony'. The humans enter the bar on a normal evening think it's a cute gimmick as they read the rules of conduct. The rules read like playground rules, with the same sentiment: If you don't want to play nice, go home... before you regret it. The humans don't realize what it means.

These bars provide the preternatural community a place to meet with the protection of the ancient Treaty of Harmony between all preternatural beings. There are rarely fights in the bars because the leaders of the different species want a safe place to meet, which means if you break the treaty your own species' leadership will come after you, if you get out of the door alive. The current attitudes over the Shadowed had made everyone a little tense. Not a lot of cool, calm, and collected going on.

Theo licked his lips and nodded a hello in Bryce's general direction. Bryce, as Eli's second, went to stand with Theo. Tempe positioned herself between the burley biker wizard and the lean sexy shifter and said soothingly, "Gentlemen, there's a task force tracking the Shadowed now. I'll admit our success rate leaves something to be desired but there's no reason to start a fight."

"Well, the task force sucks!" The savage growl came from a shifter. "Why haven't the wizards been caught?"

A female shifter added bitterly, "I just went to see my brother at the half-way house. He was missing for three years and now he won't even look at me."

Tempe focused on the female shifter, "We're searching for them. When we found the Shadowed facility in Canada we had two options: help the wounded or chase the Shadowed. I chose to help the wounded."

"Who are you?" a tall, thin wizard called out before he chugged the rest of his beer.

The majority of the bar turned to stare at the wizard. Preternaturals normally recognized the sovereign's second on sight.

"Her name is Tempest, ranked second in the shifter sovereign's Alpha Clan." The new arrival entered the bar, using wind to close the door behind her. "I'm Nova, high wizard. What seems to be the problem?"

The room went dead silent.

"We're not moving fast enough to please everyone," Tempe said.

"We aren't moving fast enough to please ourselves, Tempest," Nova responded blandly. To the room at large she added, "If anyone here has actual information we can use, present it now."

There was a lot of mumbling, but no one came forward. The angry in the bar were casting glances between Tempest and Nova. Deciding a fight against a tag team of the high wizard and the sovereign's assassin would not end well for them, no one moved or spoke.

Nova clasped her hands in front of her body and said, "Theo, perhaps a round for the bar would help everyone relax. Put it on my tab." The mumbling continued but everyone settled down and most even sat back down. The bar was no longer packed, as it had been minutes before, since those who wanted to escape a fight had exited. Nova joined Theo, Bryce, and Tempe at the bar.

"Thanks guys." Theo handed out shots of Gentleman Jack, knowing when Tempest wasn't drinking wine she turned to Jack. "This is the first dust up we've had, but a lot of bars have had problems. Tempers are running high and everyone is looking for someone to blame for the Shadowed."

"The only thing that's going to calm everyone down – including me – is finding every Shadowed facility. Shutting them down completely." Tempe downed the shot in one gulp, which wasn't her normal style. Shifters could get drunk, but it required them to drink a lot, drink fast, and keep drinking. Otherwise their metabolisms burn the alcohol too fast for anything but a momentary buzz.

"Tempe –" Bryce started.

"No. Don't Tempe me," she said crossly. "We should be better than this, stronger. How can we not find them? I've looked at the data from all sides. I can't find anything. I'm beginning to think they're smarter than we are." Tempe started out angry but ended by sounding dismayed.

"We will find them, my dear. Perhaps not as quickly as you think we should, but we will find them," the High Wizard vowed as she patted the much older shifter on the shoulder.

"But will we find them in time to keep us from turning on each other?" Tempe asked as she looked around at the anxious bar patrons who were accepting shots, draft beer or house wine. Most took the shots and downed their free drinks the same way Tempe had. No one looked relaxed or calmed by the drink, but then that wasn't the point. It was a diversion, not a solution.

The door opened, and a group came in singing A cappella. The bar turned as a group to tell them to shut up, but instead of yelling the bar patrons clapped and whistled for Waxing Moon. Their four-part harmony had made them big in country music. The band, while popular with the humans, was made up of shifters and wizards. They were doing their final tour since they don't age. After almost twenty years of performances, humans assumed they were going the plastic surgery route, but even using makeup to age their faces, they needed to retire from public life.

Bryce shook his head while the two female members of the band danced around the room singing. They were harmonizing a love song, and in less than thirty seconds the bar shifted from uptight to something approaching not quite mellow, but at least neutral.

The song ended, and the band walked over. Both girls hugged Bryce.

"Tempe, meet my sisters, Alyce and Bryana." Bryce introduced them once the bar settled down.

Alyce's blue eyes twinkled with humor. "I would be his older and wiser sister. Bryana is the younger and more impetuous sister."

"Actually, Alyce is the older and dictatorial sister, while I am the younger and more cunning sister," Bryana corrected.

"Either way I am stuck in the middle with an older sister telling me what to do and a younger sister running a scam," Bryce said in the tone of a man who knew he was doomed either way.

Bryana turned her shocked gaze on Bryce and said sincerely, "I don't run scams. I organize people's lives for the betterment of all." One of the male singers in the band walked over and put his arm around Bryana. She smiled, "Tempe, this is Shawn, my husband."

Shawn pointed to the rest of the band members to complete the introductions. "Jeremy sings alto. Taylor and Rusty play bass guitar and drums respectively. And Jackson plays lead guitar."

Once the introductions were over Taylor pointed to Rusty, "We need to stop by Eli's. If we don't check on Kaleb and Blake, Mom will have our heads."

Bryce looked surprised and Rusty added with a knowing smile, "They hate to admit they're related to us."

"Where are you staying?" Bryce asked the band as a whole.

"Well," Bryana said sheepishly, "We were hoping to stay with you, but you either sold or rented out your house. The kid who answered the door when we rang the bell looks nothing like you."

"I'm renting my house to my assistant DA. He's going through a divorce. You should have called first," Bryce explained, with no expectation of being listened to.

Tempe smiled, but before she could speak, Bryce cut her off, "No, they can't stay at Eli's."

Tempe raised an eyebrow and looked at him, as did his sisters.

Theo laughed, "I called Eli about the dust up. He heard them singing in the background and said to tell you your family is welcome at his house."

Bryce groaned, and Tempe laughed. They ordered a bunch of snacks and the bar begged for a couple of numbers. The band did a small performance, which did a lot to ease the tension.

In the car on the drive back to Eli's Tempe asked, "Why didn't you want your sisters to stay at Eli's?"

His hands tightened on the wheel. "They disrupt everything. Eventually the town will find out they're visiting, and the local reporters will be all over the place. It's harder to stay hidden from humans when Waxing Moon is around."

"I can see that, and we'll warn everyone to be on their best behavior, but it's not like they will be here more than a couple of days. They have a concert in Memphis on Saturday."

"You know their schedule?" Bryce glanced over at Tempe and his face took on a suspicious look.

"Sage had asked about seeing them in concert because Star likes their music. Their closest concerts were in Charlotte last night and in Memphis at the end of the week. There was no way for Star to see them and stay within Queen Niamh's zone of protection," Tempe shrugged.

"That's why you wanted them at Eli's." He smiled in relief. It was unlike her to want someone around who could expose shifters to the world.

When they arrived at Eli's it was obvious it would be a late night. After another round of introductions, and the kidding Blake and Kaleb took over hiding their brother's identities, Sage turned on Bryce.

"Why didn't you tell me Alyce and Bryana were your sisters?"

Bryce shrugged his shoulders, "I thought you knew. It didn't occur to me anyone wouldn't know. The clan knows. Heck, the town knows."

"Hey, I just figured it out, Alyce, Bryce and Bryana. Your mother took parts of your name to make the names for your sisters. That's so cool," Sage said.

Bryce rolled his eyes. He had been teased as a kid about their names. His name was unusual in American when he was born, although he was named after a relative from across the pond. Since shifters tended to have multiple births it was common for parents to follow some sort of pattern when naming their kids.

Catlin walked in from her shift at Harmony and said, "You guys saved the day. Even after you left, the bar stayed calm."

"How did you know to come in singing?" Bryce asked curiously. "It's not your style."

"When you weren't at your house we figured we could find you through the bar. Jackson felt the mass exodus from the bar of witches and folks with low power. Rusty found out what was going on, so we thought it would help if we came in singing," Shawn said with a shrug.

"It worked," Tempe replied.

"I don't think we did much," Jeremy said. "You and the high wizard had already taken over."

"Not really. No one wanted to fight the high wizard and the sovereign's second working together, but they were not calm." Tempe leaned back and grinned, "Not until Alyce and Bryana danced their way through the bar."

"Is this really your last concert tour?" Star asked wishfully.

"Yes. It's time, and this way we stop on a high note," Bryana said.

The next morning when Bryana came downstairs for breakfast, Bryce and Tempe were the only ones in the kitchen. Bryce offered her a cup of coffee. When she shook her head no, he almost dropped the mug. "You never turn down coffee. What gives?"

"I gave up coffee a while back," she replied mildly.

Tempe replayed last night in her head. Bryana didn't have a glass of wine either, which didn't mean anything, but still, Tempe looked over and raised an eyebrow.

Bryana saw Tempe's expression and blushed. "You know, Raven's a friend of ours. She hangs out with the band some. It's good for both of our images. She and Jackson are considered an item."

Tempe tilted her head and kept her eyebrow raised.

"Okay, but we haven't told anyone yet. I wanted to finish the final three concert dates before we announced. Then I can go into hiding and not have to worry about reporters." She took a deep breath and looked at Bryce. "Raven checked and I'm going to have twins, boy and girl shifters, in October. Since I'm not moon called I don't need a birthing bond."

Tempe shook her head. It's official. Suddenly every female shifter on the planet was pregnant.

Bryce looked at his sister like she was crazy. "Pregnant? You're pregnant?"

"Shawn and I have been married for almost twenty years. It shouldn't be that big of a surprise," Bryana replied in irritation.

"I didn't mean that. It's just… well, everyone seems to be getting pregnant," Bryce said softly. Then he picked his sister up and twirled her around the room.

Alyce walked in searching for coffee, "Guess she told you."

*****

On Friday morning, after the band left, Tempe called Jeff and asked him to meet her for lunch. She sat at the small diner drinking sweet iced tea when he walked in.

After the waitress took their order, Tempe asked, "Have you noticed how many shifters are pregnant now?"

Jeff shifted into doctor mode, "Tempe, are you –"

"No, not me," Tempe replied quickly. "But a lot of us are now. We're pushing the limits of the alpha ability to hold birthing bonds. Raven and I are the only ones capable of holding a bond who aren't. Many of my sisters are holding multiple bonds right now, meaning they can't shift or use certain powers. And then there are the females who aren't moon called and don't need a birthing bond."

He took a deep breath. "I hadn't realized. What do you think?"

"What I think is the only recent change is the inoculation we all received. Is it possible the preventive made conception easier?"

"No!" he said emphatically. He took a deep breath and added, "I'll check just to be sure."

They ate mostly in silence, reviewing the potential impacts in their minds. Preternaturals, shifters included, were slow to get pregnant and that was a good thing. With their long lives, and multiple births, if they got pregnant as easy as humans, shifters would overrun the world.

Chapter 3

The weekly clan dinner at Eli's was set up as a cookout. The June temperature peaked in the high eighties with that oh so famous southeastern humidity. At least it was still dropping to the sixties at night.

Three of the clan teenagers would be ranked after dinner and everyone was excited. Shape shifter clans rank members on their eighteenth birthday, or at the next meeting of the clan after that birthday. Clan rank was established by a dominance push. Each person to be ranked pushed with each member of the clan starting with the lowest ranked, and then continue pushing up the ranks until they face the person who can push them. Neither age nor the animal a person takes when they shift is a factor. The push is based on some internal thing, normally referred to as the individual's ability to lead. The top five members of a clan are called the cyngor.

Occasionally, a shifter will have to be re-ranked if it becomes obvious they should be. Likewise, a shifter could request to be re-ranked if they wish. It used to happen frequently but when the shifter community moved the ranking age from fourteen to eighteen – to match up to human laws on adulthood – there was a significant decrease in the need.

Bryce and Tempe sat on the deck off their bedroom in the new addition Eli added to his home, watching the kids playing tag. The seven-year-old Taylor triplets, Mitch, Michael and Mia, had talked the teenagers into a game. Ryan had taken his Great Pyrenees form and was running interference for the triplets who were too young to shift. Cinnamon was *it* and stayed in her human form. She laughed as the dog put himself between her and the kids. Nash ran over and let Cinnamon touch him, making him *it*. He shifted to his falcon and soared over Ryan and landed with the triplets between him and Ryan. The triplets squealed in delight as Ryan shifted to his fifteen-foot tall dark blue dragon and spread his wings. Although he wouldn't reach adult dragon size until he was closer to one hundred years old, he was still large enough for the kids to huddle under his wings.

Tempe smiled and winked at Bryce. She teleported and held out her hand to Nash. His wing touched her hand and she shifted to a falcon. Cinnamon's golden eagle and Nash's falcon joined her. They were joined by Nash's fraternal twin, Shan, also a falcon. The four birds dove at the dragon. Suddenly the dragon and the triplets were gone.

The feathered flying squad shifted back to human as they landed on the ground.

"No fair," Cinnamon laughed. "You can't veil the kids to protect them."

"You cheat, I cheat." Ryan's voice echoed around the yard.

"Nice." Sage drew out the word as she rounded the side of the house. She glanced at her aunt, "I can't tell where Ryan is. Can you?"

"Over by the fireplace," Tempe shrugged.

From the fireplace, Ryan dropped his veil and the triplets ran for Cinnamon. Giggling they tackled her to the ground. Nash went to her aid.

Ryan frowned, "How did you know?"

"The first echo was from there," she shrugged.

What started as a game for the kids became another training session for her nephew and sister. Both were strong shifters and would remain in the alpha clan for life, just as Tempe had.

Ryan was ranked a couple of months ago and was third in the alpha clan. Sage would be ranked next year. Like Tempe, they were both able to call multiple powers and take multiple forms, so they were training with her. It was one of the reasons they were all living with Eli's clan. They needed to be together to train and while Sage held a birthing bond it would be easier if she remained with Eli's clan.

Some of the men in the clan walked over and Theo commented, "Even when you guys play it looks like work."

Ryan directed a thumbs up at Nash, "Good move. I had to think fast to protect the triplets."

Nash returned his smiled, pleased with the praise.

Cinnamon sighed, "Wish I had thought of it. I knew I couldn't outmaneuver a dog, but I kept trying." She looked over at Nash and smiled shyly, "I didn't even think of shifting."

Tempe walked back toward the house and ran into Liz, Cinnamon's Mom. "It's so nice to see Cinnamon laugh. I'm glad she and Ryan are friends again."

"So am I," Tempe said. Ryan and Cinnamon were each other's first love but found they didn't suit. Not long after they broke up, vampires kidnapped Cinnamon. She was rescued before they could harm her, but the experience left its mark and she still didn't go anywhere alone. Ryan and Nash had taken it upon themselves to always be available when she wanted to go somewhere.

"Geez, Tempe," Star complained good-naturedly when Tempe and Liz entered the kitchen. "If you're going to get everyone shifting before dinner we'll need to make more food."

A shifter, or anyone who uses magic, must keep energy levels high. On the plus side, the members of the preternatural community – excluding vampires who rely on blood – need a lot of carbohydrates and sugars to restore energy levels. In other words, they drink soda and eat food like pizza and pasta and they have dessert at almost every meal. Another side benefit is shifters don't have common human health problems. High blood pressure and cholesterol problems are non-existent for full-blooded shifters.

Shifters also don't appear to age once they hit their thirties, when a recessive gene kicks in and their cells regenerate with wild abandon. Of course, shifters can be killed. There is no creature in the Farseen (Fae dimension) or the Seen (human dimension) that can survive having its head chopped off. Burning a shifter will kill them, as will bleeding out from a major artery cut. Crushing the brain or heart will also kill a shifter. Broken bones, minor cuts, and such, heal quickly.

After dinner, Eli's clan lined up for the ranking. Willow, born one day before Shan and Nash, went first. Normally when more than one dominance push is planned the oldest is ranked first. Willow pushed her way up the clan. When she came to Teresa, the woman who served as Willow's stand-in mother after Willow's human mother ran away, Willow balked.

Teresa smiled and said simply, "Push."

Willow smiled nervously and pushed. Then she pushed with Jeff, Ryan's father, and Phil, Cinnamon's father. Finally, she faced Star. Star, ranked two months ago, was seventh in the clan. Willow and Star pushed, and Star was the victor, leaving Star seventh and Willow eighth. Eli now had two teenagers in his top ten. Tempe looked over at him, smiled, and received his bemused smile in return.

Next up were the Clark twins, Shan and Nash. They had just moved into the clan with their parents. They would start their senior year at the same high school Willow and Cinnamon attend. The boy's father, Theo from the Harmony bar, was ranked in the middle of the clan as far as ranking went. Naomi, their mother, was human.

Shan, with an extra sixteen minutes of life under his belt, went first. He pushed his way up until he lost to Delaney. Nash lost to Dwight. The boys ended up fourteenth and sixteenth in the clan, respectively.

As soon as the ranking was over Sam indicated he wanted to speak privately with Tempe, so they went for a walk. Tempe's youngest brother moved to Eli's clan over twenty years ago to serve as the marketing manager for Eli's winery. They walked for a few minutes talking about nothing and she finally asked, "Is there something you wanted to talk to me about baby brother?"

He smiled at the phrase. Tempe was Rayna's first born and since she trained almost all of the siblings to manipulate their element as well as to use any alpha powers it was not surprising she sometimes became a mother hen with her siblings.

Sam took a deep breath and said, "I want some advice."

Tempe waited for him to continue, when he didn't, she prompted, "About…"

"What do you think of Tracy?" he asked in a rush.

"Tracy, the girl you've known for over twenty years. The woman you've been dating for at least three years. That Tracy?" she asked smiling. He nodded so she replied, "I like her. I think the important question is what do you think of her?"

They had arrived at a cave on Eli's property a couple of miles from Eli's house, and Sam sat down on the thinking rock. So many people came here to think Willow and Cinnamon put a little plaque that identifies the rock as the thinking rock a while back. He pulled a little box out of his pocket and asked, "Do you think she'll like it?"

It was a beautiful blue diamond. Tempe laughed, "Sam, if she loves you the ring will be the icing on the cake, and it's beautiful icing. You have excellent taste."

He grinned and said, "Bryce and Eli helped me pick it out. Tracy likes blue. I thought it would make more of a statement than a regular white diamond." Sam made a statement, but his tone was more of a question.

"You have excellent taste. You've never asked my opinion on much of anything in your life. Why now?" Sam had always been self-sufficient.

"Should I call Rayna first?" he asked.

"No," Tempe smiled, "Call Rayna after."

He grinned slyly, "We are going up to a little bed and breakfast in the mountains for a few days this week."

"That sounds perfect."

*****

While they prepared for bed, Tempe turned to Bryce, "You helped my baby brother pick out an engagement ring and you didn't tell me!" Even to her ears it was more of a pout than a statement.

He laughed, grabbed her in his arms and planted a kiss on her forehead. "I don't tell you Eli's clan business."

"But he's my baby brother," Tempe exclaimed.

"So is Eli," Bryce responded factually.

Tempe would have argued more but Bryce played dirty and gave her one of those feel it in your toes kisses. She liked those, and it gave her other ideas.

Next morning Bryce ran out the door for an early court appearance. Tempe sat in the sunroom with her laptop and cell phone taking care of alpha clan business. She was grumpy, thinking uncharitable thoughts about Rayna dumping all the crappy assignments on her second. Her mother was an unusual woman.

Rayna, the sovereign, married Ellwood, fae forest lord of the Northern Realm, when she was a teenager and they lived in the Farseen. The first thousand years of Tempe's life were spent with the fae. She would make trips to the Seen to visit her shifter family and train with her shifter uncle, Rayna's twin brother, but mostly she lived in the Farseen. Once her parents broke their vows, by literally taking the stone their vows were carved into and breaking it – the fae were nothing if not literal – Rayna and her shifter offspring moved back to the human dimension, where they were capable of defending themselves and others with extreme prejudice.

Rayna's mother was the shifter sovereign before her. The title passes down the mother's line, going to the offspring (normally daughter) who wins a dominance push with the current sovereign. Most people were looking to Tempe to take over. Most. Not all. One special person did not want Tempe to become the sovereign, Tempe herself.

Tempe has been Rayna's second since she became sovereign. No one had ever pushed Tempe except Rayna. They haven't entered into a dominance push since the day Rayna became sovereign. They created a dance where Rayna tells her second what she wants, Tempe recommends, they discuss, eventually agree, and then Tempe goes and does. The problem was they both knew Tempe might win a push with Rayna.

They came close a couple of months ago. Tempe ignored a direct order from Rayna, but most people assumed it was because Tempe was enthralled to a vampire. Bryce had been able to call her back to herself or she would have killed everyone there, unless they – her friends and family – managed to kill her first.

Star walked in while Tempe was reminiscing and sat down next to her and waited. Her father, Cloud, the high court envoy of the Central Realm, raised Star. Like all fae, she knew how to wait. Star was the daughter of Tempe's twin, Temperance. Temperance displayed no shifter abilities and she chose to stay with their father when the breaking of the vows occurred. When Star shifted for the first time in the Farseen, in the Central Realm Court no less, she came to live with Tempe to be trained. Lord Ellwood and the Shadowed had both tried to take Star for their own purposes. Star had decided to stay in the Seen and joined Eli's shifter clan.

Tempe smiled and looked up from her laptop, "Can I help you?"

"Now that I'm ranked in Eli's clan, I need a job of some type," she said, tossing her white blond hair behind her shoulders. As a daughter of a fae court, she would not have worked, outside of fighting and court duties. She only learned to cook after she moved to this dimension to learn to control her shifter self.

"What would you like to do?"

"I don't know. I'm good with kids," she shrugged.

"You could go to college and get a degree."

"I have no money. I'm living off you and Eli," Star groaned.

Tempe smiled, "That's what kids do. Until they are educated and working, their parents take care of them."

"But I only know how to do court stuff." Star moved firmly into whining territory.

"Then take some classes at the local community college. With the Shadowed and the fae decree I would be concerned about sending you away to school, even within Eli's territory, but you could take local classes and search for something you're interested in," Tempe suggested.

Star eyed her mentor, "What classes?"

"Let's go online and look," Tempe said as she went to the local community college web site and they dug through the various two-year degrees.

*****

Sage walked into the kitchen to fix a snack, followed by Willow, Star and Cinnamon. Cinnamon was on a mission.

"But Sage, if you don't go we have to ask Ryan," Cinnamon pleaded. "And I still feel strange going out with Nash if Ryan is playing bodyguard."

"Come on Cin, I'm a fifth wheel. I'm glad you all have guys, but I don't want to always play chaperone and watch you have fun. Do you realize that's the only time I go out now?"

"We could invite Shan or Blake," Cinnamon offered.

"Great, we've moved firmly into pity date territory," Sage replied in disgust before adding, "Besides I don't like either of them, not that way."

She was beginning to have doubts about ever dating seriously. Her empathic and telepathic abilities meant eventually she would pick up a random thought when her shields dropped, and she would hear something that would turn her off the guy. The last guy she kissed was thinking about another girl as he kissed her. A girl he still wanted to be kissing. Not romantic. No wonder Tempe shielded so strongly and hadn't dated much.

"You're right. I don't understand the whole movie thing anyway," Star replied. "Willow and Cinnamon can go with Kaleb and Nash. Then they won't need you or Ryan to guard me."

"Well, that sort of defeats the purpose," Willow groused. "Joey wants to see the movie. Besides, until the bounty on the 'girl in Eli's clan' is abandoned, we have to have a guard with us, too."

Tempe's cell phone erupted into Gretchen Wilson's *All Jacked Up*. The girls jumped and glared at Tempe as she answered the phone. "Hey Brandi, what's up?"

They had a quick conversation and made plans to meet up. As Tempe hung up the phone the girls moved to stand around her. Tempe laughed. "You guys look like you got caught with your hands in the cookie jar."

"You were listening," Sage grumbled.

"I work in the sun room daily. You know that. If you're going to discuss something you want to be private then you need to pick a private location," Tempe said.

"True," Willow agreed. "So, what do you think?"

"I think you girls need to work this out yourselves." Tempe closed her laptop. As she walked out of the room, she suggested, "You each might want to consider how you would feel if you were in the other's shoes."

Tempe stopped at the door, "Star, don't forget Ridge will come tomorrow night for his monthly check for the Northern Realm. Sage, it's your turn to be the chaperone."

Sage rolled her eyes at the use of the word she had used earlier. At least it was better than being *Shield Girl,* which seemed to be her function within the alpha community. She was one of the few alphas who could shield a large area, making it her primary contribution whenever anything happened.

Chapter 4

As it turned out, Tempe was meeting Brandi at Half Acre and Sage and Star were volunteering there so she drove them over. It was a quiet drive as the girls were deep in their own thoughts. Tempe remained silent as well, letting the girls stew. The trio walked into the halfway house Nova had created for the preternatural half-breeds who were rescued from the Shadowed in the Canadian facility.

Tamra saw Star and exclaimed in relief, "Thank goodness. All of the fae are upset today. Could you sing?" She pointed toward the living room and the piano.

Star walked over to the piano and played. The refugees gathered around, and Star sang a fae love song. Those in the room physically relaxed. Sage went to talk to a couple of the patients, Arleth and Gavin, who had refused to leave their rooms, even to visit with family. After listening for a few minutes Tamra pointed to the office and Tempe followed.

"Why are they upset?" Tempe asked, cutting to the chase.

"The Western Realm wants Drago, Ifor and Amity back in the Farseen immediately," Tamra said with loathing. "They don't bother to help with the recovery, but apparently the two half-wizards will be useful to them. I think they believe they have to accept Drago back also." Drago was a fae/shifter mix but didn't shift and had little magic. Ifor and Amity were both fae/wizard mixes and fairly strong.

"It's not surprising. The Western Realm lost a lot of the ruling fae in the Freed Fae War. They probably need fighters to fill out their ranks." Tempe shook her head, "It's not what I would like but we can't keep them here forever, especially if they want to return to the Farseen. Do they?"

"It's where they were raised. They want to go back, but they're nervous."

"I'll get with my contacts and see if we can at least make it a smooth move for them."

"Thanks." Tamra focused on her desk piled high with paperwork.

"How about Duane? He was raised here, right?"

"Yes, and he's agreed to stay here for a while. He could have left almost as soon as we got him here. Thank goodness he stayed. Since he protected the others from the Shadowed as best he could, they all look up to him."

"I've sparred with him a few times and he's powerful. I still think he could have escaped from the Shadowed," Tempe said.

"I could have, or died trying, but I wouldn't have been able to take the others with me." Duane entered the room.

Tempe raised a surprised eyebrow when he walked in without knocking. Since it was Tamera's office and she didn't object, Tempe ignored what, to her, would be a breach of protocol. "I don't think I would have been able to stay just to protect others. I'm pretty sure I would have escaped and gone back later with reinforcements."

"Lady Tempest, I've heard the songs. You would not have left the others, although I do think you would have been able to stage a successful escape for everyone." Duane slid into one of the cushioned chairs, relaxing like he belonged there.

"Have you remembered any details about your captors?" Tempe had asked a variation of that question every time she spoke with him and his answer was always the same. She kept hoping to spur a memory.

"No. They masked themselves." He smiled his apology.

"The Western Realm will come at sunset on Friday to take their members back to the realm." Tamra's eyes didn't leave her laptop screen.

"I can be here if you wish."

"Yes, please."

"What about Yarrow?" Tempe asked. Yarrow was a fae/shifter mix but she didn't shift and had been raised in the Southern Realm.

"The Southern Realm has invited her back but she's still skittish. Her cousin, Stone, visits weekly and they're making progress. Hopefully, they'll work it out."

"The big news is we tracked down Dana and Cindy's families just this morning. Both of their parents were killed in car crashes and their daughters' bodies were never found. We called the grandparents of both and they are on their way. It will be hard. Both girls are fourteen and were with the Shadowed for ten years. I'm not sure when they will be able to return to their families," Tamra sighed. "Neither girl will do anything without Duane's okay."

"I'm sure they'll get over it soon enough," he said depreciatingly.

"I'm not," Tamra said. "The twins, Brandon and Landon, are the same way, but they're showing improvement, at least Landon is. Arleth and Gavin won't leave their rooms on their own. None of them will eat anything without your okay. Arleth and Gavin had visitors the other day and they wouldn't even look at them until you ordered them to do so."

Duane shrugged.

Tempe couldn't read anything from his expression. She had opened her mind a couple of times over the past few weeks to try and read him, but she got nothing. He was probably mind blind, someone no one could read. "How about Dylan? His father, Garvey, is flying in from Scotland next week."

"He's doing rather well. We'll just have to wait and see." Tamra looked out the window at nothing.

Tempe's brow furrowed as she realized Tamra had poured everything into helping these people and she looked exhausted. Tempe made a mental note to talk to Nova. Tamra needed a real vacation.

"Where's Brandi? She wanted to talk to me," Tempe asked.

"I think she's in the garden with the twins, Lady Tempest," Duane responded with a courtly bow as he opened the door for her.

"Why do you sometimes call me Lady Tempest? Only the fae raised in the Farseen do so."

Duane smiled, "My fae father was a bard. He sang songs of you when I was young. I always thought court life sounded exciting and you were larger than life. I like to think of you as the Lady Tempest in those songs."

"If the songs he sang are some of the same ones I've heard, then you are doomed to be underwhelmed by me. I'm not that brave, that strong, that smart... or that foolish." She walked out the door laughing. He bowed with a flourish and closed the door after her, staying with Tamra.

Tempe found Brandi in the garden talking to the twins. They didn't hear her approach, so she stopped to listen.

"You tried to escape a couple of times?" Brandi asked.

"Yes, but we were always caught. After a while Duane said we should lay low and wait for the right opportunity," Brandon replied.

"How long since you last attempted escape?"

"I don't know. Maybe six winters." Landon shrugged his shoulders.

Six years? Surely Duane tried more recently. Tempe stuffed down that thought and commented as she rounded the corner of the path between the bushes, "You two look cheery today." They were both sporting Hawaiian shirts with their jeans.

Landon blushed, "Sage told us she would show us her veil if we wore something bright today."

"Then she owes you a veil. Speaking of powers, tomorrow night is the full moon. Perhaps you would enjoy running with Eli's clan. It's my turn to cook and I make a pretty good dinner," Tempe said.

"I don't know," Brandon frowned.

"Please guys. I would love to see you shift." Sage walked around a high hedge.

Landon looked at the beautiful alpha shifter in a cotton sundress and responded immediately, "Sounds like fun."

"But Duane said..."

Landon spoke over his brother, "Duane isn't going to be here forever. We must think for ourselves."

Tempe smiled. That was encouraging. Maybe the twins would be all right if they could consider life without Duane. The research into their family found their mother's wizard family was dead, killed in a massive home fire during a family get-together, and they didn't know their shifter father. The twins had been listed among the dead in the fire. The more they found out the more obvious it was the Shadowed would kill entire families to get their hands on an interesting mix of preternatural blood.

Sage remained with the boys as Brandi and Tempe walked away. Tempe looked up and saw Duane frowning as he looked out his second story window, watching the twins. She waved. After a second, Duane pasted a smile on his face and waved back. He wasn't happy but then, he might still be dealing with demons of his own.

*****

Ridge arrived at the cave right on schedule. Sage shielded Star while Ryan and Bryce patrolled.

"Hello Ridge," Tempe said calmly.

"Lady Tempest, it's always good to see you," Ridge bowed to both women. To Star he asked, "How are you Lady Star? Do you still enjoy living in the Seen?" He started every visit the same way.

"Yes, Advisor Ridge, I do. I'm happy here," Star replied formally, just as she did every visit. Since Ridge was the only person to call her by her fae title, lady, she enjoyed meeting with him.

"I'm glad," Ridge said, and he meant it. He actually wanted Star to be happy.

Ridge was Lord Ellwood's closest advisor and at one time he was Tempest's lover. Actually, Ridge was her first love. She had wondered if that's why Bryce got so jealous around Ridge. Bryce always patrolled when Ridge visited.

Ridge and Star talked about people in the realm courts for a while, as they always did, and eventually Ridge said, "I have enough for my report this month." What wasn't normal was when he continued, "Sage, if you would head back with Lady Star I would like a private word with Lady Tempest."

Instantly, an African lion and an Akita jumped into view, growling. Tempe stuffed down her laughter.

Ridge grinned and quipped, "Ryan and Bryce may stay if you need protection, milady."

Tempe rolled her eyes. The term 'milady' could only be used by fae in reference to a lover, former or current. It was an obvious dig at Bryce.

Bryce shifted, but before he could speak Tempe took one of his hands and patted his shoulder with her other hand. She turned to the lion, "Ryan, walk back with the girls. Bryce will remain."

Once the kids left Ridge said, "Your father is at the Harmony Bar. He wishes to speak with you. We gave him the full series of shots and he is himself again."

"A fae realm lord is currently sitting at the bar? Bet that emptied out the place," Bryce commented.

"Let's go see what Father wants." Tempe tightened her grip on Bryce's hand, then she grabbed Ridge's arm and teleported the three of them to Bryce's SUV.

Ridge smiled as Tempe pointed to the front passenger's seat. She crawled into the back, where she could keep her eyes on Ridge. Bryce drove.

As Bryce predicted, the parking lot was empty. They walked in and Theo let out a breath he must have been holding for a while. "Tempe, I'm glad you're here. There's a fae sitting at the bar claiming to be your father and he's waiting to talk to you. Someone recognized him as a realm lord and the bar pretty much emptied." He looked at Ridge and raised an eyebrow.

"Sorry Theo. Ridge – Lord Ellwood's advisor – just informed me Father was here and wished to speak to me. In the future, you might want to offer him a private room." The number of customers could be counted on one hand and those people were subdued.

"I did," Theo responded tightly. "He said he wanted to sit at the bar like regular folks."

"Aha, well, that's Father," Tempe murmured. As they walked over he shed his glamour and looked like the seven-foot tall forest lord he was. His white blond hair and jade green eyes contrasted nicely with his dark skin. "Lord Ellwood, father mine, what brings you here?" Tempe made a move a generous person might consider a bow. She always had trouble giving her father the respect he thought he deserved.

"Lady Tempest, daughter mine, 'tis good to see you." Lord Ellwood smiled. "I see you are escorted by Ridge and Bryce. How amusing."

"Lord Ellwood, what do you want?" Tempe clenched her teeth, not wishing to prolong the conversation by starting a fight.

"Child, I am no longer drugged, however, I still want to talk to my granddaughter," Ellwood said.

"If you want to talk to Star you need the approval of the clan cyngor, not mine."

"Bryce is a member of the cyngor. He can grant approval."

"No. Not without Star's agreement and the agreement of the rest of the cyngor," Bryce said firmly. "The decree was plain, the entire cyngor has to agree, not one member of it."

"Ah, yes, I was told you are a politician. I'm surprised my daughter would take a man who does everything by committee."

Before Bryce could respond, Ridge said, "My Lord, Queen Niamh's decree was specific, and Bryce is correct. Eli's entire cyngor must agree and since Lady Star has joined Eli's clan I suspect they will not agree if she does not. I suggest Bryce take your request to the cyngor and then Lady Tempest can inform Central Envoy Cloud of Lady Star's wishes in this matter."

Lord Ellwood scowled and turned back to his glass of wine. "I must admit the humans have finally started making good wine."

Tempe glanced over to the bar and Adelia held up the wine bottle. Tempe smirked, "I'll tell Eli you like his Cabernet Sauvignon, Father. I'm sure he'll be pleased his wine meets with your approval."

Lord Ellwood looked at his empty glass in disgust and walked out of the bar. Ridge bowed with a smile and followed.

Bryce and Tempe sat down at the bar and nodded their heads to Adelia, who was still holding the wine bottle. She poured two glasses.

"Every time I meet your father I am uncharitable enough to wish the man could not enter our dimension," Bryce said. Their glasses clinked before they took a sip of Eli's wine.

"On the plus side, Father didn't try to kill you. That's three times he has been near you and not attempted to end your life." Tempe raised her glass in another salute.

"That's right, maybe he's starting to like me." Bryce grinned, taking another sip of wine.

Theo walked past and commented dryly, "It might be better for you if Lord Ellwood continues to ignore you."

*****

They were back at Eli's early in the evening. Tempe climbed the stairs and knocked on the boys' room door. When Ryan yelled, "Come in", she walked in to see he was the only one there. "Are the others out for a while?"

"Yes," he replied.

"You've shown promise in the casting arts. I want you to try to make twinned spelled rings for you and Sage, like the ones Bryce and I have."

"Why?"

Tempe rolled her eyes. "I know you think you'll never need to be saved but how about Sage? If you can pull off this spell it will go a long way toward keeping both of you a little safer."

"I thought you were the only one in the family who could create one."

"To create the spell, you need strong abilities in the casting arts and a strong connection to the person. I think you're strong enough. You should try, but even if it works it will take some time, so it's better not to talk about it until you get it right."

Ryan sighed, and they went over the basics of what he would need to make and was surprised he would also need to purchase a few items. The next hour was spent on the mechanics of the spell and explaining to Ryan how he would need to choose the words. Later they would work on the cadence and inflection. This was a ritualistic spell and he would have to learn a lot to do this one right. It's not as easy as a one-word spell.

Before Tempe left he asked, "How about spelled clothes? Can I learn that spell?"

"It's not one spell, it's a series of spells taking months to layer over the clothes. Let's see if you can do the comparatively easy spelled rings first."

Ryan looked at the lengthy notes he had just taken for the first part of the ring spell and shook his head.

Tempe smiled as she walked out of the room. Everyone thought spells were easy, until they tried to do them. There's a reason most people with ability have a handful of spells they consider their go to spells.

Chapter 5

Wednesday dawned dreary and damp from an overnight rain that didn't appear to be going anywhere. The full moon run promised to be a wet one. Tempe was, per normal, working in the sunroom when Ryan, Star and Sage entered, sat down and waited.

Tempe looked over her laptop and asked, "Something up?"

"Tonight's the full moon." Ryan commented.

"It is."

"Tonight's also Wednesday," Sage added.

"True," Tempe agreed.

Ryan rolled his eyes, "So you have everything worked out for Cloud and Temperance to visit, but you haven't bothered to tell us."

Tempe laughed and exited email. "Actually, we only worked out the details a few minutes ago. Ryan you'll pick up Cloud and Temperance and bring them to the house just before sundown. They would like to see Star shift. They may fly some with Star running, depends on how things go. You will stay with Star this evening on guard duty."

"Of course," Ryan agreed. Yep, he was ranked third in the alpha clan, but he might as well be called *Sentinel Boy* for all the action he saw. His lot in life was to run a patrol or guard someone.

Tempe's lips twitched, but she waved toward Sage and continued, "Sage convinced Brandon and Landon to run with the clan. She'll be with them."

The three of them stared at Tempe, waiting, so she added, "I don't know which group I'll run with yet. I might not run since I'm still working through some stuff." Tempe pointed at the papers on the table.

"What happened last night?" Star asked quietly. Joey walked in, saw Star's face and moved to her side when she motioned for him to sit with her. Ryan stood to make room for Joey, acknowledging Joey's superior claim to be by his cousin's side. Tempe tried not to grimace.

"Lord Ellwood wanted to meet with me. He was waiting at Harmony. He requested permission to talk with you. Bryce and the cyngor will talk to you to see what you want. The choice is yours," Tempe said.

"Why does he want to see me?" Star asked.

Tempe chewed her bottom lip, "I don't know, and I need you to understand I must be at any meeting you have with Lord Ellwood. I don't trust him. Don't get talked into meeting with him when I'm not around."

Star nodded her head as Joey put his arm around Star to comfort her. Tempe looked down at her laptop, so she wouldn't raise an eyebrow at him.

After the kids left, Bryce passed through, leaving for work. "You looked alarmed. What happened?" He said as he laid down his briefcase and sat beside Tempe, pulling her into the warmth of his arms.

"I'm not alarmed, I'm concerned," she replied as she snuggled in properly. "I think Joey and Star are getting serious and Joey doesn't understand about Star and her sheltered life in the fae court." Tempe chewed her bottom lip.

"Don't worry," Bryce grinned and planted a kiss on her forehead. "Joey asked me a lot of questions about the fae in general and Star specifically. I explained about her sheltered life and how male members of the court get permission to approach a daughter of the court."

"You explained." Tempe laughed in surprise. "How do you know?"

"You always underestimate me." Bryce shook his head in mock sadness. "I remembered the stories you told me. Plus, I've talked with Cloud and Temperance, Clare, and your mother. I even called in the favor Saffron owed me from her apology when she attacked us." He laughed for real. "I think they thought I was asking because of you, but I noticed how Joey looked at Star and thought he might need to know."

"How did you contact Saffron?" Tempe asked, surprised.

"Clare made the arrangements for me, although she didn't want to. I thought she was going to turn me down flat, but Rayna entered the room and Clare decided to play nice."

"What do you mean Clare decided to play nice? Is she difficult to work with?"

"Ask your family, or anyone really." With the slip already made, Bryce went for full disclosure. "Everyone knows Clare is the most difficult of the alphas to deal with. She's a bit holier-than-thou most of the time. Anyway, Saffron met me at the thinking cave when you guys went after the last round of infected up north. She seemed pleased to pay off the favor in such an easy manner."

Tempe pulled him into a kiss and reminded herself to stop underestimating her man. In the back of her mind she worried about Clare's attitude. She knew a problem was brewing and had ignored it for a while. Obviously, it was time to address the issue, whatever it was.

*****

Sam and Tracy were the first to arrive for the full moon run. Tracy had the blue diamond on her hand and everyone congratulated the happy couple.

"Eli, with your approval, we want to have a private ceremony here. Nothing fancy, just the clan and our families."

"Should be okay. Have you picked a date?" Eli asked.

"Next month. We were thinking Saturday, July sixteenth, the day after the full moon," Tracy said shyly. "Like Sam said we aren't wanting fancy."

Tempe frowned, and her brow wrinkled. "Isn't your mother a wedding planner?"

"Yes," Tracy said guiltily. "That's why we want to invite them down for the weekend to run with us and then tell them about the wedding." Everyone had the same stunned look on their faces, so Tracy added, "I spent my childhood watching people go crazy over their wedding. I don't want that. I just want to marry Sam and see everyone. Mother will forgive me." She sounded more hopeful than sure.

"Okay then, let me know what I can do to help." Tempe wondered if Tracy's mother was the calm easygoing type who would be happy to get out of planning a wedding for her daughter, or if a storm was brewing.

The rest of the clan arrived and began grazing on the finger foods Tempe laid out. Brandon and Landon walked in with Sage and Brandi. Both men were nervous, but they already knew the clan members who volunteered at the house and it seemed to help. Ryan left to meet Temperance and Cloud as soon as Sage arrived.

Star rolled her eyes at the tag team protection. Tempe smothered her smile at the face Star made. When Ryan returned with Star's parents they talked for a while.

Star took Temperance to show her the information on photography classes and Joey remained with Cloud.

Tempe tried to get close enough to step in and help Joey if needed, but Bryce pulled her aside and whispered, "Let Joey handle this himself. Some things a man must do alone."

A few minutes later, Temperance and Star returned, and Tempe saw Star blush with pleasure at whatever Cloud said so Joey had done well for himself.

Outside, Brandon shifted into a brindle Great Dane and Landon to a blue Great Dane. Sage couldn't shift because of the birthing bond but she was going to walk with them for a while. The other dogs in the clan gathered around and Sage set off down the trail, looking like a dog walker, without the leashes. Akita Bryce was with them, so Tempe felt they were in good hands. Blake and Kaleb, both mastiffs, ran with the dogs as well, but Joey, an Irish wolfhound, ran with Star and Ryan. Cloud and Temperance stayed with them.

The large predators, wolves, big cats, bears, and such divided up amongst the two groups. Eli's clan was so good to help out. Tempe went back inside to pour over the Shadowed information one more time. She just knew she had missed something.

A couple of hours later, Sage screamed in Tempe's mind. Tempe focused on Sage, realized where she was and teleported to the cave. She expected to see a fae fighting force entering through a way to grab Star. Instead what she saw was masked wizards brandishing rune weapons, and no shifters. Sage must have veiled them all.

Having learned this lesson a few months ago, Tempe wore full battle gear on the full moon now, since the full moon – when most shifters have to run – is the best time for shifters to be attacked. Tempe didn't ask questions, she threw water to keep the wizards focused on breathing instead of spell casting. Of course, one shifter against five full wizards were not odds she liked. Wizards were the powerhouses of the magical community. Sure, Tempe holds a lot of power, but five wizards were five wizards. If they let loose with their best spells she was done for. She tossed a sleep spell which they easily deflected as one of them used some spell – not wind – to toss Tempe through the air and into a tree.

Temperance and Cloud joined the fight. Eli shifted to human and joined Ryan, in lion form, beside Tempe. Sage continued to veil and shield everyone else.

Temperance, Cloud, Ryan and Tempe attacked as Eli focused to siren the wizards. Apparently, they knew about Eli because one of the wizards threw a curse and Eli dropped before he could execute his siren call.

Tempe couldn't see what the others were doing, because she was busy getting tossed against another tree by the same spell. It was powerful.

As she pulled herself up after the second toss into the tree, one of the wizards called out, "Envoys of the fae high court. We do not seek a child of any realm. We have come for the twin Great Danes. Stand aside."

"The Shadowed will take no more, from any preternatural species." Cloud tossed a fireball at the wizards. A fireball they had no problems dissipating.

Ryan, now in human form, unleashed a focused freeze spell with his newly created rune weapon. He had chosen a twenty-three-inch staff as his rune weapon. Only one of the wizards froze. Cloud used water to keep another wizard from chanting. Temperance circled two of the wizards with fire.

Tempe opened her mouth to enchant the group, but as soon as she did, she was dropped by the same spell that dropped Eli.

*****

When Tempe came to, she slowly opened her eyes to see Bryce's concerned face.

"Ugh, did we get them?" Tempe asked as she tried to sit up.

"Nova sent them packing, but no, we didn't get them," Bryce replied angrily as he pulled her to a standing position.

"One was Radek and I think another was Yula, at least the size and build were right. The other three I didn't know," Tempe said. "By 'sent them packing' you mean –"

"He means when I teleported here, to the location of all the wizard magic I felt, they saw me and ran like the cowards they are," Nova replied.

"What about the one Ryan froze?"

"Radek took the frozen one with him," Nova growled.

"Is everyone okay? I saw Eli drop." Tempe continued to lean on Bryce.

"I'm here but I've got a major headache," Eli replied somewhat unsteadily. He didn't bother to move off the ground.

She looked around and asked, "So how did they know Brandon and Landon were running with us?"

No one answered. She didn't expect them to.

"Sage, take everyone to the house under your shield, Ryan, run patrol," Tempe ordered.

Both sighed, but Shield Girl and Sentinel Boy carried out their respective tasks.

"Nova I need some answers, now," Tempe demanded. Bryce, Eli, Temperance and Cloud had remained with Tempe.

Nova raised an eyebrow, "What answers do you think I have?"

"What wizards do isn't like the teleportation I do. It's more subtle, and I don't feel it."

"It's still teleportation. Yours is based on either shifter or fae magic while ours is based on wizard magic." Nova explained. "I can feel a wizard teleport but not shifters or the fae."

"Oh," she replied, feeling a little foolish. "So how would the wizards know about Eli's ability to siren and my ability to enchant? How did they know Brandon and Landon were with us in shifter form? How did they know who Temperance and Cloud were? Heck, they even knew they were here to see Star. That's a lot of knowledge considering shifters and fae haven't worked with wizards much." Tempe took a deep breath and added, "We have a leak."

"I would say it's more of a flood then a leak," Nova said.

Chapter 6

"Tempest, we need to talk, now," Charles said forcefully when she returned to the house.

Eli, Bryce and Tempe headed for Eli's soundproof office with Charles, Asilia and Adam leading the way. As the last one in, Tempe shut the door. Although she didn't see a way around it, her actions had, once again, put Eli's clan in danger they would not normally experience. They had been extremely understanding over the last few months, but maybe this was the final straw. After all, wizards were a scary lot.

Charles growled, "This has to stop." When Tempe would have spoken, he glared at her. "Please don't interrupt me Tempest. I need to say this."

Tempe was so surprised Charles was angry, not scared, she closed her mouth.

Once he saw the powerful shifter was going to listen, he continued. "Sage and Ryan cannot shield us all the time. We could have helped you, but Eli was the only one they allowed out of their shields until the fighting ended. You need us, whether you like it or not. We are able to defend our own clan. If you think we can't then you should take it over."

Tempe looked at him shocked, and then she looked at the rest of the cyngor. They agreed... with Charles.

Asilia stepped in, giving her father-in-law a chance to breathe. "Tempe, protecting the children, wounded, and pregnant is one thing, but protecting those of us who can defend ourselves is wasted energy. We need to settle this now. Either there will be some new ground rules, or we have a problem that will destroy this clan."

Tempe glanced at Adam and he nodded his agreement. She didn't need to look at Bryce or Eli. She knew what their answer would be, so she mentally called for Sage and Ryan. A few seconds later there was a knock and she said, "Enter."

"You wanted us?" Ryan questioned softly, looking at the room full of angry adults. He couldn't come up with anything he had done to anger Eli's entire cyn.

Sage was just as confused.

"Yes, come in and shut the door." Tempe took a deep breath, "We have been too quick to raise a shield around Eli's entire clan whenever problems arise. The clan cyngor will now give us instructions on who to shield and when to shield them."

Tempe looked back at the cyngor and it was their turn to be shocked. After a few seconds of silence, she said, "See the problem? It's quick and easy for Sage and Ryan to raise a shield in a dangerous situation but it's hard to come up with specific rules for when they shield and when they don't."

Tempe took a deep breath, blew it out, gritted her teeth, and offered a compromise. "This is my suggestion. Sage and Ryan will continue to raise shields when danger is present but any member of the clan cyngor can request certain people be allowed to leave."

Before the kids could question her, Tempe held up her hand in the universal signal to stop. They remained silent.

"What do you mean request?" Charles asked.

Tempe chewed her bottom lip before responding. Although Eli's clan has already learned most of it, alphas didn't normally share details of their telepathic ability. "When we are in a combat situation, I can send a message to Sage and Ryan mind-to-mind. Sometimes they have information you don't. There might still be times when you want to help, but they can't allow you out of the shield."

"Would today have been one of those times?" Asilia asked curtly.

"No."

"Let's give Tempe's suggestion a try," Adam said.

Ryan looked at each adult before raising his hand like a kid in grade school.

"Yes Ryan," Tempe said, "Do you have a question?"

"You keep drilling it into my head I'm to protect clan members before everything else, including I keep a clan member safe even if an alpha needs help. Those instructions contradict letting clan members out of the safety of a shield."

"The only real rule, set by the first sovereign, is and I quote: *We only use our alpha powers openly, in front of humans, to defend the children and human members of the clans from another preternatural threat.* We've had so many centuries without a preternatural conflict we started defending the entire clan."

Tempe took a deep breath and said, "While I hate the thought of it, the mandate of the alpha clan is not to protect the shifters who can defend themselves, but to protect the human members and children of the clan and of course the wounded."

Asilia smirked, while Adam and Charles smiled. Tempe still didn't look over at Eli or Bryce as she asked grimly, "Does this satisfy everyone?"

After a chorus of 'yes' from the cyngor Tempe faced the teenagers. "Both of you need to work on tightening up the hole you create to let someone in or out of your shield. When the shield is open magic, projectiles like bullets, and even adversaries, can get through."

Everyone filed out of Eli's office except for Tempe and Bryce. Eli was the last to leave, shutting the door after a tacit look with his second.

"You're not happy with this turn of events," Bryce said.

"No, I'm not," Tempe retorted through clinched teeth. "What I just agreed to could get your clan members killed. Why should I be happy?"

"We're not children and what Asilia said is true. You guys put yourself in danger by protecting so many. Even the Shadowed figured out you're spread too thin."

"The Shadowed had help. They have an informant and you know it," Tempe snarled.

"Tempe, look at me."

Tempe growled.

Realizing he had gone too far, Bryce added, "Please."

She looked up into his eyes. His beautiful, blue eyes always made her weak in the knees.

He shook his head. "Do you realize I have to bite my tongue every time you leave on a mission for the sovereign or for the Shadowed task force?"

Tempe nodded.

"I know if I don't let you be yourself I will lose you. So understand this. If you try to keep me in a safe bubble you will lose me." Bryce pulled her into his arms and added, "It's the same for Eli's clan. You can't protect people all the time and expect them to be happy in their gilded cage. It's still a cage."

Tempe chewed her lower lip and Bryce smiled, "Every time we argue, and you chew your lower lip it means I won. Did you know that?"

Tempe growled but he kissed her so it came out as more of a purr.

*****

Friday, the day the Western Realm would reclaim their own, Star arrived at Half Acre to sing calming songs. Those who had been captured by the Shadowed deserved some peace, but sometimes she felt like a hero in one of Logan's comic books, no, not a hero… a sidekick. If anxiety is high, call Zen Lady. Babies crying? Call Zen Lady. Feeling depressed? Call Zen Lady. Call Zen Lady and everyone will feel better. The shifters weren't doing anything new. The Central Court had done the same thing, but she had thought it would stop once she became a lady of the court. Now she wasn't so sure. Even after getting ranked in the clan everyone called her for any attitude adjustment needs.

She exited the car with a sigh, an entourage, and the realization she had become accustomed to being guarded all the time. She didn't like it, but she was accustomed to it. Joey was over the top protective because of a perceived interest he thought Duane had in her. As if! Duane was old, at least forty based on comments he had made. Ryan stuck to her like glue, which was just amusing. Tempe was part of this entourage, rendering additional guards unnecessary.

Duane leaned on the deck railing and called, "Lady Star, you're expected in the sitting room."

Star inclined her head in acknowledgement but didn't speak. She found it odd Duane called her Lady, but it was nice to hear and made her feel like an adult, almost. He did the same with Tempe, though he had been raised in the Seen. Perhaps he thought they expected courtly ways.

Star went to the piano and started her concert with a lovely ballad from the Western Realm. Ryan and Joey stayed with her.

*****

Tempe walked to the location where the fae were allowed to open a way inside the High Wizard's territory. A smooth way opened, and the Western Realm delegation arrived. Jerran and Leitha walked through along with a squadron of warriors.

"Expecting trouble?" Tempe raised her trademark eyebrow.

"Lady Tempest, we know the Shadowed tried to take two of your residents during the last full moon." Leitha, half a head taller than Tempest, shortened her stride to match the half-breed's. "I also know of your concerns for the three fae of the Western Realm. They will be well cared for. You have my oath."

"I'm glad they're able to return to the Farseen since it is their wish." Tempe was relieved to have the oath from Leitha more than anything else. "I will warn you Star is currently singing to them. She is, of course, guarded."

"Naturally," Leitha replied with a smile. "I would be insulted if you didn't consider me to be at least a possible threat."

Tempe grinned at the typical fae response. They considered it a compliment if you mistrusted them.

Leitha stopped and stared when they entered the house. "I've heard tales of Star's voice. Everyone in the Farseen knew of the Central Realm daughter of the court with the idyllic enchanter's voice, even before it became known she was part shifter. Until this day I had not heard it. Her voice is exquisite."

While others said good-bye to Drago, and Amity, Ifor talked to Duane privately. Tempe looked over at Tamra and she shrugged her shoulders. A few minutes later, Jerran opened a way and the Western Realm left.

As she turned back Tempe noticed Duane staring at Star. When he noticed Tempe watching him, he stopped and shot her an apologetic smile. Tempe wasn't the only one who noticed.

Joey had placed his arm around Star and moved to stand between Duane and Star. Duane smiled for real at the younger man's jealous maneuver and walked back into the house. Tempe almost cringed over Joey's arm, but he had the approval of Cloud, and Temperance for that matter, so she mentally shook herself and let it go.

Tempe overheard Willow talking with Brandon and Landon. They appeared to be recovering from their scare on the full moon, although Brandon kept saying things like "Duane said" or Duane thinks". At least Landon seemed to be thinking with his own brain.

*****

Fallon, Brandi's father, flew in with Garvey Waters on Sunday to see Dylan. Brandi and Adam picked them up at the airport. Bryce had already brought Dylan over to Eli's for a last medical check by Jeff. Dylan had been with the Shadowed for four years. He had moved to the states after his mother died and immediately stopped talking to anyone. At first his father thought the boy needed some time, now he knew the truth. He was alone in a new place and the Shadowed took him.

Fallon and Garvey walked up the deck and into the sunroom where Dylan was sitting. No one moved, or even breathed, for a couple of seconds, and then Dylan stood up and hugged his dad. Everyone cleared out to give them some privacy.

While working on the weekly clan dinner, Tempe's cell phone rang Fleetwood Mac's *You Make Loving Fun*. She looked in surprise at her phone since that ring tone was just for Bryce and he was upstairs. The text asked her to meet him in their bedroom. It was odd, so she excused herself and ran up the stairs. When she entered the bedroom, Landon was sitting on one of the desk chairs.

"Why didn't you guys come downstairs?" She asked.

"Can't," Landon replied. He looked like he was in pain.

Tempe went over to him, "What's wrong?"

"The pain? I don't know. I'm here because of Brandon. He's not him anymore," Landon replied. "I know it doesn't make sense, but he used to think for himself, now he just does what Duane says. Everything Brandon says or does has a certain type of logic to it, but it just feels off. I can't explain it any better."

Tempe looked over at Bryce and shared a memory, a time when Tempe was just a little off. She had been the thrall of a vampire.

"Is it Brandon that seems to be a bit off or his words?" she asked slowly.

"Both, but sometimes it seems his action, or expression, doesn't match what he's saying." Landon ran his fingers through his hair.

A thought occurred to her and she asked, "How did you get here?"

Landon leaned back in the chair and spread his legs out, hooking his thumbs in his front pockets. "Shifted and walked over as a Great Dane, why?"

He didn't seem to be in pain anymore.

"You shouldn't do that. The wizards the other night knew what your form was and they wanted you," she explained.

He gasped, "I... I didn't think. Why didn't I think of that?"

"I don't know but we'll get you back safely," Bryce promised.

They talked for a couple of minutes and decided Tempe would take Landon back the same way Landon arrived, by the deck steps. She escorted Landon back to Half Acre.

When they left Bryce went downstairs and grabbed Jeff and they went to Eli's office for a quick chat. He knocked on the door and they entered when no one answered.

"Jeff, is it possible to drug someone to have stomach pain or cramps if they disobey you?" Bryce asked without preamble.

The doctor's brow furrowed as he thought about the question. "That sounds more like a casting than a drug. Why?"

"I need you to check out Landon. He was in a lot of pain while trying to tell Tempe and me something. Something the Shadowed would not want us to know. As soon as we moved on to another topic his pain went away," Bryce replied before shifting gears to ask, "One other thing, did you find out anything about all the pregnancies?"

Jeff raised his eyebrows and Bryce blushed. "Tempe told me about your conversation. I was curious."

"My research team is working on it. It doesn't make sense," Jeff replied.

*****

"Oh, look who finally shows up to help," Sage commented dryly when Tempe walked into the kitchen. "Gee sis, you outdid yourself for tonight's dinner."

"Sorry guys, I went to take care of something and time got away from me."

"Imagine that. Bryce calls her, she disappears, and time gets away from her," Sage teased. Then she looked her sister in the eye and the color drained from her face.

"What's wrong?" Tempe asked.

"Nothing," she said as she returned to slicing brownies.

"Let's step outside so you can get some air," Tempe said, her tone just shy of an order. "It looks like most of the work is done."

As soon as they were on the porch Tempe asked, "Did you break through my mental shield?" If so, that would be a first. Excluding two powerful telepaths born of her grandmother, no one had ever broken through her mental shield.

Sage dropped into the porch swing. "Yes, I didn't mean to, but Landon was in your room and he's in trouble."

Tempe joined her younger sister on the swing, "Jeff and Nova will figure out who is messing with Landon, but right now I need to know if you pushed through my mental shield or if I dropped it."

"It felt like you dropped it. I thought you wanted me to see something, so I peaked."

"Interesting, I didn't intentionally drop my shield." Tempe took a deep breath. "Okay, my mental shield is set. Try to break through it."

Sage looked at the mountains and nothing happened, then she turned to her eldest sister, they locked eyes and she went right through Tempe's shield. She retreated, and they sat there for a minute.

Eventually Tempe said, "So you have to lock eyes with someone to push through their mental blocks."

"I guess." Sage looked a little pale. "I'll try to tighten my own shield. I don't do that unintentionally."

Tempe smiled, "That's a good idea. It also explains why you can't block some people well. For anyone who doesn't maintain a mental shield you probably read their thoughts automatically when you look them in the eyes." Sage looked appalled, so Tempe added, "Tighten your shield. I know you aren't doing it on purpose, but some might have a hard time understanding. Get Ryan to work with you on shielding your mind. He is the most focused of the alphas."

*****

"Jeff didn't find a medical reason for Landon's cramps." Tempe stated flatly as she sipped the tea Nova had just poured. Jeff had called in the results right before Ryan and Tempe left Eli's.

"Not surprising," Nova responded. "Landon has an unusual spell web over him. If he says anything the web is searching for, his stomach cramps up. I will remove the spell this evening but then we will have to protect Landon to prevent the spell from being cast again. And no, I can't tell who did it. I can tell you it was a wizard, but the wizard is not of the high coven level and the wizard is probably using other wizards or witches to beef up his or her power for the spell. A spell of this type has to be reinforced on a regular schedule so it's someone he sees regularly."

"Great, just great." Tempe's tone implied it wasn't great at all. Tempe took another sip of tea and asked, "How goes the search for Shadowed facilities?"

"It doesn't. We can't find any hint of their power," Nova said with disgust.

"I still think they might be in the Farseen. I doubt the fae checked the wastelands carefully." Tempe leaned back in the chair and stretched.

"I've heard you and Raven talk about the wastelands, but what are they?" Ryan asked.

"Each realm has a remote area the ruling fae has left untouched. It's not a true wasteland, but it's a name that's stuck. The realm wastelands can be jungles, plains, deserts, mountains, wherever the realm lord assigned the wasteland eons ago. Anyone who enters a wasteland unprepared will die. It's the land where most of the wild, more animalistic fae live and where the less cuddly fae live, those fae who like to feast on other sentient beings. It's also where the plants can and will kill you," Tempe answered. "In the Northern Realm it's the land farthest north, past the caves where you and Siri were held by the goblin."

"I don't remember the landscape from that trip," Ryan responded tightly.

Tempe patted him on the shoulder, sorry she had brought up a painful memory. They drank the rest of their tea and reviewed options for finding the Shadowed.

As they left Nova's and headed down the trail to Eli's Tempe asked, "How goes the creation of the spelled rings?"

"Frustrating," Ryan replied.

"You thought it would be easy? If it were, everyone would do it," Tempe commented with a smile.

They stopped at the cave on Eli's property and went over more of the spell requirements. Three hours later, when they stopped for the day, Ryan asked, "Are you sure these rings are worth it?"

"That's something you have to decide for yourself. If you don't think so, the spell won't work. Intent and desire are important with this type of spell," Tempe explained.

*****

Star requested a special outing for Misty's next visit as it landed on her birthday. It took a lot of coordination, but Tempe got approval from everyone and on Wednesday she and Ryan waited at the cave as Captain Tero and Misty came through the way.

The birthday girl looked around and smiled. Thorn, son of Terra, Eastern Realm envoy to the fae high court stood with the sovereign's second and third. Dawn, daughter of Elros, Cavern Lord of the Southern Realm, was also there with Stone of the Southern Realm.

"What brings so many to protected territory?" Misty asked shyly with her eyes locked on Thorn.

Captain Tero smiled. "This is an approved excursion to the Seen under Lady Tempest's charge."

Tempe returned Tero's smile, "Star wanted you to have a special treat for your birthday. She wants you to see a movie. We're going out-on-the-town as the humans say."

They met up with the partygoers at Eli's house. Bryce, Tero, Stone and Tempe would attend the movie with Sage, Landon, Star, Joey, Cinnamon, Nash, Willow, Kaleb, Misty, Thorn, Dawn and Ryan. Blake and Shan were working, and since Shan worked at the theater, the kids planned to rib him. In addition to the visible chaperons, a large number of the clan were eating out or walking around the theater. They went to the early show and then headed back to Eli's with lots of pizza.

They entered the house as Eli and Delaney headed out the back door. They would meet Brook over at Harmony to cut down on the siren sightings. The kids had a great time. Tempe was in full protection mode and was pleased Ryan and Sage also kept their eyes peeled. Good. This was the first attempt at inviting fae to Eli's for a relaxing evening and it needed to go well if it stood a chance of being repeated.

Stone raised an eyebrow when Ryan taught Dawn how to play pool. When Ryan slid his arms around her and placed his hands over hers on the pool stick, Stone visibly cringed.

Tempe smothered a smile and said, "He's only showing her how to hold the pool cue but if you prefer, I can show her."

"Lord Elros was specific. He said Ryan was trustworthy and Dawn could see what life was like in the Seen," Stone said apologetically.

Captain Tero relaxed in the recliner, secure in the knowledge Thorn had permission to court Lady Misty. He didn't envy Stone at all. If Lord Elros decided Stone had allowed his daughter too much freedom, Stone's life would be forfeited.

A screech from outside broke up the party. Tempe felt Sage's shield go up around the teenagers. Ryan came quickly into the living room.

"That's a vampire." Tempe headed for the door. She opened the door and didn't dare go outside of the threshold. At least two colonies of vampires, around fifty individuals, stood in Eli's front yard.

"What brings thee and thine here unbidden, Overseer Imani?" Tempe asked formally.

"I have information for you on the Shadowed. Protectorate Gwaednerth ordered me to deliver this to you in reparation for the actions of Rainer and Kier," Imani replied calmly. She held in her extended hand a computer disk.

Tempe sent Ryan a command and he gritted his teeth, an action she didn't catch as she was focused on the vampires. Tempe raised an eyebrow. "And you brought so many to deliver a small disk?"

Imani smiled showing the tips of her fangs, "It seemed wise. You and your young alpha male have shown great skill at killing vampires of late. Ryan killed Rainer and Tatsuo, both old and strong vampires, you both use the Farseen sun spell only the Wizard Murdoch used before."

Tempe pulled out her rune Kobudo and stepped outside the threshold. "Indeed. After I was attacked three times by vampires, Murdoch decided I needed better protection." She walked to the bottom of the porch steps and stopped.

Imani was still smiling, fangs still extended, as she walked over and handed off the disk. Tempe stared hard at the vampire's left ear, making sure direct eye contact was not made, thus protecting herself from becoming enthralled.

"I'm sure I will put this to good use," Tempe replied accepting the disk. Tempe backed up the steps.

Imani backed into her minions. Once safely surrounded by her vampires, a heavy mist covered the ground, and they disappeared.

Tempe backed across the threshold and commented, "I hope the information on this disk was worth the stress of that conversation."

"How will we know they are gone before we leave?" Stone asked.

"We'll take everyone back to the cave under Ryan's shield," Tempe explained. Bryce made a couple of phone calls to warn everyone to stay away from Eli's home until they were called.

Ryan rejoined the other kids. They seemed to think a vampire visit was icing on the cake. While they played pool and video games, Tempe opened her laptop and all the adults gathered around to look over the new data.

It didn't give them immediate answers, but it was data, so they were happy to get it. Tempe sent the data out to the task force in the Seen via email and used a communication stone to send the information to Temperance, who would pass it out to the five realms.

When it came time to break up the party Tempe said softly to Bryce, "You stay with Sage and the shifter kids, while Ryan and I escort the fae back to the cave."

Clinching his teeth, Bryce nodded.

"Dawn, in light of the vampire visit, could you teleport all the fae, plus me and Ryan to the cave?" Tempe asked.

"Yes."

"Excellent. Do you think you can teleport with Ryan's shield around us?"

Dawn smiled and looked at Ryan, "You were right." To everyone else she said, "Ryan and I tried. We can."

"Tried what?" Stone asked, aggravated.

Dawn's smile wavered just a bit. "Ryan set a shield around us, and Star. I teleported the three of us to the kitchen and back to the game room."

"While you guys were looking over the disk," Ryan offered.

"Just because you're visiting in the Seen doesn't mean you can ignore the rules of your realms." Tempe said sternly. "If you want to try something like that again, you have to make sure the adults know. And if anyone tries to say, "Star is now an adult in the eyes of the fae and shifter communities and she knew", I will not be amused."

Ryan, Dawn and Star tried to hide their grimaces proving to all of the adults they had prepped that exact response.

"Ha," Sage smirked, her comment just shy of an I-told-you-so, making it obvious she had told them her eldest sister wouldn't fall for that.

Stone held back a smile when he replied, "No harm done. I'm sure they would never do such a thing again."

"Don't bet on it," Tempe muttered under her breath as Ryan smiled his best good-old-boy-trust-me smile.

After exchanging goodbyes, Ryan set a shield and Dawn teleported them to the cave. Stone opened a way and he and Dawn left. Thorn had been invited to the central ream for a visit so apparently both realms approved of his interest in Misty. Tero opened a way and those going to the Central Realm departed.

Ryan commented, "It was nice Dawn and Thorn were able to visit."

She hid her smile and replied, "Indeed, it was."

He looked at her suspiciously. "How did that work?"

"Thorn has already received Lord Sky's permission to court Lady Misty. Mistress Dawn asked about you every time she has talked to Lady Temperance, so I decided to invite her." Tempe smiled for real and asked, "Do you object?"

"No." Ryan's face turned a nice shade of red. "I don't mind at all."

They both heard Sage's call. Tempe grabbed Ryan and they teleported to the garden outside of Eli's house, to find doors and windows were guarded. Since the caped men and women had rune weapons she went out on a limb and whispered, "Wizards." Ryan nodded his head and veiled.

Tempe opened fire, literally, with her rune weapon. Two of the three wizards she fired on burned. The third, shield in place, turned and charged directly at her.

Ryan didn't unveil until the last second and Tempe would never be sure if the wizard saw the lion that killed him. Tempe sent Ryan around one side of the house and she took the other. Tempe took out another wizard and, from the sound of it, so did Ryan.

Maybe they were just witches or low-level wizards, but it was a point of concern the wizards they fought weren't strong. For a real attack, surely the Shadowed would send strong wizards to a clan stronghold where alphas were currently living.

By the time the duo met at the front of the house there were three wizards in plain sight. Tempe recognized Radek and Yula, but she didn't know the third woman. But she did recognize what they were doing, a three-wizard chant.

Add a veil to your shield, Tempe ordered directly into Sage's mind.

I am. Sage's exasperated response could not be hidden in a mind-to-mind conversation.

Tempe opened her mouth to freeze the three wizards and discovered she couldn't speak. She glanced at Ryan and saw he couldn't either. The wizards were blocking their ability to speak. Being able to enchant didn't work so well when everyone knows you can enchant, and knows you have to speak and be heard to make it work.

Ryan, in dragon form, blew fire, but it didn't reach them. They were shielded, rendering the element powers useless. Tempe's sleep spell was absorbed into their shield as well. She felt relieved when she felt a siren's presence and waited for Eli or Brook to siren the wizards.

Too late she realized she didn't sense a shifter, just a siren. Tempe saw Ryan fall unconscious to the ground before following suit.

Chapter 7

Tempe came to with manacles around her wrists and ankles. A small pull of wind sent a nasty electrical shock through her body, meaning the manacles were fae made and resistant to magic. She could feel her clothes on her body so that was an improvement over the last time she was restrained like this. Experience had taught her to assess damage before opening her eyes and then to open them slowly. She didn't appear to be injured, not even a headache and when she opened her eyes the room did not move, but there were marks on her arm that looked suspiciously like they had taken blood, given her a drug, or both.

The room was not an old castle or fortress as recent experiences would have suggested. In fact, it appeared to be a sterile clean room, with no windows. She looked around and didn't see Ryan. She wasn't sure if that was good or bad. What was a definite not good was all of her jewelry was missing. Without the ring on her finger, Bryce would not be able to find her. Without the ring touching her skin the spell doesn't work. She had created twin spelled rings, one for her and one for Bryce. Tempe wasn't sure if her captors knew about the spelled rings or if they just removed all jewelry as a safety measure since it was no secret she spelled various pieces of jewelry.

Tempe tried to send a focused message to any alpha. The sharp pain in her head confirmed there was a dampening field around her. She suspected as much, but it had been worth a shot.

A door slid open. Radek smiled as he sauntered into the room. "Tempest, you're awake. You have cost us many subjects and a lot of research. It seems only fair you serve as one of our new half breed subjects."

"I've never been a lab rat before," she scowled looking at the pricks on her arms. "Exactly how does that work?"

"I'm no fool. The vampires allowed you to learn too much from them. I regret you are restrained but it is the only way to make sure you don't escape." Radek opened a refrigerator door and pulled out some serum and loaded up a syringe. "That vaccine your doctor worked up is amazingly strong. But don't worry, we're working on something new."

Tempe tensed as Radek walked over. When she realized there was no way to get away she tried to pull wind anyway, hoping it would loosen the restraints. The jolt knocked her back and did break both of her ankle manacles, but it didn't set her arms free. When her manacles broke a loud alarm rang. Guards ran into the room.

Tempe expected the extra muscle to use magic but when the first one she kicked blocked the kick with the precision of someone who had practiced the move thousands of times and the others grabbed her she realized Radek was using actual muscle to guard her as well as magical. Trained wizard fighters, how discouraging.

As Radek shot the serum into her arm she had time for one thought before sleep claimed her, when she escaped the best she could hope for was house arrest, again.

Tempe woke up and surveyed her surroundings. She had new manacles on her ankles. They were bolted next to the old ones and they looked to be a bit more secure. The only knowledge she acquired was they didn't move her to a new room. It would be good knowledge to have if she had a clue as to the room's purpose or where it was located.

She tried again to contact any alpha by attempting to push through the dampening field and grimaced as a thunderbolt of pain coursed through her head. She was furious with herself for getting captured and worried about who was trapped with her.

It was obviously time to escape. She had a goal all she needed was to flesh out a few details.

*****

Seven or eight shots later, and who knows how long, Tempe felt groggy but didn't feel like she was under anyone's control, however, the last time she didn't feel that way either.

She could feel the serum attempting to work. It felt like getting a shot for pain that wasn't strong enough. She leaned against the wall, manacled, and it occurred to her if she could feel it trying to work, maybe they would think it was working.

For the next shot, Radek walked in with the wizard Tempe had seen back at Eli's. The unknown wizard was a little on the short side, not even five and a half feet tall with light brown hair.

"How do you feel, Tempest?" she asked.

They had asked the same question every time they entered the room. Suspecting there might be a reason she took a chance, "How should I feel?" Tempe responded looking into her eyes.

She smiled and turned to Radek, "I think it's working."

He pushed the mousy aide aside, knocking her against the refrigerator, and said, "We'll give her another shot, just to be sure."

After Tempe submitted to the shot without the fight she had been giving them, she was careful to not change her facial expression as they turned and walked out of the room.

Later, when Radek and Alena walked in, it felt like around eight hours had passed, but when one is drugged, chained to a wall and unable to see the outside world, accurately judging the passage of time was iffy at best.

"I want proof. Something she would not do without the drug," Alena, former member of the Wizard High Coven whispered as they entered the room. Apparently, she didn't know about shifter hearing.

Radek didn't bother to whisper, "Considering how she reacted to Tatsuo, that fool of a vampire, I have just the test."

Radek walked up to the shifter, "Tempest, how do you feel?"

Tempe looked into his eyes, "How should I feel?"

He smiled, "Obedient. Kiss me as you would your love."

Not original, but she had expected something along those lines. Tatsuo had made Tempe his thrall but since Bryce was her true love, the vampire could not make her desire him, which was a little-known requirement for a vampire to seduce someone. The person must surrender freely.

Tempe could not move her hands or feet, but she leaned forward and ran her tongue across her upper lip. He smiled and closed the distance between them, grabbed her around the waist and exploring with his hands while he kissed her.

Alena tapped her foot, "Enough. I'm convinced. You can release her, but you'd better control her."

As she walked out of the room Alena called over her shoulder, "If you bed her Bryce will come after you."

Radek smiled and commented, "Might be worth it." Softly he murmured, "I think one more shot, just to be sure."

Tempe smiled up into his eyes as he gave her the shot and another kiss.

As he walked out, Radek said, "We can dance soon."

As Tempe dozed – the shot couldn't break through the anti-virus but made her drowsy – and waited for Radek to release her she held onto one thought, based on Alena's comment they didn't have Bryce and he wasn't dead, which means they didn't get inside the house. Bryce would either be dead or a captive himself before he would let them get the kids. All she had to worry about was Ryan and any other beings they had managed to trap.

Well, there was one other thing to worry about, she doubted there was enough mouthwash on the planet.

*****

Tempe looked up when the door opened and immediately schooled her expression into one of compliance. Radek walked in with Duane, the fae/wizard half-breed who had protected everyone at the facility in Canada. At least she knew who the leak was. Tempe focused on Radek and waited for him to speak.

"Tempest, do you know who this is?" Radek asked.

"Duane Hughes," she answered. "We rescued him from the facility in Canada. He's helping the others adjust."

"I still am," Duane drawled. "When next you see me, you will not remember you saw me here."

"As you wish." She kept her face relaxed and stared away from the men.

"I don't know. She's awful strong. You sure?" Duane asked with a slight frown.

Radek grinned, "Kiss her and see for yourself."

Duane walked up and said, "How do you feel?"

"How should I feel?" She asked.

"Submissive," he smiled as he pulled her into his body and kissed her. Tempe once again remembered the greater good, freedom and Bryce, as she leaned into the kiss. When he finished, and she mentally gave him a sentence of wounded, not dead, since he didn't go exploring with his hands, Duane said, "I believe you."

Radek and Duane released Tempe from the manacles. She played meek and subservient girl as they walked down the hall. It was a new role for her but she had always been adaptable.

Duane pointed at one door and commented, "Interesting he hasn't accepted the serum yet."

"Not really," Radek said, "We gave her a double dose from the beginning. This evening Yula will start doubling his dose."

In her mind she planned their murders. On the outside she walked calmly beside Radek, as if she didn't hear what they said.

They stopped at a door and Radek asked, "Do you want to join us?"

"No, I don't share well," Duane nodded and continued down the hallway.

"Your loss," Radek said as he ushered Tempe into what she expected to be his living quarters. She was not disappointed. It looked like normal research quarters, complete with a desk, computer, intercom,

TV, bed, dresser, loveseat, closet and a door that probably went to a bathroom.

Radek walked to the desk and lifted a lid off of a platter of food. "I know shifters eat a lot, so I had some food sent to my quarters."

She tilted her head to the side and asked, "You prefer to eat now?"

He smiled and sat down on the couch, "I prefer other things but I'm good with a little anticipation."

"I want what you want," she replied as she straddled him. He pulled her tightly into his body and kissed her, which should have been the last thing he ever did. Instead a loud and annoying alarm went off.

"Naturally," Radek exclaimed in disgust. "Stay here," he said as he ran out of the room.

Tempe smiled what she hoped was a drugged stupor of a smile. She noticed the jewelry and weapons sitting on his dresser. She walked over to look but touched nothing. She picked up half the sandwich, lay back on the bed and waited while she ate.

A few minutes later Radek returned. "Sorry to keep you waiting. Why are you still dressed?"

"You told me to wait. I thought you wanted to undress me," She answered, careful to avoid staring at the camera in the vent.

"Well, now, that would be a treat," Radek said as he crawled onto the bed, placing his legs on either side of her body and leaned over her, fumbling with the buttons on her shirt.

"I would enjoy a shower."

He shrugged his shoulders and pointed to the door. "That seems reasonable." He lay back on the bed.

Tempe stopped at the door as she finished unbuttoning her shirt and said, "Aren't you coming?"

Radek's eyes raked over her body, "Yes."

Tempe turned and walked into the bathroom dropping her shirt in the doorway. He hopped off the bed and followed. They left the bathroom door open and the steam from the shower filled both rooms.

After a respectable amount of time, but not too long, for whoever was watching the camera feed, Tempe walked through the steam filled room, grabbed the weapons, jewelry, and the other half of the sandwich. She headed out the door to find Ryan. Radek was unconscious, not dead. She wanted answers.

Tempe walked down the hallway wishing she could throw a strong veil but doubted she could maintain a veil a stronghold of wizards couldn't pierce. Her veil was a spell and not a shifter talent like Sage and Ryan possessed. Instead, she glamoured so anyone she passed thought they were seeing Radek. Depending on the strength of the wizard, it wouldn't work for a detailed look, but most people didn't look at him. It made her skin crawl just to see the expressions the women tossed her in Radek form. Most were scared or wary, but a couple actively shot flirty winks at his likeness. Maybe some women like an all-purpose sleaze or perhaps they were applying for promotion the old-fashioned way.

Tempe went to the door Duane had pointed to, hoping it had not been another test. She opened the door to find Ryan, trussed up like a Christmas turkey.

She smiled.

"It won't work," Ryan growled when Radek walked in. "When are you going to give up?"

Tempe lowered her voice into the male range as best she could and responded, "We won't ever give up?"

Ryan looked at Radek, shook his head and opened his mouth to speak. Tempe hit him lightly in the jaw. "Don't speak boy. Tempest is already under my control, you will follow soon enough." The dampening field even prevented her from talking mind-to-mind with Ryan less than two feet from her.

Ryan's eyes widened at the tap on the jaw, but he closed his mouth.

Tempe looked around the room, found what she was looking for and then took out her rune weapon and sent a focused spell at his manacles. They opened, and the alarms went off.

Tempe dropped her glamour and they headed for the door. She tossed him his rune weapon from the pile she had picked up in Radek's room. Ryan veiled them as they ran down the hallway, checking doors as they went, but they didn't find any more test subjects.

They continued running inside Ryan's veil, throwing spells and elements at anyone in their path. Eventually they just pushed people out of their way. There was no way to go back and interrogate Radek. There were too many wizards casting various versions of a see-that-which-can't-be-seen spell. The exit was heavily guarded, and they could both see the web spell that would trap them if they were foolish enough to try the door.

Tempe pointed her rune weapon at an outside wall and sent a blasting spell. The wall exploded as Ryan took his dragon form, still veiling them, and flew out the opening with Tempe in one of his claws.

Tempe grimaced. She was thrilled to be free, but seriously, she was being carried in a dragon's claw. At least they were veiled so no one could see her less than majestic escape.

They flew south for a while but eventually had to concede they didn't know where they were. Ultimately, Ryan needed to rest so they stopped on the side of a mountain. He gently released Tempe from his claw as he laid her on the ledge, before he shifted to human and dropped his veil.

"Any ideas?" He asked as he dropped to the ground, tired.

"We're in the human dimension," Tempe said. "Beyond that, these mountains look like mountains everywhere. We could be in the Canadian Rockies, or the Sayan Mountains in Russia, or any remote place high enough to have some snow in June. I haven't seen any obvious landmarks."

Tempe pulled her ring up to her lips, blew on it and said "Bryce". The ring glowed green when she pointed southeast. She smiled, "Maybe we're in the Rockies."

Ryan looked at her, tired, hungry and confused. Tempe explained, "Radek took my ring so Bryce would not have been able to find me. If Bryce is southeast of me he is probably still in Tennessee, or just leaving. I've only had the ring on for an hour or so."

She hadn't tried to contact anyone mind-to-mind since they left the facility, so Tempe dropped her mental shield and called Rayna. Talking mind to mind was not her favorite way to communicate, but a lot of information could be exchanged quickly. They were the only two taken and her mother said Bryce was already in the air heading for the Rockies. They were somewhere near the Montana/British Columbia border.

"Rayna says to stay put. She's sending help." Tempe sat down next to Ryan.

"Got any food?" He asked hopefully.

Tempe smiled and offered him the other half of the sandwich from Radek's room. "I saved this for you."

He smiled and raised the sandwich to his lips, but stopped and offered, "We should split it."

"Thanks, but I had the other half before I tracked you down and you've been doing the heavy lifting. You need it," Tempe replied.

He smiled and dug in. Between bites he asked, "Why don't we just open a way to the house?"

Tempe shook her head. "The alphas will need to verify we are in control of ourselves before we just appear."

He growled but didn't say anything else.

A couple of hours later she heard Sage in her mind saying to look for Ben, he was close.

She noticed Ryan was looking also. Tempe laughed. "Sage sent the message to both of us, didn't she?"

"Yes, and she needs to not scream in my head," Ryan complained.

"Tell her. She's the one alpha you can talk back to mind to mind," Tempe reminded him. He smiled and since Sage got softer in her head Tempe assumed he sent the message.

Eventually they spotted Ben about the same time he spotted them. "Tell me you have another flying form besides a dragon," Tempe requested. "Otherwise I need to teleport us."

Ryan smiled and shifted into a golden eagle. She smiled at the form he hadn't shown her yet and shifted into her falcon. His ability to take new forms was amazing. They flew down to Ben, where his team handed out food and water, which they gratefully accepted.

"Where are we and how long did the Shadowed have us?" Tempe asked Ben. He was the leader of a clan in northern Wyoming and one of her brothers. Like most of Rayna's kids he shortened his name to something more manageable. His given name was Benevolence.

Ben smiled, "You're in Glacier National Park just south of the Canadian border in Montana." His face turned serious as he added, "You've been missing for seventy-two hours. It's Saturday."

"That means around the clock alpha guards, again," Tempe moaned. Ryan looked up at her and she added dryly, "Yes, you, too."

He scowled.

Ben grinned, "At least Bryce is on the way, Tempest. Apparently, Rayna allows you alone time with him."

Tempe rolled her eyes but smiled, as Ryan bemoaned his fate. "But I don't have anyone like Bryce."

"You're too young to have found your soul mate, which reminds me," Ben said with a teasing smile. "Congratulations on your alpha ranking, nephew." Ryan rolled his eyes and accepted another sandwich from the hikers.

They hiked down to a base camp and waited.

*****

Once the alpha plane landed Pat teleported to the base camp and then teleported everyone back to the hanger where two alpha planes waited. After a round of thank you and goodbye, and an unnecessary introduction of Bryce to Ben during which Tempe found out Ben and Bryce knew each other from years ago, Ben's team went to their plane and headed back to Wyoming.

Ryan and Tempe boarded the plane for Tennessee and found Raven, Clare, Char, Lea and Lark, in addition to Pat, from the alpha clan.

Ryan looked at the ceiling and huffed, "You were right, three guards for each of us." He plopped down in a chair and promptly went to sleep.

Raven raised an eyebrow as Tempe smiled. "I'll start writing up the report now. Let him sleep. He had to fly carrying me with his veil active for a long while. He's tired."

Raven provided Tempe with a laptop and she began her report. Bryce sat next to her and she knew he was reading over her shoulder, as was Raven and Lea, so when she hit the part she knew Bryce wouldn't like, she stopped typing for a second and stared into space, but then she looked him in the eyes and found her center. She didn't say a word but renewed her typing.

Bryce knew whatever Tempe was going to type would be bad because of the way she looked at him. He was surprised when she didn't ask him to leave. Even with the warning, when he started reading about Radek his hand tensed on her leg. He was so looking forward to meeting up with Radek in the future.

Tempe could feel the anger rolling off of Bryce. She kept typing, knowing the anger was directed at Radek. When she identified Duane as a member of the Shadowed, Raven used the plane phone to make a couple of calls.

While Raven placed the call, it occurred to Tempe she should have mentioned Duane as soon as she contacted Rayna. Hopefully, she was tired and not under anyone's influence.

When Tempe finished her report, she looked over and Ryan was awake and waiting for the laptop. She handed it over and he typed. Raven and Lea moved over to read over his shoulder. Tempe decided to lie back and sleep with Bryce next to her. She could read Ryan's report later.

Bryce didn't say anything as she laid her head on his shoulder. He put his arm around her and held her while she slept.

*****

When the plane landed in Tennessee, Ryan jumped up to help unload. Since he was frequently the only male traveling with his many aunts, he normally unloaded the bags.

"Sit down Ryan," Tempe said calmly when the other alphas tensed.

"What?" He looked around the cabin. His aunts had all taken fighting stances. With a silent oh he sat back down muttering, "Sorry, habit."

Bryce sat with Tempe and Ryan as they waited to be told they could exit the plane.

"This sucks," Ryan complained.

"Indeed, it does. And since I've already been through this once this year I think I have more right to complain. You must understand it's hard on them, too. When we exit, I suspect there will be wizards and possibly Rayna. You and I are second and third in the alpha clan. Their ability to contain both of us requires a lot of effort on their part and you shouldn't do anything to make it worse. Don't grouse," she ordered.

"But we're fine." Ryan's exasperated sigh was loud.

"That's exactly what I thought after Tatsuo and I was anything but fine." Tempe took a deep breath. "Let them do their jobs."

Raven walked back on the plane and motioned for them. Bryce stood back as Ryan and Tempe exited the plane. Tempe could see his concern, but she also saw a look pass between Raven and Bryce. Apparently, the two of them reached some sort of detente on the rescue flight. Bryce had been less than friendly with Raven since he learned she carried a dart that could kill Tempe.

As they exited the plane Rayna, Nova and Murdoch were waiting. Charles, Asilia and Brook were also there.

Tempe was surprised and impressed. Brook's ability to siren would be a huge boon to the alphas if Ryan and Tempe turned on them and she suspected Charles and Asilia were there to support Brook.

They had pulled directly into the alpha hanger at the airport so obviously there would be testing before they went anywhere.

Jeff stepped from behind Rayna and said, "I need blood samples."

"Do you want to take them, or shall we give them to you?" Tempe asked. She had learned long ago when you were powerful and capable of killing a large number of people quickly, the softer she kept her voice the better.

"I'll take them." Jeff took a couple of steps before Raven stopped him.

"Sorry Jeff." She took the kit and asked Bryce, "Do you know how to take blood?" When Bryce responded in the affirmative she tossed him the kit and said, "Tempest first."

Tempe rolled up her sleeve and Jeff swore. "How much blood did they take from you?"

"No clue. Every time they gave me a double dose of the drug they took blood, and the drug made me sleepy. I think around eight or nine times," she offered.

"They were doing three shots a day," Jeff muttered to himself. He turned to his son and said, "How about you?" Ryan rolled up his sleeves and his arms looked about the same.

"Bryce, one vile from each. I want to do run tests before we take more. Did either of you get a sample of the serum they gave you?"

Ryan and Tempe each pulled out a couple of vials from pockets and handed them to Bryce.

Bryce took Tempe's blood and then Ryan's. While that was going on Tempe felt the wizards prep a shield with a spell over it. As soon as Bryce walked off she said, "Ryan, if we meditate, they can verify our minds quicker." They both sat down on the ground and assumed their meditative pose of choice.

Eventually Tempe heard a mental knock and opened her mind to allow Nova and Rayna access. They poked and prodded but eventually left as Rayna commented Tempe's mind was empty, which she assumed was her mother's idea of a joke.

After some period of time they spoke out loud and said, "They are each alone with their thoughts."

"Excellent!" Ryan said as he stood up, "Drop the shield and let's go home."

Once again all of the alphas tensed as Tempe corrected her nephew, "We aren't clear until your father finishes the blood testing."

He plopped back down on the ground and snarled at Tempe, "Why are you so relaxed? You've never been patient."

"Bryce is here," Tempe said simply. Bryce beamed and most of the alphas smiled.

Phones beeped as Rayna and Nova received text messages at the same time. Nova shook her head, "I doubt anyone will be surprised but the raid on the facility was a bust. When Satish and Kyan arrived with their teams the place was deserted, there was a bonfire of all paper in the facility and the computers were wiped."

"Kenley is examining the computers to see if anything is salvageable, but he's not hopeful," Rayna added.

Ryan glanced at his grandmother, "I wondered where Kyan was. I'm assuming Satish is the wizard Satish who's on the Tetrad Death Squad with Kyan. Kenley has to be your grandson, computer wizard that he is."

"Right on all accounts," Rayna agreed.

In due course, but not quick enough for Ryan or Tempe, despite Bryce's presence, Jeff stepped out of the van that housed a mobile lab for his equipment and exclaimed, "My team does good work."

He walked over to Lea. "Look at this. Our vaccine even works against the newest strain of the virus they created." Once everyone with enough medical knowledge to understand Jeff's results had reviewed the data, the shield was dropped.

"Congratulations, Murdoch." Tempe grinned as he dropped the shield.

"For what?"

"You sealed the weak spot in your shield." She patted his shoulder.

"I wondered if you would notice," he said with a blush.

Tempe asked, "Is Duane under lock and key?"

"Tamra, Adam and Brandi were sent to take care of Duane," Nova said quietly. "I'm waiting for a report."

"How long ago?"

"Two hours," Murdoch replied grimly.

Tempe looked at Rayna and raised an eyebrow.

"I was a bit preoccupied with my cyn," Rayna commented as she pulled out her cell phone and called Eli. Before Rayna could say anything, Tempe said, "Send Star with Sage veiling her. If Duane is using the others as a shield, and I'm sure he is, Star will be able to sing to them."

Rayna looked at Tempe and all of her sisters were shaking their heads no. She blew out air and said, "Guys. I suspect Duane has control of Dana, Cindy, Arleth, Gavin, and probably Brandon, all the ones who wouldn't do much of anything without his approval. No one is going to fight through them and he knows it. Star or Eli will be the best choice. I said Star because they are accustomed to seeing her, but Eli could siren them as well. Either way, you need Sage to set a veil, and Star must be under her veil unless there are other alphas at Eli's to guard her. If just Sage and Star go then Eli can protect the house." Not to mention his wife and unborn children.

Raven nodded. "Send Star and Sage. Tempest is right. It's going to take us almost an hour to get there."

Rayna had put Eli on speaker when Tempe started talking and he said, "I'll send Sam and Dwight with the girls. They're here working out."

Tempe chewed her bottom lip. She hated sending someone else into the fray while she brought up the rear, especially the kids she vowed to protect, but opening a way created a localized climate change the humans could track, if they knew what to look for. Currently, they didn't know what the climate change signified, but it was dangerous to toss too much information out there. Humans were getting smarter and most preternaturals didn't think it was a good thing. Besides, no one in this group had the ability to teleport themselves, much less a group, that far.

They loaded into cars and headed for Half Acre.

Chapter 8

They arrived at Half Acre in forty minutes instead of an hour. The drivers trashed the speed limits and, lucky for the shifters, law enforcement was not on the road. Rayna and Eli had stayed in touch, but he hadn't heard back from anyone who had gone to Half Acre. Rayna ordered Eli to stay at his house. Those in the car could hear him pacing in the background.

Ryan, Raven, Bryce, Asilia, Brook and Tempe got out of the cars a mile out. Ryan veiled them, and they headed toward the back door. When they arrived, it was apparent a team roster was needed. Duane had either drugged or converted some of the home team.

Tempe motioned everyone to stop and told Ryan to beef up his veil with a spell he had been working on. She knew Tamra – who was on the other team – had a knack for seeing through veils in much the way Tempe could see through glamour. Obviously, she should have warned Sage.

Tamra had been prepared for Sage and Star and she had prevented Star from speaking or singing since both girls were in a magical cage hanging in the air about twenty feet off of the ground. Sage was not up to fighting a strong wizard yet, which wasn't an insult considering most of the magical community couldn't fight a strong, battle-ready wizard one on one.

Most of the wizards Ryan and Tempe took out over the past few days were either weak wizards or new to the craft, and they had simply moved them out of the way and kept running, they didn't defeat the Shadowed wizards.

Adelia was unconscious but since she volunteered a lot of her time at Half Acre, Tempe didn't have a clue which side had taken her out. Landon, Dylan, Joey, Sam and Dwight were also down for the count, as were Adam and Brandi.

Tempe snarled. Brandi was just getting over her fear of wizards. And what the heck was Joey doing here?

Firmly under Duane's control were Tamra, Brandon, Dana, Cindy, and Arleth. Gavin was missing. Since they had been given the vaccine Tempe wasn't sure if they could have been infected again or if they were willing supporters. The two younger ones had been practically raised by Duane so there's no telling what kind of control he had over them. Dana, Cindy and Arleth were chanting together on a shield spell Duane had obviously taught the three witches.

"Tempest, I know you and Ryan are out there," Duane called. "We installed a tracking device in both of you. I must admit you have repeatedly caused us trouble, but I think we have some good half-breed replacements."

Tempe smirked but remained silent. He thought to taunt her into revealing herself. Surely, he knew this wasn't her first hostage negotiation.

He smiled and added, "We have video of you in Radek's bedroom. Do you think Bryce would like a copy?"

Bryce smiled cruelly but remained silent.

Rayna spoke, "We have shielded the area. You cannot open a way or teleport."

"You will drop the block set by your siren," Duane said coolly. "Otherwise some of my friends will kill themselves. Tamra, tighten your cage."

The cage around Sage and Star decreased in size by about six inches on each side. Had to give him credit, he was holding some good cards.

Tempe teleported out of Ryan's veil and appeared from another section of the yard. "What is it you want Duane?"

"Reveal everyone under Ryan's veil," He ordered.

Tempe sent a hand signal and Ryan, Bryce, and Asilia were revealed.

Duane smiled grimly and asked, "Where's the high wizard?

"She wasn't with us," Ryan replied crossly. He wasn't the only one wondering where Duane was getting his info. His source was good.

"Yes, she is," Clare called out.

Tempe turned to look at Clare, as did everyone. Surprise did not begin to cover what Tempe was feeling. By the five realms, this was going to get messy.

"Clare, where's Nova?" Duane asked with a smirk as he took in the shocked expressions.

"She's veiled. The plan was for her to stand opposite Ryan's veil and look for an opening to you," Clare replied.

Tempe raised her hand to throw a closely focused spell at Clare. Rayna beat her to the punch. The sovereign dropped her daughter like a stone. Jeff pulled Clare back and took a blood sample.

Rayna looked at Duane and smiled the type of smile a predator smiles before killing prey. Duane saw the sovereign's face and he backed up a step as his hostage protection ring closed in around him even tighter. Duane sent a hand single and Tamra closed the cage on Star and Sage another six inches. If she made it any smaller the cage would go through the girls.

Ryan growled.

Stop it! Tempe mentally ordered, but she agreed with him.

Tempe sent Sage mental orders that breached the cage. Apparently, Tamra didn't think mental orders would do the girls any good, or she didn't know the alphas had the ability. Sage looked at Tempe in shock, her eyes opened wide. Sage licked her lips and they prepared to share a spell. Tempe sent a spell to her sister the young shifter didn't yet know. Sage picked it up and focused it on the cage.

Tempe's eyes lit up, but she kept her facial expression bland. That's the great thing about magic. It does follow rules. Sometimes the rules are unknown or changeable based on who wields the magic and their abilities, but sometimes the rules are exact regardless of who wields the magic. For a magical cage to work the person inside cannot breach the cage's defenses. The cage is specific to the person or persons being held. Since Tamra knows Star and Sage are not well trained in the casting arts, because Tempe foolishly discussed it with her, Tempe bet Tamra didn't bother to build the cage to block spells. Tempe couldn't throw a spell from outside the cage and impact it, but she could hand a spell to Sage in the cage. Few magical beings can share their magic, but Sage and Tempe have the gift, shared just between the two of them. They don't discuss the ability and Tempe doubted Clare mentioned a skill to Tamra she didn't have. Clare hated to be seen as weak.

Thanks to alpha mind speak the other alphas knew what was going on. When Sage broke the cage Raven, in dragon form with Brook on her back for protection, flew at Tamra as Brook sirened her.

Ryan caught Star and Sage in a web created by magic before they hit the ground. Asilia and Bryce stood between the girls and the fight until Sage regained her footing and focused her shield.

Nova sent a spell and Duane's human shield wall fell where they stood, asleep.

Rayna focused a spell on Duane, who backed into the wall, eyes wide in terror.

Tempe called evenly, "Mother, we need information from him."

Rayna growled and threw her spell at an old and large oak tree. When the dust cleared the tree had been turned to kindling. The sovereign rarely shows her temper, but she does have one. Everyone walked carefully around her as they assessed injuries.

While the shifter sovereign was making kindling, the high wizard had dropped Duane where he stood.

"Jeff, we need to know how Clare and Tamra were controlled and why your vaccine didn't work on them, or the experimented on for that matter." Tempe looked over at Rayna and added, "Sooner would be much better than later."

Jeff gave her an annoyed look. "You think I don't know?"

"Sorry, I'm a bit on edge myself," She replied, certain she wasn't the only one thinking perhaps Ryan and she might be infected and who could be trusted for guard duty?

*****

Nova placed Duane and Tamra under heavy guard at her house, along with the injured wizards. The shifters did the same with the wounded shifters and Clare at Eli's. The folks already staying at Half Acre remained, also under heavy guard. They were fast running out of anyone to do anything but guard or be guarded and they weren't one hundred percent sure the guards were trustworthy.

It took Nova just under four hours to remove the tracking spells from Ryan and Tempe. By the end, they were both ready to spit nails. While they were in spell removal land, the others did medical triage.

Eventually, Tempe sat at Eli's kitchen bar eating a sandwich with whoever was in the room. After Tempe finished her sandwich, she took a deep breath and said, "Rayna, we need a complete report. With your permission, I want Landon from Half Acre, Adam who is already here along with Sage, Star, Raven and Bryce to recall what happened."

Rayna nodded and said, "Yes. Do it. I think we will need to recall what happened with Tamra and Clare as well."

Her head shot up and Tempe glared at Rayna but then she realized her mother was right. She just didn't want to put Sage through the discomfort.

Sage smiled and said, "It'll be fine Tempe, let's go."

Eli took a team to retrieve Landon while the others marched up to the bedroom Tempe shared with Bryce.

When they entered Adam said, "I get the impression this recall isn't going to be me reciting what I remember."

"No," Tempe smiled grimly. "Sage has a power we don't normally discuss. If she stands next to a person who has an experience that needs to be repeated in detail, Sage can relive their experience. She will be able to feel, hear and see it as the person did, including their emotions. Obviously, we try not to ask this of her too often. And I am requesting you not discuss this with anyone except Eli or Bryce if you feel you must. Both of them know about this power."

Star asked, "Then why do you need me? Sage was with me the whole time."

"I can't recall my own memories this way. This will be clearer than me telling what happened, so we need to use your memories," Sage replied.

Star still looked confused but replied, "Okay."

Adam looked at Tempe and Bryce, concerned, "Not to put too fine a point on this but exactly which memories of mine do you want her to remember?"

"Only what happened between when you and Brandi headed out for Half Acre and until you became unconscious," Tempe replied.

"Nothing before, right?" He asked, obviously worried.

"Right," Tempe replied slowly. Dread filled her as she narrowed her eyes on Adam.

Bryce stepped in front of his clan member and his expression sobered. "Considering what just happened with Clare, I must ask why you're so concerned about the time."

Adam's face got red, but he answered. "Brandi and I were alone at my house – in bed – just before Eli called."

Even with the stress everyone was feeling, Bryce and Tempe relaxed. Tempe said, "I don't think we need to know about that Adam. How about if I go first? Sage will recall my memories from the time Ryan and I walked back from the cave."

Sage and Tempe sat in the twin desk chairs and she recalled Tempe's experiences, including Radek's free roaming hands and her trying not to gag when Duane kissed her.

When Sage finished Tempe added with a growl, "I should have killed Radek. I thought I might be able to get some answers out of him before we left."

Bryce's expression was hard and angry, but his voice was lawyer calm, "I'll take care of Radek."

"That's detailed," Adam commented thoughtfully.

Sage had paled and sweat beaded her forehead.

When someone knocked at the door, Bryce opened it to reveal Ryan holding snacks and drinks for everyone. "If Sage is doing a lot of recalls she'll need this."

"Thanks Ryan, come in." Tempe looked steadily at Ryan and said, "I haven't read your report yet, but do you think Sage needs to recall it or should we wait?"

Ryan wanted to duck out of the room, but he didn't turn away from Tempe. "You need to read the report first and then decide."

Raven spoke up, "No, Sage does not need to recall his experience. It adds nothing to what you have reported." Her face was a mask, telling Tempe more than her words did.

"Okay, I'll read it later," Tempe replied. "Ryan, did you see the siren who dropped both of us? I didn't."

"No," he shrugged. "I'll leave if you don't need me."

"Wait. Can Ryan stay?" Sage asked.

Ryan nodded.

Tempe said, "Sure." Eventually, she was going to ask Landon to relive some experiences that might upset Sage if it turned out Landon was Shadowed so Ryan could be helpful.

"Adam, are you ready?"

"No, but let's do this," Adam grumbled. He went over to sit by Sage, her eyes lost focus as she started the recall.

Adam reached for his phone since the ring tone was the one he used for Eli, but man, he hated to break the mood. It was nice, sitting on his deck, cuddling. It had been a long time since he was this happy. The call from Eli effectively canceled the feel-good moment. When he told Brandi what Eli wanted, she decided to go with him. They got on his motorcycle and headed over to meet Tamra at Half Acre. Adam parked, and they took off their helmets as Brandon walked up.

"Hey Brandon, what's up?" Adam tried to keep his voice calm and relaxed.

"Brandi needs to leave. She upsets Arleth and Gavin."

"I'm sorry I upset them, but I was asked to meet Tamra here," Brandi replied.

"Too bad." Brandon threw a sloppy punch at Adam.

Adam side stepped the right cross and swept Brandon's legs out from under him. Brandi ran to join in, but Adam called, "Stay back. We don't want to hurt him." Adam and Brandon circled each other, sizing each other up when Landon ran around the side of the house.

"Brandon what are you doing?" Landon asked as he moved between the two men and faced Brandon. "Adam and Brandi are our friends."

"Yours, not mine. Duane is my friend, my only friend." Brandon threw a spell at Landon that dropped him.

Adam wanted to reach down and see if Landon was okay, but he couldn't take his eyes off Brandon. From behind, Adam felt another spell and out of the corner of his eye he saw Brandi fall at Tamra's feet. He ran toward her but stopped short when he saw Duane had walked out of the house. Three wizards. He was seriously outgunned. It sure explained more about why Brandi didn't trust wizards.

Tamra smiled and sent a spell at Adam. The next thing he knew, he was lying in Eli's recovery room with Jeff leaning over him.

Sage completed the recall.

Adam said, "That is the oddest thing I've ever heard or felt."

"I just call it weird," Ryan offered. "Just so you know, there aren't many who could take on three wizards. At least you survived." Ryan turned and started playfully coaxing Sage to eat.

"Not much comfort in that." Adam's eyes looked haunted.

"We've all lost battles and at the time you went in no one knew the Half Acre crowd were either controlled or Shadowed. You were trying not to hurt Brandon." Bryce clapped him on the shoulder as he spoke.

"Sage, are you ready to recall with Star?" Tempe asked gently.

She looked up after she finished chewing a bite of sandwich and said softly, "Yes, at least this time I know what I'm going to see."

Adam and Star exchanged places. Sage told Star's story.

Eli walked into the game room and told them about Rayna's assignment. Sage and Star looked at Eli like he was nuts. Once they realized he was serious, Sage went to change, and Star waited. Dwight and Sam were in the gym and they joined Star. Sage walked back in wearing the spelled clothes Tempe had made for her. Star pushed away her envy and the four of them headed out for Half Acre.

Sam drove and went over the rules. Apparently being raised in the alpha clan gave him insight in to how to run this type of assignment. He was deadly serious as he went over everyone's task. He parked on the other side of a hill so those in the house couldn't see them. Sage pulled the four of them into her veil and they started walking.

When they could see the house, and the bodies on the ground, Sam said, "We need to fall back. We can't protect you from multiple wizards."

"I can sing to them. We have to help," Star said calmly.

Sage glared at Sam and asked, "Would you fall back if Star and I weren't with you?"

Sam gritted his teeth and glanced at his youngest sister, "Irrelevant, you are."

"Sam, they can't see through my veil. We'll get close and Star will sing. She can put all wizards to sleep and we can sort out friend from foe later." Sage tried to be calm, but her voice shook a little.

Dwight, a shifter over one hundred years old, whispered, "This plan has merit, but it might work better if you and I get in the car and drive up while the girls walk over in the veil. The wizards can focus on us while the girls get close enough for Star to be heard when she sings."

"Yes, that's better."

"Sam..." Sage said.

"Sis, your job is to protect Star. Ours is to protect both of you." Sam hugged Sage and the guys ran for the car.

Star and Sage continued walking through the field while Sam and Dwight drove up. The girls were almost in place when the guys got out of the car.

"Duane, what happened?" Sam called, pointing at the fallen.

Duane smiled, "A change of leadership." He threw a spell at the men. Dwight ducked left and Sam ducked right. The first spell missed both of them. The second spell, from Adelia, hit Sam without him seeing her. Dwight fell to another spell from Duane.

Star opened her mouth to sing and nothing came out. She looked up and realized Tamra was staring at her right through Sage's veil. Sage raised her shield just as Tamra and Duane started dropping spells on it. The girls ran with the two wizards chasing them. They saw Brandon running toward them and Sage opened a hole for him to enter. Once inside he got a chokehold on Sage. Star tried to help Sage, but he was too strong physically and Star wasn't strong enough to pull elements through Sage's shield. Brandon hit Star and she fell. He never stopped choking Sage. When the girls came to they were both in a magical cage and their powers didn't work on the cage. It appeared the cage took any magic they sent toward it. The absorbed magic made the cage stronger.

Joey jogged down the road and saw the girls suspended in the air in a cage. Star tried to warn him off but without a voice he didn't understand. He ran toward the girls and was downed by a spell from Adelia.

Sage finished and said, "That's pretty much where you guys came in." She looked over at Tempe and added, "I should never have let Brandon in the shield. I thought he was trying to escape from them. I didn't know," she whispered forlornly.

"You did the same thing I did," Adam said. "You tried to help someone you thought was in danger."

"But you only endangered yourself. My job was to protect Star and I failed." She leaned on Ryan.

"Then learn from this," Tempe said brutally. "Star is safe. Review what happened and determine how you could prevent this type of thing next time."

Ryan glared at Tempe, as did Adam and Star, but Raven saw what Tempe was doing and she thought Bryce did, too. People who go into combat cannot start second guessing themselves. If a mistake is survived, learn from it and move forward.

After a couple of seconds Ryan, still trying to control his temper, said, "I think Sage needs a break."

"I agree," Tempe sighed. The last recall could be difficult for her sister. "Let's meet back here in an hour."

The kids filed out. Adam hung back and said, "I guess you had to be hard on Sage, so she wouldn't dwell on it, but you sounded a little harsh."

"I was harsh. Being an alpha isn't all fun and games," Tempe retorted.

"Never thought it was," Adam headed for the door and asked, "Do you want me here for the last recall?"

"Yes, that way you and Bryce can brief your cyngor on what happened. Adam —"

"Don't worry Tempe," Adam cut in. "I'll never mention the recall to anyone. It looks like she's stuck with the memories like they are her own." Tempe nodded, and he continued, "I hope she doesn't have to do this often."

"No, she doesn't. This is a unique situation. We have to figure out how the Shadowed are getting control of our people." Tempe froze in her tracks as she felt the fight downstairs. "Brandi's awake and she's not happy."

*****

They ran down to the recovery room. Jeff and Lea were on the ground, unmoving. Asilia and Eli were heaped on the floor and looked like they had both hit the wall.

"Brandi, stand down." Rayna didn't want to, but she was going to have to knock Brandi out since she wasn't having any luck getting Brandi to listen.

Brandi's eyes were wild as she searched the room for enemies.

Adam walked in and said calmly, "Brandi, look at me." She turned.

Tempe was sure Brandi was going to attack Adam. She braced to jump between them.

Adam held out his hand at Tempe in the universal signal to stop, but he never took his eyes off Brandi, "No wizards here, just shifters. Jeff

71

and Lea were just attempting to heal your wounds." He held out both hands to her, "Brandi, it is okay. You're safe. I'm here."

"Adam..." she said in a daze as she finally focused on him. "W...what happened?"

"The Shadowed got control of Half Acre. We all took quite a beating from the wizards, so it would be nice if you didn't inflict any more damage." He was relieved she listened to him.

"I told you wizards couldn't be trusted." Brandi said simply. She scanned the room obviously looking for wizards. When she didn't find any she focused on Tempe, "Sorry, woke up in a medical room and went a little crazy. Did I hurt anyone?"

Asilia helped Lea up as Eli assisted Jeff. "We're bruised but fine," Jeff commented.

"I discovered I cannot siren the daughter of a witch/shifter union who is part vampire." Eli shook his head.

"True, sirens have no effect on me, just as vampires can't enthrall me. Next time, if there is a next time, you would do better to put me somewhere that doesn't look like a hospital room and have Adam nearby," Brandi offered.

"In retrospect I should have waited to get his report of what happened until after you were awake." Tempe said.

"Can I take Brandi for a walk in the yard?" Adam asked. Jeff waved toward the door and the couple left.

"Any news?" Tempe asked.

Rayna frowned grimly. "News of what? Tamra and Clare are still out of it because Jeff is keeping them sedated. His team is running through every test they can think of."

"No way to test the rest of us," Tempe contemplated the ramifications. "Are you keeping the rest of the Half Acre crew unconscious until we figure this out?"

"I don't want to but we will for the next twelve hours," Jeff said. "We just don't have enough people to guard them all."

"I called for reinforcements, as did Nova. Of course, we need a way to determine who is not a member of the Shadowed or under their control." Rayna looked pointedly at Jeff.

"I know. I know," he growled.

"Is Landon awake yet?" Tempe asked.

"Yes," Landon replied as he walked in the room under guard. "I understand you need some type of report from me."

"Come with me," Tempe said and then noticed he hesitated. "Landon, we are trying to piece together what happened. We need to know what you experienced."

He still didn't move.

Sage popped her head in and said, "Come on Landon. It won't take long." He allowed Sage to walk him up the stairs.

Tempe moved to follow them, but Ryan stood in her way. "I realize what you did earlier with Sage, but that's not the way to get her to focus. It works with me, and Raven I think. I don't know about the other alphas, but if you push Sage that way she will close down."

Tempe raised an eyebrow.

Ryan snarled. "Tempe, you keep saying Sage and I are linked somehow, so listen to me. She will shut down if you tell her to control her emotions. She has to process her feelings, or she falls apart. I've had to pick up the pieces before," he added quietly as he walked off.

Tempe turned to Rayna, "Just how closely are those two linked?"

"I'm not sure. It feels closer than you and Val," Rayna offered.

"Does she feel what happens to him on missions?"

"Ask her," Rayna replied unhelpfully.

Adam and Brandi returned then and she asked, "Brandi, you okay if I borrow Adam for a few minutes to finish up the reports?"

"Sure, I'm going to work out in the gym."

"Good. And thanks," Tempe replied.

When Bryce, Adam and Tempe entered the bedroom, Raven was already there standing near the door. Ryan sat on the floor beside Sage with Star on the floor leaning against the bed. Landon was in the other chair next to Sage.

This would be tricky, as Tempe didn't want to tell Landon what Sage could do.

Tempe opened her mouth and Sage interrupted, "Tempe, I already explained to Landon that while we each hold one of these stones I can recall his memories of today's events."

Nice cover, she thought. In retrospect, she wished she had thought of that with Adam. "Okay, but first I want you to think Landon. When was the first time you remember Brandon acting strange?"

"Back at the facility in Canada." He thought for a few minutes and added, "Last fall."

"Were you guys separated during that time?"

"No more than normal. We were always separated for testing but stayed together otherwise, just like always."

"Okay, could you stand to relive that day?" Tempe asked.

"Sure." Landon shrugged his shoulders. They learned nothing important or even remotely useful, except the day-to-day life of a lab rat was rather boring.

Tempe had an idea forming but she didn't like it. "Landon, are you ready to relive today?" His face took on a haunted expression, but he turned toward Sage. Her eyes lost focus yet again and she told his tale.

Brandon and Landon argued about Duane. Landon felt Duane was exerting too much influence on Brandon. Landon walked off to cool down. He was so angry. Brandon was getting worse, not better. Landon took a walk over toward the national forest. He knew he should stay close to the house, but he was tired of being confined. He had been confined for so long. He walked for over an hour and decided to return to Half Acre. At least this cage was nicer than the one in Canada, and the girls were prettier.

Landon saw the commotion from the hilltop. As Adam and Brandon circled each other, Landon ran around the side of the house, yelling, "Brandon what are you doing?" He moved between the two men. "Adam and Brandi are our friends."

"Yours, not mine. Duane is my friend, my only friend." Brandon threw a spell at Landon that dropped him.

Sage's eyes regained their focus. Landon blushed and said, "I didn't realize my emotions would carry through the stones that well."

"Don't worry about it, everyone's did," Adam offered kindly.

"What about Brandon, can you fix him?" Landon asked. "He was never as strong a wizard as I and he could not have crafted such a spell. Someone gave him a spell to use on me. I'm not sure what it means."

"We still aren't sure what's going on," Tempe replied sadly. "We are going to do our best to help him. Ryan, why don't you get Landon set up in a room here for the night, but make sure he's not near Brandi."

Ryan led Adam, Sage, Star, and Landon out the door.

"What are you thinking sis?" Raven asked.

"I think Brandon might be a willing convert to the Shadowed."

"I agree," Raven responded. "What about Clare and Tamra?"

"I don't have a clue," she responded irritably. Tempe stared out the window for a moment and whispered the words she didn't want to say, "Maybe them too."

Adam popped his head back in the doorway. "I'm taking Brandi to my house tonight. Being away from so many people will help calm her down." When Tempe nodded, he left. Raven stared at Tempe for a few seconds and then she followed him out.

Alone in their bedroom Tempe looked at Bryce and asked him the question Raven asked her, "So what are the odds Clare and Tamra are willing members of the Shadowed?"

He shrugged grimly.

It occurred to her he didn't want to say what he thought, that Clare and Tamra are on the other team for reasons of their own. Tempe felt the same way. Even though she knew better she was afraid to utter the words out loud, as if by verbalizing her fears they would become real.

They stood in the room for a minute. In an effort to take her mind off the current disaster she couldn't do anything about, Tempe asked, "Do you know why Sage can't read you?"

Bryce looked over, surprised, and said, "Uh?" thus providing conclusive proof that even a lawyer can lose the ability to make complete sentences if caught off guard.

"Sage can't read you at all. She's never been able to. Rayna and I can both read you so I'm wondering if you know why?" Tempe asked.

He sat on the bed and thought for a moment. "When you first discussed her telepathy and empathy I thought it would be nice to be able to block her, but that's all."

Tempe thought for a minute and said, "Try to block me."

He looked at her like she was crazy. He didn't know how to do that.

She realized the issue and the corners of her mouth quirked up. "Build a box around your brain. Start with the bottom, then the four sides and then put a top on the box.

He shrugged his shoulders and said, "Okay, I'm blocking, I think."

Tempe stared at him and smiled, "You are indeed. Bryce, I think you can block anyone from your mind. That's a great talent."

"What's so great about it?"

"Are you kidding? No one can see in your mind if you don't allow it. Not a telepath or even an empath. You could lie to the enemy and they wouldn't know the difference."

Tempe wrinkled her forehead, "If you blocked Sage, why didn't you block me?"

"I don't know but I do know I've never wanted to hide anything from you." He responded simply. She leaned over and kissed him.

When they went downstairs they gathered up the available alphas with telepathic talents and verified they couldn't get a read on him and Sage could only read Bryce if he allowed it. Sage even tried to stare into his eyes and she still couldn't read him unless he allowed it. Ryan and Rayna were also unable to read Bryce.

All the alphas, Tempe included, were more than a little jealous.

Chapter 9

The weekly clan dinner on Sunday was cancelled. There were too many wounded, drugged, or perhaps just plain crazy staying at Eli's. Rayna left with Char, Lark and Pat to stay at Half Acre and work with the injured. Raven and Lea stayed at Eli's to help with the wounded, and of course Clare was still under lock and key. Drake flew in, as did Carl and Cole. With the arrival of her father and brothers, Catlin was able to take a break. The four of them took shifts sitting with Clare. Clare didn't seem to have a clue what had happened. Jeff made up some tale about possible infection and she stayed in the recovery room.

By the evening, Drake was incensed. He cornered Tempe in Eli's crowded kitchen and demanded, "Why can't I be alone with Clare?"

The other alphas started making themselves scarce, except for Raven who inched closer to her eldest sister.

Tempe raised an eyebrow, "Drake…"

"Don't patronize me Tempest. Bryce was able to be alone with you when you were controlled or whatever. What's the difference?" Catlin, Cole, and Carl were listening in silence.

"They knew what was wrong with me. We don't know what's wrong with her." Tempe took a deep breath and squared her shoulders. She didn't need this. When she turned to get her teacup, Drake grabbed her arm.

"Don't turn your back on me. I'm tired of this alpha crap!" He had a strong grip on her arm, but it wasn't deadly.

She took another calming breath.

Raven knew better than to interfere, but Bryce walked up behind Drake and said, "Get your hands off Tempe right now, or you and I will go the distance."

"Bryce, it's okay," Tempe said in what should have been a soothing voice but came out as a snarl. Bryce should have stayed out of it.

"No Tempe, it isn't," Bryce responded. "Drake, let her go."

Drake released Tempe's arm as he turned to face off with Bryce. At least this was a fight he stood a chance of winning. Tempe would have wiped the floor with him.

Great, nothing like a family fight to round out the evening. Tempe growled and teleported. She went from the kitchen to the deck off their bedroom. Well, phooey. Her tea was still downstairs. She sat on the deck for a minute and listened. It didn't sound like the guys were tearing up the house so maybe they both calmed down once she wasn't there for them to focus on. At least it's what she had hoped would happen.

A few minutes later she heard Bryce and Drake walking up the deck steps. She suspected Bryce used his ring to find her. She closed her eyes and relaxed in the high-backed deck rocking chair.

Both men stopped in front of her but didn't speak.

Tempe opened her eyes and Drake held out her mug of tea. She accepted the tea and took a sip without speaking.

"Tempest, I'm sorry."

She looked up at him but still didn't speak.

Drake dropped down into the other chair, ran his fingers through his hair and said, "I've never reacted like that before. I don't know what made me think starting a fight with you would be a good idea. I'm just so scared. What's going on with Clare?"

Tempe shook her head, "I don't have a clue. If I knew what was happening, I would tell you."

"I suppose you've already been asked if you noticed any changes in her lately." Bryce leaned on the deck railing.

"Oh yes, I've been asked by everyone. Apparently, each alpha thinks she needs to ask for herself." Drake growled and said, "Notice none of the alphas noticed anything either but they aren't second guessing themselves."

"Starless night, Drake," Tempe exploded. "I've been second guessing myself since Tatsuo made me his thrall. And I can assure you every alpha, even Ryan, has been second guessing every move I've made since."

She took a deep breath, staring at the mountains, and continued, "We've been getting our butts kicked a lot lately. Even with a strong wizard, fae and shifter task force we are not wrapping this up. Heck you're the alpha clan's chief pilot. Tell me you haven't noticed how badly we are doing?"

"Tempe, he just meant…" Bryce started.

She talked over Bryce saying, "Don't explain things to me Bryce. I know how hard it is to live in the alpha clan and frankly I've been shocked Drake stayed. He's almost as dominant as you. I'm sure it's a pain but right now I just don't care. I lost one sister to the Shadowed and I don't want to lose another... or myself for that matter."

After a few seconds of silence, Tempe added, "I should try to be nicer about this but I just don't have the energy."

She stood up to walk to the bedroom door and said over her shoulder, "Bryce if you ever step into an argument between me and anyone, ever again, you and I will go-the-distance, as you so aptly put it."

She went into the bedroom and realized she left her tea, again. Man, she wanted her tea and it was getting colder by the second.

Thanks to shifter hearing and the cracked door, she could still hear the guys talking.

"So, how do you like living with an alpha?" Drake asked after a few seconds.

"Most days it's pretty good," Bryce offered as he moved to the chair she had vacated. "However, today is not one of those days, how about you?"

"About the same," Drake responded. Then he added sadly, "On the plus side for you, at least Tempest agreed to live outside of the alpha clan. Rayna made Clare the same offer, but she wouldn't do it."

Tempe almost fell out of the desk chair she had plopped into. She didn't know Rayna offered Clare the same option and was amazed she didn't jump at it. Of course, Clare has always loved being highly ranked and enjoyed being in the know of every decision. Clare had loved being in the Northern Realm court for that matter. She loved the pomp and the fact she was considered royalty. She had even considered staying in the Farseen even though her abilities lie with shifter – not fae – talents.

Tempe thought for a couple of minutes and then opened the door wide. "Drake, how did Clare feel about Ryan beating her for third in the alpha clan?"

Drake frowned, "I'm not sure I want to discuss that."

She pursed her lips and leaned on the rail. "I won't push but I would like to know. It could be important. How about a different question? Why wouldn't Clare move from the alpha clan?"

Drake scowled at Tempest but after a couple of seconds he said, "You know she has always liked knowing what's going on, to be in the know. When Rayna offered you the chance she also offered it to Clare for the same reasons. I doubt anyone in Rayna's house could have missed the conversation. It was loud. Clare was furious you even considered it. She thought it made you weak and unworthy to be second."

Tempe dropped down on the deck and just stared at Drake, "How could I not have known? Was I wrong to move?"

"No!" Bryce and Drake said together. Drake continued, "Rayna's right. The technology is available for this to work. You absolutely made the right choice."

"For me and Bryce, I agree, but did I hurt the alpha clan by splitting us up?"

"No," Raven's voice floated toward them as she climbed the last two steps up to the landing. "If anything, the rest of us do more now. The workload is more even. You are fully devoted to training the next generation, special assignments, and Bryce, but it's working. Clare is the only one that complained."

"And you didn't mention it to me?" Tempe asked softly.

"If I had told you, you would have confronted Clare and there would have been a big dust up. I figured she would get over it soon." Raven shot an apologetic look at Drake, "I know Clare wasn't happy when Ryan won the dominance push with her. Bliss, Char, and I were grousing too. Getting beat out by our young nephew was a bit humiliating for all of us, but most of us took comfort in the fact that it took forty-five seconds for you to beat him. I figured Clare just needed a little time. After all, she's so much older than the rest of us, excluding you."

Raven looked down at the ground, careful to not look into her sister's eyes or Drake's. "I think she might have started a downward spiral when Sage was able to push her into the wall last fall. Her attitude changed around then. She was careful to stay the same old Clare around you or mother, but all of the alphas, myself included, stayed out of her way. I suspect Ryan might have been the final straw."

Drake took a deep breath and admitted, "Tempest, you know she's always envied you. You're the shifter daughter Ellwood wanted. You're Rayna's second. You're the one alpha all shifters know by name."

"Clare envies me? I'm the shifter daughter Ellwood tortured in an attempt to turn me into his assassin. I'm Rayna's enforcer. I'm the one alpha all shifters know because they fear me," she replied savagely.

"Both viewpoints are factual," Bryce said quietly.

"Does Clare hate me?" Tempe asked, keeping the tears out of her eyes but not her voice.

"I'm not sure," Drake responded despondently. He stood and walked down the steps. Raven shrugged her shoulders and followed.

Bryce and Tempe walked into the bedroom. This time she remembered the mug of tea, which was cold. She drank it anyway.

Finally, she asked, "What do I do with that information? It doesn't help us solve this problem with the Shadowed, but it does make my stomach churn."

"What do you think? Do you think Clare could be jealous enough to throw in with the Shadowed?"

"Before this weekend I would have said no. Now, I don't have a clue," she replied miserably.

Bryce pulled her tightly into his arms. After a few precious moments with Bryce she called Rayna. It was not a happy conversation.

"You suspected? You knew about Clare?" Tempe practically screamed into the phone. Bryce lay on the bed with his eyes closed, pretending he wasn't listening to his significant other explode.

"No," Rayna's voice was resigned. "I knew she was jealous of you but I didn't realize how much anger she had built up."

Tempe blew out air, "Mother, what do we do?"

"We do what we always do. We address the problem," Rayna said sadly.

*****

Monday morning Rayna returned and loaded Clare into a van with Tempe, Raven, Jeff and Drake. They went to Jeff's research facility. Clare was secured to a bed in one of the treatment rooms with Jeff's team monitoring her.

The medical review was anything but pleasant.

"I can't find any trace of drug or mind control. Neither can Nova. Not for Brandon, Clare or Tamra," Jeff said grimly. He glanced over at Drake, addressing his next comments to him. "I've double, and triple checked. I've had my work checked by every technician here. I can't find anything wrong."

"You're giving up?" Drake asked harshly.

"There's nothing left for me to check," Jeff replied simply.

"Rayna, we should check," Tempe said quietly.

Drake's face blanched as the color drained from his face. He had been around the alphas enough to realize the sovereign and Tempest had some level of telepathy. "Tempest..." his voice trailed off. When he got his voice back it was stronger. "Can I see her first?"

"Yes, Drake, that's a good idea," Rayna responded gently. Jeff took Drake to Clare's room.

"Tempest, I'll see Clare alone first," Rayna said.

"No, Mother," Tempe took a deep breath. "We go together. We succeed or fail but we do it together."

"What about me?" Raven asked.

"You keep Drake away. Like me, he's a fan of Gentleman Jack for those rare times when drowning sorrows sounds like a good idea. I brought a bottle and you might want to have it handy." Tempe opened her backpack and set the bottle down on the table.

Later, while Raven poured the first shot into a coffee mug for Drake, Rayna and Tempe stood outside Clare's room.

Rayna whispered, "I hope we're wrong."

Tempe's response was even more soft, "Me, too."

They walked into the room and Clare smirked, "You're both pathetic. Rayna, you didn't see what had changed right in front of you. Tempest, you were so busy chasing love you didn't pay attention, but then you've always refused to use the one gift you possess that would make you truly invincible."

"Clare…"

"Tempest, don't bother. We both know mother will read my mind and then you will have your answer." Clare added bitterly, "You were always the chosen one, the one both parents wanted. Every other child has been a pale imitation, even Val. Father would have kept Val alive if you had stayed with him and asked. He would have given you anything you wanted. If Father had asked me I would have stayed with him. I loved living in the Northern Realm. I was important there. I meant something there. You and Saffron are a pair. She rejected Father and lives on her own, yet he still wants her. Father would still do anything for the two of you if you would move back with him."

While Clare ranted, Rayna listened to her daughter's mind. Rayna grimaced then locked eyes with Tempe.

Tempe could only read surface thoughts, but it didn't matter. The only thoughts Clare had were of her desire to crush the alpha clan, and the Northern Realm. The Shadowed had sought her out in the past but she didn't join up until Ryan beat her in the dominance push. Until that moment, Clare thought she would eventually replace Tempest since surely one of her missions would kill her. Sage had tossed her into a wall, but she was sure Sage wasn't a real match for her if she wasn't caught off guard. Tamra had been able to infect and control the goblin and Lord Ellwood. Lord Ellwood almost escaped Tamra's control but once Clare joined up she was able to assist.

Clare smiled at Tempest. "I tried to keep all the important thoughts on the surface, so you could read them. I want to be helpful."

"Thank you," Tempe said sadly. Rayna walked toward Clare, but Tempe blocked her way, "No."

Tempe looked Clare in the eyes and said, "I'm sorry your life wasn't what you wanted."

With tears running down her face, Tempe broke Clarity's neck. One of Jeff's techs, a well-trained warrior, waited outside to behead her.

Tempe wiped her tears and turned to walk out the door as Rayna said, "That was my job."

"No one should have to kill their own child." She walked out the door and hoped there was some Gentleman Jack left for her. At this point she would take a large glass of anything strong, even Scotch, which she didn't like.

They walked back into the meeting room and while Drake had done some damage to the bottle there was enough for Tempe to toss a couple of shots down before they walked out to the van.

Bryce was sitting in his SUV and Tempe jumped in the passenger's side. She didn't know how he knew to be there, but she was grateful. Later she found out Raven had called him, and Bryce got a speeding ticket in his rush to get to her. The others went home to tell everyone the Shadowed got to Clare and they caused her death, which was true as far as it went.

Bryce and Tempe went camping for four nights, enough time to spread Clare's ashes and let Drake be somewhere where he wouldn't have to see Tempe. He flew back to Alaska with Carl and Cole, planning to join their clan.

Chapter 10

Bryce and Tempe pulled into Eli's drive from their camping trip on Friday morning two weeks before Sam and Tracy's wedding. The place was a madhouse. They got out of the SUV, grabbed their gear and headed for the house in the hopes of quietly going to their room.

Tracy met them at the door. "I'm so sorry for your loss and I'm sorry about this." She pointed at all the activity.

"What is… this?" Tempe waved at the throng of people running around.

"Mother found out about the wedding. I tried to explain one of Sam's sisters died but she won't listen. She has taken over Eli's house, the wedding, everything, and she's driving everyone crazy." Tracy was close to tears.

Tempe, her own tears spent, huffed, "Did you introduce her to Rayna?"

"Rayna is letting Mother have her way, so your sisters are following suit. No one wants to fight the force that is my mother planning a wedding. My nice little wedding is no more." Tracy hung her head.

"Tracy, what do you want?" Tempe asked. She was tired of people being forced to do things they didn't want to do. Although her track record of late wasn't great, she felt certain she could tackle this little problem.

"I want my little wedding back," Tracy sighed.

"It's your wedding day. Where is your mother?" Tempe asked firmly. Tracy pointed to a woman with the same dirty blond hair she had.

Tempe narrowed her eyes, smiled grimly, placed Martha firmly in her crosshairs and marched toward her objective. She couldn't fix everything, but she could surely fix a wedding gone out of control.

Tracy ran behind her and said, "Martha, I would like you to meet Tempest, Tempest, my mother, Martha."

"Well, Tempest, it's a pleasure to meet you. I am so sorry for your loss dear." Martha steamrolled right past her and started barking instructions at some lady in a suit.

Tempe almost smiled. This was a new experience. Normally when she approached a shifter, they stopped whatever they're doing and gave her their full attention, either out of fear or surprise the sovereign's second spoke to them. Tempe recognized a pro when she saw one. She walked fast to catch up with the wedding planner. "Thank you, Martha. I'm sorry I was away when you arrived but I needed some time alone."

"That's to be expected dear. I'm sorry for all this fuss your first day back but my daughter left so little time for planning." Martha walked away, shouting orders to the construction team.

Tempe looked at Martha's back, "I think I've been out maneuvered."

"Of course, you have, dear. Martha is a force of nature," Naomi said serenely as she walked up to stand beside Tempest and Tracy.

Tempe took a deep breath, stared after Martha, and then looked at Naomi, human, mother of two, and asked, "Do you know how to get Martha to plan the wedding Tracy wants?"

Naomi smiled, "Do you still want the wedding you and Sam were planning?"

Tracy nodded her head and sighed, "Yes."

"Leave it to me child." Naomi took off after Martha.

Tracy commented, "You know, I'm at least twenty years older than Naomi."

"Go with it," Tempe replied. "I think Naomi might be a match for your mother."

Throughout the rest of the day Tempe had all the conversations she didn't want to have. She chose her words carefully, and the story of Clare held up. By dinner time she was ready to scream and hoped no one else asked her how she felt, if she was doing okay, or if she needed anything. She just might respond with the truth.

Naomi, Tracy, and Martha went out to dinner to redesign the wedding.

When the others sat down to dinner that night Sam congratulated Tempe. "I don't know what you said but it worked. Martha is almost reigned in."

Tempe shook her head, "Wasn't me. I turned Naomi loose on Martha. They were moving too fast for me but when they stopped, the wedding was back to what you and Tracy wanted."

After dinner Tempe sat on the front porch, looking at the mountains. Ryan walked out and sat down beside her. "When do I get to read the sealed report on Clare's death?"

Never, she thought, at least not if she had anything to say about it. "You aren't ready for it. Not yet. I'm not ready for that report yet and I wrote it. Please don't push."

"You do realize not everyone blocks as well as you, don't you?" Ryan asked softly. "Sage wasn't able to block Drake since he spent a couple of days in a drunken stupor. Once she knew, she couldn't block it from me."

By the five realms! "Okay, grab Sage and let's go to my room."

Once they were in the soundproof room Bryce and Tempe shared, she asked, "What did you hear?"

Sage blushed, "Drake was drinking heavily, not mean or anything, just drinking a lot. I didn't even know shifters could drink enough to stay drunk like that. Every time he looked at Ryan he got sad. He didn't blame Ryan, but he couldn't look at Ryan without getting sad and drinking more. Then he would rotate between feeling mad at you and sorry for himself because of what happened. Eventually he would notice me and try to focus his mind, but I guess the alcohol wouldn't allow for that." She took a deep breath. "Clare joined the Shadowed of her own free will and you had to kill her."

Tempe sighed, "I wish you hadn't heard that. We want to leave Clare's memory in peace."

"I understand, but why did Drake look at Ryan and get sad?" Sage asked.

"He didn't, not really. Ryan was just the most obvious reminder since I wasn't around. The Shadowed had been after Clare for a while. She always assumed I would get myself killed and she would become second. When Ryan beat her in the dominance push she realized she would never become the sovereign's second and she accepted the offer the Shadowed made. There was a bunch of crap about growing up in the Farseen, but that's basically it."

Tempe placed a hand on Ryan's shoulder. "Clare was not your fault, if anything Ellwood got a stronger hold on her when she was a child than I thought possible. As far as I'm concerned, Clare is the second of his children Ellwood killed. This time he managed to use me to do the killing. I'll have the report opened for you to read tomorrow. Soon enough?"

"Sure," Ryan replied and followed Sage, leaving Tempe alone in the room.

She stared out the window for a while, seeing nothing.

Betrayed

*****

Tempe went downstairs early Saturday morning and sat in the sunroom with a bagel and tea, going through alpha clan emails. Catlin walked in and sat across from Tempe, who immediately braced for what was coming.

"Dad said you and Rayna were with Mother when she died." Catlin asked, "Did she suffer? I didn't have the heart to ask Rayna."

"No, she didn't. It was quick," Tempe replied softly.

"Thank you," Catlin stood to leave. "Oh, Saffron came for the spreading of Mom's ashes. I didn't understand it, but she said to tell you it's good Clare is at peace." Catlin walked down the hallway toward the gym.

Tempe looked at her laptop for a long time and didn't accomplish a thing. She sat there and wondered what Saffron knew and when she knew it.

*****

Raven returned to Eli's house later in the morning. She held up a small box and smiled.

Tempe grinned in response, ready for some good news, "Is that what I think it is?"

"Yep. Where's Ryan?"

Tempe's face fell, "He's reading the report." She held up her hands in surrender, "Drake didn't block well. Sage and Ryan already knew everything. I'm hoping reading the report will allow him to move on."

"I'm not sure that's one of your better ideas." Raven pressed her lips together, obviously to keep from saying something more.

"I know. Let's go check on him."

They reached the bottom of the stairs as he came out of the bedroom. He stopped short when he saw them, bounded down the stairs, and motioned for them to follow. He walked out through the sunroom to the deck, shifted to his eagle and flew. Tempe shifted to her falcon and Raven shifted to her barn owl. Ryan led them to a nice overlook you could only get to by rappelling or flying. It was a good sized out cropping and even had a small fissure that went about fifteen feet into the mountain. It was a favorite hangout for the shifters who could fly. They all shifted to human and sat on the ledge with their feet dangling over the side.

"That sucks!" Ryan exclaimed.

"Indeed," Tempe replied.

"Sure does," Raven agreed.

After a few minutes of silence, Ryan said, "I've decided the spelled rings are worth the trouble. I worked on them while you and Bryce were camping. When you have time, I want to review my progress."

"Okay."

They sat there for a few more minutes before Raven said, "We have something for you." She tossed Ryan the strap.

He looked at it and then he looked at his aunts.

Tempe said, "I still need to spell it so let me show you how this type of spell works." She reached for the strap, but Ryan held it away from her and said, "I still don't know what it is."

"It's a strap like the one Raven wears. Once spelled it will adjust to whatever size you become. You start out human and it fits like a strap under the vest. You shift to your dragon and it's a riding strap. The spell will keep the strap on you whenever you take your dragon form," Tempe explained.

"You saying the next time you fly with my dragon you want to ride and not be carried in my claw?" Ryan couldn't help teasing his powerful aunt.

"You got that right. I had bruises where your claws grabbed me. Don't get me wrong. It was worth the bruises to get away, but still…" Tempe's voice trailed off as she snatched the strap out of his hands, laid it out and performed the sizing spell, explaining the spell to Ryan as she went.

Raven didn't pay attention to the lesson. She had no abilities in the casting arts, so it wouldn't benefit her. She leaned back and looked over the peaceful valley and sighed. She wished she had some ability to cast spells. It would make her more useful to Tempest on missions. She shook her head. Waste of time. She would never be able to cast, and Ryan would soon be Tempe's protégé since he had beaten her in the dominance push and would eventually replace her on missions. Even with that realization, she couldn't understand how Clare's mind could have gotten so twisted.

Eventually, Ryan slipped the strap on and said, "Let's see if it works." He veiled and shifted to his dark blue dragon. Tempe motioned to Raven and once she figured out how to find a veiled dragon, she jumped on and they flew.

Tempe shifted back to a falcon and headed home. When Tempe landed in Eli's garden and shifted they landed right behind her. Once Raven disembarked, he shifted and lowered his veil.

Raven laughed as they entered the house. "No wonder you like riding a dragon. It's fun."

"How long are you staying?" Ryan asked Raven as they heated up leftover pasta for lunch.

"I'm here for a few days," Raven crossed her arms.

"Why?"

"We still have a problem with the Shadowed. Clare wasn't the only convert," Tempe explained.

"Oh man, that was so bad I had forgotten about the rest."

*****

Eli's Sunday clan dinner was somewhat subdued. By silent agreement everyone focused on Sam and Tracy's wedding. Thankfully no one wanted to talk to Tempe about Clare. The word was out the virus killed her because she fought it and the others were being closely watched. Tempe suspected Eli had warned everyone she was still upset and to tread carefully, which was the truth.

Landon and Sage spent a lot of time together and quite a few mothers in the tribe raised their eyebrows. For her part, Tempe was concerned Sage was letting her interest in Landon cloud her judgment. She wasn't sure if Sage felt sorry for him over what might happen with Brandon or if she was attracted to him. Landon was eighteen years older than Sage, which wouldn't be a big deal later, but right now it is a big deal. Tempe had not quite succeeded in reigning in her worry over the subject when Joey, Star, Landon and Sage decided to take a walk.

As the two couples walked out Ryan glanced at Tempe and asked softly, "Do you want me to go with them?"

Tempe smiled, "Do you think they need you for protection or are you playing big brother with males hanging around your aunt and cousin?"

"Both," he replied with a sheepish grin.

"Sage can shield and call us if needed." They watched the couples walk through the gardens. When they were out of view, she tucked her arm in his and said, "I'm going to the Farseen tomorrow. I would like you to come with me."

He looked at Tempe in surprise, and then nodded with a smile and walked into the game room when Kaleb challenged him to a game of pool.

After the clan left Tempe grabbed a package from her room and knocked on the girls' door. Sage and Star called, "Enter."

Tempe walked in with a pink bag and Sage grinned, "Who gets a present?"

"Star."

"Why?" Star blushed.

"I've been working on these for a while. I just finished testing them before Ryan and I took our unscheduled trip courtesy of the Shadowed." She smiled and handed Star the bag.

She opened it and said, "Oh, I can feel the spells."

"Yes, and you have the same vest Raven made for the rest of us."

Tempe smiled at her expression. "Also, I've been going through my family's book of castings and some fae can create rune weapons. I think it's time both of you try to make one. Tomorrow Nova is going to start the process of testing and then helping you create your personal rune weapons."

"What?" Sage said in surprise.

"Cool." Star tried on her new clothes and while modeling them she asked, "Did you do this because when Sage recalled my memories I was jealous of her spelled clothes?"

"No, I was working on them well before that. The spells don't work for everyone, so I never mention I'm working on it until I pull it off." Tempe stared at her niece. "This doesn't mean you run into danger. You can still be killed. These clothes will help protect you but it's still better to stay safe."

"I understand." After a few seconds Star commented, "Do you have the Northern Realm's book of castings?"

"Yes," Tempe responded, wondering where this was going.

"I have the Central Realm's book of castings. I wonder if we could compare them and see what we can learn." Star said thoughtfully. Her suggestion was radical. Sharing the knowledge outside of the realm was discouraged.

Tempe raised an eyebrow. "I didn't know you showed promise in the casting arts?"

"Dad suggested I keep it to myself. You know, because of Lord Ellwood."

"Your father is a wise man."

"Fact is I haven't done much with the book. I was afraid to ask any questions. Perhaps you could help me."

"I would be pleased to do so."

Chapter 11

Monday morning Ryan opened a way and led Tempe into Saffron's herb garden.

Tempe had sent word to Saffron she would be coming for a visit and Ryan would open the way. This would be the first check to see who would recognize a way being opened by Ryan. Ryan and Tempe had a long talk before they made the trip. Saffron had different abilities than Tempest and was extremely strong. Saffron was as fast and as deadly as her elder sister. The only reason Lord Ellwood didn't make her his assassin was she refused to play. Tempe was pretty sure it goaded Ellwood that his two strongest living offspring wouldn't do as he said. And didn't that put a smile on a girl's face.

"Welcome, sister mine. I thought Ryan was to open the way. Since I didn't feel the way open I assume it was yours." Saffron walked toward them.

Tempe smiled, "His."

"Then he must be as strong as the rumors say."

"What rumors?"

"Clare, of course, told me about Ryan but the three Western Realm fae who returned from their capture, have told many stories of his abilities," she explained.

That was not good news. Tempe didn't want everyone to know about Ryan before they needed to.

Saffron read her displeasure in her facial expressions and commented, "Did you think to keep his abilities a secret? Remember how quickly everyone learned about you and Val."

"Yes, but we were living here." Tempe frowned and then shook her head. There was nothing she could do about it.

"You didn't come here just to test Ryan's ability to open a way, did you?" Saffron asked.

"No. When did you first suspect Clare was so angry?"

"At you? She was always jealous of you and me. She felt we were the lucky ones because Father wanted us. I could never get her to understand he didn't want either of us as his daughters. He simply saw us as tools. She was angry we didn't use our abilities to rule." Saffron moved around the herb garden, making cuttings.

Tempe wondered what potion she was working on and then realized Saffron might be clipping herbs for her dinner. Tempe waited. She knew Saffron would continue the story when she was ready. Ryan became restless and started pacing.

Saffron looked over and smiled, "He needs to learn patience. As I recall, you had trouble with that also."

"Indeed, I did, still do sometimes," Tempe smiled.

Saffron turned back to her herbs. "Clare became even angrier when she realized Sage was so strong. She told me about the night Sage threw her into the wall. What you and I saw as a young person without control, Clare saw as a threat to her position. When Ryan surpassed her, she lost it. She quit communicating with me, except for the couple of times you told her to contact me. I'm now sure she did that because she knew I would warn you if I saw how angry she was. I could always read her emotions." Saffron stopped cutting herbs and stared her eldest sister in the eye, "You shield your mind too much. You would have known it was happening if you didn't block everyone from your mind."

"If I keep my mind open I hear too much. It is… uncomfortable." Tempe shook her head and asked, "Are you a telepath?"

Saffron laughed, "Telepath and empath since birth. Why do you think I enjoy being alone most of the time? Fauna knew, because she caught me listening in to her thoughts. After she died I didn't tell anyone else. I learned my lessons well. By the time I was five I knew to keep any abilities hidden if I could. I saw what Father did to you and Val. I was not going to go through that. To be honest, by the time I had my powers, I knew I wasn't strong enough. Father would have broken me, and I would have taken the mantle he tried to force on you. I was strong enough to prevent that from happening but only because he didn't know my true talents."

Ryan had stopped pacing and the shifters looked at Saffron like she was nuts. After a few seconds Tempe asked, "What else can you do that Father doesn't know about?"

Saffron laughed, "I know you don't expect an answer to that question. I will offer you one piece of unsolicited advice. Keep Ryan, Sage and Star away from Father. He knows at least some of their abilities and he would consider any one of them a prize worth the risk of war with the shifters."

"Grandmother gave you a copy of the Northern Realm's book of castings, didn't she?" Tempe posed the question, but she already knew the answer.

Saffron grinned at the question. "Yes, on my twelfth birthday, same as you. Why?"

"Do you know why the fae don't use rune weapons even though the procedure is provided in the book?" Tempe asked.

"Mostly because it only works for those of tainted blood, a full blooded fae can't create one," Saffron explained. "Since you and I both use one, I assumed you knew it would work for half-breeds like us."

"I've never seen you use one," Tempe exclaimed.

Saffron pulled out the beautiful wooden clasp she had worn in her hair since she was a teenager and showed her eldest sister the rune symbols on the underside. "Like I said, I like to keep my talents hidden."

"Saffron, it's always interesting talking to you. Peace be present with you," Tempe inclined her head and grinned.

"And with you sister, nephew," Saffron replied, nodding to each of them in turn.

Ryan bowed low.

Tempe motioned to Ryan and he opened a way. They walked through to the cave on Eli's property. After he closed the way she asked, "What did you sense?"

"Saffron is strong. In addition to her abilities with potions and the casting arts, she can call the four elements and fly, which you already knew, she is a telepath and empath, which she admitted to. She is also able to veil, shield, shift and she is not moon called." He kept his voice calm in an effort to present a report the way Rayna and Tempe liked them, concise.

"She's an alpha shifter?" Tempe exclaimed. "I never even noticed, of course back then I was a bit self absorbed. I wonder if Rayna knows. Saffron is strong to be able to keep that from us as a child. Incredible!"

"She may be right. You should open your mind more." Ryan started walking.

"No. I almost went crazy before I learned to block everyone." Tempe grabbed Ryan's arm to stop him in the path. Her glare bored into him. "You only read Sage completely. Everyone else you get bits and pieces, but not everything. Imagine if you could read everyone the way you read Sage? That's what I do. Without the blocks I would be unable to carry on a conversation because I wouldn't know if they were speaking out loud or just thinking it in their minds."

"I can see that," Ryan said slowly. He put his arm around his aunt and herded her toward the cave. He had set up a corner of the cave for his spelled rings work and he had left a spell over it while they were in the Farseen. They stayed in the cave most of the afternoon. Ryan was almost ready to spell the rings.

Rayna and Tempe had a long talk. She had suspected Saffron was a shifter who wasn't moon called, but she never sought verification. She knew Saffron kept things hidden from the family and more specifically Lord Ellwood, so Rayna never pressed. She had silently agreed with Saffron her best defense was to appear to be less impressive than she was.

And Tempe learned one other thing. You don't know everything about a parent, regardless of your age. Tempe would have expected Rayna to try to pull Saffron to the alpha clan instead of allowing her to choose her own way.

*****

The next day, after a quick flight, Ryan, Sage, Star, Brook and Tempe walked into the rehab facility in Minnesota run by Citlali. Yes, they were taking a huge risk. Tempe took Star outside of Queen Niamh's approved protected area, but they were fast running out of options. She needed Sage for the recall, Ryan and Star for her support system. Brook and Tempe were muscle, pure and simple.

Brook was the only one not wearing spelled clothes.

Murdoch met them at the private airport with a full coven of wizards and took them to the facility in what turned out to be a nice, uneventful drive. They walked down a hallway without speaking. There just wasn't much to say. Tempe had been able to spare Sage Clare's mind but they needed information and she was going to recall Tamra's time with the Shadowed, unless Tempe could think of another way to get information.

Murdoch took them to a conference room where Citlali waited, the only occupant. Because of what they were going to discuss Tempe didn't want anyone else there.

"The Western Realm killed Ifor. He was recruiting for the Shadowed. They questioned him and decided he was a willing member of the Shadowed. So far, Drago and Amity are clean," Tempe offered, skipping the small talk. "Any change here?"

"No," Murdoch said grimly. "No one has been able to get Tamra to talk." He looked over at Tempe and added, "We have a wizard who, like you, can read surface thoughts. He hasn't been able to break her mental shield. Citlali can't get through either."

Sage asked softly, "How about Brandon?"

"I read him." Citlali said. "He didn't know anything of use. He couldn't shield against me, but he couldn't tell me anything because he didn't know anything. He was the bottom of the heap. He simply followed Duane's orders."

Tempe chewed her bottom lip and stared into space for a few minutes. "Brook, can you siren someone and force them to tell the truth?"

"Sorry, it doesn't work like that. I could make her kill herself or kill someone else. I can force her to say what I want her to say, but I can't make her tell me the truth because I don't know what the truth is. I can force an emotion on someone and I can put thoughts into her head, but I can't pull thoughts out of her head," Brook said apologetically.

"I was afraid of that. Star, this enchantment thing we share, can we use it to force her to talk?" Tempe asked.

"No, and for the same reasons. I can't make someone tell me the truth because I don't know what it is." Star said softly.

Tempe looked over at Sage. "This won't be pleasant. We might have to go through a lot of memories to find the ones we are looking for."

"I know. I'm prepared," Sage responded.

"Are you going to explain how this works?" Murdoch asked.

Sage shrugged, "I can recall someone's memories. I've never done it without their permission before so there might be some problems and it may take a while, because they will try to block the memories they don't want me to find. Will I recall with Duane or Tamra first?"

"Tamra," Tempe said firmly. "I don't plan on having you recall with Duane."

"But Tempe..." Sage whined, realizing her eldest sister was, once again, shielding her.

"No, Sage. I don't want you to recall with Duane. That's asking too much."

Sage didn't say anything, but she stared at Tempe with a stubborn look that reminded Tempe of her younger self. Recalling some of her antics, it probably wasn't a good thing.

"I agree with Tempest," Murdoch said. "I've talked to Duane for a few days now and I wouldn't want anyone with a soul to remember his actions. Citlali was unable to get anything from Duane. His block seems to be spell based but she couldn't break it."

"Tempe, what are you thinking?" Ryan asked. He could practically see her plotting something.

She stretched in her chair, "I was thinking maybe we could force Tamra to remember what we want."

Everyone looked at Tempe like they were sizing her up for her straightjacket and rubber room.

"Okay, maybe I'm nuts but between my ability to read surface thoughts, Star's ability to mellow someone out, and Brook's ability to control, we should be able to come up with a plan that will work without Sage having to shift through unhealthy minds."

"Tempe, I can deal," Sage all but snarled.

"Yes, you can. I just want to make this less painful, if possible."

*****

Three days with Tamra and they had nothing. No matter what they did Sage couldn't get a reading off of her. By the five realms, they couldn't even get something along the lines of her first kiss. They reconvened back in the conference room with the same team and they were all frustrated.

"Well, that's it. I'm going to talk to Duane," Tempe said grimly. Before anyone could express their shock she continued, "Tamra is obviously a strong telepath. I'm going to see if I can goad Duane into revealing something, anything. If I can get him to think about something I might get a reading."

"We know he was using the others at Half Acre to shield his mind. He may know about your abilities. If that's true he's going to keep his surface thoughts to things he thinks will get a rise out of you," Murdoch said.

"I know, but we aren't getting anywhere, and I want to try this." Tempe looked at Sage, "I don't want you near Duane. You aren't even eighteen yet and there are some things I prefer to protect you from if I can. I have a pretty good idea what memories he is going to try to give me."

Sage would have argued but Ryan went into a stare with her. Tempe recognized a mind speak fight when she saw one, so she stayed silent. After a few seconds Sage growled but didn't say anything else.

Tempe nodded to Ryan and walked out of the room.

Murdoch followed Tempe down the hallway.

"Are you seriously going to go with me?" She couldn't help the smile, it amused her that he thought she needed protection. "You know he won't drop any information with you there."

"I'll be right outside the door." Murdoch growled. "I didn't think you wanted Ryan to be your back up, so you're stuck with me."

She couldn't argue with that logic.

They reached Duane's door and Murdoch placed a hand on her shoulder. "He's evil. If he starts to get to you walk away. No information is worth letting him get a foothold in your mind."

Tempe smirked.

Murdoch grabbed her arm. "I mean it."

"I know you do." She patted his arm. "I've been around a while and I know evil. You've met my Father."

As she walked in the room, Duane looked over and a smile spread out over his face and even entered his eyes. "I knew you would show up eventually. Tamra can block everyone out of her mind so you are forced to come to me. How exciting... for me that is. I doubt you are pleased. Did you bring Sage with you?"

Tempe ground her teeth, which was probably his goal. He grinned. "We knew about Sage's ability to recall someone's experience. Tamra identified that ability early. We've wanted Sage, even though she isn't a half breed, almost as long as we've wanted Star."

While he talked Tempe read his surface thoughts. She had to admit he had a lot of sexual partners. She was even impressed, in a grossed-out kind of way, that he was able to talk and push his sex life to the fore in his mind.

Duane looked Tempe in the eye and said, "I'm sure you realize Tamra knew about your ability to read surface thoughts as well."

"Yes, I most certainly did," Tempe smirked. "You know your sexual conquests would be a little more impressive if any of the women appeared satisfied when you finished. It appears you only care about pleasing yourself, which is not surprising."

His smile thinned before he pushed a new set of memories to her. Tempe gritted her teeth as she got confirmation of how he established control over the women he was imprisoned with. He was a smooth talker and when you're a lab rat for years it's nice to find a shoulder to cry on, and apparently do other things with.

Tempe closed her mind.

"You don't want to show me the error of my ways?" she asked. "You don't want me to understand why the Shadowed are running all those experiments for the betterment of all?"

"No. You would never be a convert," Duane said smoothly. "I admit when you allowed me to kiss you I thought Radek had succeeded."

Tempe stood and walked out the door. Murdoch was waiting on the other side with a cup of tea. She smiled and sipped what was a nice Scottish blend.

"Learn anything?" Murdoch asked.

"Yes. The next time I'll listen when you say something is a waste of time."

They strolled back into the conference room and before anyone could ask she said, "Nothing of use."

"Maybe I should try," Sage said.

Tempe shook her head. "He knows what you can do. You will not see him."

While they went over options, of which there were few, Star went to sing to some of the infected still undergoing treatment. Sage went with her in case a shield and veil were needed.

"Citlali, what will you do with the Shadowed wizards?" Tempe asked.

"The same thing you did with the Shadowed shifter," Citlali replied quietly.

Tempe made a phone call and then she stared at the table thinking they had wasted three days.

Ryan cursed and ran for the door. Tempe and Murdoch followed the young shifter.

Ryan ran to Duane's door, and pulled it open to find Duane standing with Sage in front of him, he had one hand around her neck and the other around her waist. Ryan stopped dead as did Tempe and Murdoch.

Duane grinned, "You will let me out of this building or Sage dies."

Ryan clenched his teeth and growled, but when Tempe placed a hand on his back he didn't say anything else. Murdoch backed out of the room and started issuing orders into his headset.

Angered over Sage's foolishness, Tempe forced a laugh, "You actually think we'll let you walk out of here."

"I know you will. Sage is important to you." He inched a little to the left and said, "Clear the hallway, now."

Ryan backed out of the room, once again irritated Tempe could send him orders but he couldn't respond to her. They both understood what Sage had been thinking and both were angry with her, anger he would be sure to express in detail if she survived this experience.

"Sage, my dear, veil us." Duane kept one hand around her neck and gently caressed her waist with the other.

"No." Tempe's voice was calm. Sage, as an under aged shifter, was forced to not veil herself and Duane.

"Tempest, you aren't in control here. We both know I can break her neck right now." Duane flexed his fingers to reduce her airflow just to prove his point.

Tempe gritted her teeth and nodded to Sage, who veiled them. Tempe felt them leave the room. She wasn't sure Duane would take a direct line out of the building since he was veiled. She was banking on the orders she had given Ryan.

Star's voice echoed down the hallway, singing. While Ryan and Tempe had been practicing enchanting tones, they weren't even close to Star's level of expertise. Since Star was in Ryan's veil there was no way for Duane to find her or hurt her. Duane would not know where to send his spell.

In retrospect, since everyone except for Tempe and Murdoch were veiled, she should have realized Duane would throw his spell at her. Tempe had her shield up but his spell still sent her flying. Her shield and spelled clothes took most of the impact, but the wall still hurt when she made contact, leaving an imprint in the drywall.

Even when Tempe was flying through the air, Star never stopped singing and a few seconds later Sage dropped her veil. Duane wasn't moving but Sage was still trapped in his arms. Ryan stepped in and removed her from Duane's grasp.

Murdoch took Duane back and secured him in his room.

Back in the conference room, Ryan got Sage some water and a doctor on staff checked her out.

Tempe waited until the nice doctor left the room and asked slowly and deliberately, "What did you think you were doing?"

Sage took another sip of water, cleared her throat and responded, "Getting information."

Tempe raised an eyebrow but didn't say anything. Ryan opened his mouth to speak but one look at Tempe and he closed his mouth, a bit relieved he wasn't going to be on the receiving end of her anger.

Sage looked between the two and realized neither was on her side at the moment. "Obviously Duane and Tamra were not going to give us any information. I thought if I allowed Duane to think he tricked me, he would let information slip about where the Shadowed are, who they are, or something."

She looked at Tempe and said as calmly as she could manage, "It worked."

"You are not going to use it worked as an excuse," Tempe growled. "You could have been killed. You realize that, don't you?"

"Yes, but I knew you and Ryan would save me," she replied in a small voice.

"Oh, well, that makes it better. You knew we would save you. What if we hadn't? How do you think Ryan and I would feel if we had failed you?" she demanded.

Ryan looked over at Tempe and shook his head slightly. Tempe opened her mind and realized her youngest sister was scared and had already thought of the worst-case scenario, but not until after Duane had her.

Tempe took a deep breath, "We will talk more about this later. Tell us what you learned."

Sage took a deep breath and provided a report the way Rayna demanded them, calm, concise and quick. "Tamra was not an option for me if she blocks as strong as everyone says. Duane was never going to give any information away. Based on comments Tempe made I thought he would consider me weak and easy to control. When I entered his room he offered up memories of his pain and I let him convince me I should loosen his restraints."

She looked over at Tempe and said, "Once he was free, he grabbed me and kissed me. I didn't know what to do, the self-defense moves didn't work. He countered every defensive move I made. That's when I knew I had made a mistake. That's when I called Ryan." She took a sip of water and continued, "Duane's first thoughts when we veiled were of getting to Scotland and someone named Aster. She's his contact to the Shadowed leadership. He also thought of the wizard Alena."

Tempe pulled out her cell and called Siri, currently living in Scotland, to make plans.

As the meeting broke up, Citlali asked Star to sing once more in the open area for the group. Brook went with Star and Citlali. Murdoch looked back at Tempe, Sage and Ryan and closed the door behind him.

Tempe didn't say anything for a few seconds. She looked at Sage and finally asked, "Why? Why that way? Why not tell me and Ryan what you thought you could do and let us help?"

Sage laughed at her aunt, "Neither of you would allow me to put myself in danger. Ryan is worse than you. Guys, I'm almost an adult. I can help." She stared at Tempe and said, "Just remember what you had already done before you were my age."

"You're right, if you had come to us with this plan I would have said no... and I would have been wrong." Tempe shook her head. "I know you think I try to protect both of you too much, but I wanted to give you guys a normal life. I'm beginning to realize neither of you are going to get those fun carefree years."

"Wait! That's it? That's your lecture?" Ryan fumed. "Sage could have been hurt."

"Yes," Tempe agreed. "She could have been, and I think she's learned a valuable lesson. Next time she'll talk to us first."

Tempe stood and headed for the door. Before she walked out she looked at Ryan, "You might want to beef up self-defense training. It occurs to me you have trained her to deal with people who aren't combat trained, but she will need to be able to defend against someone who is an experienced fighter."

Tempe walked out and left them alone to work out their first work related disagreement.

A couple of hours later, as Sage, Star, and Ryan ate lunch in the conference room, Tempe entered with Loane, the person she had called earlier.

Sage looked over and asked, "Tempe called you?"

"Yes dear, she did." Loane replied serenely.

"What I did was that bad?" Sage asked, distressed.

"No. I called Loane before you yelled for help," Tempe replied dryly. To Star Tempe said, "This is Loane, one of Rayna's younger sisters. She is the strongest functional telepath and empath in the family."

"Hello ma'am," Star said.

"My dear, it is a pleasure to meet you." She looked around the room and smiled, "Tempe you are the last alpha I would expect to be training the next generation."

Tempe smiled, "It caught me by surprise, too."

"Hello, Loane," Ryan grinned.

Loane smiled, "I'll bet everyone keeps comparing you to Val, but you're nothing like him."

Star looked confused and commented, "I read about Ryan's push with the alpha clan. I don't remember anyone but Rayna's children being there."

"There was no reason for Rayna's sisters to be there. None of us were ever allowed in combat and while we hold birthing bonds, it's the only function we do for the alpha clan now. Once a new sovereign is in position and her children are old enough to take over the duties, the sovereign's siblings are allowed to withdraw from active work if they wish." Loane grinned and admitted, "Of course, we were also the first to still be alive when a new sovereign took over."

"Why weren't you allowed in combat?" Star asked.

"Jocosa and Katell are both healers and were always protected from battle so they could help the wounded. That's their only gift aside from shifting. My telepathy and empathy make me unsuitable for fighting. I feel too much," she responded calmly. Loane turned to Tempe and asked, "Who am I here to read?"

Tempe chuckled as she realized her aunt had found the truth without help, as always.

"My dear niece, you could never block me. And before you ask, yes I knew about Saffron's gifts. I have always been blessed with the ability to keep my mouth shut and I think everyone will agree my keeping my mouth shut is a good thing." She inclined her head.

"Then let's get to it." Tempe switched to business mode. "Loane, this will not be pleasant. If there were another way I wouldn't have called. Tamra has strong blocking abilities but she might know the membership of the Shadowed and I hope she has the location of their main facility."

"You should have called me first. I read the report as I flew in. Sage is too young for this type of reading." She looked over at Sage whose eyes flashed in anger. "You need to train with me if you have the ability to break into someone's mind. As Tempe said, it's not pleasant. I will leave Tamra brain dead. You can't force your way into someone's mind without causing permanent damage. If she fights me I will destroy her brain to get the information. I have only done this one other time in my life and I had hoped to never do it again. With this type of battle there are no winners. I will have to live with the pain I inflict on her."

Sage, Ryan and Star were suitably subdued.

"I need thirty minutes in a private room to prepare," Loane said softly.

"Citlali has prepared a room for you." Tempe headed for the door with Loane in tow. When she returned the teenagers were still silent.

Finally, Sage said, "Do you think I need to train with Loane?"

"I don't know. Rayna and I were going to wait until you were ranked and then we were thinking one summer between college semesters you might spend time with Loane in upstate New York, with Jes's clan. You would be able to visit with Phoenix and work with Loane and she can determine how strong you are."

"That makes sense, I guess." Sage looked at her soda and added, "It's sort of scary. To know someone can destroy a mind and I might have that ability."

"Yes, it is, but Loane is almost as old as I am, and she's only done this once before," Tempe shrugged.

"But it seems like a power someone could corrupt."

"That's why few know what she can do. The fact that she chose to tell the three of you means she trusts you with the knowledge. The only other people who know exactly what she can do are Rayna, Serenity and yours truly, because she trained us outright or augmented our training. Citlali suspects but she has never asked for verification." Tempe replied. She didn't bother to state the obvious. Loane was strongly protected from people like Lord Ellwood.

When Loane was prepared Tempe went with her to Tamra's room.

Tamra smirked at the shifter assassin, until she saw Loane, the mind walker, behind Tempest. The wizards knew and feared Loane, although few had seen her in the flesh. Tamra had not expected the sovereign to send the mind walker. They are rare in the preternatural world. A mind walker can pull any information from someone's brain. Any experience. Any knowledge, even hopes, dreams, and fears.

Loane ignored Tamra's emotional grid as it flamed to panic. She walked calmly to the bottom edge of the bed.

Fear obvious on her face, Tamra's eyes widened. Loane's face was unreadable. As an onlooker, that was all Tempe saw. No movement, no screams, just a stare down of sorts. After maybe ten minutes Tamra's eyes lost focus. Loane turned and walked out. Tempe followed like a little puppy.

They returned to the conference room with Citlali and Murdoch in tow. The teenagers hadn't moved, but Brook had joined them.

Loane looked around the room and said, "Tamra did not know the location of the Shadowed main facility or any other. The Shadowed are divided into cells of no more than five. Tamra, Clare, Duane, Brandon, and Adelia made up one cell with Duane as the leader. He reported up to a woman whose name Sage has already gotten. The others at Half Acre that helped the Shadowed were manipulated by Duane and to a lesser extent by Tamra." Loane sat down in the chair and said quietly, "Her mind is gone."

Tempe looked over at Citlali and asked, "Would you like me to…"

"No, Tempest, this time the duty is mine." Murdoch said grimly.

She sighed as he walked out of the room. Sage let a single tear fall down her face. Ryan and Star had their game faces on and didn't show any emotion.

Chapter 12

Tempe breathed a sigh of relief as soon as they were wheels down in Eli's territory where Star was protected. Never had Tempe been so glad to be back in Tennessee. Dwight and Bryce met them at the airport. Ryan loaded Star and Sage in his pickup truck and they headed out.

Brook was delighted to see Dwight and she waved bye as he loaded her suitcase in his pickup truck. Tempe smiled at Brook's obvious happiness.

Once the others had left and Bryce and Tempe were in his SUV she said, "Did you know about Brook and Dwight?"

"I suspected." Bryce smiled, "Dwight spends a lot of time with Brook and Chev."

"How do I not know this?" she whined.

"You're gone a lot, and you've had other things on your mind," Bryce said kindly.

*****

Tempe sat Landon down and told him the Shadowed killed his brother the same way they killed Clare. She purposefully had this talk alone without Sage or Ryan. If he ever found out the truth she wanted him to have only one person to blame for the lie and his brother's death.

He listened in silence and then sat for a couple of minutes. Finally, he looked at her and said, "Thank you for the lie to preserve his memory, but we both know Brandon was a willing member of the Shadowed. Since you are saying Clare, Tamra and Duane died the same way I suspect they were too. Please tell everyone I prefer to not discuss Brandon." He managed a sad smile and admitted, "I have suspected for some time he was of the Shadowed. I will not be able to lie well enough to keep it to myself if too many people ask me questions."

Landon walked out of the room as she sat there, stunned at his comprehension. Then she shrugged and walked down to the kitchen for a cup of tea.

When Tempe arrived in the kitchen Ryan was waiting for her. He cut his eyes to the porch, so she joined him, sipping her tea.

"The rings are done, and they work," he said proudly. "I made one change."

"Change? What change?" Changes to complex spells could have nasty side effects.

"I made one for Sage, one for Star and one for me," he replied.

"You…" Tempe looked at him and asked, "You did what?"

"I looked over the mechanics and talked to Nova. I just have the feeling the three of us will need to be able to find each other."

"That's amazing. Before you hand out the rings there is one other thing we need to do. We need to lay a spell that keeps the rings on their fingers, and makes them invisible to anyone else, like the spell on a bracelet of honor. I worked that up after my ring was removed when we were taken by the Shadowed."

"Will I be able to create a bracelet of honor?" He wanted to be able to make one of those at some point.

"Yes, I believe one day you will. But it will require a lot of effort and you have a few other things to learn first."

They walked up to her sound proofed room and she taught him the final spell to layer on the rings. Once he finished, he mentally called Sage to the room and told her to bring Star with her.

The girls walked in and Ryan gave them each a box. They looked at their rings and then they looked at Ryan. Sage was the first to break the silence. "You made spelled rings, like Tempe did. How did you make them to allow Star and I to find each other?"

Tempe snorted, "You're missing the big picture. He made three, one for each of you. The three of you will be able to find each other."

"That's amazing," Sage said.

"How do they work?" Star asked.

Ryan launched into an explanation of the rings and how to use them. Eventually, they put their rings on and watched as each wearer could only see the ring on their own hand. Star looked over and grinned hopefully, "Does this mean I don't need to be guarded so much?"

"Sorry. There is too much interest and there is still a high bounty on your head. Taking you to the rehab facility was a big risk and we won't do it again." Tempe said softly.

"I suspected as much, but a girl can dream," she replied with a sigh.

They headed out to the yard to engage in a little sparring in the hot July sun. This was Tempe's first opportunity to see the rune weapons

Sage and Star had created. She was amused to see they both chose six-inch Kobutan sticks, like hers.

Sage saw the smile. "It makes sense. They fit in the pocket on our vests and in our purses."

"True. That's why I like mine."

Ryan rolled his eyes and pulled out his twenty-eight-inch rune baton. "Let the mock battle begin."

*****

Saturday evening Bryce and Tempe met up with Adam and Brandi at Harmony. Brandi and Tempe disagreed over how things were proceeding, Tempe was pushing the slow-and-steady approach while Brandi was firmly in let's-take-action mode. Bryce and Adam remained silent.

Eventually, Brandi turned to Adelia behind the bar and asked, "What do you think? Shouldn't we be more aggressive in our dealings with the Shadowed?"

"Well, I'm not much of a strategist or warrior," Adelia said slowly. "I see both of your points, but I don't think I'm qualified to even have an opinion on how to proceed."

"Come on," Brandi cried passionately. "It's just a friendly discussion. Surely you have an opinion. Neither Tempest or I will get mad if you don't support our view," she added with a smile.

Adam laughed, "Not even Bryce or I are weighing in on this so called friendly discussion between you and Tempe. I think Adelia has it right, it's duck and cover time."

Adelia shot Adam a quick smile and went to wait on a couple who grabbed two seats at the bar.

Brandi loudly proclaimed she could beat Tempe at pool. The challenge was accepted. They had a noisy game ragging on each other and eventually most of the bar took sides, betting on either the shifter/fae or shifter/witch/vampire. Bryce and Adam remained at the bar talking with Adelia.

Waving goodbye to Brandi and Adam as they took off on his motorcycle, Bryce and Tempe climbed into Bryce's SUV and headed for Eli's.

Later that evening Brandi showed up and asked if she could have a room at Eli's for the night. She and Adam had a fight, called it quits and she needed someplace to sleep for the night. She was heading out at daybreak for parts unknown.

Adam went back to the bar to drown his sorrows. Adelia proved to be supportive when she heard about the split.

Betrayed

The next morning Brandi took off, putting Vitvarg Farms firmly in her rear-view mirror.

Chapter 13

Asilia, Bobby and their triplets showed up early Sunday afternoon to cook the clan dinner. It would be another cookout but no hotdogs and hamburgers this time. She threw a selection of elk roasts and tenderloins on the grills and the smoked salmon was already in process. Bobby and Charles took regular hunting and fishing trips and the freezers needed to be cleaned out before their next excursion. As is the case for many outdoor cooking events, the men folk took charge of the grills and smokers, with Bobby issuing orders every so often.

Sage, Star and Tempe helped with the side dishes in the kitchen while Delaney sat at the kitchen bar resting. The twins were taking their toll today.

"How am I going to learn about life in the Farseen if you guys never talk about the good stuff?" Sage grumbled.

"I've told you what I know. I was a child of the court, protected and sheltered. If you want real information Tempe will need to tell you her stories," Star said.

"No. Most of the stories of my life in the Northern Realm are not good pre-dinner conversation," she said firmly.

"You could tell us about Ridge," Star suggested slyly.

"Yes, I wondered why you split with him. He's kind and so protective, not to mention handsome," Delaney sighed. When she saw the looks from the others, she added, "What? Ridge and his niece were good to me when I was first rescued from Crystal's caves. They were the first to offer me kindness. I wouldn't have survived a week without their help, especially the way I threw fire when frightened. I know Bryce doesn't like Ridge, but I'll never forget how kind he was to me."

"No," Tempe stated flatly. "I'm not discussing Ridge. I'm glad he was kind to you, but I won't discuss that time of my life."

Asilia smiled, "Even I have to admit Ridge is a fine-looking man, and he always displays such good manners."

Tempe shook her head, "Please don't say that in front of Bryce."

"Gee Tempe," Sage responded with an eye roll. "Even I know better than to talk about Ridge's most excellent good looks and pleasing manners in front of Bryce. He's the only guy who can get a rise out of him."

Star turned to Asilia, "While I was still living in the Central Realm I heard stories of a female shifter, with skin the color of chestnuts, who took the form of a lioness and lived with a forest lord in the northern tip of the Central Realm for many years. The description of the woman, and the lion, matches you."

Tempe turned to Asilia, "This sounds promising. Is this the forest lord you promised to tell me about one day?"

Asilia blushed, which was interesting to see with her dark skin. She looked out to verify the men were hanging out with Bobby at the grills. She took a deep breath and said, "If I tell this story it stays between us. Bobby doesn't like to hear Aran's name any more than Bryce likes to hear Ridge's."

They all nodded their agreement. Asilia looked at the teenagers and said, "Sometimes love isn't enough."

"I was almost twenty years old and hunting in the jungle where I was born. I had tracked an antelope in my human form and was just getting ready to shift and kill the deer. It would have fed my village well. Right as I shifted and lunged at the deer a hunter's arrow flew through the air. I caught the deer by the throat as the arrow landed in my backside.

"This hunter was like no hunter I had ever seen. He was almost seven feet tall, with oak colored skin, white blond hair and jade green eyes. He was beautiful. Even with an arrow in me I couldn't look away from his eyes. He apologized to my lioness form and took out his knife to slit my throat. It was painful, but I shifted to beg for my life. He stepped back and introduced himself as Aran, a forest lord of the Central Realm. He asked if he could tend my wound and I agreed. It wasn't like I had a lot of choice. I couldn't reach the arrow, and my family didn't know where to look for me. I had tracked the herd for a while and was nowhere near where they would have searched. It would have taken them too long to track me.

"While he healed my wound, for he had that gift, he talked to me about my family. He helped me take the deer back to my village. He used glamour to hide his true form and my small village was pleased to accept a young strong man. Aran stayed for two seasons and then said he must return to his home. He invited me to go with him.

Betrayed

We became close and I decided to leave with him. My family was not happy, but they judged him a good man and my father thought I would be safe with him. We left and once we were in the jungle he opened a way and we entered the Farseen. He introduced me to all at his residence as his mate.

"Most of his household accepted me, but there were a few who were unhappy to have a shifter as the lady of the house. For many years we were happy, but I couldn't have children without an alpha female around and Aran wouldn't invite one to his residence. He was afraid news would reach Lord Ellwood's attention of a shifter in his house. Aran's home was right on the edge of the Central Realm and the Northern Realm.

"Even so many years after the fae shifter war, Ellwood was not happy to see shifters and it was well known amongst the fae that, excluding the daughters of his blood, alpha females were not welcome in the Northern Realm or near his realm. At the time I didn't understand how strong Ellwood was. I didn't realize he could bend the other realm lords to his will.

"Lufu was a servant in Aran's house, who had long desired him. When I first arrived, she thought I was just a passing fancy. Aran had brought many women home. He would eventually tired of them and sent them back to where he found them. When I was still there after fifty years, Lufu decided to do something about me.

"She was given leave to visit her sister in the Northern Realm. When she returned, there was another forest lord with her, one from the Northern Realm. He came in under the guise of escorting Lufu since they were going in the same direction. His name was Cada.

"Cada met with Aran privately and they argued, loudly. Eventually, they quit talking and starting fighting. Once the swords came out I rushed to Aran's side. Lufu tried to hold me back but she wasn't able to hold onto a lioness once I shifted.

"I was too late. Cada beheaded Aran about the same time I killed Lufu. I was mad with grief. I attacked Cada, which should have been a stupid thing to do, but he was as cocky as he was powerful. He decided to play with me. He didn't use magic only his sword. It was his downfall. He apparently had never hunted a lioness with human intelligence. He was going to put all of his power behind the thrust of his sword, but his stance telegraphed his plan. I hunched down and then lunged as he was drawing the sword back. I caught his throat in my jaws and that was the end of Cada.

"I ran from the house in my lioness form. I could not open a way and didn't know anyone who could. There was no one I trusted in the Farseen. I had never made friends with the fae, trusting in Aran for everything. I roamed. Thank goodness Aran had hunted with me over the years so I knew what creatures to avoid. Eventually I neared a residence with a female fae of the ruling class. She appeared to live without a man or any servants besides pixies. That was enough to get my attention.

"I watched her for days, but she didn't seem to notice me. One day she was working in one of her many gardens and I inched closer to her than ever before. She didn't look at me but asked, 'Would you like to shift and have lunch with me?'

"I growled. She smiled and shifted into a tiger. We looked at each other, big cat to big cat, before she shifted back saying, 'I haven't shown anyone my other self for a long time. So now we both have information on each other. I vow you will take no harm from me this day.'

"I shifted. It had been months since I was last in human form for more than a few moments and it felt good. We talked and eventually she offered to open a way for me. She did not have the necessary knowledge to open a way back to the jungle where I was from, but she could open a way to the new world, near where one of her mother's children lived. I accepted her offer and came through the way at Eli's cave.

"While I was getting my bearings, I ran into Eli. When I explained how I ended up on his land, he offered me a safe place to stay. He explained about slavery, but we were so far from other settlers it wasn't much of a problem. It was an odd time for me.

"I decided to stay in the new world rather than go back to Africa. The Taylors moved here in the seventies and Bobby and I hit it off right away."

"Wow," Sage looked over at Tempe. "Is…"

"Wow is right," Tempe agreed before Sage could say anything else. "Most people don't know Saffron can shift and she prefers to keep it that way."

"No problem. When Saffron came here when Ellwood was infected with the virus it was the first time I had seen her since she sent me back," Asilia replied. "I didn't even tell Eli. I merely said a kind fae opened a way for me, but I never wanted to talk about it. Eventually, he stopped asking." She looked over at Delaney, "I suppose you can tell Eli."

"I don't think Eli needs to know this story," Delaney said softly. "Unless something happens, making it important for him to know, I won't tell him."

"You know, the song of Cada's death is nothing like your account," Tempe smiled. "I'll bet Father didn't want everyone to know a lone shifter took out one of his senior guards."

Most of the teenagers went for a short run with some of the adults. Sage put the finishing touches on the salad while Landon sat at the kitchen bar. They were deep in conversation. Asilia raised an unhappy eyebrow but didn't say anything since Tempe was in the room.

Mia walked in and moaned, "It's not fair."

"What's not fair, sweetie?" Asilia said as she checked a casserole in the oven.

"Everything. Mitch and Michael are playing video games. They have each other. There are no girls my age around and I can't even shift." Mia pouted as only a seven-year-old can.

Everyone smiled except Landon. He responded, seriously, "That does seem unfair."

Mia correctly identified Landon as an understanding soul and sat down beside him. "I wish there was something to do," she sighed, laying her head on the counter.

"Yes, that would be good. But what, what could we do for an hour or so until dinner is ready?" Landon mused.

Mia appeared to think about it for a few seconds and offered, "Well, you could teach me to drive a golf cart. Mitch got to drive one a couple of weeks ago and it's all he's talked about since."

"You know, I was just thinking it would be amusing to take one of the golf carts for a spin," Landon admitted.

Mia grabbed Landon's hand and called to Sage, "Will you come too?"

Sage glanced over at Tempe before she agreed and the three of them went to experience Mia's first driving lesson.

After they walked out Tempe asked, "Does Bobby know how much trouble he's going to have when Mia starts dating?"

"Dating? Who's dating?" Bobby asked as he walked in to get the platters for the food on the grill.

"No one dear," Asilia grinned, "Tempe was just commenting on how well Mia just wrapped Landon around her little finger."

"Oh, I thought I was the only one she did that with."

Tempe laughed, "Have you never watched her with Eli or Bryce? They have no ability to say no to her. I think being the only young girl in the clan has made her a trifle spoilt. She gets every male in the clan to do what she wants, except for Mitch and Michael."

The clan dinner was excellent, and everyone got to hear Mia expound on Landon's excellent teaching ability. Mitch and Michael were suitably jealous, and Mia had a wonderful evening, even if there were no other girls her age to play with.

*****

Half Acre was almost empty. Yarrow had finally gone back to the Southern Realm with Stone. Dylan flew back with his father to Fallon's clan in Scotland. Dana and Cindy were completely brainwashed by Duane, but Nova found them a good witch run facility closer to their grandparents. Everyone was hopeful they would have a full recovery, but no one expected it to be fast.

Arleth and Gavin showed marked improvement and their families had arrived to stay at Half Acre. They should be leaving within a couple of weeks.

Landon moved into Eli's for the time being and had been talking with Eli about maybe joining his clan. He was already employed at Eli's restaurant and was a big hit with the staff. His organizational and people skills had made him popular.

Chapter 14

Star walked slowly into the sunroom on Monday morning where Tempe was working. She sat calmly and waited for her aunt to look up from her laptop. She knew Tempe wouldn't like what she was going to say but her mind was made up.

Tempe looked over and asked, "What can I do for you?"

"I've decided to see Lord Ellwood," she stated calmly.

"Star…"

"I know, it's a risk, but maybe if we meet, he'll give up and go away."

"I don't think it will work that way," Tempe replied flatly.

"I'm tired of tippy toeing around this issue. Let's meet with him and get it over with. Will you set it up?"

"If the clan cyngor approves, yes," Tempe admitted. "But you need to understand everyone will be nervous about this visit. We can't have it at Harmony because you are not yet twenty-one."

"I didn't think of that. Perhaps we should go to him," she commented out loud.

"No," Tempe replied angrily. "I will not take you into the Northern Realm or any realm. Star when you leave the safety of Eli's territory then you are no longer protected by Queen Aerten's decree."

"Okay," Star said slowly, "I didn't realize this would upset you so much."

Tempe took a deep calming breath. "I shouldn't have said that so sharply, but I'm worried about you. If you want to see Ellwood, Eli's cyngor will agree and I'll set it up."

Tempe smiled, "Heck, just giving the news to Father might shock him to death."

*****

Tempe decided to follow the advice of the Northern Realm the last time she visited. Ridge's sister, Lady Sierra, said she should warn her or Ash if she was coming for a visit, so she did. The thought being, if they knew Ellwood's shifter daughter was coming to the residence there would be less clean up for the staff afterwards.

Like always, she opened a way to her childhood bedroom and the first thing she noticed was the listening device she had blown up the last time she was there had been replaced. She smirked and placed the thimble of honey she brought for Briar's family on the dresser.

She walked out the door and down the hall in full battle gear. When she turned into her father's receiving hall – the place where those wishing to speak with the realm lord waited his pleasure – it was empty, except for Ash, Ridge and Ellwood's staff and guards. Normally the room was packed.

"Gentleman," she inclined her head. "Is Father not receiving today?"

"Lady Tempest," Ash responded with a bow and a smile. "When I informed those who were waiting that you would be seen first they decided their business with Lord Ellwood was not so urgent and they could return tomorrow."

"How considerate," Tempe pressed her lip together to keep from smiling.

Ridge held out his arm and she walked with him to the door. The guards bowed low as Lady Tempest walked by and entered Lord Ellwood's receiving room. The room was about the size of a basketball court and there was one seat, his throne.

As she expected, Temperance stood to Ellwood's right. What she didn't expect was Algar, Father's oldest assassin, standing on his left. If Algar was in the room, then Cayenne would be available, but just out of sight."

Tempe took in a breath and bowed, "Father, I bring news from Star."

His lips curled into a scowl, but no sound escaped his lips.

"She wishes to meet with you."

He sat up straight and a small smile lit his eyes and lips. "Why did you not bring her here with you today?"

"Father, I'm no fool," Tempe raised an eyebrow. "You will have to come into Eli's territory to visit with Star since that is the only place where she retains the protection of the Queen's decree."

"Ah yes," he replied placidly, "As you wish. When shall I meet my granddaughter?"

"This evening at six you will open a way to the cave on Eli's property. You and two of your court may enter. If any more enter the way, the meeting will be over."

"This evening, that's not much time to prepare," he replied.

114

"Then don't come."

"I'll be there, daughter mine," Ellwood replied. "I wonder if Star will solve the mystery of who her mother is."

"I didn't realize there was a mystery. Do you now suspect she is not your granddaughter?"

"Child, you have your mother's tongue," he snapped.

"I am pleased, Father."

"That was not a compliment," he snarled.

Tempest smiled.

"If you have no further business I'll see you this evening. I assume you will be there," Ellwood said.

"You assume correctly, Father," she bowed and turned to leave.

"Daughter mine," Ellwood called after her.

"Yes Father?" She didn't bother to turn around.

"I was saddened to hear of Lady Clare's passing. I understand the Shadowed caused her death."

Tempe buried her pain and took a deep breath, "You heard correctly."

Ridge walked Tempest out of the receiving hall to the living bridge and toward her old quarters. She looked at him and smirked, "Why are you walking me to my room?"

"To make sure you don't have to kill anyone to leave." Ridge's enigmatic smile lit up his entire face.

Tempe shook her head and reached for the door. Ridge grabbed her hand and pushed her gently into the wall and pressed their bodies together, like he was going to kiss her. Her eyes flashed before he whispered into her ear, "Peace. He will bring Algar and Cayenne with him tonight. They will be searching for holes in your defenses. Don't let them find any."

Anyone who saw them would think Ridge was back to playing her lover. It angered her, but the warrior in her was smart enough to realize it was a safe way to pass information. So she played along, slapped his face and said, "Ridge, I am not yours anymore. Never do that again."

Tempe opened the door and walked in. As she turned to close the door he winked. She shut the door and smiled. Maybe that would give the court something to talk about, and hopefully someone would taunt Ridge for losing her to a mere shifter.

She picked up her empty thimble (her pixie friends would eat well tonight), opened a way, and returned to the cave on Eli's property. Bryce waited on the other side. He had been pacing but when she exited the way he grabbed her and kissed her. She returned the kiss in full. When they separated, he asked, "How did it go?"

"About like you would expect. Father will probably bring Algar and Cayenne with him."

"The assassins? Won't that be fun?" Bryce quipped.

"Bryce, why were you pacing? It was just a quick trip to the Farseen."

He ran his fingers through his hair, looked at her and growled, "I don't like waiting here when you go to the Farseen, where Ridge is. He was close to you. I can smell him."

She pulled him in for another kiss. After a few minutes, when he could breathe again, he added, "Of course I enjoy welcoming you back."

*****

"Are you sure this is the best option?" Eli asked for the fourth time.

"Eli, stop," Tempe ordered.

He growled but shut up.

Tempe chewed her lower lip already sorry she had issued such a direct order to the prif in his own home. "We know Ellwood wants Star, Sage, Ryan, or any combination thereof. I hope to put him off by showing they work together and they are stronger together than any force he might send. And I want him to see their support system. I'm taking Ryan on a mission into the Farseen tomorrow. I don't want Ellwood to think making a play for him is a good idea. If we're going to search the wastelands of the five realms for a Shadowed outpost I don't want to fight off Ellwood at the same time. Ryan and Sage are under no decree."

"I understand but it seems dangerous," Eli replied.

"It is dangerous. If this blows up I'll never forgive myself, and I suspect no one else will ever forgive me either." She blew air out between her teeth.

Eli came and sat beside her. "Sis, it'll work out. I'm just grousing 'cause I can't be there."

"You're the house siren. I'm the cave siren." Brook walked in the door with Dwight.

Dwight asked, "Can I go with Brook to the cave?"

Tempe looked over at Eli and raised an eyebrow. He shrugged, "Talk to Bryce, he's our senior cyngor member at the cave." Dwight went off in search of Bryce.

When he walked away Brook turned to Eli, "Do you object to my relationship with Dwight? I don't want to do anything that would cause problems for Dwight in the clan. He says it's not a problem, but I want to be sure. I'm still not sure how the clan stuff works. Since Mother wasn't moon called she wasn't active in a clan after she met Father."

Eli looked over in surprise. "My sister is a fae/shifter mix. My niece is a fae/shifter mix. My wife, your sister, is a fae/shifter mix. Why would anyone in this clan object to you?"

"Because I can't shift," she said sadly.

"Has anyone said anything to you?" Eli's even tone promised trouble if someone had.

"No," she replied, surprised at the question.

"Then don't look for trouble. Dwight's happy, you're happy, so it's not anyone else's business."

Eli walked off and Tempe asked, "Is there another question you want to ask?"

Brook frowned, "Is it okay? If we were to have kids they might not shift. Would that upset anyone?"

"Have kids? You guys are talking about kids?" Tempe asked as she carefully locked down her mind.

Brook smiled nervously, "I'm pregnant. We just found out today. I honestly thought I couldn't get pregnant. I'm old. Not compared to you, but I'm well over four hundred. I've been married twice, to humans both times, but never got pregnant. I will have this child and I don't care who objects. I will leave if I have to, but I would like to stay and Dwight has asked me to stay and get married. I'm not sure about marriage because I don't understand clan life, but I want this child."

"I'm happy for you. I'm also a little surprised. It's amazing how many women in Eli's clan have gotten pregnant," Tempe mused.

"I'm not in Eli's clan," she replied with a smile.

Tempe chewed her lower lip. "You might need a birthing bond to carry the child to term. If the child is a shifter, your body might reject the fetus like a human female will without a bond."

"How can I find out?" Brook demanded.

"I can check now."

"Yes please."

"Then let's go to my room." Tempe led Brook up the stairs and down the hall to the room she shares with Bryce.

"What a nice room. It's peaceful." Brook sat on the fainting couch and asked, "What do I need to do?"

"Nothing, just relax and let me check." Tempe joined her on the fainting couch.

Tempe has always been amused for the name someone came up with for that type of chair. She remembered in the mid eighteen hundreds the fainting couch was for looks and gave women a way to escape whatever they wanted to escape, when they would 'faint' and be allowed to relax on the couch for a while. She took a deep centering breath and focused on the child. Well, children, twins. Both girls displayed shifter markers. She centered back into herself and said, "Brook, how pregnant do you think you are?"

"Two to three months. Dwight and I met years ago, and we were friends. When he showed up here, and I was here, we picked up where we had left off. Why?" She asked.

"Because shifter pregnancies are only five months long, you will deliver about the same time as Delaney. We need to get you in a birthing bond now." She mentally called for Sage.

There was a knock at the door and Tempe called, "Come in."

"You called?" Sage asked before she saw Brook.

"Yes, I called," she responded dryly. By now most of Eli's clan knew the alphas had some telepathy but there was no reason to make a show of it. "We have a little issue. Brook is around three months pregnant. Since she is part shifter and doesn't shift she might be able to carry to term but I'm not sure. We either put her in a birthing bond or I call Lea to come check her out."

Tempe turned to Brook, "Lea is our sister and a healer. She has probably dealt with this type of pregnancy, but I haven't. There's a chance you can carry to term without a birthing bond, but it's a risk I don't want to take without verification."

"It has taken me over four hundred years to get pregnant. I want this child Tempest, whatever it takes," Brook said plainly. She looked at the alpha and said, "Can you give me details like Sage did with Delaney?"

"Yes."

She sat up a little straighter and said, "Please."

"You will have two shifter daughters. We will have to wait and see what talents they each have."

She smiled.

"Let me call Lea and see what she can tell me."

While Tempe talked to Lea, Sage told Brook about the birthing bond.

Tempe hung up the phone, "Lea's driving over. She will be here in a few hours. She does have experience with this type of pregnancy and you might be able to carry shifter offspring to term without a bond. She's coming to verify and if there is any doubt she will hold your birthing bond for the remainder of your pregnancy."

"I didn't mean to put anyone out," Brook said in a small voice.

Sage laughed, "The job of a female alpha is to hold birthing bonds. It's more important than anything else we do. Otherwise the next generation can't be born."

Brook grinned. "Can I tell Dwight?"

"Yes, and tell your father, sister and the rest of Eli's clan. Everyone will be happy for you. Sage, track down Dwight and send him up here."

Sage walked out, and Tempe turned to Brook. "Change of plans for tonight. I will never put a pregnant female near the fae. We will make do without a siren at the cave."

"No, you need me," Brook said.

"Perhaps I'll take Eli and leave you at the house but there is no way I will let a fae know about a pregnant woman. There are things about the fae you don't know. Trust me on this."

There was a knock on the door and Tempe called, "Come in."

Dwight stuck his head in and said, "Sage told me to come up here?" He looked nervous. It's not often a low-ranking member of a clan drops into the bedroom of a member of the clan cyngor.

Tempe smiled, "Brook has something to tell you. I'm going downstairs. Stay as long as you need."

She patted him on the shoulder as she walked out and shut the door.

Down in the kitchen Tempe said, "Eli, change of plans. Brook will stay and protect the house. If you wish you can come to the cave and be the cave siren or you can stay here and have two sirens on house patrol."

He looked over at his sister and raised an eyebrow.

She smiled, "Just go with it. I promise you will understand soon."

Eli turned to Delaney, "You okay with that?"

"Yes, honey. I trust my sister."

"Okay, I'm going to the cave."

*****

A few minutes before the agreed to time, the shifters arrived at the cave. Sage, once again in her guise as Shield Girl, held Star in a shield and veil.

At the appointed hour Lord Ellwood, flanked by Algar and Cayenne, entered the Seen.

"Fairly met, Lord Ellwood," Eli greeted him with something between a smile and a snarl.

"Eli, son of Rayna, fairly met."

"Father, allow me to present Star, daughter of Cloud of the Central Realm, and your granddaughter," Tempe said formally as Sage dropped her veil and her shield, revealing both of them.

Lord Ellwood stared at his daughter and not his granddaughter. It was the first time anyone had admitted Star was his granddaughter.

Tempest smiled.

Star walked up and said formally, "Grandfather, Mother told me you desired to meet me. Now that I am a member of the Smoky Mountain Clan I thought it might be a good idea. I have chosen to remain in the Seen and embrace my shifter self. I have joined Eli's clan and here I will stay. Once the Queen's decree is over I would like to visit the Farseen, but if it will cause problems I will not."

"Granddaughter, I am pleased to meet you. Which of my daughter's is your mother?" Ellwood ordered.

Star smiled, "She's here."

Ellwood looked at Tempe in shock. Ryan released his veil and revealed Temperance and Saffron.

Saffron asked, "Lord Ellwood, can you not tell by looking which of your daughters is Star's mother?"

Ellwood fumed.

Tempe forced the smile from her lips, "Father, do you want to argue parentage, or would you rather talk to your granddaughter?"

Ellwood suppressed his anger, which surprised everyone, and talked to Star about life in the Seen. Temperance, Saffron and Tempe had carefully prepped Star, and she did not mention Joey or any male except her cousin Ryan, uncle Eli, and mated members of the clan. She talked of taking Misty to a movie.

Ellwood surprised everyone with his knowledge of movies. Movies and books were things he traveled to the Seen for. He loved them and gave Star a list of movies he thought she should watch. Surprisingly enough, he watched a wide array of movies, and entertained everyone with his rendition of *Oh What A Beautiful Morning*, from the musical *Oklahoma*.

While they talked Tempe watched Algar. They had what Ryan later called a smile off. Temperance stood beside Tempe and tried to look calm. Saffron had Cayenne in her sights and Cayenne was coming off the worse for wear in that stare down. Cayenne had never been friendly with any of Ellwood's daughters, but Saffron was the one she hated for reasons Saffron knew well.

As their meeting drew to a close, Lord Ellwood asked, "Have you no desire to live in the Northern Realm Granddaughter? You would be treasured there."

120

Star looked him dead in the eyes and replied, "I am treasured here, Grandfather. For the time being I choose to stay here with my shifter family. Eli is a wonderful uncle and an excellent prif."

Lord Ellwood turned to his daughters, "What does the Central Realm think of this?"

Ryan dropped the veil around Cloud, who responded, "My daughter is happy here. I can visit whenever I wish. I am satisfied for the moment she is where she should be and where she wants to be."

Ellwood almost swore. Tempe kept her face neutral, time for the final surprise. She sent a small hand signal. Asilia walked out of the woods in her lioness form. She shifted and walked up to Ellwood. "Lord Ellwood, we've never met, but I remember Cada from the Northern Realm fondly. He made an interesting meal."

Algar looked at Asilia and his eyes got wide for a fraction of a second before he settled into his normal bored expression. It was the first time Tempe could remember the assassin giving anything away and if she hadn't been focused on him she would have missed it.

Ellwood snarled and turned on Tempe.

She laughed, "Father, please let Eli know when you next wish to visit your granddaughter. She has a full schedule but I'm sure a suitable time can be agreed upon."

Lord Ellwood glared at her, ignoring Temperance and Saffron and said, "Daughter, you have always been the most extraordinary of all of my children." Then he smiled and added, "I have never had a more worthy adversary in all my days."

"Thank you, Father," she inclined her head.

He opened a way and Algar and Cayenne walked through, before he left Lord Ellwood said, "Good hunting Lady Tempest." He walked through the way and closed it.

"Well, that went better than I hoped," Bryce said.

Saffron shook her head, "When Father left he issued a challenge to Tempest. He now considers the hunt to be in motion. Father isn't the forest lord of the Northern Realm for nothing." She looked around and said, "He isn't hunting for Star anymore. He plans to kill Tempest. He thinks that by killing her he will get Star and perhaps Sage and Ryan as well."

"You could have kept that to yourself sister," Tempe snarled.

"Tempest, you lose sight of the big picture where Lord Ellwood is concerned. The last time you played this game with Father, Val was the price. We've lost enough siblings. Take care." Saffron's even voice was more telling than if she had yelled. "If Lord Ellwood schedules another visit with Star I will be here, and Temperance will be with me.

Grandmother will see to that." With that Saffron opened a way and walked through it, followed by Temperance and Cloud.

The shifters all looked at Tempe. She sighed. "Better that Father focuses on me rather than Star, Sage, and Ryan. Surely you guys see that."

"I don't!" Ryan retorted.

"Then it's a good thing I outrank you," she replied calmly. "Ryan, we leave for the wastelands of the Northern Realm tomorrow." To everyone else she added, "We should return to Eli's house. I think we'll hear some happy news and that would be a welcome change."

She took off walking down the path to Eli's house with the shifters following behind. When they arrived at the house they found Delaney bouncing around the room. She didn't speak as plates were filled and everyone took their seats.

Eli slid into the seat next to his wife and asked, "Honey, why are you so happy?"

Dwight cleared his throat and said, "Lea, Tempe's sister, arrived while you guys were at the cave."

Brook came over and held Dwight's hand. He smiled and continued, "She confirmed Brook is pregnant and she can carry our children to term without a birthing bond. We're going to have two girls around the end of August." The room exploded into congratulations. Tempe leaned on the door and smiled as Eli congratulated his sister-in-law and clan member.

Bryce came over and raised an eyebrow. Tempe grabbed his hand and they snuck out the back door and went up to their room via the outside stairs to the deck.

As she closed the door he said, "So, you chose to make yourself a target?"

"Would you prefer I let Father make Star, Sage, or Ryan his target?" She chewed her lower lip. "It's the lesser of two evils."

Bryce pulled her into his arms and said, "Will we ever have a time when you don't make yourself a target?"

"It's what I do," she replied softly as she pulled him into her for a long slow kiss.

"No fair," Bryce replied huskily. "You're distracting me." But instead of pulling back he maneuvered her to the bed.

Chapter 15

Tuesday dawned, and the strike force prepared for the wastelands. Research indicated if the Shadowed had a camp in the Farseen it was either in the Northern or Western Realm. Based on the actions of the goblin a few months ago, Tempe was betting on a camp in the north.

Lea had agreed to stay with Sage, Star, and the two pregnant sisters until Ryan and Tempe returned.

Ryan, Raven, Tempe, Murdoch and Siri met at the cave. Tempe opened a way to the mountains on the northern side of the Northern Realm Mountains. They walked through, and Tempe asked, "Does everyone remember what I said about the wastelands?"

"Yes, you've been drilling it into our heads for days," Ryan replied in disgust.

"The wastelands will kill you quicker, and more painfully, than a realm lord," Saffron said as she released her veil.

Tempe looked over in surprise.

Saffron smiled, "Sis, you'll need help on this one. I want the Shadowed out of the Farseen so I'm here. Deal with it."

Tempe smiled and mentally upped the odds of a successful mission.

"Let's go folks." Ryan and Raven shifted to their dragons. Murdoch on Raven's back and Siri with Ryan flew into the air. Saffron smiled and flew without shifting, which was so cool. Tempe shifted to her falcon and followed Saffron. Ryan veiled the dragons and Saffron pulled Tempe into her veil.

Tempe lowered her mental blocks and pushed a question at her sister, *why are you showing us your veil?*

Saffron laughed and replied, *Ryan read my powers the other day, so you already know.* They both enjoyed a mental laugh as sisters.

Thinking about it, Tempest decided it was the first real laugh they had ever shared as adults.

The veil was great for preventing fae, shifters, wizards, and the like from seeing the strike force, but the wastelands were home to a few creatures that see through veils with no problem. Tempe threw fire at a flock of harpies, winged beautiful female-looking creatures with sharp talons, and the harpies went in search of easier prey to torture or punish, depending on your point of view.

Siri tapped Ryan's dragon neck each time he veered toward the harpies. Even with her corrective actions, Ryan continued to stare after the harpies. Harpies entrap men with their beautiful faces and sensuous bodies. Once trapped the men see the other side of the harpy, the one with talons and sharp teeth.

They had covered almost all of the Northern Realm wastelands and Tempe was beginning to think this would be a bust. They flew around a solitary tree house, giving the home and its owner a wide berth, past a forest, and topped a hill where they found a makeshift facility. From a distance it would not be visible. Up close it's harder to hide something that large even with magic. Murdoch verified it was a Shadowed facility by the type of magic surrounding it. Using a device created by the shifter tech team, Siri found five half-breeds – a.k.a. prisoners – clustered together.

The ground, twenty feet in any direction, was covered with assassin vine. Assassin vine entangles its prey when they wander too close to the plant and the vine automatically reacts to constrict around the ensnared creature. The vine's thorns cut prey while the vine constricts its victim to death and tosses the remains near the root structure for nourishment. Assassin vine needs meat, bone, and blood to survive.

Saffron, with her well-known affinity for plants, flew ahead and cast a spell that caused the assassin vine to backtrack away from her. Tempest flew in next and landed within the safety of the spelled area. Ryan continued to veil dragon Raven and rider Murdoch as they descended toward the now open ground. Raven shifted once Murdoch jumped off of her back.

Once they landed Ryan and Siri, still veiled, took to the skies. They didn't like it but they were back up for this run.

Saffron walked them in her veil to the wall closest to the prisoners continuing to spell the vine out of the way. Murdoch focused a spell on the wall. As soon as he flung open his hands there was an opening. No noise was made when he created the opening. He didn't blow a hole in the wall, he just created a hole. A door-sized section of the wall was just gone.

Wizards were amazing, Tempe marveled. What she could do with brute force and raw power, leaving a mess like a bull in a china shop, they did with finesse and intelligence.

Inside, two adult males stood ready to fight. Behind them three children huddled close together. No one spoke for a second while the men checked out the new arrivals. Finally, one of the men asked, "Murdoch, is that you?"

"Elijah? You show up in the oddest places."

The corners of Elijah's mouth curved into a smile. "It's okay kids. We're being rescued."

Murdoch created a wagon out of wind, much along the lines of the wind chariot Tamra had created, but his could hold a lot more. Test subjects loaded into the wagon, Raven shifted to her dragon while Murdoch attached the wind wagon to her sling. Murdoch jumped on her back and they flew with Tempe and Saffron following.

While the others attended to the prisoners, Ryan and Siri planted detonation devices around the outside of the facility. They flew away from the building as Ryan extended his veil around the others. Once they hit the necessary distance, Siri blew the charges.

Finally, they dealt a blow to the Shadowed without injuries to their side.

*****

The five prisoners were half-breeds and newly acquired. They took the two adults to Half Acre. Gabriel and Elijah were both witch and shifter hybrids and they had been together for almost thirty years and were only captured by the Shadowed three months ago. It didn't appear it would take them long to recover and return to their home in Arizona, where they lived outside of a clan or coven. The duo was reported missing in the human world, but not within the preternatural community.

The seven-year-old French triplets had only been with the Shadowed for a little over a month, their family didn't take long to track. Their entire family, wizards and shifters, were together for the triplets' seventh birthday on the seventh of June. The house and grounds were burned down, along with over fifty members of their family. The responders thought the kids were killed with the rest of the family. They had one cousin left alive, a twenty-four-year-old shifter, Jeannette Moreau, currently studying veterinary sciences at the nearby University of Tennessee, getting ready to start her last year of her doctorate.

They spoke English well, but Star, Naomi, Adam and Tempe were fluent in French while Tracy, Liz and Bryce dusted off their high school French. Star, with the fae ability to learn languages, picked it up in a couple of days.

Jeannette made the one-hour drive immediately. She sat in the car for a couple of seconds and just watched the triplets. She had family. After burying her entire family and trying to move on with her life, she had family. She wiped her tears and stepped out of the car.

Chanel looked over and squealed. Chanel and Janel jumped into Jeannette's arms throwing her off balance, knocking all three to the ground in a heap. Darnel added himself to the pile as hugs and kisses were exchanged.

"You won't leave us, right?" Janel whispered.

Jeannette's heart healed a little at that moment. All the pain from burying her family ebbed. She hugged her young cousins tightly, "I won't leave."

After the initial reunion, the triplets went back to playing. The kids ran back and forth, mostly checking on Jeannette.

After a few minutes of watching the kids Jeannette asked, "What do I do? There are only six clan members left counting the four of us. The other two members of our clan are single men. If I drop out of school how will I support us? I'm not even sure I should try to parent them."

"Let us help," Tempe said simply.

Naomi smiled and said, "You need to finish school, so you can support them. We're close enough you can visit easily."

Jeannette chewed her bottom lip, and everyone smiled, except Tempe. Jeannette looked confused and Tempe said, "Ignore them. I've been trying to stop chewing on my bottom lip for centuries."

"Oh," she said in a small voice. "I've only been trying to break the habit for three years."

"Maybe you'll have better luck."

Eli sipped his tea and offered, "My clan is happy to help. The triplets could live here, I've got the room, and you could visit as much as your school schedule allows. Are you going to school right now or are you working this summer?"

"I was working at a vet clinic near the university. I told them about my cousins and I gave my notice. There's no way I can work and go to school now." She shrugged her shoulders. "I was working for the experience. I don't need the income. I think I can budget the insurance money to get through school without working, but I need help with a budget. I have no clue what they will need. Until the accident my mom and dad managed most of the money and gave me a monthly budget so all I worried about was my monthly costs."

She felt overwhelmed. "I was devastated when the fire happened. I went home and sold everything, planning to never go back. Do you think I should go back now, for them?"

Tempe placed a gentle hand on Jeanette's shoulder. "That's something you'll need to decide, but you don't have to decide right this minute. If I may recommend, finish school, get your degree, and then decide. Here, the triplets can go to school with the Taylor triplets. They would have a clan with them and wizards nearby. They can get any wizard training they might need at their current age." Tempe took a deep breath, "You should know that with me around, there's a lot more interaction with the fae than you're probably accustomed to. I don't want you to think we're keeping anything back."

"Since, as far as I know, I've never met a fae you would almost have to have more interaction with them than I'm accustomed to." She grinned, and the grin almost relaxed her face. She turned serious again, looked at Eli and commented, "I did talk to both of the men from our clan and they said I should trust you. They both think highly of you."

Eli looked surprised but pleased, "Why don't you stay here for a while? School won't start up until the end of August so that would give you a solid month to see if the triplets would be happy staying here for a while."

"That would be nice if you have the room."

Liz laughed, "Oh honey, I'm sure Eli can find an empty room in his house for you."

Delaney, Liz, and Tempe took Jeannette to the house for a tour.

"Jeannette, where are you going?" Darnel ran toward her and grabbed on. The girls were right behind him.

"Don't worry Dar," she replied using the nickname only she ever used. "I'm just going to see the room I'll be staying in."

"Then we'll go with you." Darnel sounded much older than his six years.

"You may come if you wish, but truly I am just going to see how Eli's house is set up." She smiled.

Darnel looked at Tempest, the powerful shifter that had always been honest with him.

She inclined her head but didn't speak.

The decision was truly his. He grinned, feeling important, as he realized the adults were waiting for him to decide. "Okay, we'll finish our game of tag."

He ran back to the others. Janel and Chanel followed him.

As the adults continued walking Tempe asked, "How come they speak English so well?"

Jeannette smiled, "My mother. She was from the states and she made sure all of the kids in the clan spoke English. She thought everyone should speak at least two languages."

They walked into the kitchen where Ryan and Blake were making sandwiches. When they walked in Blake almost dropped his sandwich. "Jeannette? So, you're the cousin."

"Guilty."

Blake looked over at Tempe and said, "We ran with Jeannette and some of the older shifters on campus a couple of times."

They continued walking, Blake's eyes following Jeannette. Tempe smiled to herself, suspecting Blake had a little crush on Jeannette. And man, if those two got together they would make beautiful babies.

They showed her the Birch Suite on the second floor and Jeannette said, "It's wonderful but you don't have to give me a room with its own private bath."

Liz hooted, "Honey, all the bedrooms in this house have their own bath. Eli's good to his guests."

"Nice." She smiled as she looked around the well-appointed room.

On the way back down the hallway they showed her the Aspen Suite, right next to her room, where the triplets were currently staying. A set of bunk beds had been added so the triplets could stay together while they adjusted. Then she saw the girls' suite and the boys' suite where everyone expected the triplets' would stay after all the college kids went back to school in the fall. When they went back downstairs, Blake offered to show her the first floor and the grounds.

Dinner was simple, salad from the garden and pasta for a crowd. The triplets fought over who got to sit by Jeannette, but it was a happy, joking fight. After dinner the kids showed off their video skills to their cousin.

As Jeannette walked the kids up to bed Chanel asked, "So it's just us now?"

"Yes," Jeannette said softly.

"Will we ever have to go back to that scary place?" Darnel asked.

"No, Tempest took care of it. No one will ever go there again," she said firmly.

"Good." Janel added. "It wasn't a nice place." She stopped on the stairs and asked, "What about Elijah and Gabriel? They were nice, and they tried to keep the bad people away."

Jeannette smiled, "They're safe too. Maybe we can visit with them before they leave."

128

Tempe heard the conversation and made a note to have Gabriel and Elijah come over to visit before they left.

Chapter 16

The July full moon was on Friday. Since it was the night before Sam and Tracy's wedding it was an all out party.

Naomi and Wayne, the human members of the clan, were on babysitting duty along with pregnant Delaney and birthing bond partner, Sage. Star decided to do a quick shift for an hour and then help with the kids. Jeannette, Ryan and Joey joined Star in her quick run. Ryan took his Great Pyrenees form and it turned out Jeannette also took the form of a Great Pyrenees. The triplets found that amusing. They sat in the sunroom waiting for Jeannette to return.

Once Jeannette, Star and Joey returned to the house, Ryan, Raven, and Tempe split up and patrolled. No reason to get lax now. All in all, it was a quiet run. Sam and Tracy ran with both of their parents. Tempe couldn't stop smiling at how Martha handled Rayna. Like Naomi said, Martha was a force of nature.

In addition to Raven, sisters Lark and Wren showed up from the alpha clan. Phoenix arrived from New York and that put all of Wes and Rayna's children – Sam's full brothers and sisters – together in one location. They partied. Bryce and Tempe sat out on the deck after their run. It was pushing two in the morning and the pre-wedding party was still in full swing.

"That's nice to see," Tempe said.

"Yes, it is." Bryce stretched his legs across the deck, resting them on the railing. "What time do you have to get up to help with the wedding day stuff?"

"I'm strictly support. I'm on standby if needed but I don't have any assigned tasks."

"So, we could have a little play time ourselves?" Bryce asked.

Tempe didn't answer, she just pulled his body into hers and they kissed. That was probably all the answer he needed.

*****

Regardless of what she told Bryce, Tempe rose early on Saturday and went downstairs to see if she could help. Last minute stuff always came up on the wedding day. She started off making a big plate of breakfast sandwiches for anyone who stopped by. She wrapped them, so the sandwiches could be nuked as needed.

She finished up just as Naomi opened the door and held it open as Nash and Shan carried in the cake. It was a beautiful three-tier cake with icing flowers streaming down the side like a waterfall. The wedding topper was an eagle, Sam's animal, and a golden retriever, Tracy's animal.

"Nash, the cake looks amazing. Where did you find the topper?" Tempe asked.

He smiled, "Shan carved and painted it."

"It's amazing. The retriever even has Tracy's markings. Excellent."

Cinnamon walked in with a box and said, "It is, isn't it? They both out did themselves."

Martha walked in a short time later, saw the cake and stopped dead. After a couple of seconds, she whispered, "I can't believe I almost prevented you from making that cake. Nash, you need to open a bakery."

"That's the plan," he said with a shy smile.

"Well, when you do, let me know. I have contacts in the wedding world and a few tips for running a business." Martha patted him on the shoulder as she went by.

The rest of the morning was spent with delivery trucks pulling in and out of the driveway. When the big moment finally arrived, the bride was beautiful, the groom was handsome, and the entire day went off without a hitch.

*****

Sunday morning, in the aftermath of the wedding, Bryce volunteered to drive Martha and Jerry to the airport for their early flight. Tempe once again prepped breakfast.

"Morning dear," Rayna said as she poured herself a cup of tea. "Did Martha and Jerry get off alright?"

"You know they did. You waited to come downstairs until she left. Martha's something, isn't she?"

"She wore me out. It was easier to let her have her way than to argue with her." Rayna kept a straight face, but her eyes were smiling.

It wasn't often a shifter spoke up around Rayna and even more rare one gave her a task list. Rayna had stuffed her dominance down deep and let the mother-of-the-bride order everyone around. As the sovereign did so did the rest of the alphas. For a couple of days, a wedding planner, mid-ranked shifter in an average clan, ordered every alpha at Eli's around.

Wesley walked in and Tempe placed a plate of Eggs Benedict in front of him. He smiled, "Tempest, this is why you are my favorite stepdaughter."

Sage walked in and feigned hurt, "Nice, Dad. You like Tempe better than your own flesh and blood."

Wesley gave Sage a look of mock horror, "My child. I specifically called Tempest my favorite stepdaughter. I could never choose between my own daughters."

Sage kissed him on the check, "Then all is forgiven Daddy, especially since I see Tempe made you Eggs Benedict. No one could blame you for your declaration with your favorite breakfast in front of you."

Raven, Wren and Lark walked in and Raven groused in a good-natured way, "Tempe's making us look bad again, isn't she?"

"Yep," Sage replied as she bit into her own plate of Eggs Benedict.

"You know guys, I could let the rest of you make your own breakfast," Tempe threatened.

"No, ignore my young and foolish sisters." Phoenix kissed his eldest sister on the cheek and grabbed a plate, organizing his own Eggs Benedict. "Your breakfast makes getting out of bed worth the effort."

Phoenix, the only non-alpha born to Rayna, and Tempest, the most powerful of Rayna's offspring, didn't get along most of the time, probably because Phoenix had to obey orders from no one, even though he was ranked last in his clan. He was completely outside clan rank structure. He also had no powers other than the ability to fade to shadow. He had always been the weak link in his powerful alpha family and Tempest was a shining example of everything he would never be. He didn't hate Tempest but it's hard to look at the person who had everything you wanted and not feel jealous. He had made a vow to himself to try to get along with everyone, even Tempest, for Sam's wedding. As an added benefit, he realized his compliance shocked Tempest more than if he caused a scene. It amused him.

Landon walked in behind Phoenix and she handed him a plate as well.

"You cook?" Landon asked in surprise.

"Landon, my ignorant friend," Phoenix said between bites as he waved his fork in the air, "Tempest studied cooking in one of her bids for education. She is the best cook of all my sisters."

A flood of napkins assailed him.

"Eggs Benedict," Ryan said in appreciation as he, Blake, Kaleb and Joey entered the room.

"Okay, if I'm going to keep making them we need an assembly line."

The boys lined up and, after some instructions, cooked and served Eggs Benedict for everyone in the house who had not eaten. Star, Catlin and Jeannette were suitably impressed with the boys.

The triplets were the only naysayers. They wanted pancakes, which Ryan whipped up and served with a flourish, despite Jeannette's protest that she could and should fix the pancakes.

After breakfast and goodbyes, all of Rayna and Wesley's children, except for Sage, headed for the airport. As she watched them leave Star commented, "You certainly have a large happy family."

"Large, yes, happy, not always," Sage replied. "This was a wonderful visit."

"Being away from all the other alphas probably helped," Tempe offered.

"Not to mention the fun of watching Martha with Rayna," Sage smirked.

"That too," she agreed.

*****

Bryce was on the hook to head over to the Harmony bar for the evening and Tempe invited Jeannette to go with them.

"Thanks, but I should stay here with the kids."

"Jeannette, you haven't left their side since you arrived. It's been five days. We'll only be gone a couple of hours," Tempe reasoned. "They need to know you can leave and will return."

"There shouldn't be a problem, but I'll be here and can sing if they get upset," Star offered.

"You'll only be ten minutes away," Sage added.

Jeannette walked into the game room where the kids were watching a movie and asked, "Would you guys mind if I went out for a couple of hours?"

Star walked in behind her and added, "I can tell you more about living in the Farseen."

"Stories about dragons?" Darnel asked.

Ryan looked up from the book he was reading, "You like dragons?"

"Yes, but I've never seen one," Darnel said wishfully.

"Then I think Star should tell you everything she knows about dragons." Ryan smiled and returned to his book.

"You won't be gone long, right?" Chanel asked.

"No, I'm just stepping out with Tempe and Bryce. I'll be back to tuck you in."

"Sounds okay," Darnel said.

As they left Tempe called over her shoulder, "Ryan, don't scare anyone."

He grinned his best good old boy grin.

Tempe expected Harmony to be fairly quiet on a Sunday evening. It wasn't packed but it was pretty full. Adam sat at the bar talking to Adelia. He was at the bar most every night now. They walked over and Adam introduced Jeannette to Adelia.

"You're the girl who just found her young cousins. Are they well?" Adelia said.

Jeannette smiled, "Much better than I could have hoped. Eli's clan has been wonderful."

"Jeannette, my pet, what brings you to this neck of the woods?"

Jeannette scowled, then planted a smile on her face and turned to face the newcomer, "Hello Matt. Do you live around here?"

"Not yet, but I hope to." Matt walked over, encroaching heavily into her personal space.

Bryce intervened, placed his body between them, stuck out his hand and said, "Hello, I'm Bryce. How do you know Jeannette?"

Matt gave Bryce a startled look as he craned his neck to look up at a tall Native American with blue eyes. "Vet school. I graduated last spring."

"Congratulations. Where are you working?" Adam gently pulled Jeannette into the seat beside him while Bryce sat on her other side.

Amused by the macho display, Tempe leaned on the bar next to Bryce and simply watched.

"Still looking, I have an interview tomorrow with Dr. Cruz in town," Matt responded bravely. Neither Adam nor Bryce gave the appearance of being interested in Matt, their questions notwithstanding.

Tempe smothered a smile and offered, "Good luck in your interview."

He walked off in something of a daze.

"Thank you," Jeannette whispered. "He's a leach and he hit on every single female in our department. He knows his stuff and he'll be a great vet, but he has roaming hands." The last sentence she said to Tempe.

Adelia laughed, "He's already hit on any female in this room that doesn't have a man by her side, even staff. Tempest, if you were to toss him out every woman in the place would buy you a drink tonight."

"I'll leave it to the men folk." She grinned, "How about a glass of wine?"

Matt of the roaming hands left a few minutes later and Adam joined them in a game of pool, women against the men. Jeannette was a good pool player and she and Tempe slaughtered the guys, which gave the bar a good laugh.

Jeannette, Bryce and Tempe left when Adam returned to the bar to talk to Adelia.

*****

When they walked up to the sunroom door, the triplets ran out to Jeannette, surprising her. "Did you miss me that much?"

"What?" Darnel asked pulling on her arm. "No, you gotta see what Ryan can do."

Ryan, Sage, and Star had followed the triplets out. Tempe raised an eyebrow.

Ryan blushed, "It was good to see them laugh."

"Okay, show off for Jeannette."

The triplets were holding Jeannette and saying, "watch this" and "wait till you see" and even "we got a ride".

Ryan shifted into his dark blue dragon and flew a low sweep around the yard. Jeannette laughed, "Well, that's a treat, isn't it?"

Ryan shifted back and they all walked into the house.

Jeannette went to tuck the kids into bed and Bryce and Tempe went to their room and sat working at their desks. When there was a knock on the deck door, Bryce opened it to find an unhappy visitor.

"How much longer do I have to keep this up? I'm tired of feeding information to Adelia. I'm tired of acting like I like her. And mostly I miss Brandi." Adam plopped down into Bryce's desk chair. He stretched his neck and admitted, "I'm not cut out for this stuff. I'm not a spy."

"Adam, I know it's hard but the Shadowed have made a couple of moves based on the information you're feeding her. It's working. And believe me this type of maneuver never moves fast enough." Tempe chewed her bottom lip and asked, "How's Brandi?"

He looked over at Tempe in disgust and ran a hand through his hair. "How would I know? She sneaks over once a week if that. Mostly she's hiding and making sure she's seen elsewhere. I want her back full time and I don't want to pretend to the clan we're no longer a couple. I've always been a one-woman guy. I don't play the field. Some guys might find this fun, but I don't. I've told more lies in the past couple of weeks than I've told in my entire life."

Tempe would have spoken, but Bryce cut his eyes to the door. She patted Adam on the shoulder and left them alone.

Tempe went downstairs and fixed herself a cup of tea.

Jeannette walked in and said, "Thanks. It was nice to get out even if Matt was there. I guess if he gets the job I'll deal with him."

Tempe smiled, "Well, Dr. Cruz is Wayne, Teresa's husband. Somehow I think Bryce or Adam will warn Wayne about Matt with the roaming hands."

She blushed, "I don't want to cause a problem for him. Just because I don't like him doesn't mean he's a bad vet. He is good at vet stuff."

"Well, that's for Wayne to decide, but a small town practice doesn't need a vet who makes a percentage of his clients uncomfortable."

"It was nice of Bryce and Adam to shield me. My dad would have been pleased," she smiled. "You guys have been great. Are you sure having the triplets stay here won't be a problem? Delaney and Brook are both going to have kids. This place is going to fill up fast."

"It's a big house and what kind of clan would we be if we didn't help?" Delaney sat down at the kitchen bar and groaned, "The kids are kicking. Eli thinks it's wonderful when they kick, but he doesn't feel the kidney shots."

"This, too, shall pass." Tempe patted Delaney on the shoulder and turned to Jeannette, "The triplets will have a good support system here, both wizard and shifter. We're the closest clan to your university. It's a good fit."

"I guess but I feel like I'm taking advantage of you. Eli won't let me pay him for their room and board. I've tried to insist, and he ignores me. You know, your brother is a bit dictatorial sometimes." Jeannette added softly, "In fact, your entire family is good at ordering everyone. I just feel like I should be doing more to help out."

"Get your degree. That will be the most help." Tempe walked out of the room with her cell phone blaring Fleetwood Mac's *You Make Loving Fun*. She took the stairs two at a time and walked into the bedroom. Adam was gone.

"Is he feeling better?"

"He won't feel better until he's done playing spy or dup or whatever, and he has Brandi back." Bryce pulled her into his arms.

"Well, I think it's almost time to spring the trap anyway," she said.

"Adam will thank you for that."

She smiled sadly, "But I don't think you will. You sure about this?"

"It is the best way to find their hideout." He grinned and said, "Ha, I just used hideout in a serious sentence."

136

Tempe smirked, "Would you prefer lair, den, or perhaps stronghold?"

"No, I like saying hideout." His grin covered his entire face.

*****

Over the next few days, the task force, including Saffron, checked out the wastelands in the remaining four realms. No additional Shadowed facilities were found but the task force got an intense education in some of the less cuddly fae. Since they were searching the wastelands only, they didn't need realm permission, as all wastelands were enter-at-your-own-risk sectors.

In the Western Realm they hiked through a forest where it was rumored there might be a facility near the same mountains where Raven and Tempe met Crystal. On foot, they outran hellhounds – which are close in size to a werewolf, but they work as a pack. The hellhounds shot fire from their mouths. They don't breathe a steady stream like dragons, they shoot fire in short bursts, like a gun. Ryan used water to circle the pack until they could get away.

Once clear of the hellhounds they continued the trek and walked into a family of gorkongs – ten-foot tall gorilla like creatures with pale blue-gray coloring. They were so focused on the task of finding a lair they didn't pay attention and walked into the family group, right between a mother and her child. Ryan set a shield as Tempe teleported to the child and teleported with the child to the other side of his family. She set him down, shifted to her falcon and flew up out of reach.

The entire pack continued to beat on the shield until the mother heard her child crying behind her and not inside the shield. She ran to her son and held him. The dominant male looked at the child, looked at the team in the shield and then looked up at Tempe in falcon form. He grunted and walked away with the pack following. They were much more careful about their surroundings after that, but they didn't find a facility.

The Central Realm introduced the team to a herd of doppelgangers, mist like creatures in their true form, they pull a form from the mind of their prey and duplicate it. It could be a person or creature. If they take the form of a person, their speech reflects the memories of the person they take the recollections from. If multiple people invoke the same form each individual doppelganger can only use the memories of one person.

Unfortunately, fully half of the herd took the form of Lord Ellwood, so Tempe was fighting off her personal nightmare. Apparently, it was Saffron's nightmare too since half of the Ellwoods attacked her. If the multiples of Ellwood hadn't been so scary, Tempe would have laughed at a six-feet, six-inch-tall Murdoch cowering before multiple copies of a five-foot nothing female who must have been the wizard he apprenticed under. Ryan fought off faceless fae warriors while Raven fought a slew of plain looking women.

Everyone has demons of their own, weird though they might be.

They survived an encounter with a family of white dragons in the mountains of the Eastern Realm. White dragons freeze prey with fog, wind or ice. Saffron and Tempe poured fire at the mother dragon until she gave up and took her kids in search of easier prey.

In the Southern Realm they met a blue dragon. She created an illusionary terrain that almost trapped the task force in its lair. But it was the dragon's ability to mimic sounds and speech that caught Ryan's attention.

The dragon encounters had the most interesting result for the task force. Once Ryan and Raven realized different dragons had different abilities they started researching their dragon forms to check for new abilities. Since shifters get the abilities of the creatures whose form they take, they found a couple of new talents.

It got Tempe thinking about dragons, too. Sage and Tempe started doing a little research of their own.

After they searched each wasteland, Tempe met up with Bryce at Harmony. This time she found Bryce and Adam playing pool so she sat at the bar talking to Adelia.

When the guys finished their game and sat down at the bar Tempe leaned toward Bryce, "Could you take a few days off? I'm going to meet up with Siri in Scotland. We could work a mini vacation into the business trip."

Adelia gushed, "That sounds wonderful… and romantic."

Adam grinned, "A vacation in Scotland. How could you possibly say no to that?"

Bryce smiled, "I don't think I can."

Chapter 17

Bryce and Tempe landed in Glasgow. Tempe's daughter Kacy and her husband Gabriel met them at the airport. Kacy stood by the gate, waiting as they exited customs. Tempe dropped her carryon bag. Kacy was pregnant! Bryce picked up Tempe's bag as Tempe continued to look at her daughter.

"How?" she finally asked.

"Really Tempest, you want to know how I got pregnant," Kacy grinned. "To be honest, I didn't realize I was pregnant until after your quick visit in February. I'm due any day now."

"But..." Tempe paused, and then her voice got louder, "How could you drive down here? You should be home resting. And who has your birthing bond?"

Charity, one of Tempe's younger sisters, barely 260 years old, rounded the corner. Char and Kacy were close to the same age and grew up more like sisters than aunt and niece. Tempe turned on her, "Char, I seem to be missing some reports from you. I thought it was because you weren't on assignment." She tapped her foot.

Char looked at Bryce for help. He laughed, put his arm around Tempe and ushered her to the exit.

She allowed herself to be herded away since she noticed they were drawing a lot of unwanted attention. Gabriel, Kacy's husband, pulled the van up and everyone hopped in, except for Kacy who Char carefully assisted into a nice plush captain's chair.

Once they were underway, Bryce spoke before Tempe. "Kacy, you shocked your mother. Now I think you should apologize."

She grinned but her eyes looked worried. "Tempest, we didn't do it to upset you. The only way I could get you here for the birth was for Siri to call and ask you to come for work. I knew you would come for a problem. It was useful that she did need you right now."

Tempe stared out the window. Since Siri only called because they were setting a trap for the Shadowed, Kacy's statement didn't help her mood. She turned from the window and asked, "You didn't think I would fly in for the birth but I would for trouble?"

"Well, that's always been the way with you. Alpha business comes first," Kacy whispered.

Tempe stared out the window for a few more seconds. "I'm afraid you're right about my track record. Recent events have caused me to rethink some of my past choices." She smiled sadly and asked, "Are you sharing details, or do I have to wait for the birth?"

Kacy grinned, "Two girls, one boy, all shifters."

"That's wonderful," Tempe replied, meaning it.

*****

Devlin, like most prifs, had a rambling house set up to support various clan members for periods of time. The original part of the house was built by his father, Tempe's husband, just before the triplets were born. Kacy and Gabriel were already staying in the largest room since they would need three bassinets. Char was in the small room next to them. Devlin walked Tempe and Bryce down the hall to the guest room as far away from the hub of the house as possible.

They only brought carryon bags, so the unpacking didn't take much time at all. Tempe hung up an outfit and asked, "Does everyone else already know?"

Bryce managed to keep a straight face, "Well, Ryan read the reports. They forgot to remove him from the distro. Sage knows because he knows. The rest of your sisters know, and I was told."

"Am I unapproachable? Did my daughter honestly think she had to trick me to get me here?" Tempe asked softly as she sat on the edge of the bed.

"You always put everyone else before you, and frequently you put everyone else before your family." Bryce kissed her. "And you always tried to protect everyone from association with you. I think it backfired on you this time."

"Well, I guess I won't improve things by feeling sorry for myself." Tempe stood up and pulled Bryce up as well. "Let's go see the kids."

They walked into the family room as Kevin, Kacy and Gabriel's first born, came into the house. Tempe finally got to introduce someone to Bryce.

Siri walked in with two pints. When Tempe raised an eyebrow, Siri's face broke into a wide grin. "I told them it would be better if I told you about Kacy. Your kids are stubborn. Can't imagine where they get it."

"Is one of those pints for me or are you a two-fisted drinker now?" Tempe asked.

Siri held one out to Tempe and gave the other to Bryce.

Before they finished the pints, Kacy looked over at Char, who nodded.

Tempe took another sip and asked, "How far apart?"

"How did you know?" Char looked over at her eldest sister.

"Gee, Char, I've had kids and I've held birthing bonds. Plus, that drive to the airport and back was not good for her."

"True. They're about nine minutes apart." Char pulled out her cell and made a call.

Less than fifteen minutes later Linsey, Devlin's clan doctor, arrived. In the wee small hours of Wednesday morning, under a full moon, Kacy delivered Ashley, Bailey and Riley in short order with a doctor and two alphas standing by to help.

Tempe got to hold each of her new grandchildren.

Gabriel was in full proud papa mode, thrilled that Bailey and Riley had red hair like him.

*****

"Good morning Tempest. Did you get any sleep last night?" Kevin asked as he walked into the kitchen.

"Yes, but I wanted to get a jump on some work for Rayna before everyone else got up." She closed her laptop. "What do you have there?"

"I thought everyone might like some breakfast scones." Kevin went about the important business of making tea and coffee.

"Who in this house drinks coffee?" she asked surprised.

Devlin walked in. "Mom, the only way Bryce would keep the secret was if we promised to have good coffee for him to drink while he was here."

"That's the one flaw with Bryce. He wouldn't know good tea if it hit him over the head." Tempe shook her head.

"My love, I will drink cold sweet iced tea with lunch and dinner and even hot tea upon occasion. But for breakfast I must have coffee." He kissed Tempe on the forehead and went to get a cup of coffee. He took one sip and looked at Kevin, "You drink coffee."

"Me? No," Kevin objected with a smile.

"Yes, you do. No one can make coffee this good unless they drink it." Bryce smiled and looked at Tempe, "You have a grandson who drinks coffee. Ha!"

"So, your job while we visit is to keep Bryce in good coffee?" she laughed.

"Yes," Kevin replied, blushing.

The triplets woke up and let everyone know they needed to be fed, changed, or admired. Tempe patted Kevin on the back and headed off to help Kacy.

*****

Tempe received an urgent text later in the afternoon. Someone sent an anonymous note to the alpha mailbox. A small Shadowed nest was located close by and she was to check it out.

Kacy looked up from changing a diaper. "Mom, it's what you do. You were here for the important part. Once you and Siri take care of whatever you'll be back."

"I don't like the timing," Tempe commented to Siri as they walked out the door, only to find their way blocked by Bryce, wearing his spelled clothes, and Devlin.

"Seriously, you think you can prevent us from going on a mission for the high wizard and the shifter sovereign?" Tempe asked, making use of titles instead of names.

"No, but you need backup." Devlin said just as evenly.

"With a nest close by you need to protect your clan. We know the Shadowed have taken newborns in the past and killed their families to do it," Tempe growled.

"We're in agreement. Tristin, Finley and Michael will go with you, Siri and Bryce," Devlin replied.

Tempe frowned at her son, took a deep breath, and asked, "How are your wizard lessons going?"

He pulled out a rune weapon and demolished an old shack he was planning to take down anyway.

Tempe smiled and said, "Tristin, Finley, and Michael have three minutes to get here."

"We're here, Tempest." Tristin was the oldest member of Devlin's clan and the snowy owl who found Siri and Tempe when a vampire held them captive a while back.

"I'll drive." Siri made a move to take the keys from Devlin.

Devlin's entire clan yelled "No!"

"Lass, you still don't drive on the correct side of the road," Devlin said as he kissed her on the forehead. "Be careful." He tossed the keys to Finley.

As they left they passed most of Devlin's clan on the road driving in to protect the children.

They drove into the Grampian Mountains and followed the directions Tempe received. The nest was in an old abandoned residence. They worked out the plan on the way up so when Finley pulled the car over about two kilometers from the building, everyone had their marching orders.

Finley and Michael shifted to their wolf forms. Tempe shifted to her falcon and flew over to do recon. It should have worked. Falcons are darn near everywhere and most people can't tell one falcon from another.

A shot rang out and she fell out of the sky. Someone shot her, or rather winged her. She gritted her teeth and landed before shifting. The wound was in the fleshy part of her upper arm. The bullet had gone clean through. Painful but not deadly, she cursed under her breath as she ripped the bottom of her t-shirt and wrapped it around the wound. She had not set her shield because a shifter in the infected group might have had the ability to see a shield and known the falcon was magical.

Now she set her shield, which was lucky. Someone, with serious juice, threw a spell at her. She sent a mind-to-mind warning to Bryce.

Tempe focused her rune weapon and threw fire at the wizard who turned it toward the two wolves that burst out of the bushes. Since the wizard now had the fire, Tempe pulled water to shield the wolves.

The wizard screamed.

"What's your name?" Tempe asked conversationally as her water kept the fire at bay.

"I am death to those who challenge the new order," the wizard retorted.

"Hello, death," Tempe replied, her gaze taking in the five-and-a-half-foot tall wizard. "I thought you'd be taller."

Tempe threw a spell and the wizard absorbed it. Tempe snarled. So few wizards working alone had the ability to simply absorb her spells, she hadn't expected it.

"Go check on the vampires." When the wolves disappeared back into the bushes, Tempe turned her full attention on the wizard. After a few minutes of exchanging spells, Tempe realized it was a set up. She reached out with her mind and couldn't hear any of her team, except for Tristin and he was injured. Her rage exploded.

The wizard cringed as she looked into the shifter's solid black eyes, as Tempe drew all the power she could.

"If you throw that spell your friends will die," Radek said calmly as he appeared. He was holding Siri. Yula, another known Shadowed wizard, had Bryce in a bubble floating in front of her.

Radek looked at the wizard Tempest had been fighting and said, "Aster, we have what we came for. We leave now." He smiled at Tempest.

Tempest smiled back grimly, manipulated the vines growing on the hill behind Radek to pull Siri out of his arms, and unleashed her spell.

He and Aster fell as the fire she threw circled them. They were on fire when they teleported.

Yula had already disappeared with Bryce.

Tempe snarled. She realized even though everything went pretty much according to plan, she was livid. She checked Siri, who was unconscious but alive. She rounded up Tristin, still in human form, and the two still in wolf form. Everyone was unconscious, so she teleported to the car and drove it to a more central location and then she used wind to carry each to the car and drove back to Devlin's. Devlin's clan ran out to meet the van as she parked the car. Linsey started triage in the van, giving orders as she checked each person.

"There are no serious injuries," Linsey said a few minutes later.

Devlin came and stood in Tempe's path, "Where's Bryce?"

She pulled out her cell phone, called Rayna, put the phone on speaker and said, "It was a set-up, as we expected. Three wizards of the Shadowed were waiting for us. One kept me busy and I foolishly thought I had the only wizard on me. Radek and Yula were also there." She took a deep breath and gave Devlin and Rayna the details.

"Mom, you saved Siri over Bryce. Why?" Devlin asked softly.

"Because it was the plan," she responded angrily.

She raised her right hand to her lips and breathed "Bryce". She made a circle until the ring glowed green, facing south.

"Rayna, I'm heading south," Tempe said as she headed in to pack her weapons.

Chapter 18

"Tempest, you are a fool." Siri punctuated each word as she followed Tempe out the door. "You can't go alone."

"No one from this clan is to leave here. I want my grandchildren safe," Tempe said before looking at the fae/wizard and adding, "Please."

"That's going to be a problem," Kevin said, "I'm the only shifter pilot available in the area who can fly internationally. I'm your pilot."

"No," Tempe snarled.

"Mother!" Kacy walked into the room holding a baby girl in each arm.

Gabriel was behind her with Riley. His hair did match Gabriel's.

"Kevin is over thirty and an accomplished pilot. He can get you to Bryce. If he weren't your grandson you'd be thrilled to have him. And another thing since I'm on a roll, Siri is the best backup you could get. You need her, and you need Kevin. Devlin and the rest of the clan can protect the babies." She sat down in a chair and looked surprised at what she had just done.

Tempe stared at her daughter. She had never taken that tone with her, ever.

She looked up at Tempe sheepishly and said quietly, "Mother, your odds of success go up with Kevin and Siri. Please take them."

Devlin was as shocked as his mother over Kacy's unusual response, but he managed to say with only a slight smirk, "What she said."

"I don't have time to argue. Okay, fine. Siri, Kevin, let's go."

Kevin breezed through the airport and got them up in the air faster than Tempe would have thought possible. She acted as co-pilot and talked to the resources on the ground. The ring kept them going south. When they were over Spain the ring's glow turned ever so slightly southwest.

Tempe glanced over at Kevin. "I think we're heading toward Morocco."

"I agree. How's the ring?"

"Still green." She silently commended herself for adding the spell to keep the rings invisible except to the wearer.

They landed at Marrakech with the help of the local shifter clan. Ryan, Raven, and Murdoch met them there. They had opened a way directly to the land the leader of the local shifter clan owns. A place Raven knew well.

They gathered the supplies they needed and headed for the Haut Atlas Mountains, following the green glow of her ring. Since Tempe was the only one who could see it, the group kept glancing at Tempe. It was driving her nuts. The only bright spot in the trip was Ryan's reaction to the first camel crossing sign he saw.

Abbas, their guide and second in the Marrakech clan, turned down a dirt road and drove around the base of the mountains. They were jostled so much Tempe commented, "We should have ridden camels. They would have bounced less."

"Obviously you have only ridden gentle camels," Abbas replied.

Eventually they left the trucks and took off on foot. Ten miles later they arrived at a compound, complete with wired fence, current running through it, and guards, lots of guards. They were within a fourth of a mile of the fence, somewhat hidden by some prickly shrubs. Tempe was pretty sure the cameras could see them.

"What's the plan?" Kevin asked.

"Sweetie, your grandmother is going to express her displeasure at someone taking her man." Tempe's soft response did not match the anger in her eyes.

Tempe heard Ryan give Kevin and the other shifters orders about staying within his shield. She smiled.

Personal shield in place Tempe stood up and waved at the guards. They didn't do anything for about three seconds. They just looked at her. While they were looking she drew power and threw fire at the fence and any guard without the brains to duck and cover. She started walking toward the newly created opening in the fence.

A trio of wizards started chanting so she focused the modulation of her voice to say "silent" and the chanting wizards fell silent. The enchantment would only last a few minutes.

Murdoch pointed his rune weapon at the wizards. Sparks flew, and the wizards dropped.

Tempe's smile widened. Looked like the wizards would be out of it for a while.

Another group threw individual spells at Raven in dragon form. She simply returned any spell back to its point of origin. It was a neat ability. Whatever Murdoch did to the wizards Tempe enchanted, he also did to the wizards attacking Raven.

They got to the front door and Tempe sent a spell to negate the electronic alarm. She pulled the door open and they went in. There was a line of wizards who looked intimidating until Murdoch laughed and sent a spell with his rune wand.

The wizards dropped.

"Dang, remind me to not piss you off," Ryan chuckled. That had been seriously impressive.

"That lot hasn't even passed their final wizard tests," Murdoch shrugged.

Tempe smiled grimly, if there was a test maybe they do have a School for Witches and Wizards after all. When this is over Tempe just had to ask Nova if she has her own Hogwarts somewhere.

They blew through another door and entered the next section of the building.

Tempe's anger flamed, and she drew more power. Everyone backed away from her, which was smart.

Bryce was suspended in a bubble over a deep pit with flames flowing up toward him. He wasn't moving. Bryce had tiny cuts on his body, the kind used for torture.

"Tempest," Alena, formally of the high wizard coven and the suspected leader of the Shadowed, smiled. "If you do not cease your activities, I will kill Bryce."

"Threatening me is a bad idea. Ask my father," she replied.

"That's why I'm not threatening you, I'm threatening your love," Alena said. "I have watched you for years and you will do a lot to protect others, so I suspect you will do anything to protect him." She pointed at Bryce.

Tempe growled.

"You and your friends are surrounded, but you already know that." Alena, hands held high in a classic conjuring position, smiled. "You should have brought Nova with you. She is the only one who could possibly stop me."

The wizards closed in and Tempe looked around. "Murdoch, have all of the wizards surrounding us passed their final exams?"

"Yes," he replied grimly.

They were outnumbered three to one and none of the shifters, except for Ryan, Raven and Tempe would be able to defend themselves much at all.

Tempe took a deep breath, "Stand down."

"Wonderful, I didn't think you would surrender." Alena's smug smile landed on Tempest.

"You misunderstood," Tempe replied. "My team walks out or I will flatten this facility killing all of us."

"You wouldn't," she gasped.

"Yes, she would." Radek was burnt horribly and the vindictive aspect of Tempe's genetic makeup was pleased. "She sacrificed Bryce yesterday to save the others. She will kill everyone before she allows us to have them."

"What do you propose?" Alena asked.

"I will stand here and once I hear one of the shifters tell me everyone else is out, including Bryce, I will not fight you," Tempe said.

"Simple, but why should I trust you?"

"Because I'm one of the good guys and I gave you my word. I don't lie." Tempe smirked. "You have no clue which shifter will tell me they are clear, so you can forget about forcing one of them to contact me."

"True, however there is one exception to your lovely plan. Murdoch stays." Alena pronounced.

"No."

"This isn't negotiable. Murdoch stays, or we can all die," Alena explained serenely.

"I expected as much." Murdoch replied calmly, "Tempe and I stay, Bryce goes with the others".

"No," Radek yelled.

Alena smiled, "Bryce goes with the others. Tempest will protect the man who just saved her love. It's a good trade."

Yula, untouched by the fire Tempe had sent at Radek and Aster yesterday, moved Bryce's bubble and popped the bubble over Ryan's head. Ryan shifted to his dragon, caught Bryce, and expanded his shield to include them.

Kevin and Abbas took Bryce in a fireman's carry and the team backed out slowly under Ryan's shield. Ryan shifted back to human and looked ready to argue, but he followed orders. Raven was last out. She stared at Tempe hard and then backed out of the room.

Murdoch and Tempe stayed right where they were. They didn't move. Two and a half hours later Tempe received the message she was waiting for. The others were driving down the road.

Tempe nodded to Murdoch and then to Alena. The wizard guards closed in.

So far, the plan was working perfectly.

Let the good times roll.

*****

As torture goes, Alena wasn't a pro, aside from snide comments she didn't even try. Radek, however, had some seriously impressive skills. Tempe even considered burning him might have made him a tad touchy. Radek was healing fast and she didn't know if it was some wizard ability or if somehow his healing was augmented. Murdoch and Tempe were never tortured at the same time. If Tempe was being tortured, Murdoch was in the holding cell and vice versa.

Murdoch and Tempe were kept in the same cell, which was not smart. Neither of them pointed out the error to their captors.

Tempe learned one thing. Alena was just the figurehead, but she didn't know it. Alena had the magic power, but she didn't know how to run the show. Aster always took her orders from Radek. Of course, that could be because she was burned worse than Radek and she wasn't healing nearly as fast. Both Aster and Radek seemed to be taking that personally. Yula also took her orders from Radek. She was subtle, and it didn't look like Alena noticed, but Yula verified every order with Radek either by a glance or hand single.

Tempe was tired, hungry and waiting for a signal from Murdoch. Like most wizards, he had an impressive internal clock. On his signal they would unleash the next phase of the plan. They just had to hold out that long.

Since Tempe's internal clock was crap she didn't have a clue how long they had been in the Shadowed stronghold, but it was her turn for torture. The fae made restraints were never removed from their arms and legs, preventing any use of magic. They simply unlocked the restraints from the wall and floor in the holding area and reattached them to the wall and floor in the torture room. Once the four extremely competent wizard warriors hooked up her magic resistant restraints to the wall and floor bolts, and she tried one more time to pull magic and shocked herself, she waited. The guards left when Radek walked in. Somehow, he had healed to the point he was barely scarred. Tempe was so tired her surprise showed.

Radek smiled, "Yes, Tempest. I am almost completely healed. I'm surprised you haven't asked about Bryce."

"You would lie, so I didn't waste my breath. I don't need to ask to know you tortured him," she replied evenly.

"I can't take all of the credit. Yula and Aster were willing to assist. Aster was extremely attentive. I also find it interesting some of your jewelry is now spelled to stay on your body. So is Murdoch's. I wonder why?" he asked as he touched her necklace.

He must have been talking to the walls because she wasn't answering.

"When we were last together we were getting ready to have some playtime together. Now that I'm feeling more myself, shall we pick up where we left off?" Radek asked.

"I don't think that's going to happen."

He walked toward her, and she couldn't stop herself from backing into the wall. It was as far as the manacles would let her move.

He smiled and placed a hand on each side of her body. "You know, I will take great pleasure in telling Bryce about this moment."

She smiled right back at him, "And Bryce will kill you, unless I beat him to the punch."

Since her magic was short-circuited, she tried to physically push Radek away, but some spell held her. She couldn't move her arms or legs. Once again Radek took his time to feel his way around her body before he unbuttoned her shirt.

Tempe was pressed into the wall with no place to go. She still couldn't move her arms or legs, so she did the next best thing. She slammed her head into his. Thank goodness her neck could move. Radek stepped back dazed and she smiled. He backhanded her, causing her head to hit the wall and then she slid to the floor. It took a few seconds for the room to stop spinning. Radek also kicked Tempe, and a couple of ribs felt cracked and possibly broken.

Guess she shouldn't have smiled.

The four wizard guards carried her back to the cell. They hooked her magical restraints to the bolts in the cell and left.

Murdoch asked, "You okay?"

"Peachy," Tempe growled.

"Tempest, look at me," Murdoch ordered, before he hastily added, "Please."

She looked over at him and he asked, "What did Radek do?"

"Not what you think," she replied as she realized her shirt was mostly unbuttoned. "Oh, he tried, but I head butted him. Then he decided to beat me up. I think my ribs are going to be unhappy for a while."

Murdoch swore.

"Why does Alena hate you so?"

He barked a laugh. "Years ago, her son went rogue. I killed him. She thought I should have restrained him instead."

Tempe snorted and the movement made her ribs hurt. Most mothers get vindictive when you kill their kids.

*****

Tempe must have passed out, again. When she came to Murdoch was gone. Thanks to the metabolism of shifters, her ribs were healing, although not properly. Which meant someone would have to break and reset the bones. She knew from past experience it would hurt and she would not be happy about it.

When they brought Murdoch back in he was unconscious. After the warriors left she tried to get his attention but he didn't move.

A little bit later, Radek walked in. "Did you think we would allow him to mark time for you?"

"I didn't expect it, but I was hoping," she admitted.

Radek pushed the hair out of her face and said, "This could have been much more pleasant for you my dear."

She laughed, "I think you mean this could have been more pleasant for you."

"That too," he replied agreeably. He touched her ribs and, after she sucked in air from the pain, said, "I am sorry you forced me to break your ribs."

She snarled, "You should ask before you touch."

Murdoch must have been faking it because suddenly he said, "Radek, you take too many liberties." He whispered, "PENLEASE."

She smiled since the allotted hours were obviously up. The pendent around her neck and the pendent around Murdoch's neck released smoke and two forms appeared.

Nova turned on Radek in disgust and said something under her breath. He dropped to the ground even as recognition and then fear registered on his face. Tempe would have been happy with dead, but he was breathing. Unconscious would have to do, for now.

Citlali turned to their restraints and used some murmured word to shatter them. Tempe fell to the ground. Murdoch showed off and managed to stay standing.

Tempe looked up at Nova and Citlali and said, "Don't wait for me. Find Alena and the others. Destroy them." They both veiled and left.

As she grabbed the hand Murdoch offered her, several ribs expressed their displeasure. Tempe let go of his hand, dropped gingerly to the ground, and said, "Go without me. Come back after the battle."

"No. We go together." He leaned down and lifted her, despite her hiss of displeasure. He kicked Radek into the wall as he carried Tempe out of the cell.

Later, he would reflect that he should have killed Radek.

Chapter 19

"Murdoch, put me down. I can walk," Tempe said in disgust.

"Okay, but if you can't keep up I will carry you. I'm not explaining to Bryce I lost you." He gently lowered her to a standing position.

Walking hurt, but she didn't slow down. "So how did you do it?"

"Do what?" he asked.

"You looked like you were half dead and then suddenly you were fine." She almost stopped walking. "Geez. You projected wounds you didn't have?" she exclaimed, suddenly impressed. She had never thought of doing that, and all things considered, she could have used that ruse a time or two.

"The spell is somewhat similar to the glamour the fae project." He checked then opened a door and they were in another hallway. Once out of the shielded and soundproofed holding section, they could hear the battle.

When Tempe tried to pick up the pace, her ribs reacted badly. As she moseyed down the hall she thought about how many times she had cracked or broken ribs, often enough she did know something of wounds and the pain that would go with repairing the damage. They reached the room where they had been taken for their quality time with Radek. Murdoch opened the door and they retrieved their weapons.

Walking down the hallway they could hear the fight getting louder. Their capture had been a delay to allow time for preternaturals to gather at the site once they knew, for sure, where it was. She cursed under her breath, "Murdoch. Go. Help the others. I'll be right behind you."

"No way Tempe, we stay together," he said as they reached the next door.

She shook her head in disgust and tried to open the door. She sucked in air when the motion caused her ribs to protest loudly.

Murdoch smothered his concern and opened the door while she snarled, rune weapon ready for action.

Tempe sent a focused sleep spell at Yula's back before she even knew the shifter was there. She dropped and Tempe felt immense satisfaction, until she looked around the room. It was a warzone. She set her shield, Murdoch nodded and ran into the fight.

Quinn appeared at her side. She dropped her shield as he gently pulled his sister into his arms and then teleported her inside Ryan's shield. She tried to argue but he smiled and said, "You are too wounded to be of help. Stay here, please."

Tempe snarled but admitted to herself someone would probably be hurt helping her if she joined the fight. She watched as Quill, one of her brothers, fought fire to fire with Aster. Despite the fact she was still burnt badly she wasn't as afraid of fire as Tempe would expect her to be. In addition to keeping a shield around the wounded, Ryan was healing the most injured enough to keep them alive until the fighting was over and real medical attention could be found.

Nova and Citlali were nowhere to be seen but then Tempe didn't see Alena either, and she was still looking for at least one powerful mystery villain.

Siri was tag teaming a couple of wizards with Devlin. Tempe couldn't wait to hear Devlin explain how the heck he was protecting his sister and her babies while he was here.

Ryan finished with an injured wizard and walked over, "How bad?"

"Don't worry about me. I'll have to have some ribs broken and reset," She said, watching the fight.

"If I heal your ribs you can fight. You're needed," Ryan explained. "No one else is that bad off right now and I won't be able to heal many more anyway."

Tempe rolled her eyes but nodded. She felt a massive jolt of pain and then relief flooded into her body as he healed her ribs properly. When he finished, Ryan was tired, and Tempe was feeling good.

"You put too much into healing me." She caught him before he fell over. "I need you with me, not too weak to fight. You have to pace yourself in battle. You can't heal everyone."

"I'm fine. Just give me a minute."

Tempe heard Citlali in her mind. Grabbing Ryan, she said, "No time, battle mode."

Ryan veiled them as Tempe teleported them. They both had their rune weapons drawn as they arrived near Citlali.

Radek used wind to push Citlali, who looked close to unconsciousness, to the rim of the ledge where the flames that reached for Bryce not so long ago now reached for Citlali. She was hurt and couldn't block Radek's wind.

Radek was using a coven of thirteen witches to focus his power. The witches were somehow shielding themselves, but Tempe could deal with that. Since they were veiled, she modulated her voice and said loudly, "silence" as her voice echoed around the room. The witches could no longer chant. Unfortunately, all witches in the room were now unable to speak.

Citlali glared as Ryan dropped his veil and ran to shield Citlali. Tempe winced, "Sorry."

On the plus side, Radek screamed in silent fury. Tempe turned to Radek, "It's time for us to finish our dance," she said determinedly. She sent a mental order to tell Ryan to get Citlali to safety and took a fraction of a second to be happy she couldn't hear his response as his face turned into a rather furious scowl before he opened a way.

Radek's expression was priceless as they circled each other. They were both mad because neither of them drew power, moving immediately into bar room brawl mentality.

Tempe smiled, "For what you did to Bryce, and Citlali, I am going to kill you. I just wanted you to know this is personal."

"It certainly is," Radek rasped as his voice partially returned. "I had great plans for you and you destroyed them."

"You're welcome," she replied. They circled closer and closer to each other, both making sure to keep an eye on the ledge.

Tempe lunged, and the fight began in earnest. It was immediately obvious that without using magic they were well matched in a fistfight. Both were well trained and blocked each other with ease. Ultimately Radek came in close with a punch and Tempe ducked. His follow through on the punch sent him rolling over her back and toward the rim of the floor. She twisted to kick him, but he grabbed her foot and pulled. She landed on top of him and he grabbed her around the waist, rolling with the motion, landing on top of her.

Radek smiled and Tempe growled. They both pulled wind, which was standoff, wind wise, but he had a good forty pounds on her and Tempe couldn't throw him off. He was sitting on her thighs and had her arms pinned to the floor. She tried to move and realized she was in that same frozen arm/leg spell Radek had used before. He leaned down and whispered in her ear, "I've been waiting a long time for this."

"So have I," Bryce said as he grabbed Radek in a chokehold and pulled the creep off of his woman.

Tempe still couldn't move.

Bryce snapped Radek's neck and threw him over the rim of the floor.

"Sorry I'm late," Bryce apologized.

"Your timing was perfect" Tempe replied. The spell dissipated with Radek's death and she was mobile once again. She grabbed the hand Bryce offered her and jumped up. "Come on, I need to find Citlali."

They ran out of the room and found Citlali inside Ryan's shield. He looked over and shook his head. Murdock was holding one of her hands. Tempe dropped down beside her and took her other hand. Citlali opened her eyes and smiled weakly, "Tempest, find the source."

Citlali flooded Tempe's mind with information. Tempe wasn't sure how long they stayed like that, staring into each other's eyes. It couldn't have been too long because her legs didn't cramp up. When she finished, Citlali took her last breath.

Tempe said, "Good journey," in the way of the fae and added, "The sun will not shine as bright tomorrow," in the way of Citlali's people from centuries ago.

Tempe walked out of Ryan's shield. Murdoch made a hand motion over his grandmother's body and his expression turned angry.

"Ryan, go help the main fighters. Murdoch, Bryce, with me," Tempe said. "Citlali gave me directions."

They ran while the others fought the Shadowed troops.

Tempe reached to open the door and Murdoch pushed her hand away. "Tempe, the door is spelled. Look at it for pity's sake," he snarled.

Tempe looked at the door and then had to refocus her eyes. "Sorry. Wizards see magic different than shifters and Citlali gave me her sight to find the source."

By the time Tempe finished her explanation Murdoch had cancelled the spell and opened the door. He replied, "Then you point the way and I open the doors."

They entered another hallway. Tempe stopped at the next door, which turned out to be spelled too, but again it was no match for Murdoch. They entered a room that looked like a high-end office filled with carved maple furniture. Bryce took the filing cabinets. Murdoch took the desk drawers and Tempe took the computer. As passwords go, the computer was hardly protected at all. She found the research and downloaded it to a flash drive she pulled out of her vest. She also found out what the source was.

Tempe read quickly as she downloaded files. "The source of the virus is a tree and we need to find it." It wasn't a tree from the Seen or the Farseen, but from another dimension the Shadowed called Brimstone because every plant was dangerous, if not downright fatal, to both dimensions. The sap of the slave tree, as the Shadowed called it, had many uses as a pharmaceutical and none of them were good.

Bryce looked over a stack of papers he had just finished scanning. "There's a climate-controlled arboretum in this facility. The flames in the entrance are from the heat needed to keep the room at the right temperature for the tree housed there."

"Guess that's why they called the dimension Brimstone," Tempe commented to herself. Louder she said, "Can you lead us there?"

"Yes. That's where Radek, Yula, and Aster chatted with me," he said grimly.

Tempe still didn't know what had happened to him while he was their prisoner. She must have made a noise because he looked over and said, "It was worth it. That's how we found this place."

Tempe growled again.

Murdoch opened the door, "Don't let my grandmother's death be in vain."

Tempe took a deep breath, nodded, and they took off with Bryce in the lead. As they ran they could hear the battle raging. She asked, "Does anyone know what happened to Nova and Alena?"

Neither man answered which didn't give her a good feeling.

Bryce stopped in front of a non-descript door. Murdoch checked it out, did some wizard maneuver and then opened the door. There were chains on one wall and blood on the floor. Tempe looked at Bryce, but he had set his face in lawyer mode. She decided she could ask later. They walked past the blood and saw the tree.

As soon as they neared the tree its branches reached toward the trio.

Bryce pulled Murdoch and Tempe back and said, "That tree eats blood. That's how they keep it alive. They feed it the blood of their prisoners. At one point I watched them throw a live person, with many small cuts, into the tree to feed it."

Murdoch snarled, "How do we destroy it?"

"No clue," Bryce replied tightly.

"Hang on. It needs the heat of the flames, right?" Tempe asked.

"I heard them discuss that, yes. Of course, they could have been feeding me misinformation."

"If the flames help it and it uses blood for nutrients, then perhaps water is bad for it."

She pulled water and doused the tree. As luck would have it, the tree liked water just fine and it grew a couple of feet.

"That wasn't helpful." Murdoch crossed his arms.

Tempe tried water again. This time to put out the flames but there was more flame than she could find water. Murdoch tried a freezing spell that did nothing.

"A chipper would be nice about now." Bryce watched them try various spells with no positive results.

The trio continued to stare at the tree when Tempe smiled. "It likes the heat, but I've never known of a tree that likes flames."

Murdoch grinned and they both pulled their rune weapons and sent focused fire at the tree. It caught on fire. Just when they were beginning to congratulate themselves, breathing got hard.

"The tree… is poisonous," Bryce coughed.

Tempe pulled water again and put out the fire. The tree recovered within seconds from the burns. The water seemed to speed up the healing and apparently let the tree grow another foot.

"I guess when we implode this building we will just have to bury the tree with it," Tempe groused.

"But if we don't get all the Shadowed they will know where the tree is." Bryce said.

"Then we'll get them all," Murdoch vowed.

They searched the room for any additional information and came up empty. They were getting ready to leave the room when Tempe had a duh moment before she mentally called Raven and told her to have Quinn teleport her to Tempe.

They arrived, and Tempe said, "I have a job for your dragon." She pointed to the tree and turned to the guys, "You guys go back to the fight. I think Raven's dragon can take care of this tree."

Bryce and Murdoch wanted to argue, but even though he looked confused, Quinn trusted Tempe. "They don't need our help. The others do." With Bryce and Murdoch in tow, he teleported back to the fight.

"Raven, your green dragon can control plants. The only concern I have is this tree is from a dimension I don't know or understand. I'm hoping you can control it anyway." Tempe went on to explain about the dangerous nature of the tree and what had already been tried.

Once she was prepared, Raven shifted and attempted to control the tree. Initially, nothing happened, but then the green dragon squawked and doubled over in pain.

Tempe looked over at the tree and realized somehow the tree was accessing Raven's green dragon ability to manipulate plants to allow the tree to grow stronger.

Tempe ordered Raven to shift back to human, a direct order from alpha to lower ranking alpha. Raven tried but was unable to comply. The tree continued to pull power from her dragon.

Tempe snarled and turned on the tree. She shifted into her new form, a gold dragon and breathed out a gas that weakens those who breathe it in, hoping it would work on the tree. The tree lost control over Raven's green dragon, allowing her to shift, and drop to the ground. Throwing a sleep spell in an attempt to put the tree into a state of hibernation, Tempe shifted back to human and dropped by Raven's side, "Raven, speak to me. Say something."

"Ugh, that did not work," she stated weakly.

"I'm sorry. I should never have asked you to do that. That tree seems to be intelligent, like the treemen in the Farseen except it hasn't talked. My dragon was able to use spells on the tree but in my human form I couldn't. Somehow the tree was able to use your dragon's power to help itself to more power." Tempe helped Raven stand up. "You okay?"

She smirked, "You owe me for this one, sis. My head is going to pound for a while." She took a couple of steadying breaths and said, "I like the golden dragon."

Tempe smiled, "Thanks. Stay here and be prepared to drag me out of the room,"

"What are you going to do?"

"I'm going to open my mind and try to talk to the tree," Tempe replied as Raven growled.

Tempe rolled her eyes and added, "We were getting our butts kicked here. Maybe the tree will tell me how to send it home. We can't kill it here."

"No," Raven snarled. She took a deep breath and added, "Please Tempe, I don't have a good feeling about this."

"Neither do I, but you're my safety net. I need you to drag me out of the room if my mental conversation with the tree goes south."

Tempe removed Raven's hand from the death grip on her arm. "We have to do something. This facility can't be destroyed with the tree here. It could spread its poison who knows how far if it manages to adapt to our dimension."

Raven set her face in battle mode and said, "Do it. But if I have to pull you out of here don't complain if I break a bone or two on the way out."

Tempe smiled grimly, "Deal."

Tempe turned to the tree and opened her mind just a little bit. The tree, Celeborn, flooded her mind with images.

Other two-legs ripped me from my grove and brought me here. To a place where nutrients are hard to find except when they feed me two-legs, and the air is too cold. My grove is gone. I can't hear them anymore. I need my grove as much as I need nutrients and warmth. The others cut me and took my leaves. They hurt me. I want to go home.

Tempe responded in kind, giving him information on the Shadowed and how they had used pieces of him to kill and enslave the people of two dimensions.

You are deadly to this dimension. We want you to go home as much as you do.

Celeborn leaned his branches toward her. *Send me home.*

I can't open a way to a place I don't know. Show me the two-legs who took you and I'll find out from them how to send you back.

The image he sent was of Radek, Duane, Adelia and Crystal. Great, only one left alive.

I'll do everything in my power to return you home if you don't kill anyone else.

You have three sunrises. Then normal seed germination starts, and the seeds will spread out and become part of this dimension's ecosystem. I have no control over the germination process.

She sighed even as she agreed. Less than seventy-two hours.

Tempe sent a mental message to every alpha. Adelia was needed alive, Alena, too, on the off chance she knew how to open the way.

*****

Raven and Tempe teleported back into the entrance where the battle was almost over and the Shadowed were losing.

Ryan and Murdoch were in a yelling match. Tempe ran over in time to hear Ryan say, "We need to question her."

"She dies. She's too strong to keep alive," Murdoch snarled.

"Murdoch," Tempe planted herself between the two men. "The only way to get the tree out of here is to open a way to Brimstone. We need someone in the Shadowed for that. The tree is going to germinate soon, and the seeds will spread throughout earth. We can't allow that to happen."

Murdoch's face blanched, "Tempe, we can't trust the Shadowed. More importantly, I can't hold Alena. Not a wizard here can. Nova is unconscious. If I don't kill Alena before she wakes up she will kill us, all of us."

Tempe arched her shoulders, blew out air and asked, "How about a coven of wizards working together to boost your power?"

"Look around," Murdoch gestured angrily. "There aren't thirteen healthy wizards here. No chanting. We took heavy casualties."

"Do you need wizards? Will chanters with power do?" Tempe asked.

"I prefer wizards. But I can control the chant if I can get the power boost and have thirteen people who know how to chant."

Her eyes darted around the room as she asked, "How many wizards do you have?"

He ticked off names, "Siri, Janel, Odelia, Bianca, Arnie, Sumner, Aalem, Jackson, and Abbie."

Tempe looked around the room at the shifters who knew how to chant and said, "Devlin, Ryan, Landon, and Kenley. Come here."

She turned back to Murdoch. "These shifters can chant. Use them to round out your coven. That gets you thirteen." As she walked off she called over her shoulder, "I suspect at least three of them would rather chant than explain to me what they're doing here."

"Right," Murdoch said with a grim smile and issued orders to his makeshift coven.

The chanters started doing their thing and Murdoch did whatever the lead wizard does in this case. Tempest didn't have a clue what that was and, as much as she wanted to watch and learn, she didn't have time.

Tempe grabbed Raven and Brandi, "Where's Nova?"

Brandi said, "In Ryan's bubble, unconscious."

Tempe felt a presence that shouldn't be in a war zone and turned toward the entrance as Katell, Jocosa and Loane entered the battlefield. She could feel their mental shields tightening as they walked.

"Are you three nuts?" The sovereign's second yelled in exasperation, "This place is too dangerous for you."

Loane smiled serenely. "You hold no sway over us."

"I meant no disrespect," the sovereign's second responded through gritted teeth. "But you have always been protected from the battlefield for reasons you well know."

"But in this case, it is necessary," Jocosa said. She walked into Ryan's bubble and knelt over Nova.

Loane walked to the edge of the floor and talked to the tree much more efficiently than Tempest did. After a few minutes she said, "Tempest, the one you seek will not know how to open the way."

"The others are dead," she replied grimly.

Loane looked at Alena's unconscious body and then she looked at Murdoch. "Was this one truly in charge?"

He had sweat beading on his forehead from the force of his concentration on his controlling spell, but he managed to say, "We think so."

Loane said, "Then I will check."

Loane stood over Alena. After a few minutes she looked at Tempest, "She might be a strong wizard, but she does not have the brains to run this operation. She doesn't have a clue how to open a way to Brimstone. That knowledge belongs to…" Loane screamed and fell.

Tempe had already opened her mind to Loane, so she knew who the leader of the revolution was. She looked up on the walkway over the flames on the third level. There stood River, Water Lord of the Western Realm, the name Loane didn't say aloud.

Tempest growled. Everyone else was completely silent. They knew something was up, but they didn't know what.

"Lord River, I tire of cleaning up fae chaos," Tempe said deadly calm. "You will open a way to Brimstone and we will return the treeman to his home."

"Why?" he sneered. "To send me back to the Farseen, so the other realm lords can kill me? I think not. Brimstone gives me power beyond everyone. I will keep that information for myself."

Tempe heard Murdoch break Alena's neck and the chanting stopped. Ryan ran to Loane's side. Tempe motioned for everyone else to stay where they were.

"Why do this? The treeman from Brimstone is just as deadly to the Farseen as it is to the Seen."

"Which is why I convinced Alena to keep him here," he boasted.

"It was you? You organized the Shadowed. You used Crystal, Savannah and Amber to do your dirty work in the Farseen. You were never under their control. You have destroyed entire families in the Seen and the Farseen, for what? Power?" Tempe asked in disgust.

"Yes. This plan was centuries in the making. I've wanted to destroy your father since the fae/shifter war. He caused the war just because he wanted you and Val. If he had left the shifters alone my children would not have been killed. You killed them Tempest. You were so mad at your father when he killed Val you leveled three of my squadrons. My three youngest were leading those squadrons. You killed them," he yelled.

"By the five realms, you blame me for the fae/shifter war? A war started because the fae kept stealing the people of the Seen to be slaves, albeit without drugs that time. What was your master plan? Even with the Brimstone poison you could not defeat the five queens and they would never allow one fae lord to rule multiple realms."

"Don't you get it yet? The poison will kill the queens and I will rule the five realms," River said.

Tempe looked at him in disgust, before turning eyes to the sky. "Do you need anything else?"

"No, that is sufficient," Mistress Kainda, daughter of the hunt, replied as she unveiled.

Lord River blanched and backed away from Kainda, right into the arms of Theron, Master of the Hunt. River did not improve his position at all. The fae might call them the master and mistress of the hunt but Theron and his daughter were the queens' assassins. They worked for all five queens and they had never failed to track and kill their prey.

Theron smiled and said, "Lady Tempest, I send you greetings from the queens. They acknowledge your service in this matter." He opened a way and pointed River toward it.

Tempe called, "Before you take River away, I need the instructions for opening a way to Brimstone."

"I have that information." Loane leaned on Ryan for support as she stood.

Theron looked at Loane and there was a flicker of some emotion in his eyes. Loane blushed.

Theron and Kainda stood on either side of River, Kainda opened a way, and they left. Tempe wasn't the only person to breathe a sigh of relief when the hunters were gone.

She turned to Loane, "Give me instructions. I want to get the treeman safely home, sooner would be much better than later."

Chapter 20

Everyone else was out of the building. Bryce, Ryan, Murdoch and Tempe stood around the treeman. Tempe needed Ryan and Murdoch but she was unable to order Bryce away. He simply ignored her, which was a first. She knew he could only ignore her direct order was if Rayna gave him a counter order.

Tempe snarled. As soon as her feet were firmly on the ground in the States, she and the sovereign were going to have a long talk. Ryan and Murdoch took great pains to be looking anywhere but at Tempe, while she and Bryce disagreed. No matter how she phrased the order, Bryce was able to ignore her.

Finally, Murdoch glanced at Tempe and said in a soft, apologetic tone, "Tick, tock."

Tempe glared at him but realized he was right. If Bryce wanted to throw himself into danger, and her mother gave him the means to do it, maybe she should just let him. It wasn't like she was having any success protecting him.

The four of them wormed their way into the uncomfortable environmental suits the Shadowed had on hand. At least they would be able to breathe in Brimstone. Tempe explained to Celeborn she would open a way to his home dimension and Murdoch and Ryan would help move him to his dimension. He agreed to withdraw his roots from the ground as much as possible to help with the move. He now stood around twenty feet tall after all the magic that was thrown around and at him. He explained the forces they call magic were full of life sustaining nutrients for his people.

Once Celeborn, Ryan and Murdoch were ready, Tempe took a deep breath and opened a way. She heard the treeman send a mental warning to his family his traveling companions were helping him, and they were not to be harmed. Ryan, with his telekinesis, helped spell-wielding Murdoch 'carry' the treeman.

They walked through the way and were surrounded by treemen, irritated telepaths all.

The force of their minds pressed on Tempe. She was suffocating. Her mind was overloading. She couldn't keep them out. They pressed harder and harder. The information entered her mind too fast. She could not make order out of the information or even determine which thoughts came from which tree.

She didn't know what was happening to the others. On some level, Tempe recognized this was not a physical fight. Mentally she wasn't strong enough to beat them back. She couldn't see, hear or feel, except for what the trees pushed at her, all of their anger and fear when one of them was taken, their inability to open a way, and their sadness when their grove member did not return.

Suddenly, the pressure was gone from her mind, but she couldn't focus her mind or her eyes. She tripped.

Bryce dove underneath her and caught her. He had barely caught her before she hit the ground.

During the mind attack, Ryan and Murdoch had carefully released Celeborn and his roots were burrowing down into the loose soil.

Tempe carefully opened her mind and showed them what had happened to their child. A huge tree walked up to Tempe as all the other trees backed away. Tempe wasn't feeling too confident about the outcome.

The tree opened up her mind to all four of travelers.

I am Momoye, matriarch of this grove and the great-great-great-grandmother of Celeborn. I offer regret over the assault on your female. My children thought since she was the strongest mind talker she could communicate with us normally. They stopped when they realized she wasn't strong enough for that.

She turned to Murdoch and didn't speak so much as show him her sorrow at his great-great-grandmother's return to earth, their way of saying death.

Momoye focused on Tempe. *I recommend since the two dimensions are not healthy for each other the ways should remain closed.*

I agree, but I'm not the only one who knows how to open a way to your land. Those who kidnapped Celeborn have broken our laws and we are searching for them. Tempe then exchanged information with the matriarch on how they could contact each other and then Momoye backed away.

Celeborn thanked them for their efforts on his behalf with the entire grove standing around him.

Tempe stood up with Bryce's help and leaned on him while she opened the way back home. Before she left she took a good look at

Brimstone. Mini volcanoes spewed up fire and smoke, but no lava. Plants moved across the sandy ground either chasing food or playing. The sky was orange and there was a haze over the valley. There was no water within eyesight. Brimstone was a good name for it.

The four of them returned to their dimension and the massive cleanup that waited. Ryan jerked off his hood and gloves, pulled out his cell phone and sent a text message. The group waiting outside entered the building.

Tempe, still unsteady and leaning heavily on Bryce, tried to walk over toward her aunts and stumbled. Bryce caught her and then he picked her up and carried her.

"Bryce, put me down. I don't need to be carried," she said angrily, anger that changed to all out shock when she realized he ignored another direct order from her.

He ignored the sovereign's second and called, "Loane, Tempe got something of an unintentional telepathic attack from the tree grove in Brimstone. What can we do?"

Loane walked over and said, "Set her down and let me see."

"Loane, I'm fine. Bryce is being overprotective." She stood up to prove her words, and promptly felt her knees collapse underneath her. Bryce caught her again and sat her back in the chair.

Loane raised an eyebrow. "You are not fine, and Bryce is not being overprotective. You received a telepathic overload. Apparently, they stopped as soon as they realized what they were doing to you. You were lucky."

Tempe rolled her eyes.

"You may not feel like it but you were lucky they listened to their sapling," Loane said mildly. "Sit for a few minutes while I check you out."

While Tempe sat, attempting to ignore Loane in her mind, she looked around the room. The cleanup was pretty well done and some of the soldiers were setting the charges to implode the building.

Devlin walked over, "My clan is protected. Fallon and I joined our clans until this is finished. Both clans are in the safety of Fallon's fortress." He went down on one knee and looked her in the eye and whispered, "Mother, I would never have left the children unprotected."

"I had a feeling that you had managed to protect them. You have always been the careful and deliberate one," she grinned at him. "Only you would find a way to secure everyone in a fortress in the twenty-first century."

Kenley had walked up behind Devlin and said, "I didn't realize you knew I had started my wizard training and could chant. Of course, I shouldn't be surprised. Did you think I would stay safely in Italy while everyone else was fighting?"

"No, but I was hoping," Tempe replied mostly to herself.

Landon, with Eli by his side, walked over and said, "Does that mean it's my turn to confess?"

Tempe inclined her head.

"I felt I should make reparations," he explained.

Her brow furrowed, "Landon, you didn't do anything."

"You're right, I didn't!" he replied heatedly. "I should have figured it out sooner. I should have stopped him. I had to be here to finish this, otherwise, I wouldn't be able to live with myself or move on with my life."

"You are not responsible for the actions of others," Tempe explained kindly.

Ryan looked over and said, "Please tell me someone recorded that."

Tempe blew out a breath and closed her eyes while everyone enjoyed a chuckle at her expense. When Tempe opened her eyes, Nova was standing in front of her. Tempe took in her disheveled appearance, and commented, "You look like you've had a hard day."

"As do you. Lord River and Alena levied a joint attack on me. I might start training with you to learn how to better fight the fae," Nova replied with composure.

Tempe looked at the man standing behind Nova. "So, Eli, why are you here and not with your pregnant wife?"

"Remember the siren that captured you and Ryan?" he asked. She nodded her head and he continued, "We still don't know who that is. Brook is protecting the house and I'm here in case someone needs to fight a siren."

Loane finished her check of Tempe's mind and said, "You will be unsteady on your feet for the next couple of days. Take it easy and I recommend you not fly home until Friday."

When Tempe balked, Loane smiled and said, "Child, a mental assault takes longer to heal than a physical one does. Besides, Ryan and Bryce have never been in Marrakech and I think they will enjoy the vacation." Then she opened her mind to Tempe and offered, *I know you are mad at Bryce for going with you to Brimstone, but it was his presence that kept you from falling completely into the minds of the treemen.*

Tempe looked up at her aunt and growled. Loane smiled serenely and walked away.

Chapter 21

Since the logistics of getting everyone back where they belonged required someone had to wait for a plane, Loane, Eli, Ryan, Landon, Bryce and Tempe did hang out in Marrakech for a few days, along with some of the wizards. Those who had entered the country with passports needed to leave the same way and some of the others stayed to offer protection.

Their first day resting in Marrakech, Loane and Tempe met for a private breakfast. Katell and Jocosa had flown out with the first wave. Bryce helped Tempe get to the restaurant and then he left them. They ate and talked about the old days for a while.

Finally, Loane suggested, "Why don't you ask me the question you want to ask?"

"I do that to people sometimes," Tempe smirked. "It's rather irritating to have it done to me."

She took a deep breath, realized she didn't have the guts to ask the real question, so she commented, "I noticed Theron recognized you."

Loane looked bemused. "Do you think you are the only person besides Rayna to have had a fae lover?"

Tempe almost choked on her food, "You and Theron? A telepath/empath hooked up with the master of the hunt?"

"Yes, he was exciting and new. And not to put too fine a point on it, he was an excellent lover." Loane smiled.

Tempe smirked, Loane might be her aunt, but Tempe was one hundred years older than her, as she shook her head. "So, do I get to hear this tale of love and romance? I'm also curious as to how you managed that without my knowing about it."

"No child, you do not, maybe one day, but today is not that today," Loane said serenely.

Tempe laughed and changed subjects. "Do you know of anything that would cause a lot of shifter females to get pregnant at the same time?"

"Yes, Twin solar and lunar eclipses. The last time it happened was back when Rayna was with Ellwood and you were with Ridge, living in the Farseen. It was when Katell, Jocosa, and I were born to your grandmother, and when Rayna birthed Saffron, Fauna, and Clare. You had a child of your own during the same time."

Tempe coughed as her food went down the wrong way, but Loane continued without seeming to notice. "There was a twin solar eclipse in the Farseen and the Seen. Fourteen days later there was a twin lunar eclipse in the Farseen and the Seen. It created a mystic convergence that made shifter females more fertile and it even allowed many moon-called females to carry their babies to term without a birthing bond. It lasted almost a year. I suspect you and Rayna didn't remember because you were both living in the Farseen. I've always known I was born during that time."

Tempe pulled out her cell phone and searched the Internet. Sure enough, there had been a solar eclipse on April eighth and fourteen days later a lunar eclipse on April twenty-fourth. She would have to check with the Farseen, but she suspected it was the answer.

They finished breakfast and met up with the guys at Menara Gardens for a lovely walk. After a few minutes of leaning heavily on Bryce and watching her feet to make sure they were where she thought they were, Tempe found a nice place to sit and people-watch while the others continued their walk.

When the others left Landon, came over and sat beside Tempe. She looked up, startled. "You didn't want to walk around the gardens?"

"I wanted to talk to you," he replied. After a few minutes of watching people walk by he asked, "How old is Sage?"

"She'll be seventeen in a week and a half," Tempe replied gently.

He watched a couple walk by hand in hand and sighed, "I was afraid of that." He blushed but continued, "When we first arrived at Half Acre I didn't think about it. Eventually, as I started being me again, I realized she was much younger than I thought. I am a little amazed no one in your family told me to back off."

Tempe opened her mouth to speak but he talked right over the powerful shifter. "It's okay, she's safe with me and I'll keep my distance for now. But just so we're clear, she completes me. I know that sounds sappy, but she does. When Sage isn't around I feel a void, when she is with me, I feel whole. I'll never do anything to hurt her. I don't think I could. I'll wait until she's older and then we'll see if she'll have me."

He stood up and walked off while Tempe sat in wonder.

Her sixteen-year-old kid sister has found her true love. Not just her soul mate, her twin flame. Tempe had opened her mind enough to realize that. She doubted they even realized what they had. Give Sage another handful of years and she will be able to be with Landon and be extremely happy.

Good thing she had Bryce, otherwise, she would be jealous.

The second morning of their forced vacation, Eli came down the steps looking edgy, tense and just plain annoyed. He had been that way since the fighting stopped. Tempe smiled and winked at Landon who was sitting with her having a cup of tea.

"Eli, how are you?"

"Fine," he growled. He looked over and said, "Sorry, I know it's silly, but I feel like I should be with Delaney. It's only four more days before we fly out. That's a full week before her due date. I just feel like I need to be there. I'm going for a walk to try and burn off my tension."

"I don't think you have time," Tempe commented.

"I have four days," Eli grumbled.

"Well, I thought Delaney might want to have you back home. I booked you on a commercial flight. It takes off in three hours. You're flying with Loane to Newark and one of the alpha planes will be standing by there to take you back to Tennessee." Tempe made a show of looking at the ticket and said, "Of course, if you would rather take a walk, perhaps Landon or Ryan would like your ticket."

Eli grabbed the ticket, hugged his sister, and ran up the stairs to his room, almost knocking Bryce down in his haste.

"I guess you got the ticket for Eli," Bryce commented as he sat down and looked at the tea with a grim expression. A waiter came over with a pot of coffee and Bryce's face was transformed to an expression of joy as the waiter filled his cup and left him the pot.

After just a few minutes Eli and Loane came down the stairs together. He was carrying his and Loane's suitcases. After some quick goodbyes they left for the airport.

As he walked out Tempe murmured, "I hope he left his weapons with Ryan. They'll never let him on a commercial flight with them."

"He did. He came barging into my room and threw them on the bed," Ryan, bleary eyed and not quite awake, grumbled as he sat down and poured himself a cup of tea.

They made plans for more sightseeing while they ate breakfast.

Betrayed

On forced vacation day three, Murdoch was still dealing with customs to return Citlali's body to the States, along with the other dead. Odelia, Bianca and Abbie stayed to help him. Once the paperwork was done, showing they died in a cave-in at a ruin in the mountains, Nova had a plane on standby to take the remaining wizards back to the states.

Tempe walked slowly down to the lobby and saw Odelia sitting alone, looking miserable. Tempe carefully made her way over to the wizard, mindful of her legs and feet to make sure she didn't stumble. Loane was right. A telepathic attack leaves your brain and limbs a bit out of sync for a while.

Tempe sat down next to Odelia and said without preamble, "I'm sorry about Adelia."

"And I'm sorry about Clare." She shook her head. "I can't believe I didn't notice anything," she laughed bitterly. "Oh, I noticed I was out of the loop, but I didn't have a clue why. Right before I joined the wizards and shifters for the battle, Kaisho told me everything. I yelled, screamed, and even called him a liar. Kaisho, Rayna and I confronted Adelia. You know, she didn't even try to lie to us. She admitted it all. She was jealous. Can you believe that? She was jealous because I was stronger than her. How idiotic is that?"

Tempe managed a sad smile. "It's basically the same thing Clare said to me."

Odelia looked over at the powerful shifter, shocked. "You've got to be kidding."

"No, I'm not."

She glanced at Tempe under her lashes and said, "Rayna killed Adelia. I was going to do it, I thought it was my job to do, but she said she didn't want me to live with that."

"Rayna was right," Tempe replied tightly.

"Adelia was dead before the battle even started. I heard you somehow contacted the alphas and said you needed Adelia alive, but it was already too late," she said.

Tempe nodded. One of the first things she heard when the fighting was over was Adelia had already been killed and none of the captured Shadowed had a clue about the Brimstone dimension.

They sat in silence for a few minutes and Odelia asked, "Even Lord River said he was jealous of your father. Did all of the Shadowed feel insecure or weak?"

"I don't know. They were strong enough to seriously kick our butts a few times. And, at a minimum, there is still a siren out there we haven't identified and don't know how to find." Tempe chewed her bottom lip.

"Maybe one of the fallen Shadowed was the siren," she offered.

"I'm not that lucky," Tempe replied. She didn't want to say the words out loud or heap more burdens on Odelia, but she was pretty sure someone other than Lord River was the power behind the Shadowed. River was, in the opinion of many, the weakest of the realm lords.

All of the realm lords pack a powerful magical punch, but it was generally agreed they ranked strongest to weakest as Ellwood, Elros, Sky, Leaf, and finally, River. Some people flipped Sky and Leaf in the order but most of the warriors agreed Ellwood was the most dangerous and River was the least dangerous. Of course, being the least dangerous realm lord is a lot like being a weak category five hurricane, still deadly.

*****

The night before they flew out, Tempe stood on the balcony off their bedroom, taking in the view. Bryce joined her. "When are we going to have our argument about my ignoring your orders to leave when we were taking the treeman to safety?"

Tempe smirked, "I was sort of saving that until my limbs obeyed my mind again and I wanted to talk to Rayna, first. I want to know how she phrased her order to allow you to ignore mine. It was masterfully done."

"Yes, your mother is intelligent." He leaned on the wall.

"Are you going to tell me the order the sovereign gave you?" She continued to look out over the city.

"I'm not sure I should." Bryce confessed, "You might be able to find a way around the order."

She turned from the cityscape and looked up into his eyes and whispered, "I was angry when you ignored my order."

"Tempe, I knew you were angry. Ryan and Murdoch knew you were angry. I wouldn't be surprised if everyone within one hundred miles who possess even a small pinch of empathy felt your anger," he shook his head. "I just wanted to go with you, to keep you safe. It turns out you did need me."

"Did Loane tell you?" she asked surprised.

"Yes, she thought I should know," Bryce replied with a small grin.

"We've been through this before. You can't always go where I'm going," she stated firmly.

"True and I don't usually tag along," he blew air out between his teeth. "I hate watching you leave for this mission or that mission, but I normally keep my concerns to myself. But this time I was here. There is no way I will let you go without me if I think I can help you. I left you and Raven with Celeborn and joined the fighting because I knew I would be more useful fighting. But I will not go be safe for no other reason than you want me to be safe."

Tempe heard the truth in his voice. She took a deep breath and said, "I understand."

She snuggled into his arms, kissed him and asked one more time, "What was Mother's order?"

Bryce laughed and kissed her on the forehead. "Her order was, I can disobey any order from any alpha if the order is issued simply to keep me safe while there is still work for me to do."

"What?" Tempe stood there, dumbfounded. Every alpha knew that order. It was the order all healers, telepaths and empaths are given by the sovereign on the day they are ranked in the alpha clan. She had begged Rayna not to give the order to Ryan, but Rayna told her it would be a disservice to him. That she gave the order to Bryce means both of them can disobey her if they think she gave an order just to keep them safe. The problem with that order is the person who receives the order, in this case Bryce, decides on the intent of the alpha giving the order.

Tempe shook her head, "Don't worry. There is no way for any alpha to override that order, until a new sovereign is selected. Even then, the new sovereign normally reaffirms it to the ones who received it. Did Rayna explain who normally gets that order?"

"Yes, telepaths, empaths and healers."

"Currently Loane, Jocosa, Katell, Serenity, Ryan, and you are under that order." Tempe replied.

Bryce asked, "How about you?"

"Yes, me, too, but only Rayna can give me an order. And for the record, she has never ordered me out of danger just to keep me safe. I doubt she would even consider it. She is blessed with the ability to understand for the safety of many, some must be sacrificed. I understand it, but I find it hard to accept when it's the people I love," she replied. "Did she say why she gave you that order?"

"Yes. She said that she was concerned you would need me, but you would send me away to keep me safe rather than use my skills. This order allows it to be my choice. She gave me the order back around Thanksgiving and this is the first time I've used it."

Tempe hugged him tight and whispered back, "You are without a doubt the most amazing man I've ever known." She spoke louder and added with a smirk, "There are few shifters who would have waited so long before proving they could disobey me."

He laughed, picked her up and carried her to the bed.

172

Betrayed

Chapter 22

They arrived back at Eli's house just before midnight Friday night. Even with a private plane the trip was long, and everyone was tired from being cooped up. Tempe would even go so far as to say they blew past tired and flew into cranky. They had planned to sneak into the house through their bedroom, giving Ryan and Landon a straight shot at their rooms without waking the house.

No such luck.

They walked in from the deck and the guys headed for the door to the hallway. Before they took the ten to twelve steps that would take them to the hallway door, they heard a knock.

Ryan growled and opened the door.

Sage blocked the doorway, smirking. "You thought you would sneak in without my knowing?"

"We were hoping," Ryan admitted. "We're drained. It was a long flight and we just want to go to bed."

"Okay," she said with a smile. She hugged all four of them before walking down the hall with the boys. She turned left into the room she shared with Star, Ryan turned right into his room and Landon went upstairs to his room.

Bryce and Tempe dropped their suitcases and fell on top of the comforter. When next they opened their eyes the sun was shining and they had managed to get under the covers at some point during the night. They showered, dressed and headed downstairs in search of food and caffeine, lots and lots of caffeine.

Star and Sage were on cooking detail while Delaney and Brook sat propped up in chairs with expressions that said they were tired of being pregnant.

"Welcome back. The clan dinner is tonight. Mary's cooking and some of the clan will be going on an overnight run with the full moon."

Delaney ran down the day's events as she searched for a more comfortable position in the chair.

"Sounds good. I'm heading into town to see what state my desk is in." Bryce accepted a cup of coffee and a breakfast sandwich as he left.

"Excellent! Breakfast to go," Kaleb said as he and Joey each grabbed a breakfast sandwich and kept moving.

"We're due at the winery," Joey waved as he closed the door.

"Twelve-hour shift. See you guys tonight." Blake followed them out the door, breakfast sandwich in hand.

Landon entered the kitchen a few minutes later. Unknowingly, he continued the grab and go trend of the morning. He took a sandwich and headed for the door. "I'm opening the restaurant today so I'm heading in to check inventory and such. I've been gone a while."

Sage watched him go in surprise, and then turned back to her cooking. He didn't even speak to her!

"The zoo!" Darnel yelled as the triplets grabbed sandwiches and headed outside.

"You can eat at the picnic table. Do not get in the car with food and open juice boxes," Jeannette ordered. "Eat fast, the Taylor triplets are waiting."

Tempe grinned. The zoo staff would be busy today. The zoo was always more active with shifters around. Predators sense new predators and react accordingly. Prey animals also sense a new predator in the area and become extremely tense. Jeannette, who had worked in a zoo, planned to teach the kids how to walk through the zoo without upsetting the animals or at least how to minimize their impact.

A little while later Tempe sat in the sunroom attempting to reduce the size of her inbox, when Sage walked in and sat. She apparently had taken lessons in waiting from Star because she remained calm while Tempe finished an email. A month ago, Sage would not have waited without trying to catch Tempe's attention. Tempe looked up, "Need something?"

"Advice," she said.

"General advice or do you have a topic in mind?" Tempe asked with a sigh as she leaned back in her chair and stretched her arms.

"Landon. What have I done to make him angry?" Sage asked.

"He's still recovering from the loss of his brother. I'm sure he's still your friend," Tempe replied slowly.

"Friend? You think we're just friends? Tempe, I like Landon, a lot. He helps me center better than Ryan for pity's sake. He makes me feel whole." She looked at the expression on Tempe's face and rolled her eyes. "At what age did you hook up with Ridge? And he was what, almost seven hundred years older than you?"

"Bad relationship example," Tempe snorted. "I enchanted Ridge. He didn't have a choice. By the time I dropped the enchantment we had been together a while. Do you want a guy you had to enchant to get?"

"No, of course not. But we're good friends and he suddenly backed off. I don't understand." Sage groaned and stretched out on the chair in a manner only a teenager can pull off. It looked uncomfortable, but experience had taught Tempe teenagers could contort their bodies around hard furniture in ways adults can only dream of, or, at best, remember vaguely from their own youth.

"Sage you'll turn seventeen next Friday. Landon is eighteen years older than you. Right now, that's a big age difference. Heck, right now that makes you jail bait."

Sage rolled her eyes again.

Tempe shook her head, "When he first arrived at Half Acre all he saw was a strong alpha shifter. He didn't realize your age until later and then he backed off. You may not like it, but it's the right thing for him to do, for now."

She set her face in an expression Tempe knew well from her own youth. The girl was trying to figure out how to get around the age thing. Tempe looked her youngest sister seriously in the eye and said, "Don't do something you will regret or something that will hurt Landon. He's been through a lot and doesn't deserve to be tricked or manipulated into doing something he will regret later, especially if you regret it later. I don't think he's going anywhere anytime soon, unless you push him."

Sage walked off and Tempe wasn't sure if she helped or not. She did remember that age and she did remember how badly she wanted Ridge. Of course, back then girls were considered women as soon as they bled for the first time, and they were normally married at that time. Times change but teenage girls haven't, not really.

Tempe returned to her work, and tried to not think about Sage. When her cell phone blared *We Are Family*, she answered with relief, after checking caller ID. "Hello, Raven."

"Hey sis, come out and go for a drive with me," Raven said as she honked her horn.

Tempe spied the Prius in the driveway. She looked in the kitchen and told Star, "I'm going out with Raven for a while if anyone is looking for me. Be back soon."

"Okay," she responded as she put clean dishes away and reloaded the dishwasher.

Tempe jumped into the passenger seat and off they drove. Raven pulled off at a hiking trail and said, "Let's walk."

After a while Tempe suggested, "Shall we shift and find a nice quiet ledge?"

"No, no shifting," Raven said softly.

Tempe stopped and repeated, "No shifting." She took a calming breath and said, "No shifting because you want to talk or no shifting because you can't."

"Can't," she replied even more softly.

Tempe asked hopefully, "Birthing bond?"

"No." She drew out the word, her voice barely above a whisper.

Tempe did a guppy impression for a few seconds but couldn't manage to speak.

"I know. That's why I'm here. I need your advice," Raven moaned. "Jackson and I have been seeing each other for a couple of years now."

"I thought that was just for the tabloids."

"It made a nice cover, but we married almost a year ago."

"You what?" Tempe eyed her sister like she had sprouted a new head.

"We were waiting to announce until after the last concert date, which was last Friday by the way. We flew back together after the mess in Marrakech. I went to the concert and then we celebrated. I was planning to formally introduce Jackson to Mother this week. It's just like you guys told me. I knew within an hour of conception I was pregnant. Jackson's a wizard, not a shifter, so he thought I was joking... at first. He wanted to tell Mother right then, but I was afraid." She smiled, "He's thrilled about the babies, and so am I, but I want backup when I tell her. Raven held up her hands in submission. "I know. I can fight all day but telling Mother I married without her approval scares me."

"So, you want the one sister who went wild and enchanted her way into her first relationship as your wingman. Are you hoping Rayna will be happy you didn't go that route?" Tempe smirked, "And you're the second sister to evoke the memory of Ridge today."

"Why would Sage... oh my. She likes Landon, huh?" Raven shook her head. "He's too old for her."

"Well, don't say that to her. Speaking as a sister who bucked the system, don't force Sage to prove she can make her decisions without us." Tempe narrowed her eyes on Raven. "Otherwise, you will face Mother alone with your confession."

Raven smirked and bowed with a flourish, "Who am I to cast stones?"

As they walked back to the car Tempe explained about the twin solar and lunar eclipses and how they created a mystic convergence making shifter females fertile.

Mystic convergence? How ridiculous. Raven shook her head and buckled up for the drive back to Eli's.

*****

Raven and Tempe walked into the kitchen and it smelled heavenly. "Fried chicken. I love you," Tempe said as she hugged Mary.

"That's because you don't have to worry about cholesterol," Brandi commented as she entered the house with Adam. The clan had been informed of the sacrifice Adam and Brandi made to expose the Shadowed and had decided Brandi was as good as a member of the clan already. Adam was happy again and pleased about the support they received. Brandi was even able to eat with them as long as she knew the food had been prepared in the house and she knew who had prepared it. No take out for Brandi.

The down side of her half vampire status was if she ever ingests someone else's blood she becomes a full vampire. No one knows the exact amount, so Brandi had always refused to eat anything she didn't prepare herself. She also embraced a vegetarian lifestyle, as no one could tell her if animal meat would finish the conversion or not. She still doesn't eat with clan often but she's coming out of her shell some.

Willow walked over and asked quietly, "Do you think I could spend the night here after the run?"

"I don't see why not, unless..." Tempe looked at Willow and over toward Kaleb. "Are you two planning to hook up tonight?" she asked plainly. The last thing the clan needed was for the teenagers to start getting pregnant.

"No! Well, not like you think. We plan to run together but that's all. I promise." Willow's face turned red.

Everyone ate early and went out to run. The shifters without early morning commitments headed for the mountains and an overnight run. Tempe told Bryce she and Raven were going to talk so they wouldn't be running. He kissed her on the cheek and left with the clan. Since the Cruz kids were under the weather, Wayne had kept them home and Teresa was just going to shift quickly in their house, which is a nice benefit of taking a small animal as her shifter self. Her ferret could roam the house and play. The Taylor triplets were out with the Moreau triplets at a skating rink. Jeannette did an early shift and then took the kids out for some more fun.

Brook and Dwight stayed with Chev in his secure full moon room. As a werewolf, Chev must be secured and under Brook's siren call during the full moon. Until the children were born, Dwight would stay with Brook while she controlled her father's wolf. Once everyone was gone, Brandi, Delaney, Sage, Raven and Tempe remained.

"Raven do you want to talk in my room?"

"No, Sage will figure it out and the others will understand." She took a deep breath, "I married Jackson Green a year ago. I'm pregnant and I haven't told Rayna yet."

"You married Jackson? Cool," Sage said, and then she gushed, "Your babies are going to be gorgeous. Why haven't you told Mom? She loves grandbabies." Sage's eyes widened, and she said, "You mean you didn't talk to her before you married Jackson? Oh, my…"

"What's the big deal?" Brandi asked.

"Mother likes to approve a future son-in-law before the marriage. I don't think she's ever said no but she likes the formal asking permission thing," Sage said quietly.

"She'll get over it," Brandi said.

Raven, Sage and Tempe burst out laughing. After a few seconds during which Brandi and Delaney looked at each other wondering if the alphas had gone crazy, Tempe managed to reply, "You would think so, but Rayna holds a grudge well and for a long time. I'm going with Raven to tell her tomorrow."

"Boy, I'm so happy to be holding a birthing bond right now," Sage said to the room.

Tempe looked toward the door, as did Sage. Tempe sighed, "Mother just arrived. I suspect she felt your pregnancy."

"Starless night," Raven managed to say as she dropped into a chair.

Rayna walked in the door without knocking. She was not happy. Tempe motioned for Brandi and Delaney to leave. They stood up in a near perfect choreographed pregnant female move. Delaney displayed massive bravery by walking, well, waddling since it's the last week of her pregnancy, over to the sovereign, "Hello Rayna. What brings you here?"

"I need to speak with Raven, privately," Rayna said in a tone that was just shy of an order.

This was not going well. Tempest looked at Rayna. "Mother, if your mood forces Delaney or Brandi into early labor Eli will not be pleased, and neither will I."

She stared at her eldest daughter who simply raised an eyebrow. The raised eyebrow kept them from falling into a dominance push. No one moved for a few seconds, and then Brook said, "I've never understood this shifter stuff. I guess it's because I can't shift. Delaney, let's go into the game room and leave the alphas to it."

"Sage, why don't you go with them?" Tempe offered.

Sage looked at the three retreating figures and said, "No, I believe I'm needed here."

"Everyone knows before me? You're pregnant and I don't even know who the father is."

Raven took a deep breath and said, "My husband is the father."

Rayna turned an interesting shade of red. Tempe stepped in and said evenly, "Mother, Raven has been married for a year. I found out today, as did Sage. Raven was on her way to tell you when I asked her to stay for dinner which turned out to be a good thing, otherwise she would have passed you on the road."

Rayna snarled at Tempe. Sage bravely stepped up beside Raven.

Tempe once again raised an eyebrow. "Rayna, do you want to have a go? Wouldn't you rather hear about her child or children? I don't know the details yet and I'm curious."

Rayna took a deep breath and proved her superior diplomatic abilities by saying in a level voice, one without the hint of a snarl or growl, "Yes, I prefer to hear about new grandchildren and apparently my new son-in-law."

Tempe released the breath she had been holding.

Raven smiled and said, "Jackson Green and I were married a year ago."

"Jackson? You married that guy from Waxing Moon, the wizard?" Rayna asked calmly, which was interpreted as a good sign.

"Yes Mother, he's a wizard," Raven replied softly.

"Well, that's acceptable. He's strong and brave. From the reports I read he fought well in the battle outside of Marrakech."

Raven added, "We're having triplets, one male wizard, and a male and female shifter. They should be born in January."

Rayna beamed, two more shifters in the Alpha Clan. Truthfully, the identifying of the species was a little looser than that. The wizard may be able to shift, and the shifters may have some wizard talent. The identification was more of a benchmark as to where their strongest talent lies.

Tempe motioned for Sage and they left the room. As they moved down the hallway Rayna called, "Sage, we need to talk later."

Tempe shrugged her shoulders as Sage's eyes widen.

"What do you think she wants to talk about?" Sage asked quietly.

"You already know," Tempe replied mildly. "I think it would do you good to talk to Mother before she leaves."

"Did it ever help you?" She asked.

Tempe smiled, "I've always considered you to be smarter than I am about some things. Please try to learn from some of my more foolish mistakes. Don't repeat them."

Delaney pounced when they entered the game room. "Is everything okay?"

"Yes, as soon as Rayna knew she had shifter grandchildren she calmed down." Tempe replied.

"That and Tempe." Sage looked at her eldest sister, "I never realized you and Mother were so evenly…"

Tempe shook her head slightly and Sage closed her mouth. A few minutes later Rayna came in with Raven and the talk turned to babies. Before all of the runners returned, Rayna took Sage up to the girls' room for a talk. As soon as they left the room Raven called Jackson.

Tempe looked over, "Where is he?"

"Nova's."

"Well get him over here so mother can look him in the eye." Tempe ordered. "It'll go better here than if the rest of our sisters find out Rayna was blindsided."

She smiled and conveyed the order to Jackson.

As the shifters returned from their runs Tempe threw out a general announcement that Rayna had stopped by and was talking to Sage upstairs. Star and Willow, both smart girls, understood they did not want to walk into the bedroom until they were given the all clear.

Jackson showed up and Raven introduced him as her husband. Congratulations were still being expressed when Rayna and Sage came downstairs. They both seemed happy which made Tempe just a little concerned. She had fully expected Sage to be angry or heartbreakingly cheerful to hide her sadness.

Rayna hugged Jackson and then looked around the room and said, "Have you told them the rest of the news?"

"No," Raven replied. "You may have the honors."

Tempe smiled. Allowing Rayna to make the announcement would make Eli's clan, and the other alphas when they heard, think Rayna had known for some time. And the other alphas would hear about it, even if Tempe had to spread the word herself.

"Raven and Jackson are going to have triplets, two boys and a girl." Another round of congratulations was offered up as everyone closed in on the food Delaney laid out.

Tempe watched as Rayna talked to most of the clan members. She has always been able to do that. She was a great politician. She managed to sit next to Landon for a few minutes. At first he seemed nervous and Tempe was going to go rescue him but Sage looked over and shook her head. When Rayna left Landon's side he looked relaxed. Tempe was impressed.

Eli offered Rayna a room for the night, which she accepted. When the rest of the clan went home it was late and those staying at Eli's went to bed.

Bryce shut the door as they entered their sound proof bedroom and said, "Whew. That was a somewhat more eventful clan dinner then we normally have."

Tempe smiled, hugged him and commented, "You have no idea." There was a knock at the door. She looked at the door and then at Bryce, "Do you think they will go away if we ignore them?"

"Your family? Just go away? I doubt it." Bryce opened the door.

Sage once again blocked the doorway.

"Bryce, we need a minute please," Tempe said.

"Sure thing," Bryce replied as he walked down the hallway.

Sage shut the door as she entered the room. Tempe shook her head, "Sage, we don't need to have this conversation."

"Tempe, are you stronger than mother?" Sage asked.

"I just said…"

"Yes, Tempe, I heard you. But it might explain something." Sage shrugged.

Tempe looked over in concern and asked, "What?"

"Anytime you and Mother disagree I don't follow orders until I know what you want." Sage said softly. "So far it hasn't been an issue because I've been too young to be given big orders."

"Starless night," Tempe sat down on the fainting couch and for the first time understood its name. She looked at the floor for a minute and asked, "Did you tell mother this?"

"No!" Sage replied, sporting the obligatory are-you-crazy look for such a foolish question.

"Please don't." Tempe closed her eyes to center her thoughts before looking at her youngest sister. "For the past few centuries, Rayna and I have had an unspoken agreement. She doesn't order me. She suggests, I recommend, we discuss, we agree, and then I go do. It takes a certain kind of person to be the sovereign, someone who can negotiate, more so now than in the past. The sovereign is a politician. I'm a general. Do you understand the difference?"

"I… I think so," Sage said but her eyes were confused.

Tempe took a deep breath and explained, "I could easily be a realm lord. They are dictators, ordering everyone around. I can do that. I have a hard time letting anyone else go into battle while I stay behind. Can you see me sending everyone in to fight while I stay back to negotiate the peace? I can't."

"Tempe, I understand. I do, but I don't know where that leaves me."

"I do." Smiling, she ordered, "Until such time as you are ranked in the alpha clan, if the sovereign and her second disagree on a task, you are to obey the sovereign. Do you understand?"

Sage laughed but said the words that are binding to shifters, "Your word is law."

"After you're ranked on your birthday we might have this discussion again. Once ranked, these types of orders must be reissued," Tempe smiled and added, "Unless you outrank me."

Yeah, that's gonna happen, Sage smirked and asked, "I wonder if any alpha has ever ordered another alpha to disagree with them?"

Ignoring the question, Tempe asked, "Can you keep this from everyone, including Ryan and Rayna?"

"I think so. I've been closing my mind tighter."

"Speaking of birthdays, you turn seventeen next Friday. What do you want?"

Sage smiled, "I would like to not be in a birthing bond for a while."

"That seems fair, but problematic," Tempe replied, and then she went on to explain about the twin solar and lunar eclipses and the increase in shifter births.

"Figures it would happen when I'm available for holding birthing bonds," Sage whined.

"Before you leave, I have a question. If it's too personal, then you don't have to answer." They were both still sitting on the fainting couch and Tempe faced Sage. "What happened with you and Rayna? I expected you to be angry or hurt and you weren't."

Sage grinned, "She sort of said the same thing you did, but she was much clearer. She said if I pushed Landon he would run away to protect me because of the age thing and if I enchanted him he would leave as soon as I released the enchantment because I had trapped him. She also explained a little about the turbulence you and Ridge unleashed in the Farseen when you released his enchantment. I don't think I want to go through that. Also, Mother said she approved of Landon. I guess I'm forced to wait for my turn at love," Sage admitted. "I would rather have Landon as just a friend for now if anything more would hurt him."

"Yet another example of why Rayna is an excellent sovereign."

Sage left, and Tempe sent a text message to Bryce. He wasn't far because with the bedroom door open, she could hear his cell phone playing *Green-Eyed Lady*. He walked down the hallway and shut the door.

"How's Sage?" Bryce asked.

"She's going through a little something, but she'll be fine," Tempe replied.

"Interesting, so is Landon. On the plus side, Rayna seems to like him."

Tempe was still sitting on the fainting couch, which just seemed more and more appropriate, as she asked, "Landon talked to you?"

"Just now," Bryce confirmed. "When I left the room, Landon was coming up the stairs and he asked if we could talk. He had a lot of questions about Rayna and the alpha clan. He wanted to make sure he understood what Rayna had said to him."

Tempe stopped herself from asking for specifics. "I think we need to stop talking about Sage, Landon and Rayna. We should be rejoicing in the fact that we're back home."

Bryce pulled her off the fainting couch and onto the bed, "You have excellent good sense, just like your mother."

Chapter 23

Sunday, the Smoky Mountain clan woke to a light steady rain, the kind of rain that can last for days if the conditions are right. Tempe walked into the kitchen and stopped short as Landon, Joey, Kaleb and Ryan made breakfast: bacon, sausage, and pancakes for a crowd. There was a pot of tea ready and coffee was brewing.

Tempe leaned on the doorframe and grinned, "You boys are going to make some women happy one day."

Ryan matched her grin. "We were thinking if we cooked, someone else would clean."

Tempe laughed. With so many living in Eli's house, new rules for peaceful cohabitation had been established. One being if you cooked you didn't have to clean up. The boys have been doing a lot of cleaning lately.

Blake dragged his body in the house and plopped down at the kitchen bar. "A little food before bed would be nice," he said, hopefully.

"Another twenty-four-hour shift?" Tempe asked the future doctor. He had spent his summer working as an emergency medical responder. She handed over the plate Kaleb had just given her.

"Yep," Blake dove into the plate of pancakes and sausage. He finished about the time Tempe accepted another plate. Blake threw a "thanks" to the room and crawled up the stairs to sleep. Bryce passed him on the stairs and came in search of coffee. Star, Sage, and Willow were right behind him.

"Do the guys always fix breakfast?" Willow asked, impressed.

"No," Sage chuckled.

"Aw, now why did you have to go and tell the truth?" Kaleb pouted as he handed Willow a plate of food. "I was hoping to impress her with my kitchen skills."

"Kitchen skills," Joey snorted. "Kitchen skills you seriously lack." He handed Kaleb another two plates for Sage and Star before continuing. "Notice we only allow him to hand out the food. He can't even plate the meal without dropping or spilling."

"Hey, I'm not that bad," Kaleb's playful pout turned into a frown.

"Yes, you are," Ryan laughed. "Sorry man, but you burn boiling water."

Once fed, Tempe offered to clean up the kitchen. Dwight and Bryce helped. Once the kitchen was cleaned, Bryce went into work to get a jump on a couple of upcoming trials. Tempe went to her usual place in the sunroom, working on her laptop.

After she finished the bulk of her catch-up work, she decided to go ahead and prepare the casseroles for tonight's dinner. Since they had the clan dinner last night she planned to make dinner for whoever was around. She was slicing veggies when she felt the way open.

Ryan ran into the kitchen and said, "Sage is shielding the house."

Eli walked in the kitchen behind Ryan as Tempe said, "Let's go see who opened a way into your territory."

They walked outside as Tempe prepared to teleport the three of them when Bryce drove up. "Hurry," Ryan called. "We're teleporting to the cave. Someone opened a way."

"I can't teleport three other people. I'm not that strong," Tempe retorted.

Ryan said, "I'll meet you there." He jumped over the side of the railing, shifted to his eagle and flew while Tempe teleported the others.

Sitting on the clan's thinking rock was an adult male fae who looked a lot like Ridge but had green eyes. He was already soaked from the rain, but it didn't seem to bother him. He looked up and said, "Lady Tempest, it was not my intention to arrive unannounced, but Lady Temperance could not contact you and the matter is urgent."

Ryan shifted as he landed beside Tempe.

"Layton, you have never been interested in visiting the Seen. What brings you here?" Tempe asked.

"Queen Weindrych chose me as one of her competitors. I will fight Kairav and Leitha. The winner becomes the new Water Lord of the Western Realm," he explained miserably. "I need a private place to practice and I hoped I could prepare in the Seen with you."

Tempe's heart fell. She didn't say anything as the enormity of Layton's statement hit her.

"Why would you come to Tempe for help?" Ryan asked.

"Ryan, this is not the time," Bryce sighed.

Ryan stared at Bryce. Tempe nodded for Bryce to explain since her mouth still wouldn't work.

"Layton, this is Eli, the prif of my clan, and one of Rayna's sons. And this is Ryan, third in the alpha clan. Layton is the son of Lady

Tempest and Ridge." Bryce calmly performed the polite introduction as if this wasn't a shock to the shifters. "It's nice to see you again Layton, but it doesn't sound like this is a friendly visit."

Under Ryan's shocked stare, Tempe got her voice back. "When a realm lord dies, his replacement is determined by contest. The queen of the realm selects three competitors and they fight to the death. The winner becomes the new realm lord."

No one said anything as the rain fell harder and every inch of them was thoroughly soaked. Finally, Eli, who knew about Tempe's fae son but never expected to meet him, said, "Layton, why don't we return to my house and get dry. Then you and Tempe can talk."

They started the hike back and Bryce motioned to Ryan, "Will you run ahead and find some dry clothes for Layton?"

Ryan shifted and flew. He should have thought of that himself. He would give everyone in the house fair warning about the visitor.

By the time the others arrived, Ryan and Dwight, Brook's husband, sat at the kitchen table. No one else was around. Ryan handed Layton some dry clothes and pointed down the hallway, "These should fit but they might be a bit baggie. There's a bathroom on the left."

When Layton returned to the kitchen Ryan was leaning on the door jam in what was probably supposed to be a laid-back manner, but it was obvious he was a guard. Layton smothered his smile at the young shifter's actions and sat down at the kitchen table.

Eli, Bryce and Tempe returned to the kitchen together. Tempe commented, "We might as well have a cup of tea and sit in the kitchen."

She passed out mugs of tea and continued talking, "Layton, why would the Central Realm pick you? You've never participated in court life."

"I don't know. I assumed she knew who I was, but I was surprised when Queen Weindrych appeared in my house. Between you, Ridge, Rayna, and Ellwood, most of the ruling fae know who I am. It's no secret. What was a surprise, was her knowledge. She knows I'm able to shift and not moon-called. She said my unique gifts will make me an excellent realm lord since we are once again 'harmonizing with the Seen', her words. I also suspect she thinks I will be able to work with Rayna better than most since I'm family." Layton took a deep breath, "You know the rules. If I refuse to fight, she will kill my descendants. I will fight and, win or lose, Nolween and the kids are safe."

"You have kids. Tempe's a grandmother?" Ryan commented mostly to himself, confusion etched his face.

"Ryan, I am many times a great-grandmother, which you well know. Please be quiet and deal with my age later," Tempe replied coolly before turning back to her son. "Who's with Nolween and the boys now?"

"Father came as soon as the competitors were announced. Her father is there as well."

"That makes Ridge a father and grandfather too," Ryan said in wonder.

"Ryan, I'm fast losing patience," Tempe warned.

"Sorry, I just didn't think..." Ryan stopped in mid-sentence when Bryce thumped him on the head. Ryan looked at Bryce in shock as Ryan outranked him. Bryce gave Ryan his best get-your-act-together look, which Ryan took in the spirit in which it was given, counsel, not an order. Ryan had to reign in his comments before he angered Tempe.

Tempe took a deep breath, scowled at Ryan, and turned back to Layton, "Would your family be safer here?"

"No. As long as I agree to compete, no one would dare go near them or threaten them. The queens kill anyone who does. They are safe."

"Okay, when's the competition?" she asked, dreading the answer.

"Thirteen sunrises, that will be Friday the twenty-sixth of this moon cycle on your calendar," Layton replied.

"Eli, may I help Layton train here, in your territory?" Tempe asked formally.

"Of course, what equipment does he need?"

"No equipment. It's combat with no weapons of any kind, but he can use any magic he can access," Tempe replied. "He needs to practice with as many types of magic coming at him as possible."

"I'll help," Ryan said.

Tempe glared at her nephew and he blushed. "I'm sorry, Tempe. I just never thought about you having a child older than the triplets. I'm over it. You know I can help with his training."

"Yes, you would be helpful," she agreed. Turning back to Layton she forced her voice to be steady, "You said the other competitors were Leitha and Kairav?"

"Yes," he replied.

"If I had thought about it I would have expected both Kanja and Kairav. Leitha is also an obvious choice." To the shifters in the room she said, "Kanja and Kairav are brothers and both are strong and ambitious within the court."

"Both wanted to fight but the queen only wanted one of them. They dueled in contest and Kanja lost. His ashes were cast to the waters right before I came here," Layton said quietly.

"Leitha is the one I would be the most concerned about. She's an excellent warrior," Tempe said.

Layton laughed, "That's the first time, in a long time, you and Father have agreed. He said the same thing."

Tempe smiled.

"You may stay at the cabin or here. At the cabin you get privacy but no central heat and air conditioning or running water. Here you get the latter but not the former," Eli explained. Bryce left the room as soon as Eli made the offer.

"Which will be the least trouble for you?" Layton asked. "On the plus side, you won't have to worry about any fae visiting to disturb Star. Only Theron or Kainda, serving as the queen's messengers, will be allowed in your territory with me here, except for those training me, of course."

"Is there any fae you want with you, for training?" Tempe asked.

"No. I am well versed in fae fighting techniques and workout with fae daily. I still practice the techniques you taught me but working out with shifters might be the best thing for me." He managed a smile, "I'm hoping it gives me an edge."

Bryce returned with Dwight and the women as Tempe promised, "As soon as I finish prepping the casserole, we'll have our first sparring session."

"I can finish the dinner, Tempe. I think you'll have other things on your mind and you tend to burn the bread when you aren't focused on cooking." Sage walked up to Layton, hugged him and said, "It's nice to finally meet you. I'm Sage, Rayna's youngest."

Layton was shocked by the hug. No female in a fae court would embrace a male – even a relative - if they didn't know each other well.

Star grinned, "Well met Layton, and don't worry, Sage hugs everyone. How are the boys?"

"Wait! You two know Layton and you know who he is?" Ryan asked.

"Of course," Star replied. "I've watched Breton and Delton, his youngest twins, numerous times. Lady Nolween is from the Central Realm and they visit her family frequently."

"Didn't you have to pass a test on the family tree?" Sage asked. "I did."

"I've focused his training on his powers and not the family stuff," Tempe explained.

"Well, somebody send me the info and I'll read it for myself," Ryan said in disgust, most unhappy at being blindsided.

Bryce introduced Delaney, Brook and Dwight. Everyone embraced the concept Tempe had a kid with Ridge and she had to admit to herself that for once she did the right thing. Taking Bryce to the Farseen a while back and introducing him to her son and his family had been a good choice. Bryce was handling everything pretty well considering he was going to have to live with the walking, talking reminder of Ridge for a while. Tempe just hoped Layton would be alive on the twenty-seventh to continue to be a reminder.

Tempest called Rayna and explained what was going on, and then mother and son got down to business. Layton and Tempe spent the afternoon checking out his fighting skills in what remained a heavy rain. Ryan, Sage and even Star helped, but while Ryan and Star shifted, Layton didn't.

After a fast-paced fight between the two of them, Ryan dropped to the soaked ground to rest, which would have been irritating if he had a dry spot on him, and asked, "What shape do you take?"

"I can take the form of most any dragon of the Farseen." Layton dropped beside Ryan and leaned on a tree.

Ryan tilted his head and verified, "Multiple dragons?"

"Yes, white, silver, red, green, gold, brass, blue and black. Although most believe I only take a black dragon form. It's the form I take when others are around."

"And you can use any magic you can call, right?"

"Yes," Layton frowned. He didn't understand where the conversation was going.

"Excellent," Ryan looked over at Tempe. Tempe's grin matched his.

"When we, as shifters, take a dragon form we have access to the magic they have, even if we can't use that same magic in human form," Tempe said.

"You mean I could..." a grin spread across his face, "Well, that's something to consider."

Sage smiled, "When we finish today's workout, I'll bring down all the research on dragons. Layton will need to read through it."

Tempe leaned back on a tree of her own – thoroughly soaked – and smiled. It would be nice to have a surprise prepped and ready. "Okay, we break for today. We'll want to get dry before dinner." Tempe stood and headed back to the main house.

Layton met the rest of the folks staying at Eli's when they sat down to dinner. Afterwards, he joined Tempe in her sound proof bedroom to start the dragon research. After a couple hours of determining which skills and dragons would serve him the best, he closed the folder and leaned back in the chair.

"Tempest, I'm the one who wanted to prepare with you. Ridge didn't suggest it," Layton smiled, "I've heard Father and Bryce do not like each other. I just wanted you to know Ridge didn't use this competition to send me here to bait Bryce."

"I never thought he did. Ridge would do a lot to bait Bryce, but he wouldn't use you to do it." Tempe smiled, "Ridge is a good father. He would never use you. Speaking of fathers, what did mine say?"

"Considering I left the Northern Realm because I refused to be part of the court, Lord Ellwood is amused that I'm now forced to take up the mantle of realm lord, or die trying," he replied, coolly.

"Sounds about right."

"In addition to all the realms sending numerous representatives, I am allowed to invite my family and three guests. You, of course, are invited as my mother. I would like to invite Bryce as one of my three guests."

"Are you sure? That might be baiting Ridge."

"Father suggested it. He knew Bryce would dislike you sitting close to him while your son competes to the death." He grinned, "Either Ridge secretly likes Bryce or he's setting Bryce up to owe him a favor."

Tempe shook her head and leaned back on the fainting couch. "Either way, if you invite Bryce he will attend, and I would appreciate having Bryce with me."

As he stood to leave Layton added, "Breton and Delton are both showing some signs of shifter talent."

Tempe looked up in surprise and he continued, "Nolween knows what to look for. If I'm not around, she will contact you."

"Layton…"

"Mother, I need to get this said. In two weeks I will either be dead or a realm lord. My two youngest show signs of shifter talent and I have prepared them as best I could. If I die, they will need you," Layton said sharply. "Orton and Kelton are adults and able to care for themselves and neither shift. My one request is if the boys shift and Nolween wants to be with them, please let her live in the Seen with them while they learn to control the shift."

Tempe nodded, "Of course."

Layton left a few minutes later. She was still lying on the fainting couch when Bryce entered.

"Did you faint or are you relaxing?" Bryce asked.

"Neither. Breton and Delton both are showing shifter talents. If Layton dies in the competition, I'll need to train the boys." She looked up at Bryce and her voice cracked as she said, "My first born may die because of stupid fae politics."

"Your first born may become a realm lord because of fae politics," Bryce responded as he joined her on the fainting couch and gathered her in his arms.

"It is bizarre, isn't it?" Tempe asked as she snuggled into him. "It's not just me. I was born in the Northern Realm. My only fae offspring left the Northern Realm and the Central Realm to get away from fae court life and now he's being forced to compete for the position of Water Lord of the Western Realm."

"It's bizarre," Bryce agreed.

"What do you think it means?" Tempe asked softly. "There has never been a realm lord who wasn't a pureblood. Before I chose to move back to the Seen when Rayna and Ellwood broke their vows, many fae were concerned I might one day become the Forest Lord of the Northern Realm. Their main concern was I wasn't a full-blood."

"I don't have a clue. Maybe the queen wants someone ruling the realm with a broad range of knowledge and contacts, as she told Layton."

"Or maybe Layton is a throw-away, someone the queen thinks looks good on paper but will be an easy kill for the queen's true choice," Tempe whispered. Bryce pulled her tightly into his arms and they sat like that for a while.

The next morning, Tempe distributed a training schedule that made everyone involved groan. It was a good schedule. Most of the alphas, male and female, were scheduled to spar with Layton. Since he didn't know most of them, or all of their abilities, he got a quick education in fast adaptive maneuvers. His control over his various dragons was impressive.

Tempe hoped it would be enough.

Chapter 24

Eli cursed as he shuffled papers. He had worked from home the past few days. Delaney was due any day now, was in fact past due, and he was nervous as a long-tailed cat in a room full of rocking chairs.An old expression, but a valid one. Any noise, no matter how loud or soft, and Eli jumped to check on Delaney. He knew he wasn't helping. He wasn't even sure whom he made more nervous, Delaney or Dwight.

As Dwight watched his prif get more and more nervous over Delaney's pregnancy, Dwight started fussing over Brook's pregnancy. Dwight and Brook were living at Eli's until their babies were born. Dwight had rented a one-room apartment and Chev and Brook's place was a small two bedroom. They were currently looking for a place that would house the parents, babies and grandfather.

Jeff stopped by to check on both women every day on his way to work. They were both doing fine, and he was sure both women would deliver soon.

Before Jeff left Dwight asked, "Is there anything I need to prepare for?"

"Yes," Jeff said with a smile. "Once labor starts, your main function is to agree with your wife and let her vent on you." He patted Dwight on the shoulder and walked out of the house.

Sage walked downstairs to a course of "Happy Birthday". The teenagers were planning to go out for pizza and a movie later to celebrate.

After breakfast, the regular cast of trainees came into the sunroom to grab Tempe for their daily training session.

"Sage, you're off training today," Tempe said as she closed her laptop.

"What? Why?" she asked.

Tempe inclined her head toward the kitchen where Delaney and Brook were. "I have a feeling they might need you soon and Eli is driving them crazy. Run interference for them."

She rolled her eyes, "Eli needs to get a grip."

"Sage, he lost his first wife and child during labor. He's nervous. Cut him some slack," Tempe whispered in irritation.

"Okay, baby patrol. I'm on it," she saluted and walked into the kitchen.

After a hard four-hour workout, they returned hungry and ready for lunch. As they entered the kitchen, Delaney expressed a surprised, "Oh."

Tempe walked into the kitchen, saw her, and said unnecessarily, "Your water broke, do you know how far apart the labor pains are?"

"I haven't felt any," she said in a small voice.

"Neither have I," Sage answered as she walked into the kitchen from the sunroom where she had been reading.

"Okay," Tempe drew out the word. "You get Delaney comfortable in the bedroom and I'll call Jeff."

Before Tempe finished the sentence, Sage had started Delaney toward the stairs saying, "It's no big deal. Sometimes the water breaks before labor starts."

Eli came into the kitchen at a dead run, "What happened?"

"Delaney's water broke. She and Sage…" Tempe started but Eli was already taking the stairs two at a time. "…Went upstairs." She finished the sentence to the air where Eli had been standing.

She shook her head and prepped food to feed anyone who stopped by. Tempe had already made and frozen lasagna for this day, so she pulled out the nine and a half by eleven containers and started baking. She sent Dwight to the store for bread and salad fixings and the others outside to continue training under Ryan's leadership. No sense wasting training hours.

Jeff showed up a couple of hours later. He and Sage had been texting back and forth. He blew through the house and headed up to Delaney and Eli's room.

Brook walked into the kitchen and said softly, "I'm sorry."

"Sorry, about what?" Tempe questioned over the sounds of tired folks dragging in the house after a good hard workout.

"My water just broke."

Tempe smiled, "It's all good. Let's get you settled and I'll let Jeff know. I'm here, so if nothing else I can deliver the babies. I've done it often enough."

"Star, go find Dwight and bring him to their room. Don't let the lasagna, or the bread, burn. Someone put the salad together," Tempe called over her shoulder as she helped Brook up the stairs.

Just before midnight, Delaney gave birth to Sydney and Rodney Shaw. Eli actually passed out once he verified everyone was healthy and safe. Not to be outdone by her younger sister, just after midnight Brook gave birth to Kayla and Jayla Turner. Dwight scored points by not passing out. Mothers and children were all fine. When Eli passed out he landed on his left hand and broke it. Lucky for him shifters heal fast, but he wasn't able to hold his kids without assistance for the first forty-eight hours.

Tempe passed Sage in the hallway as she was heading to bed. "So, you got to deliver babies for your seventeenth birthday. Sorry you didn't get to go out with your friends."

"It's okay." She yawned, "We're planning to go tomorrow night, or tonight since it's after midnight."

Chapter 25

The day before the realm competition, Layton, his mother, and his guests went to the Farseen. He would spend tonight with his family at his residence. Ryan and Landon, who had spent the most time training with him, joined Bryce as Landon's chosen guests.

Layton opened a way and they came out at the front door of his residence. Nolween and the young twins ran out to greet him.

Ridge joined them and exchanged nods with Bryce. They would never be friends, but at least for this visit, they could be polite.

A few minutes later, Kelton arrived with Orton, who brought his wife and grown triplets. Darious and Landon found common ground as Darious owned several restaurants, while Terrious and Ryan shared an appreciation of all things sports related. Jarvious, a known bard, regaled the family with amusing songs, including a couple detailing some of Tempe's childhood antics. The songs helped to calm the children but didn't do much for the adults, who were thinking about tomorrow's contest.

Later in the day, Lord Ellwood arrived to wish his grandson good hunting. He didn't speak to Tempe, Bryce or even Ridge. When he left, Bryce commented softly, "That's the fourth time in a row Ellwood has seen me and not tried to kill me."

Ridge overheard him and commented, "That probably means he has something truly despicable in the works."

Layton nodded his agreement, as did Orton and Kelton.

As guests of one of the competitors, Bryce, Ryan, and Landon were in a unique position. On penalty of death by the queens' order, no harm can come to the guests. If a hellhound were to drop down in front of the three men every fae in the five realms would have to jump between the men and the hellhound. It was a matter of honor. It would have been the most relaxing visit to the Farseen ever, if Layton weren't about to be in a battle to the death.

As tradition demands, the remaining realm lords stopped by, either to introduce themselves to the competitor or to simply say hello.

When Lord Elros arrived, his wife and eldest daughter were with him, which was not tradition. It took everyone about two seconds to realize Dawn used her influence to get her father to bring her to a location where she could visit with Ryan for a few minutes.

When the Southern Realm left, Terrious clapped Ryan on the shoulder. "Nice choice, but I recommend your first dalliance be with a daughter of the court who isn't so high up the pecking order, especially one who won't attain her majority for a few moons. It's safer if you wish to remain single."

Jarvious smacked the back of Terrious' head and leaned over to look at Ryan. "And that's why he's called Terror. He has at least one girl in every realm and all of their fathers want his hide."

"Not all," Darious grinned. "I'm pretty sure Cypress still thinks Lord Ellwood will force him to exchange vows with Eucalyptus."

"Lord Ellwood wouldn't," Terror growled, before he looked over at Ridge and cringed, "Would he?"

Ridge shook his head, sure he had never been that young. "If you are not looking to exchange vows then you should not chase after proper daughters of any court."

As Ridge walked off Tempe stared at her great-grandson, the one who reminded her of Ridge. "Why would Cypress, who is level headed, expect or want you to exchange vows with his daughter? And why would Lord Ellwood need to force the issue?"

Terror blushed and stared at the ground.

"Terrious! You're too old to still be breaking hearts," Tempe exclaimed.

"Lady Tempest, Terror didn't break her heart. What he did was contribute to the gene pool in the Northern Realm," Jar smothered his laugh.

Tempe turned on Terrious. "You're telling me Lady Eucalyptus is pregnant, has acknowledged you as the father and you haven't come to an agreement with her?"

"And I thought Lord Ellwood was the one with the temper," Terror commented under his breath.

Lady Seotia walked over to stand beside Lady Tempest and glared at her son. "It sounds to me like you did not spend the last three weeks in the Northern Realm working out the agreement, as you were told to do. If I never get to see my grandchild, except in public, you will suffer."

Jar and Dar grabbed Ryan and Landon and headed for the relative safety of the house. Lady Nolween had joined the other women and they saw no reason to be in the line of fire when the three powerful matriarchs lit into Terror.

Kelton turned from the fire as the boys entered the house, "Where's your mother?"

Jar grinned, "The ladies Seotia, Nolween, and Tempest are talking with Terror."

Anger brought a flush to Kelton's face, "Did Eucalyptus reject his proposal?"

Jar dropped his grin and shrugged his shoulders.

Dar winced but answered, "I'm not sure he talked to her."

"What?" Kelton's roar reverberated throughout the room.

"Son, you might want to reign in your anger and go check on Terrious, before the ladies of this family kill him," Layton said mildly.

Kelton nodded to his father and left.

Layton shook his head and looked over at Ridge. "Ter is too much like you, Father."

Ridge raised an eyebrow. "Perhaps, but I suggest we go rescue him. They are probably projecting their fear for you as anger at him." He looked over at Bryce, "You will be of value with Lady Tempest."

Bryce sat his drink down and followed Ridge.

*****

Landon woke up to a buzzing sound. He batted the sound, wishing death to the fly. When he heard a yelp, he opened his eyes and saw a pixie flying circles a couple of inches from his face. He jerked back, banging his head on the headboard.

"Morning, honored guest. I am Itzal. Have you needs prior to first repast?"

"Uh, no, tha..., that is, no." Landon caught himself before thanking the small fae. Man, he needed to wake up. He was in the Farseen. Thank no one was the rule of the day.

Itzal bowed and disappeared.

Landon rubbed his eyes and his newly banged head, while he looked out the window. Everything in the Farseen seemed a bit brighter, but otherwise looked like the Seen, as long as you didn't notice the three moons, especially Corentin. That was one huge ball in the sky. He looked at the Kaveri River and smiled. He watched water nymphs playing something similar to tag with a creature that looked to be a jellyfish, but it flew in and out of the water. Unicorns and centaurs were visible in the open fields and a flock of dragons flew overhead. Okay, not so much like the Seen after all.

He met Darious on the stairs. "Is Terror still among the living?"

"I think so, but if he doesn't work out something with Lady Eucalyptus, the ladies of this family will kill him."

"Doesn't a male fae have any rights to his child?"

"Sure he does, but the female must acknowledge him first. She did, but he didn't move quickly to secure her approval and now she's probably a bit irritated."

"A bit?" Terrious joined them. "You always did have a gift for understatement. And Mother is going to kill me if I don't get this worked out."

"If she does I'll write an ode to you," Jarvious offered from the bottom of the stairs.

Terrious made a grab for him but Ryan interceded, planting himself between the brothers. "Makes no difference to me, but if you get bloody before breakfast your mother and grandmother will go postal. And I don't want to see Tempe, um, Lady Tempest, angry this morning."

Terrious was in the process of reaching around Ryan when he stopped and looked at the shifter, "Postal?"

Landon laughed, "It's a human expression. It means enraged enough to inflict great violence."

"Ah, they would, indeed, go postal." Terrious took off after Jarvious anyway.

The others headed for first meal where everyone tried to keep it light as they ate. Tempe opened a way and the family and honored guests made their way to the killing field of the Western Realm.

"The place is actually called a killing field?" Landon whispered the question to Ryan.

"Seems so."

Jarvious slid between the two, "Yes, any sanctioned to-the-death fight is called a contest and they take place in the realm's killing field." He pointed toward their destination.

"That looks like an arena," Landon exclaimed.

"It is. All sanctioned contests are attended by any who wish to observe, so there's plenty of seating. There hasn't been a battle for the title of realm lord in over seven thousand years. Representatives from all over the Farseen will be here," Jarvious explained.

Landon looked around and wished there was a book on beings of the Farseen. He wasn't sure what he was seeing. It must have shown on his face because Jarvious started a running commentary. "Nymphs are easy to identify. Adults are five to six feet tall, slender with delegate wings that allow them to fly. Their coloring – blue for water, green for meadows, brown for woodlands and silver for mountains – usually identifies their habitat, but not always."

Jarvious bowed to a family, short in comparison to most fae. As they walked away, he straightened up, "Dryads from Dad's land. They are pleasant and helpful, unless you try to remove them from the land." He pointed to Darious, who was talking to a diminutive, shriveled, old man, "Gnome," and to a tall, muscular, grotesque looking guy, "Goblin."

Ryan tapped Jarvious on the shoulder and inclined his head toward a creature, "What is that?"

Good question, Landon thought. Tempe was talking to a creature that looked like a gargoyle from a fifties horror movie.

"Gargoyle."

Okay, that made sense. Landon ducked, as did nearly everyone, when ten huge dragons flew low over those approaching the arena. They spread out and flew to land on a platform that looked to be made for each dragon.

"And those are the supreme matriarchs of each dragon tribe. A dragon tribe is made up of all dragons of a certain color. Each dragon family has a matriarch, but those matriarchs must obey the supreme matriarch, ruler of all dragons of their color. And yes, they are the strongest of the dragons."

Landon took his assigned seat and continued to be amazed. Four elementals arrived and took their platforms. Finally, something he could identify: water, fire, air, and earth. The elementals of the Farseen looked like the elementals of the Seen, at least they looked like the drawings he had seen. To his knowledge, he never met an elemental.

Mistress Dawn made a point to stop by and talk to Ryan for a few minutes. As a daughter of the Southern Realm, everyone in the stands noticed the attention she gave to the young alpha male shifter most of the Farseen compared to Valliant the Bold, Ellwood's eldest son and Tempest's brother.

"Watch it or you'll be in my shoes soon," Terrious grinned to Ryan when Mistress Dawn left.

Ryan blushed but didn't comment.

*****

At the appointed hour, Leitha, Kairav and Layton entered the ring. Each walked to a pedestal with their crest emblazoned on it and stood ready.

Theron, Master of the Hunt, spoke from the stands, using a spell to project his voice. "Welcome all. Queen Weindrych has chosen her three champions. The last one standing will become the Water Lord of the Western Realm. Let the challenge begin."

As soon as the last word was spoken, Leitha sent fire at Kairav and Layton. Both men blocked with water. Layton pulled the ground from underneath Leitha, but she jumped up and hovered. The crowd responded with astonishment as most of the observers didn't know she could fly.

Kairav leveled a spell at Layton and Leitha and both were tossed into the stands. They landed on hard surfaces as spectators dove out of the way. To aid or hinder a combatant would result in death for the observer.

Layton rolled with the fall and was the first to recover. He teleported to Kairav's pedestal and grabbed him in a chokehold. Kairav grabbed Layton's shoulders and pulled him over his head slamming Layton to the ground, which had turned to mud from both men's earlier call of water. Layton landed on his back in a puddle and spat out water and mud. He shook his head, clearing his eyes in time to see Kairav poised over him, ready to deal a deathblow. Layton turned to a silver dragon and used freezing breath to turn Kairav into a Popsicle from the shoulders down.

The silver supreme matriarch spread her wings and shrieked in approval.

Before Layton could shift, Leitha teleported to his back and created a knife of fire. Silver dragon Layton reared up and as Leitha lost her grip he used his spiked tail to toss her into the wall at the base of the stands. He shifted back to human, grabbed Kairav by the neck and snapped it in two. Kairav didn't fall because he was still frozen from the shoulders down.

The crowd screamed, some with joy, others in anger. Later, most would agree it was somehow worse because Kairav couldn't fall. Since his neck was broken, his head bobbled atop his frozen body.

Layton blocked out the sound of the crowd as he searched for Leitha. He shifted into a gold dragon and set an invisible shield. He completed his shield just as the tornado formed. It hit his shield and vaulted out of the arena and into an open field. Lord Ellwood dispelled the storm without taking his eyes off of the battle. Layton's dragon sent a fireball at Leitha, which she blocked with water.

Leitha unleashed an ice spell and Layton shifted to a white dragon. Ice is home to a white dragon, so Layton ran across the ice straight at her, his dragon claws digging into the ice and keeping him upright. Leitha was crafting another spell when Layton shifted to human and tackled her.

They fought hand-to-hand for a few seconds, but Layton couldn't win that battle. Leitha was the advisor of the Western Realm because she was the best combat solider in the realm. Layton would die in simple hand-to-hand fight.

Layton shifted to his blue dragon and held Leitha in his claws. No one could tell what he was saying but his whispers worked. She stopped fighting. Layton took her neck in his dragon claws. The resulting crack as her neck broke reverberated throughout the arena. Layton laid her gently on the ground and shifted.

Layton stood on the killing field and didn't move. A soft sound grew louder and louder as the crowd repeated, "Lord Layton."

Queen Weindrych appeared and the spectators fell silent. "Layton, Water Lord of the Western Realm, what is your first command?"

"Bury the dead, with honor."

Queen Weindrych inclined her head.

The warriors came out and gathered up Kairav and Leitha and took them away, with honor, as instructed.

Each dragon supreme matriarch and each elemental appeared before Lord Layton, and introduced themselves, followed by various other leaders of the lesser fae, including unicorn, centaur, dryads, pixies, brownies, and nymphs. Harpies, goblins and other groups without an organized structure did not attend, except for one. Father Aldous, oldest of the known fae had watched from Queen Weindrych's box and tilted his hat to Lord Layton before disappearing.

The queen and lord walked off the killing field.

Breton asked, "Is it over?"

"Yes," Ridge replied. His face still didn't change expression, but the relief was plain in his voice.

Tempest handed Nolween a veil to cover her face. It was a sign of respect for those her husband just killed that she would not show her face for twenty-four hours. It was also a handy way for the victor's wife to express relief and joy without appearing to gloat over the deaths of the others.

Ridge turned to Tempe and whispered, "How long have you known shifters who take a dragon form can access the dragon's power?"

"A while," she replied with the same bland expression she had kept throughout the combat. Tempe looked at her grandsons and commented, "Lady Nolween, you have need of girls. Your court needs females."

"Indeed, Lady Tempest, you might be right. Perhaps now would be a good time to mention I am, in fact, pregnant. I found out while Layton was training, and I didn't mention it for fear it would distract him from his fight. Since you are here I was going to ask you to tell me about my children."

Ridge and Tempe stared at Nolween, dumbfounded. There are only so many surprises a parent can handle in one day, no matter how old the child. Tempe finally managed to say, "Once you're settled, I would be pleased to do so."

*****

As was the custom, according to the archives that had been researched frequently over the past few weeks, the first group of visitors Lord Layton would receive was his family and invited guests to the combat. They filed into the receiving room.

Jerran, master-at-arms for the Western Realm, met them at the door. He bowed, "Interesting that the parents of the Western Realm lord are the Northern Realm advisor and the second most powerful shifter in the Seen. I suspect this will be an interesting court."

"I suspect you are right," Tempe replied before Ridge could take offense, but not before he growled.

Jerran grinned, opened the door wide, and announced the family and guests. They walked in.

No one said anything for a few seconds, so Tempe took charge. "Lord Layton, your lady is tired. Have you no seat in this residence to offer the woman who bore you four strong sons?"

"Of course, Lady Tempest," Layton replied with a smile.

Even as Tempe spoke a chair was produced and Lady Nolween sat, though she protested she didn't need to sit. Tempe was sure she didn't, but something had to be said. The court needed instructions. Most of them were thinking they were about to be fired and being fired by a new realm lord meant death.

Layton looked over at Jerran and said, "Master-at-arms. Walk with me." By not so much as a breath did any of the guards and attendants react, but everyone watched to see if this would be the first death.

Ridge, and to a lesser extent Tempe, had prepared Layton in case he was the victor. He had to already have made his decisions on his court. Otherwise, everyone would become nervous and the backstabbing would start. For good or ill, the fae are not accustomed to having their ruling structure changed.

Layton and Jerran walked around the room, and eventually returned to Layton's throne. Layton announced, "Jerran is the advisor to the Western Realm." You could feel the relief. Jerran was an excellent fighter and the warriors would not have to worry about changes for change sake. The master-at-arms was a logical choice for realm advisor when the advisor dies, but after a new realm lord ascends, nothing could be assumed.

Lord Layton sent Jerran on a quick mission. While the court waited, Layton gave out some minor orders about his schedule and such. When advisor Jerran returned, Agwe, son of Kairav who Layton just killed, was with him. Agwe was one of the senior officers over the warriors.

To give Agwe his due, he did not flinch at what could become his final moment, he bowed, "You wished to see me Lord Layton?"

"Indeed. Jerran has agreed to be the advisor to the Western Realm. I find myself in need of a master-at-arms, a position you are well suited for. Will you accept?"

Agwe bowed again and said, "It will be my honor, Lord Layton."

Agwe was a good choice. By all accounts, Agwe was well respected by the officers and warriors alike. By promoting Agwe, Layton was telling the realm he considered Kairav's family to be valuable to the realm.

While Agwe and Layton talked, Jerran stepped out again, returning this time with Lady Aerten, Leitha's mother, and according to rumors no one had the guts to verify, River's lover for centuries. Lady Aerten pretty much ran the western court household for River since he had never taken another wife after his died in childbirth. There was no title for what she did but everyone from the court staff to the stable hands obeyed her.

Lady Aerten curtsied, "You wished to see me Lord Layton?"

"Yes, Lady Nolween and I desire you continue to arrange the court household. There might be a few minor changes, but I believe you and Lady Nolween will be able to work those out. Will you accept?"

Lady Nolween was well known in the realm for her well-run house and most knew she did not need anyone to arrange her household for her, but if the new lord kicked Lady Aerten out in the cold he would lose supporters. No one had been able to tell Ridge or Layton how Aerten would respond to the man who killed her daughter. They couldn't even find anyone who would hazard a guess.

Lady Aerten bowed again and said, "I will be pleased to continue serving the realm."

The entire room breathed a sigh of relief. The rest of the court relaxed as they realized a blood bath was not in their immediate future.

Lady Aerten turned to her new mistress, "Lady Nolween, for tonight I have prepared rooms for the children. Would you like to inspect them?"

"Yes," Nolween replied. They walked out together with the two younger boys. Her older sons, Orton and Kelton, followed playing dutiful sons and bodyguards. It would be some time before any member

204

of the new realm would feel safe alone. Orton's wife and children would not leave the receiving room until they returned. Layton had to remove any remaining Shadowed or anyone who felt their allegiance to River would require them to injure the new Western Realm lord by killing off the weaker members of his family.

The visitors from the Seen left, allowing the fae time to embrace the changes. Ridge left with them, a sign Lord Layton's parents were sure he could handle his court himself.

Chapter 26

Tempe, still recovering from the fact her first born had just become the Water Lord of the Western Realm, headed for the kitchen to start dinner. Mary was already cooking. "Geez, is Eli paying you to cook for his house now?" Tempe asked the question in jest, but part of her was worried his clan was once again picking up the slack for her.

"Now Tempe, this is the last home cooked meal the college bound crowd will get for a while. They're moving to campus tomorrow." Mary put the finishing touches on the chicken potpies.

"Mary, I think I'll miss you most of all," Ryan replied as he hugged her. She blushed and kicked everyone out of the kitchen, so she could cook in peace.

Dinner was loud with talk of college. Once the boys left to finish packing, it was quiet enough to hear the Moreau triplets in the sunroom with Jeannette.

"Do you have to go?" Darnel asked.

"Couldn't you stay here and drive into school every day, like we do?" Janel added.

"It's too far for me to do that easily. Would it be better if I waited to go back to school?"

Mary walked into the sunroom from the kitchen. "Jeannette has nine months of school left and she'll be done. She will graduate and be a vet before you finish your school year." Mary sat down and gathered Chanel in her lap since Darnel and Janel were clinging to Jeannette. "You guys are going to school so don't you think Jeannette should, too?"

"Yes," All three replied slowly and with little conviction.

"Jeannette will come to visit often. She's less than an hour away," Mary added.

Tempe leaned on the wall just outside the sunroom listening to Mary. She was the mother figure everyone dreams of having. Star and Sage joined Tempe since they had been listening too.

Sage walked into the room, "Are you guys ready to start my French lessons?"

Chanel groaned, "If you aren't living in France why do you want to speak it?"

Star smiled, "I came from the Farseen and I speak English, French, and Italian. It's rather useful."

The girls took the triplets to help them get ready for bed.

Jeannette watched the triplets leave and sighed.

Tempe cut off Jeannette's question before she asked it, "No, you don't need to wait a semester. You're planning to come home the first few weekends anyway. They'll adjust. Finishing your studies is the best thing you can do for them, and for you."

She smiled but looked worried as she walked up the stairs.

Next morning, Jeannette had already loaded her car when the boys came down and piled bags and books into their cars. Blake and Kaleb shared a car and Ryan's truck was loaded down, as was Joey's car. It turned out Jeannette rented an apartment with another female shifter in the same townhouse complex the boys were moving into, so they were going to caravan to the school.

The triplets grabbed Jeannette for a last, long hug. Landon walked out and commented, "I wonder if anyone wants to learn to drive the golf carts? The Taylor triplets enjoy their lessons."

Darnel ran over and grabbed Landon's hand, "That would be awesome." Chanel and Janel gave Jeannette another hug and walked over to where Sage and Star had joined Landon. The six of them went off to find golf carts.

"Get settled in school. Come back when you can." Mary shooed the college bound into their cars. The triplets turned to wave bye as the caravan drove out of the driveway.

It only took a couple of hours for everyone to realize that, without the boys, the house was a lot quieter and required less food.

When the triplets came back from their golf cart-driving lesson and were settled in the game room with Bryce and Landon, Tempe motioned for Star and Sage to follow her.

They went up to the girls' room and settled in for a talk. Sage preempted her and commented, "This is where Tempe tells us we have to be extra careful. There is still a two-million-euro bounty on the head of a blond shifter/fae in Eli's clan and we have proof they will kidnap any blond in the clan." She looked over at Star and continued, "With any luck they'll try to kidnap Tempe and she'll solve the problem for us."

Tempe snorted, "You think so."

"I know so," Sage replied. "If they tried for you they'd be toast."

Tempe smirked but shook her head, "Be that as it may, I doubt they will try for me. My face is fairly well known. Star, you start community college tomorrow so there are some new ground rules."

"Naturally." Her voice was calm, but there was a flash of anger in her eyes.

"I'm also taking a class at the school."

"What? Why?" Star asked in disgust.

"Because being enrolled in bird watching classes – don't laugh – will give me an excuse to be on campus. I'm not going to follow you all the time because, frankly, I can't. Sage is also taking a couple of classes at the community college to get a jump on her college credits. Landon is taking cooking and business administration classes."

Sage looked up and smiled. She hadn't realized Landon would be at the school.

Star saw Sage's happy expression and couldn't hide her anger. Her guy had left for another university. "I've put up with all the supervision but Starless Night… can't I even go to a local community college without body guards?"

"Someone besides Lord Ellwood still wants you and they aren't concerned about the queen's decree. I know it's hard and we aren't going to be with you all the time. But we will have a presence on campus," Tempe explained.

Star emitted a growl that would have done her jaguar proud.

Tempe ignored the growl, "You will drive yourself to and from school since you are taking a full load, but Landon, Sage, and I will be around."

There wasn't more to say so Tempe left the room to give Star the chance to vent about the unfairness of life.

Landon looked up as Tempe entered the kitchen. She looked frazzled and he correctly deduced the reason. "I guess you told Star about the classes and she's angry."

"It's to be expected," she replied mildly. "I wouldn't like someone always looking over my shoulder."

He smiled, "Guess I wouldn't, either. I'll pay you back for the loan."

She smiled, "I know." He was too proud to take a hand out even though there were scholarships for shifters who don't have the ability to pay for their own schooling. He refused the scholarship saying it was for young shifters. Eli offered him a loan, which Landon flatly refused. Tempe convinced him to take a loan from her under the guise of watching out for Star and Sage on campus, when she laid out her concerns about the girls he finally agreed.

Tempe was less than enthusiastic about her birding class, but it was only one day a week and gave her a reason to be on campus.

*****

It didn't take long for everyone to settle. The Moreau triplets quickly learned they could charm Bryce and Landon into almost anything. Eli was also a soft touch but with kids of his own they found Bryce and Landon had a little more free time. Jeannette came in almost every weekend, and one of the boys, usually Joey, made the trip with her. Ryan had to learn how to juggle his alpha duties, light though they were, with his schoolwork. He knew a few evenings of irritation at being highly ranked in the alpha clan. The weekly visits with Star's family continued without incident. Everyone was doing well in school, even Tempe.

Ridge surprised everyone when he came for his monthly visit with Star in October. In an effort to prepare his grandchildren, who were almost sure to shift, he brought Breton and Delton. On the plus side, since Ridge was focused on his grandsons' first visit to the Seen, he quit baiting Bryce, and Bryce wasn't interested in causing problems with the kids around. Ridge and Bryce would never be friends, but they could at least be in the same area without the temperature dropping significantly.

Both boys were showing strong shifter talents so occasional visits to the Seen would allow them to be comfortable with shifters if they needed to visit for an extended period of time. Star and Ryan explained to the twins what they could expect and how to prepare for the bloodlust. While the kids were eating pizza, Bryce stepped away to answer his cell. Tempe snagged another slice of veggie pizza and put it on her plate when he walked in smiling. He picked her up and twirled her around. As he sat Tempe down he announced, "I'm an uncle. Bryana delivered Triston and Aaron just a little while ago. Everyone is healthy and happy."

Much happiness and many congratulations ensued.

During these fairly quiet months, the alpha clan had only one issue they hoped would go unnoticed, the only alpha female who was not pregnant, or in a birthing bond, was Tempe. In addition to Raven, Bliss was also pregnant. Rayna was holding multiple birthing bonds over distance, which worked fairly well for shifters that had given birth before and had a doctor in the clan. The rest of the sisters were spread thin throughout the world to hold birthing bonds for multiple clans from a central location. If anything were to happen, Tempe would have to go solo or pull Ryan out of school.

Tempe thought calming thoughts and it worked… for a while.

Chapter 27

Star and Sage were on campus for their last day of classes before Thanksgiving. Landon and Tempe left a couple of hours later since they both had just one class that day and the time synced up. Landon drove Tempe's BMW, practicing shifting gears. She was calm considering she hated anyone else driving her car, perhaps Bryce was a calming influence. Tempe gasped and grabbed the dashboard.

"Tempe, what's wrong?" Landon asked as he down shifted.

She grabbed his arm and pointed down the road. "Don't slow down. Sage is in trouble."

He shifted up a gear and they practically flew into the campus parking lot closest to Sage's class. They hopped out of the car to find students and teachers milling around in shock.

David, a kid in Tempe's birding class, hurried over and asked excitedly, "Did you see it?"

"No, we just got here. What happened?" She masked her fear with a look of confusion.

"A door opened up. Sort of like the Stargate event horizon without the metal border, but it was smooth. It didn't poof out or anything. Two masked guys walked through and grabbed a girl and took her into the whatever." David shook his head, "I know it sounds crazy and I swear I'm not drunk, or high. All I saw was blond hair but it looked a little like your sister, Sage."

Tempe couldn't even open her mouth to say she believed him, but she did. Someone had opened a way into a college campus, in front of who knew how many humans, and took Sage. She knew it was Sage because she couldn't feel her sister and she could feel Star. Landon, bless his heart, stood next to her and didn't scream or break anything, although Tempe could feel his emotions and knew that was what he wanted to do.

"Hey Dave, did you see it? What was it?" Another student pulled Dave into their group for details.

Star ran over, "Did you hear?"

"Yes," Tempe managed to say. "We need to get out of here and regroup. We go in my car. Now," she ordered.

Landon didn't say anything but got in the driver's side and started up the car. Star and Tempe had to share a seat, but the alpha wasn't about to drive the other car and let her niece out of her sight.

Tempe was livid. How could she have been so foolish as to think the girls would be safe without a guard? She started her focused breathing for meditation, pulled out her cell phone and called Eli to circle the wagons, at least they did have a plan if something like this happened. Just as they pulled into the driveway her phone blared *Rough & Ready*. Ryan was frantic. She spoke over his tirade, "Someone opened a way to the campus and took Sage. Star is safe. What's your schedule?"

"I'm on the way." Ryan hung up.

Tempe ran to her room, dressed in her spelled clothes, and grabbed the accessories she thought would do her the most good.

As she came down the stairs she saw Star was in her spelled clothes, as well.

Tempe simply said, "No."

"But Tempe…"

"No, you stay, but keep those clothes on in case they attack here." Tempe walked into the kitchen to grab a snack. Brook walked in with her kids and Brandi. Tempe looked at Brandi in relief, "You willing to go to the Farseen?"

"Of course," came the automatic response. Brandi didn't know what Tempe wanted but it didn't matter. Tempe wouldn't ask if it wasn't important.

Tempe turned to Landon. "I have no right to ask but I need…"

"Anything." He replied before she finished asking.

Tempe nodded her thanks. "Star, when Ryan gets here he's to guard you and the house." She held up her hand, "This isn't a negotiation. He needs to be here to lead the second assault if I fail."

"Yes, Tempe" Star kept her irritation to herself. This was her fault. She should be with the team going to rescue Sage.

"We're going to Saffron's home. That's where Ryan starts if I don't make it back. Understand?"

She nodded.

Eli walked in. "I'm going with you."

"Excuse me? You have a clan to protect and a death sentence in the Farseen," Tempe replied. Her tone leaving no doubt she wasn't taking him.

"And Brook is here to protect the clan until Ryan gets here to protect the clan. Have you forgotten about the Shadowed siren we never found?"

Yes, she had, but this was no time to admit she was capable of making mistakes. Everyone looked to her to do the right thing, always. "Fine, let's go." She was out of options as she opened a way to Saffron's. Tempe walked through first, followed by Landon, Brandi and Eli.

*****

Saffron's herb gardens looked good, even in November. Tempe mentally called, and her sister flew out a window and landed beside the shifters.

"Someone opened a way into the Seen and took Sage. I want to use your home as our base," Tempe stated.

"Of course," Saffron tilted her head in agreement.

Tempe turned to Landon, "I suspect you possess a strong enough link to Sage that I can use your heartstring to find her."

He looked confused but was ready to do what was needed.

Tempe felt for his heartstring and discovered he was a loadstone for Sage. She glanced over at Saffron who could feel the heartstring as well, and they both shook their heads. Their baby sister found her true love as a teenager.

"Is everything alright? Will this heartstring thing work?" Landon asked. He mistook their expressions over his heartstring for a problem.

"It'll work perfectly," Tempe replied honestly.

Before they could make plans, a way opened, and Jackson walked through with Siri and Kenley. "What are you guys doing here?"

"I've been in Italy training Kenley. He opened a way to Rayna's when the call went out and Jackson came with us from North Carolina," Siri explained.

"Before you say something foolish like, it's not my fight, try to remember I'm family now," Jackson leveled a stare at his powerful sister-in-law.

Saffron raised an eyebrow. Tempe nodded, "Saffron, meet Jackson Green, Raven's husband. Raven is pregnant and will not be joining us."

"You mean it's true?"

"What?"

"Shifters are in some type of high fertility phase and you're the last alpha available for combat. At least that's the rumor," Saffron said.

"I'm afraid it is almost true. Neither Ryan nor I are pregnant or in a birthing bond," Tempe said dryly. She looked at the assembled team and took a deep breath. "Let's go find Sage."

Jackson created a large wind wagon like the one Murdoch had created. Tempe took her gold dragon form and Jackson attached the wagon. Everyone hopped on and Saffron veiled them. Landon's heartstring was strong and steady. Tempe followed it with no problem.

Tempe felt Eli shield her mind from a possible siren attack and she rushed to explain to Saffron what was happening before she attacked Eli.

"Eli, next time warn a sister before you shield her mind from a siren. I almost blasted you," Saffron growled.

"Do you think you could?" Eli growled back.

Do you want me to pull this wagon over? Tempe asked Eli and Saffron in their minds. Both had a moment of confusion before their faces lit up with understanding. The Adams Family has nothing on Rayna's children for weirdness.

Tempe followed the heartstring to the Western Realm's wastelands. As they homed in, she noticed they were close to the place where they met the gorkongs a while back. It looked like they were heading straight for the gorkong lair. Saffron and Tempe exchanged a few thoughts and Saffron warned the others about the gorkongs.

With the heartstring, Saffron and Tempe could feel the entrance to the possible Shadowed facility, but they still couldn't see it. Brandi suddenly pointed to a small slit in the rock and sure enough there was an entrance. Tempe landed, and everyone stepped off the wagon. Jackson dropped his spell, the wagon disappeared, and Tempe shifted back to human. Saffron still had them veiled.

The gorkongs could smell, but not see, the intruders. Jackson added a shield to Saffron's veil just before the most dominant male gorkong ran into it. He hit the shield so hard those inside the shield felt the vibration. Tempe looked over at Jackson and grinned, as did Siri. Saffron simply kept walking. Tempe had the impression her sister knew Jackson could and would set a shield.

They walked into the crevice in the rock where the heartstring pulled. The tunnels were high enough to walk upright, but just barely. It didn't help that they used a single dim light to mask their approach. There were complaints as people bumped into stalactites and outcrops. After maybe three miles of tunnel they came to an open area that looked like a natural meeting hall. Out of the corner of her eye, Tempe saw movement.

Tempe smiled and bowed, "Tace, friend gnome, it has been a while. We are weary travelers searching for a teenager taken from our shifter clan in the Seen. What price do you charge for passage through your tunnels?"

"Lady Tempest, Lady Saffron, and assorted traveling companions," Tace said with a bow. He looked like all of his species looks, about four feet tall with a long flowing beard and he was sporting a gnarled walking cane that was for defense rather than a walking aid.

Tace pointed to Landon, "If you track the heartstring for his love, I give you free passage and a warning. The one who has her is a siren. She plans to trap and use you, Lady Tempest. I expect you are prepared for her."

"I am, indeed." Tempest smiled showing all of her teeth. At least now she had proof gnomes could see a shifter heartstring. Tempe was surprised he realized Landon was Sage's love but that was nothing to the surprise of Tace allowing them free passage. She would have to think up a suitable gift for his kindness in her hour of need.

"Good journey ladies, and traveling companions of the ladies," Tace said as he faded away.

Kenley made the only comment as they crossed the large room and started uphill through another tunnel, "My first gnome."

Landon gritted his teeth. He had seen gnomes and more at Layton's challenge. The only sight he wanted to see now was Sage.

They hiked another few miles through the tunnels and Brandi commented, as she scrambled over another set of rocks carefully placed to slow down intruders, "I suspect they're hoping we'll be too tired to fight when we finally arrive."

"Won't they be surprised?" Landon ground out each word.

They walked mostly in silence, straining their ears to hear... anything. Suddenly, right when Tempe felt Sage, Eli moved up beside her and held her back. He mouthed one word, "Siren".

As much as Tempe hated it, she let Eli go first. No one else would be able to stand against a siren. Their only real hope was for Eli to be the stronger of the two. Weapon of choice at the ready, they followed Eli, forming an arc behind him.

Tempe had racked her brain for weeks to determine who the siren was. Lady Aerten was actually seventh on her list. If she had been any higher, Tempe would have interrogated Layton's subject, fae politics or not. As they rounded the edge of the cavern, Lady Aerten moved up to number one. She was sitting on the only chair – a throne of sorts – in the room. Lake, the Western Realm envoy to the high court, and Nolween – Layton's wife – were standing on either side of Aerten. Sage was unconscious on the floor. In the background, Orton and Kelton – Layton's eldest set of twins – stood at parade rest, along with Agwe and a couple of squadrons of warriors.

Aerten and Eli fell immediately into a siren reverie, which would determine who was the strongest and also allowed them to see the truth of each other's life. If it wasn't Eli, they were in a world of hurt. Aerten got a look of fear in her eyes that made Tempe's heart soar. Eli was winning.

Tempe was so focused on the two sirens she didn't notice Nolween. Apparently, no one else did either. Nolween walked up to Eli and drove a short sword into his side.

Brandi screamed as her prif fell to the ground with the sword still in his body.

Aerten ignored everyone else. She looked at Tempe and smiled.

As Tempe's mind blanked out, she sent a mental stay-away order in a vain attempt to keep everyone else away, but she wasn't sure anyone would actually hear it as Tempe dropped to her knees.

Her mind cleared in an instant. Tempe looked up as Aerten's body fell to the floor and her head flew across the room.

Brandi's stance was impressive. She stood with her sword raised, ready to kill anyone that threatened her comrades. Brandi, as a vampire half-breed, was immune to a siren's call.

The squadrons attacked.

Tempe snarled. She may not be proof against a siren, but two squadrons she could handle. Still on her knees from Aerten's attack, she called wind and crushed them into the ground with the force of a hurricane.

Later, they learned Aerten had given the two squadrons – who were faithful to her and her alone – orders to kill everyone if she died.

Lake, Nolween, Orton, Kelton and Agwe stood there for a few seconds and then Nolween asked softly, "What happened and why am I here?"

Tempe looked over at Landon who was holding Sage and talking quietly to her. He looked up and said, "She's alive, but unconscious."

Tempe breathed a sigh of relief as she dropped to Eli's side. She removed the sword, which was still in his side, and ripped the bottom of her shirt to slow down the bleeding. Kenley handed her his shirt as well and she used it to tie off the wound. It was a clean wound with no organ damage. He would heal but medical attention would speed up the process.

Tempe ignored the fae, leaving it to Saffron to explain what had happened. She nodded to Kenley and he opened a way to Eli's house. Landon walked through with Sage, Jackson and Tempe walked through carrying Eli. Brandi and Kenley followed with their weapons still poised against possible attack. Tempe was surprised Kenley opened a way to

Eli's patio instead of the cave, but it was the quickest way to get medical attention. Ways were normally opened in secluded settings to keep humans unaware. Anyone driving past Eli's could have seen the way.

They rushed into the house and took Eli to the recovery room with Jeff and Ryan in pursuit. Delaney cried out but they didn't slow down.

Jackson and Tempe laid him on one of the beds and stood back and waited. Ryan healed the wound as Eli moaned and tightened his muscles. Eli took a deep breath and commented, "I didn't expect Ryan's healing hands to actually hurt."

Tempe kissed Eli on the forehead and went to find Sage.

Landon had taken Sage to the guest room on the first floor. Ryan reached for her, but Tempe stopped him. She reached for Sage's mind. Sage forcefully ejected her from her mind and then tossed her into the wall. Nightmares had been placed in her head and Tempe couldn't break through them.

Tempe hit the wall and slid down to the floor. As she stood she grabbed Ryan. "It was a mental attack, not a physical one. You can't heal this. Get Brook," Tempe said and shoved him toward the door.

Ryan grabbed the door and pulled so hard he took it off the hinge. He came back a few minutes later with Brook and Chev.

"Can you help?" Tempe asked softly.

Brook looked horrified and seemed unable to speak. Chev answered, "This is the reason sirens have a death sentence in the Farseen. A siren can do this to anyone but mostly they use this type of attack against those who are able to resist them. They send nightmares the person can't escape. Anything another siren does will simply make it worse."

Chev backed up as Tempe's eyes turned black.

"Everyone leave," Tempe ordered as she grabbed Landon to keep him in the room. They didn't move fast enough so she yelled, "Now."

Ryan looked at Tempe but all she said was, "Set the door in its place." He backed out of the room, grabbed the door and set it tightly in front of the opening.

"Landon, when I felt your heartstring I confirmed you and Sage are twin flames, closer than soul mates. You're the only person who can pull Sage back from an attack of this type. I know you have been staying away from her because she is young and normally I would agree, but right now you are the only person who stands a chance of reaching her. When I attempted to touch her mind, she didn't even recognize me."

"I… I don't know what to do," he whispered, with his eyes on Sage.

"Tell her how you truly feel about her. Tell her about your hopes, dreams and even fears for the two of you. Open your mind to her and let her in. She will enter your mind if she knows it is open to her and if she trusts you enough. Share your memories. I hope she'll get past the nightmares for you." Tempe walked to the door.

As she touched the door she felt the magic Ryan had used to wedge the door in place. Rather than break the spell, she teleported out of the room. Everyone looked at Tempe. She shook her head but didn't speak.

Ryan walked toward the door and she stopped him. "Not this time." She hugged him knowing he felt as helpless as she did. She looked up after a second and asked, "Where's Loane?"

"She should be landing at the airport in a few minutes. Bryce is waiting to drive her here," Ryan said.

Tempe dropped into a chair. After a few seconds she cursed and said to whoever was listening, which was everyone in the house, "Guard the house. A way has opened from the Western Realm"

Tempe stood up and grabbed Ryan, "Let's go."

She teleported with Ryan and they arrived at the cave everyone knows about. Saffron stood there, alone.

Relief flooded through Tempest that this wouldn't be another battle. "Is Layton and his family safe?" she asked.

"Yes," Saffron replied. "It turns out your son cannot be controlled by a siren. Aerten was controlling his family to prevent him from telling anyone what was going on, however, he managed to get word to the master of the hunt. Theron had informed the queens and they were moving to attack Aerten when you arrived. They decided to let you handle it."

"Of course, they did," Tempe replied savagely. "Wouldn't want the queens to bother themselves over the life of a teenage shifter," She spat the words.

"Tempest, watch what you say," Saffron whispered.

Tempe growled, and her eyes turned black. Saffron backed up. Ryan walked from Tempe's side to Saffron's. He stared at Tempe's eyebrow and waited calmly.

"By the five realms! Can someone explain to me why this teenager is calmer than I am?" Tempe asked the sky.

"Because, my granddaughter, you were accurately named. You are a tempest. You attack a problem with all the subtlety of a controlled cyclone. It makes you a great warrior, but it doesn't serve you well when you must wait," Queen Niamh said serenely as Tempe turned to yell at her.

The queen was wearing a flowing forest green dress and cape. She looked like she just stepped out of a storybook. Niamh held up her hand in the universal stop signal, "I understand you are upset and I'm willing to make some allowances, but I don't think you want to speak just yet."

Tempe growled but kept her mouth closed. Threatening a fae queen, even if she's your grandmother, is nothing short of suicide.

"I have dealt with those who saw the way open on the college campus," Queen Niamh said.

"Dealt with... how?" Tempe asked fearfully as she ran down the options. The queen could have killed them all or caused them to lose their memories, all of their memories.

"Have faith Tempest," Niamh smiled. "All media of the campus way and kidnapping has been destroyed. Most of the humans have already decided it was a painted van the men came out of. The few who believe what they saw will have no proof."

Tempe didn't like it. Those that believe will be ridiculed forever but there was no other way to deal with it. She hoped Dave would have a new explanation for what happened when she next saw him in class, but she doubted it. He possessed a strong mind.

"Sage is in good hands. You are right. Landon can pull her back from this. Trust the two of them." With those words of wisdom, Queen Niamh walked through a way Tempest couldn't see or feel. It must be nice to be that powerful.

Tempe took a deep calming breath and glanced at Saffron, "Do you think the queens have known all along about Aerten?"

She barked a sarcastic laugh, "Who knows? The queens almost always know more than they say. They have a deep-rooted belief in moral liberty. I believe humans call it free will." Saffron opened a way and said, "With your permission I will return again tomorrow to provide you a status, and to receive one as well. I am currently staying with Layton, as is Ridge. We will keep them safe as we search for more Shadowed among the Western Realm."

Tempe nodded her head and Saffron left.

Tempe looked up at the sky and took a deep breath. Ryan and Tempe walked the two miles back to the house in silence. When they walked in she looked over at Jeff and he shook his head. Tempe went to stand by the door and wait. She leaned on one side of the door and Ryan leaned on the other side. Star came over and sat down between them, a little way back, turning the three of them into a triangle.

After an hour or so Bryce walked in with Loane. She walked up to Tempe and said, "You're right. Landon is the answer. We wait."

Tempe was getting tired of hearing that. Excluding Ryan, everyone looked confused, but she didn't offer any explanation. Sometime later, Bryce brought sandwiches and sodas to the trio. Tempe tried to eat, but the turkey sandwich stuck in her throat. As she tried to force down the sandwich, it occurred to her it was Thanksgiving, and someone had apparently cooked the turkey and ham they had planned on having. Now that she thought about it, the house smelled of Thanksgiving foods.

A little bit later, both Ryan and Tempe had dropped down to the floor, but they still waited. Everyone tippy toed around them. Star curled up on the floor and fell asleep. Bryce tucked a pillow under her head and laid a blanket around her body.

Just before midnight Ryan and Tempe heard a sound. They both looked at the door. When nothing happened, they decided they hadn't heard anything. After another minute, there was a louder noise and then Landon's voice, "I don't know what magic Ryan used to close this door, but I can't budge it. If I remove it with magic I might hurt someone on your side."

Ryan jumped up and ripped the door open. They looked past Landon's smiling face and saw Sage, weak but awake. Ryan ran over and hugged her.

Tempe hugged Landon as he whispered, "I need to understand how you knew that would work."

Tempe kissed him on the cheek, "Later,"

Star moved quietly into the room and hugged Sage as Tempe commented in relief, "Please don't scare me like that again."

Sage smiled weakly.

Loane walked in and checked out Sage's mind. "You will be fine child, but you will have to stay in bed for a few days and walk carefully even longer. Tempest can tell you how long it takes to recover from a telepathic attack and she had a rather mild one, nothing like what you experienced."

As she walked out, Loane patted Landon on the shoulder and kissed him on the cheek, "Excellent work, and welcome to the family."

Landon's face went beat red as Ryan and Star said, "What?" They looked between Landon and Sage. Sage implored Tempe with her eyes.

"Sage managed to find, not just her soul mate, but her twin flame, before she reached adulthood. That's why Landon was able to help her when no one else could. And if it bugs you she found her true mate so young just remember, it took me almost seven thousand years to find mine. Life is not fair." Tempe walked out the hole where the door should be, grabbed Bryce, and walked up the stairs to their room.

Bryce closed the door and asked, "Landon is Sage's 'what did you call it', twin flame? How is that different from a soul mate?"

Tempe smiled and went into lecture mode. "Twin flames are like turbo-charged soul mates, they share a closeness and similarity of spirit. The connection is somewhat telepathic, and the simple act of hugging each other sustains their souls. When twin flames are together there is nothing between them to block their closeness. Twin flames are always couples. Soul mates are our soul family – siblings, parent-child, best friend, and even romantic relationships. The ones who help us grow, and evolve, or create and dissipate karma."

"Sage and Landon are twin flames?"

"Yes, just as we are soul mates," Tempe replied.

"We are?" Bryce asked.

"Yes. We share a deep love for each other, and a spiritual bond. Most important, soul mates are better together than apart. While Sage and Landon share a similarity of spirit and a telepathic connection, soul mates make each other grow and learn." Tempe took a deep breath, "Without Landon I doubt we could have gotten Sage's mind back. The siren had truly broken her."

Tempe looked down at her filthy clothes and said, "I want to take a shower and go to bed. Would you like to join me for either, or both?" she asked.

Bryce didn't speak. He just picked her up and carried her to the shower, clothes and all, which was, in a way, his answer. At any rate, it was the response she wanted.

Chapter 28

The day after Thanksgiving, Bryce and Tempe slept in. By the time they put in an appearance downstairs and gave thanks for caffeine and leftovers, Ryan was carrying in a new door for the guest room on the first floor. Landon followed behind, carrying the replacement parts for the doorframe. Bryce grabbed his coffee and went to help with the door. Between the three of them it was fairly obvious none of them had carpentry skills at even the most basic level.

Blake and Kaleb came downstairs, saw the mess and started laughing.

"Dang Ryan, I never thought of you as helpless before," Kaleb laughed and then held up his hands in surrender when Ryan threatened to throw the hammer at him. Blake beat feet out the door heading some place safe, dragging his twin with him.

A handful of curse words later, Bryce pulled out his cell phone and placed a call. Twenty minutes later Charles, a plumber, electrician, and carpenter by trade, and Bobby, his son, walked in the house. With the addition of skilled hands, the door was installed in short order. In the end it opened, closed, and locked, just like a door should.

Later in the day, Landon popped his head in the sunroom and asked Tempe to go for a walk. They headed out toward the cave and thinking rock on Eli's property. He didn't speak while they made the two-mile trek, so Tempe didn't either. Once they were at the cave he sat down and asked simply, "What's the deal with this soul mate thing?"

Tempe quirked a smile as she sat down beside him, "You and Sage are not soul mates, you're twin flames. Bryce and I are soul mates. We're better together than apart but our attraction is physical and emotional. Don't get me wrong, being soul mates is great, but as I understand it twin flames is much more. You and Sage are attracted on a physical, emotional and spiritual level. What you have is extremely rare and should be protected. It doesn't change the fact that the physical part of your relationship will need to wait for a while, but emotionally and spiritually you guys are already a couple. Don't get me wrong. You can still drive each other crazy but in the end you will both put the other first."

"So, we're meant to be together?"

"To answer simply, yes, but, and there's always a but, that doesn't mean you will end up together forever. Like everything else, timing is important. Your relationship could be troubled just like anyone else's. The real difference is you have a strong link that will serve you well, if you let it. Trust in yourself, and Sage, and I suspect you will have a wonderful life together."

"Will you explain all of this to Sage?"

"I doubt I need to. All alphas are educated on soul mates, twin flames and other such matters. It's part of our training. Right now, she may suspect you are simply soul mates. She'll ask when she's ready. I have only met two other twin flame couples in my life. Like I said, you have a rare and precious gift."

"Should I leave until Sage finishes high school and college?" Landon's eyes looked dejected. He obviously didn't want to leave.

"Only if you think you need to. To be honest, you have the worse end of this wait. Sage is young and inexperienced. She doesn't know what she's missing, but she might try to move the physical part of your relationship along. You will have to be the adult and keep her grounded."

Tempe gave Landon an apologetic smile, "This is an odd conversation for me to have with a male interested in one of my younger sisters."

"Odd doesn't even begin to cover it from my point of view," Landon retorted. He had spent most of the conversation with his eyes firmly focused on the ground.

Before they could start back to the house, they both looked toward the entrance of the cave and watched the way open. Landon jumped up into a defensive pose.

Tempe smiled, "It's Saffron. She's coming through alone."

Landon relaxed and shook his head, "I would like to know how you can tell that."

Saffron walked through the way wearing the coat of arms of the Western Realm. "Did you move from the Northern to the Western Realm?" Tempe pointed at the cloak.

Saffron laughed. "Hardly, it was cold this morning and I didn't have anything warm to wear."

"Don't let father see you in that cloak," Tempe warned. "Have you learned anything of Aerten's plans or reasons?"

"Some, but there's probably a lot of questions we will never be able to answer. What we do know is Aerten's husband lost the realm fight to River over seven thousand years ago. Based on her diaries, which I've been reading, she'd been plotting revenge ever since. She hid her siren powers, obviously. No one had a clue she was one. Now most of the Western Realm who participated in politics is questioning everything they've done over the centuries. A few families have decided their feuds were caused by Aerten to keep alliances from forming. On the plus side, the realm is settling down and old feuds – even blood feuds – are simply no more, but Layton is busy."

Into the silence that followed Saffron's explanation, Landon said, "I suspect you have some family issues to discuss. I'm heading back to the house."

Before he could leave, Saffron said, "Welcome to the family."

He looked back at her, shock written on his face.

"Did you think Rayna, Tempest, Loane, and Sage were the only telepaths in the family?" she asked with a smile.

"No, but I was hoping," he muttered as he walked off.

Saffron turned serious as she commented, "I have a message from Layton. He will send his youngest sons with Ridge to visit each month but for now, it would be better if there were not a lot of shifter activity in his realm."

"Don't worry, we weren't planning on visiting. I knew if he became a realm lord I would see even less of him than I already do," she sighed. "I also know Eli can't enter the Farseen again. I suspect the fae are even more anti-siren than they were before."

"Indeed." Saffron stood for a few seconds as if waiting for Tempe to say something. When she didn't, Saffron asked, "When are you announcing your pregnancy?"

"Oh geez… I just got pregnant, literally. Last night for pity's sake." Tempe sat back down on the rock and moaned, "Bryce said he wanted to get married before kids. Once again, I'm doing things out of order."

Saffron smirked, "At least you didn't enchant him."

While Tempe was thinking of a suitably cutting reply, Saffron opened a way and left. Sisters!

She pulled out her cell phone, called Bryce and asked him to meet her at the thinking rock next to the cave. She sat down on the rock to put her thoughts in order. A short time later, Akita Bryce arrived with a dog pack on his back. Laughing, Tempe removed the pack, which turned out to be a picnic, complete with wine, water, cheese, bread, and fruit. They even had plates, utensils and wine glasses.

He shifted while she laid everything out and poured him a glass of wine. She poured herself some water. He raised an eyebrow but didn't say anything. After they had consumed about half of the food he finally said, "So, why did you call me out here?"

Tempe looked down at the ground. "Well, do you remember when we found out Eli was going to be a father and you made the comment that you wanted to get married before you had children?"

Bryce put the food in his hands down carefully and reached over to gently pull her chin up so he could look into her eyes. "Yes, I remember."

She tried to smile as she asked, "Are you firm about that order of events?"

"Tempe..." no other words came out of his mouth.

"I started using protection as soon as I realized we were in a high fertility cycle for shifter females, but I'm pregnant," Tempe said softly. "I know we were planning on waiting but the little embryos had other plans."

Bryce still wasn't talking so she placed her hands on his cheeks and said, "Bryce, you're scaring me. Say something. Are you happy, sad, distraught, or in shock? Say something!"

He looked at her, took one of her hands and kissed the palm. Then he smiled and pulled her into his arms for one of those kisses you can feel all the way down into your toes, her favorite. "I'm happy. How could I be anything else?" he asked.

"Well, you've always talked about an order of events and this doesn't fit into your ordered universe," Tempe commented.

"Tempe, I love you. I even love the craziness of our life together." Bryce pulled her in close and said, "The only thing that matters is we love each other, and we're going to be parents together. Everything else will work itself out."

Bryce leaned down to whisper in her ear, "I would like details."

She smiled and leaned on Bryce. "Prepare yourself. Sometime in the first half of April we'll have one girl and three boys in our room. I wonder if Eli wants to expand his house again."

"Four. We're having quads!" Bryce exclaimed.

"Yes, and I don't know why. No one in my family has ever had quads." It bothered her because family genetics are needed for a shifter to have more than three.

It was Bryce's turn to look guilty as he replied, "Quads run in my family on both sides."

Tempe laughed. For once his family was responsible for the weirdness.

As they walked back to Eli's, Tempe admitted something to Bryce she normally wouldn't say out loud. "This leaves Ryan as the last alpha standing. Everyone else is holding birthing bonds or is pregnant. If anything big happens, we are in a world of hurt."

As they approached the house Tempe started walking slower and slower.

Bryce pulled up and asked, "You'll fight any creature in any dimension, but you balk at telling everyone you are pregnant?"

Tempe's face fell as she realized something. Tempe whipped out her phone and called Rayna. "Hello Mother. How are you?"

Rayna laughed, "I already sensed your pregnancy. I guess you finally told Bryce."

"It's only been a few hours," she replied guiltily.

"Tempest, relax. Are you sharing details?"

"One girl and three boys, obviously all shifters. Bryce just admitted that quads run in his family."

Rayna actually squealed in delight, loud enough that Bryce heard her and laughed. After Rayna congratulated Bryce and talked to Tempe for a while, the couple continued down the trail.

Before they reached Eli's garden, Bryce asked, "Can you teleport now? Is it safe?"

Tempe raised an eyebrow at the odd question, but answered, "No. I can't do anything that transforms my base form. No shifting, teleporting or glamouring. Why?"

"Let's sneak to my SUV and go for a drive," Bryce said with a smile.

"Okay, we can call once we're away from here and tell them we won't be there for dinner." Tempe realized she was looking forward to just a little time with Bryce before the world knew.

They made it to the car without being detected and headed north from Eli's. One mile down the road Bryce turned off the main road and onto a newly paved road. Tempe looked over in surprise. "Do you know who bought this land?" There had been a lot of work crews out here and everyone at Eli's house had been speculating on what was going on. The land housed one of the favorite overlooks for shifters who could fly.

"Yes, I do," Bryce smiled. Tempe waited but he didn't say anything else. As the only person she's ever met no telepath can read unless he allows it, Bryce was wearing a huge grin. She decided to not ask any more questions. She wasn't going to give him the satisfaction.

They had gone about half a mile when he rounded the bend and there was a beautiful Victorian house.

"Merry Christmas." Bryce grinned, "I was going to bring you out here on Christmas Eve, but I think now is the time."

"You built a house? For us?"

"Of course, for us. I know I should have included you in the process, but I wanted to surprise you. As luck would have it, it's a five-bedroom house so, when they hit the teen years, each kid can each have their own room. Of course, that means we won't be able to have other visitors unless we turn the offices into guest rooms." His grin turned sheepish as he added, "I didn't think quads when I thought of a future with kids."

She laughed and hugged him. Then they went in to tour the house. It wasn't completely finished yet, but it was mostly done and she didn't find anything lacking, nothing at all, which made her suspicious. "How is this house perfect? I love everything about it, every detail. How is that?"

Bryce ducked his head and admitted, "I talked with Loane, a lot. She was a wealth of information."

"I didn't realize she could read me this well. It's wonderful, and so are you."

Tempe pulled him into her for their first kiss in their new house. "I noticed the kitchen isn't stocked so what are we doing for dinner?"

"We're going to stop by Alan's house on the way to dinner."

"I'm hungry. Do you have some business to do?" She tried not to whine considering how wonderful the house was, but she wasn't sure she succeeded.

"No business, pleasure. I called Alan while you examined the master bath. He's going to marry us, special license, just one of the perks of being in the justice system."

"Shouldn't you ask me to marry you first?" She wasn't sure if she should be mad or pleased. She knew she wanted to marry him, but he was taking a lot for granted with the house and now the marriage.

Bryce turned slowly and looked at Tempe. Realization dawned as he walked over to stand in front of her. "I'm the one who did things out of order this time. I had originally planned to ask you to marry me when I showed you the house at Christmas. Let's start over."

He went down on one knee and took her right hand in his. "Tempest Wray, will you do me the great honor of becoming my wife? Since the first time I met you, when you came to Eli's to hold the birthing bond for Asilia, I have been yours. No other woman captivates me the way you do. I want to spend the rest of my life with you." He smiled clumsily, "The ring is sitting in a box in the dresser at Eli's."

She shook her head with a smile and answered, "Bryce, I would love to marry you. I'm more myself with you than with anyone else I've ever met. But be forewarned, I'm cranky when I'm pregnant and can't do what I want."

Bryce stood up and kissed her and asked tentatively, "Do you want to go see Alan or shall I cancel?"

She laughed and put her arm through his, "Let's get married, Mr. Reynolds."

One wedding and a meal later, they headed back to Eli's.

Unknown to them, Alan called Eli and told him Bryce and Tempe were married so when they walked into the house most of the clan was there for an impromptu party. Once the initial festivities were over, Bryce stood up and said, "We have one other announcement."

Eli barked out a laugh. After the ribbing he took for his rushed marriage when Delaney was pregnant, he was ready for payback. "I knew it."

Tempe rolled her eyes as Bryce continued. "Tempe and I will have quads in April."

"Quads?" For all of his bluster that was all Eli managed to say.

"Yes, quads, one girl and three boys."

"Geez, Tempe, do you do anything the easy way?" Ryan asked when he hugged her.

"No, I don't," she said as she returned his hug and growled softly in his hear, "By the way, you are the last alpha standing." Ryan looked suitably subdued.

Willow nudged her father and looked pointedly at Brandi. Brandi smiled so Adam stood up and, with a red face, announced, "As long as we are making announcements... around the first part of April, Willow will become a big sister to one brother and one sister. Loane checked and since Brandi doesn't shift, but carries shifter genes, she will be able to carry to term without a birthing bond."

There was a moment of silence before everyone started talking at once.

When everyone calmed down, Asilia commented, "By April our clan will have thirteen children under the age of one."

Everyone stopped and did the math in their heads. The Cruz triplets, Shaw twins, Turner twins, Baker twins and Reynolds quads. Yep, thirteen kids under the age of one. Oh my.

Charles stood up slowly and said, "Fourteen, actually. Mary will have a child in March. It's been so hectic we were waiting to tell everyone. Rayna is holding her birthing bond from a distance. We're having a girl."

The rest of the evening was spent talking about babies and how all of their lives were about to get busy.

*****

Saturday morning, Ryan and Tempe opened a way to the Farseen to the caves where Tace lives. They walked through the tunnels in the cave until a mist formed and turned into the gnome.

"Friend gnome, 'tis good to see you. I bring thee a small token," Tempe stated formally.

"Indeed, I know of no service performed that required payment, Lady Tempest," he said.

She nodded her agreement, "That is why I bring you a token of my appreciation, a gift. This is not offered in payment." She presented Tace with a bracelet of honor. He seemed to be awed by the gift few ever give or receive. This bracelet would allow Tace to enter the Seen, take it off his arm and it would call to Tempe and protect him until she arrives.

When Ryan and Tempe returned to the cave in the Seen he stopped her and asked, "Do I need to take next semester off from school?"

She had ragged on him last night to hide her concerns over alpha business and to hide her embarrassment. She was already sorry she had done so. "No, I don't think so. I'm hoping we'll have a quiet few months. The siren that created the Shadowed is dead. Don't go looking for trouble." She took a couple of steps but turned back to Ryan, "I am sorry this has happened now. Until a short time ago, I didn't even know about the twin eclipses. You will probably be pulling more duties for a while but overall, unless there is an emergency, Rayna is pretty much halting all unnecessary assignments. Raven should deliver her kids in January before you go back to school, so we should be okay. You have less than a month left of this semester."

*****

Sunday afternoon the college crowd left. No one expected to see Ryan or Jeannette until Christmas break. Joey, Blake and Kaleb would fly home to Texas for the winter break. Joey and Star had spent most of the day away from everyone and Star held back tears as Joey drove off.

As Star, Sage and Tempe turned to walk into the house after the UT students left, Tempe asked, "Should I ask how serious you and Joey are?"

Star blushed and offered, "I would prefer you didn't."

Tempe raised an eyebrow, shook her head but refrained from speaking. It took most of her will power to keep her mouth closed. Star's parents and Lord Sky had given their permission for Joey to court Star.

In the Farseen, permission to court a daughter of the realm was permission to have a full adult relationship.

After a few seconds Star added, "Tempe, we aren't doing anything that would result in another pregnancy for this clan if that's what you are worried about. Even though the Shadowed seem to be destroyed we don't plan to advance our relationship for a while. My protection runs through March nineteen next year and I still don't know what Lord Ellwood might have planned. I guess we'll wait and see what happens after that."

"That's well thought out," Tempe said, impressed, in spite of her personal misgivings.

Sage took a deep breath, leaned on the carved walking stick she had been using to steady herself since the siren incident, and jumped into the fray. "As long as we're on this topic, when Loane was talking with me this morning I confirmed with her that Landon is my twin flame. I can tell he also talked with someone and I'm sure I will be waiting at least until next year before I get to even consider doing anything. Landon has been clear about that." The last part she said in disgust. "You know, I always thought it was the girl that said 'no', not the guy."

Tempe hid her smile and said, "You should be thrilled you have a guy who thinks so much of you he's willing to wait."

"Oh goodie, advice on waiting from the sister who enchanted her first lover," Sage snarled.

"For the record, I'm tired of every member of the family bringing that up lately. It happened over six thousand years ago," she muttered. Her phone rang and she used that as her excuse to step away from her sister and niece.

"Hello, Kenley, how are things going?" She asked in surprise. "You're what?" Tempe stopped walking and stood on the patio as Sage and Star stopped to stare at her. "Sure, see you then." She hung up the phone but didn't move otherwise.

"What's up?" Sage asked.

"Kenley's moving here for a while. He's apparently a strong wizard and he's going to train here with some of Nova's people. Apparently, he's stronger in the casting arts than Siri and needs more training than she can provide."

"He must have major juice," Sage exclaimed.

Before she could drop her phone back into her pocket another call came in, "Devlin. How are you?"

"What?" Tempe practically screamed into the phone. "Yes, of course I'm thrilled. How's Siri?" Sage and Star were walking into the house, but when she asked about Siri, Sage turned and grinned.

When Tempe hung up the phone Sage was still staring at her with a huge grin, so Tempe answered the question she didn't ask. "Yes, Siri and Devlin will have twins around the first of April."

"You know, I think I'm going to make a family tree of all the new family members," Star muttered.

"If you do, make copies. Otherwise, we'll be saying things like 'hey you born during the twin eclipse cycle' and that sounds silly. Not to mention a dozen heads will turn," Sage replied.

*****

Monday was a hard day. Tempe had to force herself to let the girls attend their classes, alone. Sage was still too weak to drive so she rode with Star and would study at the library until her afternoon classes. It was Landon's day off, so he and Tempe spent the entire day watching the clock and checking their phones.

When her phone eventually rang, she lunged for it so fast she knocked it off the table. She dove for the phone, retrieved it from the floor, and pushed the speaker button, "Hello."

"Bliss gave birth to Kiran and Elaina. Everyone's fine," Serenity laughed. "Did you toss your phone?"

"Yes," Tempe muttered.

A short time later her phone rang again. This time Tempe carefully reached for it. It was Bryce. Kenley's flight was delayed so they would be home later than expected.

By the time the girls came home from the college campus, Landon and Tempe were both jittery, but they survived their personal anxieties. They had prepped dinner to give them something to do.

The girls walked in the door laughing. Sage looked over at Star and said, "Pay up."

Tempe raised an eyebrow as Star handed a ten-dollar bill to Sage.

Grinning sheepishly as she put the ten in her jeans pocket, Sage explained, "I bet you would both be making dinner to pass the time. Star bet you would be outside tossing powers at each other as a stress reliever."

Tempe growled but didn't say anything.

Landon was simply relieved the girls were home.

Life settled down and they all got back on a schedule of sorts. Brandi verified the Shadow's 'kidnap' web site was disabled after the siren was killed, but the girls in the clan were still under restrictions to make sure they were safe.

As November settled into December things were calm for everyone except Ryan. The alphas were pulling him into a lot of stuff and he was feeling frustrated. Tempe and Ryan communicated almost daily, and she talked with the other alphas reminding them Ryan needed to pass his first semester of college. Of course, Rayna was the one sending him on assignments, so the jury was out on whether or not it did any good.

Kenley stayed with Eli for a few days but ended up moving into the Half Acre facility to train with the wizards. He started visiting Tempe frequently and was surprised to learn he liked his mother. He had always felt Rita, Ryan's mother, was the woman who raised him. While Tempest was out saving the shifter world, Rita was the one who made sure he was fed, proofed his homework, and was always there if he scraped his knee or just needed to talk.

At least one or two shifter families gave birth every week all over the world. The birthing explosion had shifted into high gear.

Chapter 29

"Are all pregnant women this cranky?' Bryce whispered as he poured himself a cup of coffee.

"Shh, you want her to hear you?" Eli replied even more softly. "Tempe has always reacted badly to restrictions."

"Yeah, but dang… it's still four months until the birth and she's driving me up the wall. Today she yelled at me for daring to move her to a new house."

"That's probably the caffeine withdrawal," Delaney offered.

From the sunroom, Tempe commented surly, "You guys do know I can hear you, right?"

"Yes, dear," Bryce replied with a feigned tone of contriteness. "You do know you're being overly cranky, don't you?"

"No, I'm not. Ryan is going nuts trying to take final exams and do work for the sovereign. I should be available to help him," she growled.

Eli and Delaney slithered away, wisely leaving Bryce to dig his own grave.

Bryce filled a mug with herbal tea (which means no caffeine) and set it down in front of Tempe. "He comes home in a couple of days. This crunch time is almost over for him. By January, Raven will be available, as well as a couple of your other sisters."

She growled, took the mug of tea and sipped, even though it was lacking caffeine. "I feel bad for him. He should be having fun in college. Not running around taking care of alpha business. Bliss is the only other alpha available now and she's just delivered her twins."

"Your pregnancy is not letting Ryan down." Bryce looked her in the eyes, "Do you regret being pregnant?"

"No. Never," She sighed. "I guess I am hormonal."

"Well, we move tomorrow and the next day Ryan and Jeannette will come in for the holidays," Bryce said. "You can fuss over him then."

"Ryan is bringing a shifter from UT to stay with us over the holidays. And before you get any romantic ideas, her name is Heather and she moved to Tennessee to start her doctorate in January. She has no family. She's a friend who needs someplace to go for the break."

"Okay, you got the trivia out of the way. What's the real issue?" Bryce asked, focusing on his coffee as he took a sip.

"What do you mean?"

"Tempe, don't hedge with me. What are you worried about? It's not just hormones."

Tempe sighed, and the words rushed out. "In the past, when I've been pregnant, except for Layton who was born in the Northern Realm, I've managed to stay away from the fae to keep Father uninformed. Star will lose the queen's protection on March 19. My due date is April 11. There is no way to keep the fae in the dark."

Bryce pulled her into a tight hug, "You know we'll protect the kids."

"But the end of March would be a perfect time for an attack," she sighed.

Bryce snaked an arm around her and pulled her in close and whispered, "Then we prepare for that."

*****

A couple of days later, Bryce and Tempe were preparing for a house warming party. All they had to do was move their clothes from Eli's to their new home. All the furniture and such were purchased for the house, making it a relatively easy move, so they had invited the clan over for the grand tour.

"Where's the flour?" Tempe asked hopefully. Mary, Delaney and Tracy took it upon themselves to go grocery shopping and to stock the pantry. She hated to be ungrateful and whiny, but she couldn't find anything.

Bryce laughed and called from the bedroom where he was putting clothes away, "Not a clue. Did you look in the kitchen cabinets?"

"Why would it be there instead of in the pantry?" she replied grouchily as she opened kitchen cabinets. Sure enough, flour, sugar, cornmeal and such were in glass containers on a shelf in a cabinet. "I will never figure out the system they set up," she growled.

She was still irritated over a call with Rayna and she was pretty sure she was taking it out on the kitchen organization. Tempe had tried to convince Rayna Ryan needed some quality 'non-alpha' time to focus on school. They finished their call nicely enough but neither woman was happy.

In the aftermath of the housewarming party and Christmas, they settled into their new home.

*****

Bryce plopped down in a chair at the kitchen bar and commented, "It's quiet, isn't it?"

"Yes. It seems odd not to have a ton of folks around us all the time." Tempe hugged him from behind, her hands rubbing his chest.

Bryce grinned. "Of course, it also means we don't have to run to the bedroom if we want to be alone." He turned and pulled her into a kiss while they moved toward the rug in front of the fireplace.

The doorbell rang.

Bryce groaned and whispered in her ear, "If we pretend we aren't here, do you think whoever will go away?"

"Not a chance," she said with a sigh as she straightened her hair and clothes. "It's Wren and Lark."

A quick kiss and she went to answer the door. Opening the door, she didn't bother with pleasantries, "Your timing sucks." She took a calming breath and added, "But it's nice to see you anyway."

"Mother sent us," Lark said without preamble. Tempe must have looked surprised because Lark added with a smirk, "Come on. You expressed concern over the birthing explosion, your condition, Ryan going solo so much, and Star's status. What did you think would happen? Mother has never sat quietly when she could do something."

"And before you say anything, there are plenty of alphas at home to take care of business," Wren added.

As Bryce came to stand behind Tempe, she smiled, "It's a good thing my man built a house with lots of bedrooms."

Wren grinned. "Oh, we aren't staying here. I called Eli before we left. He's putting us up. That way we're close to Star if needed... and we can keep an eye on Sage and her" disgusted sigh "twin flame."

Tempe raised an eyebrow and Wren had the decency to blush. "Oh, you know what I mean. I'm happy for her. I am, but geez, she didn't even have to search for him. Landon practically dropped into her lap."

"I know what you mean. I truly do," Tempe replied as she ushered her sisters into the house for the tour.

"Your commiseration would mean a lot more if you didn't have Bryce," Wren groused.

*****

The weekly clan Sunday dinner fell on January the first, which was a cold and rainy day. Since it was Tempe's turn to cook, she took over the kitchen at Eli's and made a huge pot of stew with bread and cake for dessert.

Sage ran in squealing, "I'm an aunt!"

Ryan laughed, "You were born an aunt." He pointed to Star and himself, both older than Sage, but niece and nephew anyway.

"Silly," Sage smiled as she hugged Ryan. "Aden, Dena, and Dean were born a few minutes ago. Raven is doing fine, but apparently Jackson fainted."

Eli laughed. When everyone looked at him, he shrugged, "Well, it's nice to not be the only father who's done that."

"At least he didn't break his hand when he fainted," Sage smirked.

Wren walked in smiling, looked at Sage, snarled and then shrugged, "I was hoping to be the one to tell them."

"Tell them what?" Sam asked as he and Tracy walked in from the sunroom, along with some of the other clan members.

Sage bowed low to Wren, who smiled and said, "Raven and her triplets are fine. Born a little while ago."

Sam put his arm around Tracy and asked Wren, "How long are you and Lark going to be here?"

"As long as needed, at least until Tempest delivers. Why?"

Sam, the only child Rayna ever delivered that never got flustered, said, "I… that is we… Tracy and me… I mean I, Tracy and I… we need an alpha female."

Sage squealed and grabbed her brother in a hug. Lark and Wren smiled and also hugged their brother.

Tempe simply laughed, "Sam, I'm your alpha." Amid the surprised expressions she continued, "Alpha females can be pregnant and hold a birthing bond, although it's not normally necessary. For now though, Sage, Lark and Wren need all of their powers so I'm it."

Tracy, Sam and Tempe went into the bedroom on the first floor. After all, there had been so many birthing bonds of late it had become commonplace. As she shut the door she asked, "Will you want details?"

"Yes, and there's one detail I should tell you," Tracy said in a soft voice.

Tempe prepared herself for family genetic issues but was unprepared for Tracy's next words.

"Quads run in my family."

Well, that is a genetic issue, of a sort. Smiling, she sat down. "Let's find out, shall we?"

A short time later they walked back into the kitchen where Tracy found herself to be the focus of the room, which was not a position she liked to be in. She tucked herself into Sam. As his arms went around her he manned up and explained, "Around the end of May, we're having quads, two males, two females."

While everyone circled around Tracy and Sam to congratulate them or offer words of wisdom, Tempe followed Ryan out on the front porch. He had ducked out as soon as Sam made his announcement.

Both of his hands had a death grip on the deck rail as he stared at the mountains.

"Penny for your thoughts." She sat down on the porch swing. She was pretty sure what the problem was but knew he had to say it out loud, just to force him to face the reality.

He plopped down beside her and ran his fingers through his hair. "If I had stayed with the alpha clan after my ranking, would all of the alphas have deferred to me, on every freaking thing?"

She managed to keep the smile to herself. "About alpha business, yes, except for Rayna and me, of course. Is there a specific problem?"

"No," he leaned back and sighed. "It's creepy. Wren and Lark were adults before I was born. Now if I disagree with them they immediately back down. I can't even joke with them anymore. If it weren't for Sage and Star, I would either become a tyrant or a hermit. I've been around when all the alphas have given their opinion without all the backtracking around you and Rayna."

"Yes, you have. What was different about those times?"

"I don't know," he growled.

"Think about it," she said calmly as he growled again.

Staring off into space, Ryan didn't move for a few minutes and then he shook his head with an appalled expression, "You or Rayna asked for their opinions. Seriously, I need to ask them to offer up their opinions every time? Even about stupid stuff, like how some minor task Rayna wants done, gets done?"

"Yep," she bobbed him once on the shoulder to get him to look at her, and smiled, "It gets easier as you work on it. For any alpha task they will defer to you. You need to make sure and ask for their opinion before you throw out yours. It will serve two purposes. First, you will get the benefit of their experience and knowledge. While Lark and Wren haven't done a lot of fighting, they have a lot of experience with the more mundane housekeeping tasks of the alpha clan. That, my dear nephew, will free you up a lot. Second, they will see you still value them."

"I know Wren was the one you and Sage both went to if things weren't going great or if you needed advice on dating, clothes, or anything else. I also know Wren and Lark were your most frequent babysitters. The new reality is you are responsible for their lives now and they take orders from you. I suspect they are as unsure around you as you are around them. Just make sure they know you respect them, and for

236

pity's sake, ask for their opinion before you say what you think. They are used to it since Rayna expects the senior alphas to do that."

Tempe stood up and headed for the door. Over her shoulder she called, "You coming?"

"Not just yet. I think I'll sit here for a few." Ryan stared at the mountains, but he didn't see them at all.

Inside, Delaney and Star had finished up dinner and most of the clan had already filled their plates. Joey, Blake, and Kaleb had returned a couple of days early for the return to school. Joey and Star were talking quietly, as were Kaleb and Willow. She suspected the quartet would be heading out for a stroll as soon as they finished eating. Kaleb and Willow were something of a mystery. She was dating a human in town, but Kaleb always sought her out. Perhaps they were good friends, confidants like Sage and Ryan.

Looking around, everyone seemed happy, except for Craig, Sam's friend. Tempe sat her dinner down next to Craig, "Mind if I join you?"

"Please," Craig waved to the chair, polite but distracted.

"I don't mean to pry... oh who am I kidding? Of course, I mean to pry. Are you okay? If you don't want to talk you can tell me to back off, but you look downright gloomy," Tempe smiled encouragingly.

Sam laughed as he sat on Craig's other side. "Give it up. Tempe will keep at you until you talk to someone, even if it's not her."

Craig sucked in a deep breath. "Tammy dumped me. She knows there's something I'm not telling her and she, yeah, she dumped me. Can't say I blame her. And before you guys ask the answer is no."

"No?" Sam asked.

Tempe was glad he asked since she didn't want to be the one.

"No. As in no I don't see her marrying into this world. She's great and I enjoyed being with her, but she likes nice and normal. I don't believe she would want to learn shape shifters, vampires, witches, and fae exist. You know?"

"Unfortunately, I do," Tempe said softly as she patted his arm. Relationships with humans were hard for that reason. Before bringing them into the preternatural world, shifters have to be sure it was forever, or at least for the lifetime of the human. Discretion was a must. Adam's human wife left him, and the alphas kept tabs on her ever since. She hadn't done anything to out shifters, so they left her alone, but still she would be watched until her dying day.

Craig offered a small smile, "I'll be fine, really. Just give me a couple of days to lick my wounds." To Sam he added, "Congratulations. I'm happy for you and Tracy."

To keep the change of topic going, Tempe looked over at Sam. "Your quads are going to follow too close to mine for me to give you the cribs and such when yours are born."

Sam laughed. "I did think of that. And I called Mom and Dad after I told the clan. I waited until we knew the details. Mom was thrilled, of course."

"Of course she's thrilled," Wren said as she and Lark placed their bowls on the table and sat down. "I swear she wishes all of us would get pregnant right now. She loves the whole massive pregnancy thing."

Tempe laughed. She couldn't help herself. While the four of them stared at her she managed to get herself under control. "Can you imagine if Mother got pregnant right now?"

As all of the alpha females that knew what the sovereign was like when pregnant joined Tempe in laughter, everyone else stared in confusion.

Chapter 30

In January, Ryan went back to UT with the rest of the college students. Wren and Lark made a vast improvement in Ryan's life. Truth be told, it vastly improved Tempe's life as well. She shifted a lot of work their way, as she grew as big as a house. Quads for pity's sake!

January gave way to February as shifters continued to give birth. Among the births, Lisa and Harry – formally of the Smokey Mountain clan – had triplets. Cinnamon was ranked in the Smokey Mountain clan. She remained dead last in the clan rank structure. She wasn't interested in being in charge and was pleased to just have a ranked position in the clan and to be considered an adult.

Landon was the big surprise, to everyone but Tempe. He asked to join Eli's clan and he ended up in a stare down with Sam. At the end of the push, Sam remained sixth in the clan and Landon became seventh, beating out Star.

Wren and Lark trained daily with Sage and Star and all four of them were getting stronger and surer of themselves. Sage showed remarkable improvement and control of her powers. Tempe put her in charge of the training sessions and invited any of Eli's clan that wished to participate. Her maturity grew along with the class size.

Eventually, the day of Star's choosing arrived. March the nineteenth dawned with sheets of rain falling from the sky. Sam, Liz, and Mary had joined their individual shields over Eli's house and the result was almost as strong as Sage's. It wouldn't last more than a few hours but would be good enough for the fae queens' visit.

Rayna, Serenity, Bliss, and Raven arrived before noon. Cloud, Temperance and Saffron arrived shortly after. Cloud had refused to allow Misty to attend just in case problems arose. Sage and Ryan were with Tempe and Star but everyone else at Eli's was told to stay away.

They gathered at the cave to wait for the arrival of the fae queens. Sage set one-layer shield ten feet off the ground serving as a tent to keep everyone dry. No shifter or wizard could block a fae queen for more than a few seconds. No reason to waste the energy.

Queen Niamh and Lord Ellwood from the Northern Realm arrived with Queen Ceridwin and Lord Sky from the Central Realm. The decision was to be announced at sunset, which no one would see with the rain pouring down. Those who could feel a way open were the only ones that knew the fae were arriving. Theron and Kainda were the last to enter the Seen.

Queen Ceridwin was the first to speak. "Star, your father has informed me you have chosen to remain in the Seen with your shifter clan but you would like to visit the Farseen from time to time. Is this true?"

Star cleared her throat but spoke clearly, "Yes, my queen."

Queen Niamh smiled, "You mother provided the same information to me."

Ellwood sputtered. His mother knew who Star's mother is but he still didn't know for sure.

Ignoring her son, Niamh continued, "Lady Star, you are unique. You hold status as a shifter in a clan and as a daughter of the court in two realms. While you can continue to hold dual status in a shifter clan and in a realm court, just as Lady Tempest does, you can only be a daughter of the court in one realm. You must choose your realm allegiance."

Star had been prepped and knew she would have to choose. The choice had to be hers alone and no one else could know what her answer was going to be. That way, no one could say she was manipulated to choose one court over the other. She was strong and would be a valuable member of either court. Kainda's main purpose at this gathering was to verify none of the shifters or fae knew ahead of time what Star's choice would be.

Star smiled and curtsied beautifully to Queen Niamh. "The protection you initiated for me allowed me the chance to grow as a shifter." That was as close to a thank you as a fae could get. She turned to Queen Ceridwin and curtsied again, "I prefer to remain a daughter of the Central Realm court, where I was raised."

Both queens smiled their agreement to her choice. Lord Sky beamed, as did Cloud. Ellwood hid his snarl but not the dagger look he gave his first-born.

Tempe was simply relieved. Since Star chose the Central Realm, Ellwood would not be able to make a play for her directly without declaring war on the Central Realm.

In the silence that followed, Cloud took Temperance's hand in his and walked forward to his realm lord and queen. "Queen Ceridwin and Lord Sky, I present to you Lady Temperance, Star's mother, and my wife. Queen Niamh released Temperance to the Central Realm after we carved our vows."

Temperance curtsied perfectly to her new queen and realm lord as Rayna, Saffron and Tempe exchanged surprised looks. Star had a satisfied expression that made it apparent she already knew.

Ellwood was back to being livid. Normally the realm lord releases a subject to the care of another realm, but a realm queen certainly had the ability as well. Now there was no way for him to go after Temperance either.

Tempe was pleased with how things were going until she noticed Ellwood was not watching Temperance. He was looking at her. Specifically, he was looking at her stomach. She had worn clothing she hoped would hide her current condition but the fae were good at sensing pregnancies and she was rather large. A grin spread across his face, and even hit his eyes.

Tempe put on her game face to keep him from seeing her concern.

Ryan glanced at Tempe and then looked at Ellwood. Her nephew quickly came to stand beside her, as did Saffron. Rayna, not to be outdone, moved to stand in front of her first born. Tempe heard her mother tell Ellwood mind-to-mind to stay away from all shifters.

Ellwood smirked at Rayna, and then he inclined his head toward Cloud. "Take care of my daughter." Turning toward both queens he bowed. Without another word or glance, he opened a way and left.

Queen Niamh opened a way, and along with Queen Ceridwin, Theron and Kainda, left for the Farseen.

After the way closed, everyone turned to Temperance and Cloud. Before anyone else could speak, Star smiled at her parents and said, "You should tell Rayna now."

Temperance placed one finger over Cloud's lips, "My love, I need to do this." Turning to her shifter family, she spoke to her mother, "The triplets are due in June, two boys and a girl."

"That's wonderful. And how did you manage to get your grandmother to carve your vows without Ellwood's knowledge?"

Cloud grinned, "Temperance was inspired"

Blushing, Temperance admitted, "I told Queen Niamh about the triplets and she called Cloud to her residence."

"Masterfully done," Saffron clapped. "We might make a rebel out of you yet."

"No offense sister mine, but I would rather you didn't," Temperance said quietly, tucking herself into Cloud's side.

*****

The Sunday clan dinner on March twenty-sixth turned into a whine fest, at least for Mary, Brandi, Tempe and Tracy. Pregnant and cranky, they sat in the sunroom and discussed swollen feet, upset stomachs, and difficulties doing normal tasks due to the tummy bulge. For some reason, no one else wanted to sit with them. Those not on cooking detail in the kitchen hid outside.

Tempe had been watching Mary for a while and she had already sent Jeff one informational text. She sent another and stood to help Mary rise when Liz announced dinner was ready.

Mary stood but immediately sat back down. "You know, I feel tired. I think I would like to just sit in the sunroom for a little longer." She looked up at Tempe and added, "Yes, I know my labor started but the pains are fourteen minutes apart. You guys go eat. I want some ice chips but we both know I shouldn't eat. And for goodness sakes, make sure Jeff eats before he checks on me."

Tempe walked into the kitchen planning to tell Jeff and Charles what was going on and then go back out to sit with Mary.

"Eat." Star handed Tempe a plate of food, "Sage and I will sit with Mary until Jeff finishes. Sage called Rayna and they worked out the plan." Rayna was holding Mary's birthing bond at a distance but having an alpha nearby to help certainly makes it easier on everyone.

Jeff and Charles were already eating so Tempe joined them as everyone else lined up at the buffet.

She grinned, "I'm beginning to feel unnecessary."

"Sage and Star have grown up over the last year, but I have a feeling you still have a couple of useful years left." Jeff said with a smile.

Between bites of food, the rest of the clan glanced toward the sunroom. Everyone knew Mary was in labor.

About the time Jeff took his last bite of food, Mary groaned.

"That's my cue." Jeff said as he stacked his plate and hurried out.

"Mine, too," Charles grinned. "Mary said she would skin me if I missed this birth. When Bobby was born, fathers hung out in the waiting room."

"Aha yes, the good old days," Theo commented under his breath, but everyone heard him thanks to shifter hearing. A flood of napkins rained down upon his head.

Naomi raised an eyebrow. "Maybe you should shift and sleep in the dog house for a few days."

Theo, who shifts to a Rottweiler, was appalled. "Come on, baby. You know I was joking."

Everyone quietly left Theo to dig his way out of that hole all by himself.

Less than three hours later, Robin Taylor entered the world. Loudly.

"Sis certainly has lungs that work," Bobby proclaimed as he and Asilia took their triplets down the hall to meet the newest family member.

Two hours later, Robin was still displaying her vocal talents.

As Bryce and Tempe headed out the door she suggested to Star, "If you want to get any sleep tonight you might want to sing to her. I believe everyone in the house would be happier."

Lark looked over and murmured, "Please."

Star smiled and walked down the hallway. Although Ryan and Tempe could enchant, she had much more control than either of them. Both were a little jealous and it made her feel good about herself, which was probably a bit petty, but there it was. At least she was honest with herself.

*****

Bryce and Tempe pulled into their garage, but their house wasn't empty.

Chev, Dwight and Brook along with their twins, Kayla and Jayla, had left Eli's earlier and were already in the house, staying with Bryce and Tempe until the renovations on the house they bought were complete. They had moved in a month ago and would remain for at least another two weeks if their renovations remained on schedule.

The house was big enough and Tempe was pretty sure Bryce was thrilled to have Brook and her ability to siren in the house while she was pregnant. Dwight had the ability to become invisible in shadow, giving him an edge in a fight. Chev, as a former master-at-arms for the Eastern Realm, would be an excellent addition in a fight with the fae, as long as it wasn't a full moon.

Tempe had wondered about the timing of their need of a place to stay and she worried about putting their twins in danger, but she always tried to be honest with herself, and was glad they were there.

She tried to keep it to herself, but Tempe was concerned about her father. Star and Temperance were off his menu for the time being, but she wasn't. If he could get Tempe to his realm and kill her after the quads were born, by fae law, he would be their guardian and the only way anyone, fae or shifter, could remove them from his realm would be with his blessing – not a chance – or to win a war against the Northern Realm.

With the fae, possession wasn't nine-tenths of the law. It was the law.

As they walked into the kitchen from the garage, Chev poured tea. "Tempe, sit and have a cup. A cup of herbal before bed is always nice." He placed a mug in front of a chair at the kitchen bar.

Tempe growled, "I miss caffeine."

"You went the first thousand years without it. This, too, shall pass," Chev replied soothingly.

"She what?" Bryce plopped down in the chair next to his wife with a confused look.

A smile played across Chev's lips. "There is no caffeine in the Farseen. All teas are herbal. Coffee doesn't exist, and neither does chocolate. The only way to get caffeine in the Farseen is to bring it from the Seen. Didn't you know?"

Bryce hooted with laughter. Tempe ignored both of them and drank her herbal tea.

*****

A few days later Chev sat on the living room floor telling his seven-month-old granddaughters tales of the Farseen. It was a beautiful spring morning as Tempe waddled into the kitchen. Yep, she had reached the much hated waddle stage.

"You're just in time for breakfast," Brook said.

Tempe could smell the bacon and eggs Brook was fixing but she wasn't interested. "No thanks, I just want toast and tea... herbal tea."

"Tempe..."

"Just tea and toast," She growled. After a few seconds she started laughing.

"What's so funny?" Brook's eyes widened, unsure what the powerful shifter was laughing about.

"Back when Teresa was nearing the end of her pregnancy she and I had the same conversation. Only she was the one wanting nothing but tea and toast. I get it now."

Brook smiled.

An explosion shook the house and the door to the patio blew off its hinges. It would have hit the twins, and Chev, but a shield saved them.

Brook sirened for ruling fae, but she couldn't actually see who was on the other side of the hole in the house. It was a good guess. It was also wrong.

A single goblin entered through the hole. Tempe called wind and knocked the goblin back, which gave Brook time to siren the goblin.

While they were attending to the goblin, Sam became visible and dropped his shield from the twins. Chev moved the twins to their playpen and activated the spell he and Tempe had set to shield them and their playpen.

Ruling fae burst through the patio and one of them launched an arrow at Brook. Tempe tossed a return-to-sender spell and the arrow embedded in the fae who shot it. He fell instantly so it must have been dipped in a sleeping draught.

Brook would have sirened the ruling fae but another goblin grabbed her, covering her throat in a tight grip and cutting off her air. She was too busy trying to breathe to siren anyone. Sam shifted to his falcon and went for the goblin's eyes.

Chev proved to be an excellent fighter and had already taken out a handful of the intruders.

Tempe tried to enchant the fae, but her voice was gone. She looked up to see Dyfri, who had obviously spelled her voice away. Excluding Father Aldous, Dyfri was the strongest ruling fae to live outside the five realms. To choose to live as an outcast meant he had no realm to support him. He has no way to bring charges against another fae or to even be heard in their court system. He could be killed by any fae from any realm without facing charges of any kind. Most ruling fae who do so are those who are anti-social or insane. Dyfri does it because he's strong enough to do so. Tempe had heard he died, an apparent exaggeration.

Dyfri threw a web spell at Tempe. She countered with a spell that froze the web as she tossed one of her bracelets into it. The small explosion destroyed the web.

Tempe called to the golden pothos vines she has potted throughout the house. The vines grabbed Dyfri around the arms and legs, but the vine that got him under control was the one wrapped around his neck. For the fae – as with most living beings – breathing was a necessity.

With Sam's help, Brook broke free of the goblin and she sirened the remaining ruling fae, putting them to sleep. As Dyfri became unconscious Tempe was able to speak again.

"Anybody hurt?" Sam asked.

"I'm good," Chev responded.

"Never better. How are the girls?" Brook responded, pleased her voice sounded calm as she walked toward her girls.

"Wait. Let's do a full sweep before you drop the shield around them," Tempe said as she headed for the door.

"No, you don't." Sam grabbed his sister's arm.

Tempe raised an eyebrow. He blushed but plowed on. "You're the prize. You're what they were after. Stay here while Chev and I check it out."

Tempe would have argued but concern for the quads held her back.

They heard cars pulling into the driveway. Peaking out the window Brook commented, "They're going to be bummed when they find out they missed the action."

Wren, Lark, Sage, Landon, Charles, Theo, Teresa and Joe hopped out of Joe's truck, weapons drawn.

Wren's voice carried throughout the house, "Everyone but Tempe, Teresa and Brook, check to make sure there aren't any fae still moving around outside."

Teresa passed Chev and Sam as they went to join the search.

Teresa smiled, "Call Eli. As agreed, he remained at his house to protect the children there, but he was beside himself when your sisters said you were under attack."

Tempe pulled out her cell and dialed. "We're fine. Things would have gone bad indeed if Sam hadn't been here. Your insistence that we always have a hidden clan member at our house was a good one."

Tempe looked over and realized Dyfri was gone. He must have passed out from the vine choking him and not from Brook's siren call. When he came to he managed to sneak away.

"Eli, I think I'll take you up on your offer and move back into your house until the kids are born. I don't like dividing resources like this," Tempe whispered.

Eli chuckled, "It's about time you came to your senses. The clan is safer if we keep those needing protection under one roof. And until the quads are born, you are one of the ones we need to protect."

Tempe growled but didn't argue with him.

All of the ruling fae that attacked were outcasts, so they couldn't take action against Ellwood because they couldn't prove he did it. In the back of her mind she wondered if Ellwood would kill Dyfri for his failure. She hoped so. She was Dyfri's first failure as a contract-for-hire. He might want revenge at some point.

Chapter 31

Bryce and Tempe moved back into Eli's. Everyone was pleased, and tried not to show it, she finally saw reason. As Bryce brought in the suitcases, she sipped herbal tea (still no caffeine) in the sunroom. Devlin called from Scotland to say Siri had given birth to Nevin and Nyla. A couple of hours later Quinn called from Italy to say Jas had given birth to Santino, Piero, and Mirella.

"April Fool's Day seems to be a big day for delivering babies." Adam brought in suitcases for him and Brandi. She was due within the next week. Brook, Dwight, Chev and the twins were going to stay at Adam's house with Willow since Eli's house was so crowded.

Although they were in the sunroom they heard Brandi in the kitchen cry "Oh no!" followed by "You've got to be kidding me."

Sage calmly called out, "Adam, you might as well move into the recovery room. Brandi's water broke. Tempe, please call Jeff."

Tempe couldn't stop her smile as she reached for the cell.

Just before midnight Ginger and Basil Baker were born.

*****

Eleven days later, time had stopped. Tempe just knew she would be fully pregnant forever. Quads. It was all Bryce's fault. She had thought triplets were bad. She was wrong!

She shuffled into the kitchen and sat at the table with a growl.

"Tempe would you like some breakfast? I'm making pancakes and sausage," Star asked timidly.

"Just tea and toast," she grumbled. The thought of syrup was not agreeable, and the smell of the sausage cooking was enough to persuade her not to eat that.

Star frowned as she handed her a mug of tea, when Teresa walked in and agreed. "Tea and toast it is. I'll make the toast while Tempe drinks her tea."

"You know, it's not tea without the caffeine," she continued to grumble.

"I suspect you will be able to have caffeine soon." Teresa patted a shoulder as she laid the toast in front of the grumpy alpha.

Tempe managed to refrain from ripping Teresa's arm out of the socket, so it occurred to her perhaps her mood was improving. Then again, it could be she was too tired to bother.

Before she could take a bit of her toast she realized another contraction was in progress. That put her contractions at sixteen minutes apart. She sighed and pushed the food away.

"Is something wrong?" Teresa asked.

"No, but my labor is sixteen minutes apart. I shouldn't eat anything. Not even the toast," she responded. She knew labor was easier on an empty stomach, but she wanted to eat, even if it was just toast. But having upon numerous occasions been the person who did the clean up after a woman in labor ate, she didn't want to do that to anyone else.

She could hear Sage in the background calling Bryce.

Tempe asked, "Do you think he needs to rush home right this minute? It could be hours before I deliver."

"I don't want to be the one Bryce is mad at if he misses anything," Sage said with a smile as she bounced out of the room.

Wren and Lark walked in dressed for battle.

Tempe looked them over, "What's going on?"

"Relax Tempe, we're going to patrol while Sage assists you with your labor," Lark answered.

Wren added, "Yep, it's all worked out. Eli will remain in the house and Sage is going to shield the house. Everyone in Eli's clan is prepared for battle if needed. We worked out the assignments days ago."

Sage returned wearing her spelled battle clothes. "Nothing and no one will harm the quads."

"You got that right," Kenley walked in the back door with Odelia from the wizard's compound. "Don't worry Mom, we've got you covered."

Tempe smiled, touched that so many were making sacrifices just for her kids to be born.

A few hours later on a beautiful spring day, with absolutely no interference from any big bad out there, Vivian, Tavian, Julian, and Adrian were born. All four were healthy and happy. Well, the happy part came after they were fed, and Star sang to them. Bryce was there for everything, from Tempe yelling at him for daring to have quads in his family, to taking each child from Jeff and handing them off to Sage to get cleaned up and checked out.

He didn't pass out.

Books by N. R. Tucker

Farseen Chronicles

Deceived
Enthralled
Betrayed
Revealed

The Farseen Chronicles is a fantasy series set in the Seen (current human dimension) and the Farseen (fae dimension).

Finding Earth

Drifters Rising

Finding Earth is a science fiction series, set throughout the stars, that chronicles the journey of select ships as they travel into the unknown and away from their dying world.

With earth's resources depleted and the planet dying, the world leaders built twenty-five transport ships capable of space travel. The ships were population ships and carried 5,000 people per ship into space with the hope of finding a healthy planet to populate.

More information about the worlds of N. R. Tucker's mind – including flash fiction, character lists, glossaries, and maps – can be found at

NRTucker.com

www.ingramcontent.com/pod-product-compliance
Lightning Source LLC
Chambersburg PA
CBHW061613170626
46811CB00001B/413